D0034507

The Null Quotient

By
Philip F. Margo

Eloquent Books

Copyright 2010
All rights reserved – Philip F. Margo

No part of this book may be reproduced or transmitted in any form or by any means, graphic, electronic, or mechanical, including photocopying, recording, taping, or by any information storage retrieval system, without the permission, in writing, from the publisher.

Eloquent Books
An imprint of Strategic Book Group
P.O. Box 333
Durham CT 06422
www.StrategicBookGroup.com

ISBN 978-1-60860-011-3

Printed in the United States of America

For Bunckie: My gorgeous bride who is spectacular in any and all of the Universes.

Acknowledgements:

Abbie Sue, our children and grandchildren in order of appearance: Noah P. Margo, Joshua M. Margo, Neely Margo Irwin, Lynne Ginsberg-Margo, Laura Rose Margo, Daniel Irwin, Ethan Cordover, Solomon Alexander, Jax Ilias, Jacob Moses, Benjamin David, Reese Diamond, Zoe Kolette and Gabriel Malcolm.

My brother Mitch Margo, and my sister Maxine Margo Rubin and Dr. L. B. Rubin.

And of course, my incredible mom Ruthie Margo, and Leon.

Also John Paine and Beth Lieberman who believed I could write a novel ... and made me believe it as well. Special thanks to Jeff March of Editpros who finally enabled me to let the work go, and Ari Margo whose eagle-eye editing was indispensible in propelling "The Null Quotient" across the literary finish line.

Finally, the staff at Eloquent Books whose patience and continued support are greatly appreciated.

CONTENTS

PROLOGUE

SHIVA AND THE PILOT
IN
"THE LOST WORLD"

Almost a billion years ago, at an anonymous crossroad along the temporal continuum …

… she knew for certain that it was the end of her world. It was written on the far horizon where the scorching flashes from the antihydrogen fusion-pod explosions swallowed up the stars and turned the carbon-blackness of night into a ghostly, pale-gray dawn.

Her name was Ahneevah, and as she stood on the transit-deck of her residence inside the Orbital Interceptor Base, the pairs of concentric, slate-gray pupils within her expansive, jade-saucer eyes, instantly contracted to their minimal aperture. This autonomic response served to protect her highly evolved inner-optics against the ravages of the searing white-light generated by the unyielding bombardment. She recognized that whatever living creatures were within range of actually hearing the thunderous detonations would be incinerated by the tritium-particle firestorm before any sound could be perceived.

All diplomatic channels had been explored and exhausted. Regrettably, an overwhelming majority of her civilization had succumbed to the primeval forces—hate and fear. Hate and fear—the malevolent twin-insanities that suffocated the voices of dissent coming from those who knew better; the sound thinkers who attempted in vain to convince the war-driven leadership to halt their stiff-necked, irrational march down the path of total destruction. *Now it was war,* she solemnly reflected. *'The' war ... the war to end all wars ... the war to end all.* An intense wave of frustration coursed throughout Ahneevah's comprehensive analytical system. "Why does leadership almost invariably make the wrong choices?" she said aloud in her silky, alien tongue. "How is it possible for the outrageous deceptions of an inept, warp-minded few to enable the extinction of every living creature on this world?" These words, however, were rendered moot as they passed Ahneevah's lips. Experience taught her that as a highly decorated, Supreme-Echelon Officer, she had a vitally important responsibility to think outside the impending cataclysm. Her background and training demanded that she focus on her mission and erase, from every tier of her diverse mental network, all thoughts of the inescapable madness and horror to come. With her mindset rapidly shifting into full combat mode, she reached for an area above the crook of her elbow on the inside part of her uniform's left sleeve. At the precise instant her fingertips made contact with the cerulean, organic-carbon-fiber material, a hidden compartment opened and from it she withdrew her thin, rectangular, Neuronal Logic Unit which activated at her touch. "Standing by for tactical evaluation," announced an authoritative but natural-sounding voice emanating from the instrument. "Relay all combat area recon from the geo-synch satellite arrays," Ahneevah instructed. "Negative," was the response. "All orbital transmissions across the entire bandwidth have been compromised by the enemy's cyber-storm of cannibal rover-waves. Digital acquisition of any visual or telemetric signals from the primary terrestrial observation network is unachievable." Ahneevah considered this information. "That should have been anticipated by Sat-Net control ... scan secondary analog mode to circumvent."

"Seeking," was the composed reply and at once, through a protected back-door server, an up-link was established with a system of lunar-based, analog surveillance installations which transmitted a succession of ominous battle-zone visuals. Ahneevah *gasped* at the sight of the real-time holographic display generated through the small, flat, multi-purpose logic device. A sequence of striking, three-dimensional views confirmed that the remote defense colonies were under a vicious, unremitting attack. One particular image both stunned and chastened her. As a consequence of the pulverizing shock-waves brought on by the squall of nuclear air-bursts, stem-like pedestals of dust arose and trailed the rising fireballs. When the blossoming, mushroom clouds reached the freezing, higher altitudes, their reddish brown color changed to a pure white due to the condensation of water droplets and ice crystals. The panoramic depiction made the entire landscape look to Ahneevah like a hellacious garden of blooming annihilation; a field of grotesque, *holocaust lilies* that within the fleeting passage of a nano-span vaporized over three-million of her people and wiped out the first-line air defense force along with the entire borderland security network. Ahneevah breathed out a shuddering sigh, and then her attention was drawn to the glow of the ascending day-star which was just breaching the horizon. She gazed awestruck as webs of blood-red, triton-plasma-flares crisscrossed the fiery orange crescent. *It looks like a sunrise that has run amok,* she thought, *it's as if the stellar disk itself had been mortally wounded and is... bleeding ... dying.* She considered the agonizing spectacle a poignant allegory for the once-flourishing civilization which the benevolent daystar nurtured—*her* civilization. One that was now steeped in lunacy and irrevocably spiraling down out of control to meet its ignoble end. Sharply, with piercing long—short—long—long—short staccato quavers, the alertklaxons abruptly halted any further inner deliberations. Emergency intercept status had been reached and she resigned herself to the implications. The anti-warhead missile defense system had failed and the roiling inferno and noxious fragmentation funnels created by the impact point turbulence-flames were merely an overture to the ferocious and chilling carnage to come. Ahneevah knew that the final assault was under way—and so—she had to go up.

She had to go up even though she was certain that a suppressive darkness would preempt the natural fall of the coming night. She further realized that practically every level of plant and animal life on her planetary home would be reduced to ashes well before the day's end, and whatever creatures somehow survived would suffer unbearable pain and anguish and eventually perish in the aftermath—but still—she had to go up. It was her sworn duty. She was the Air Arm Commander; a flag rank in the elite Orbital Flight Wing which represented the last line of defense, even though she totally recognized that there *was* no defense. Despite this demoralizing awareness, the sheer hopelessness was overridden by the oath Ahneevah took. She avowed to serve until her final breath, and now this desperate circumstance was upon her. The pledge that she affirmed represented part of the price she paid for her illustrious and rewarding military career. A calling that provided her with the opportunity to pilot the most advanced flight-vehicles that her aeronautical science could conceive. Preeminent among these craft was the StarStream. This advanced trans-orbital combat platform represented a giant leap in airframe and power-plant technology. At its core was an ion-fusion propulsion-train composed of oxy-hydro, bio-metallic lattices formed by trillions of coalescing micro-stars infinitely smaller than a molecule. The continual processing of all forms of ambient radiation provided a virtually inexhaustible fuel supply and each energy-web produced a sun-like nuclear reaction which generated limitless power without the excessive stellar-surface temperatures and hazardous radioactivity.

Ahneevah took a deep breath, exhaled, and walked across the transit-deck to the day-side terrace overlooking the back garden where, at the beginning of each new warm season, she and her mate would watch their young ones stumble and fall and play and laugh and grow. Several of her thought-pathways were still immersed in the terrible futility and waste that lay ahead while the majority of her mind tracks were reviewing the operations profile for what would unquestionably be her final mission.

The *whooshing* sound of the approaching Verti-craft Transport Module that would carry Ahneevah to the flight-line prompted her to turn and make her way over to the sky-pier extension. As the conveyance silently hovered, others in her circle came out of the residence shepherding her offspring who rushed to gather around her. She tried as best she could to explain the concept of forever to them but they tearfully fought the notion, though the eldest two tried to understand and be brave. Holding them tightly, she again considered the complete lunacy of what was about to take place and felt deep remorse that she was powerless to do anything to stop it.

The deployment of the Verti-craft's frozen-plasma embarkation walkway signaled that the time-chain segment had arrived for her to make her final departure. Ahneevah always imagined that when her physical existence ended, her eternity would be spent with her essence resting close to those she loved. She couldn't know that her impending forever would be far, far different from the one she had envisaged.

Ahneevah whispered a last agonizing farewell to all those around her and expressed the hope that they would see each other again in a better place, although she did not really believe that there was a *better place*. Finally, the gallant pilot crossed over the walkway, boarded the Verti-craft and took one last heartrending look at her progeny and the others so dear to her, others whom she would never see again. Then, facing the most courageous moment in her existence, with golden tears welled up in the corners of her exotic, verdant eyes, Ahneevah was *whisked* away to her improbable and incomprehensible destiny.

EPIJODE ONE

LESLEE ROSE MYLES
IN
"TIME AFTER TIME"

Nearly a million millennia later …

… Counselor Leslee R. Myles was pleading a major intellectual property case before the nine robed figures seated on the
bench of the United States Supreme Court. The legal action
concerned the patent rights to a revolutionary, nano-tech, medical
device known as the Cardio Event Monitor. Though worn on the
wrist like a watch, the CEM had the capability of providing far
more than the time of day. It could detect the onset of a heart-
attack by sensing any irregular cardiac contractions or erratic
electrical impulses and, with remarkable accuracy, was even able
to identify and evaluate the minutest changes in the blood
chemistry and vascular system. The invention had the potential
of saving millions of lives by recognizing an imminent cardiac
crisis, alerting the victim, and automatically contacting the
appropriate Emergency Responders within the medical *golden
hour* of maximum survivability. The CEM was also capable of
activating a companion, subcutaneous, micro-miniature defibrillator to restart cardiac function if necessary. Unfortunately, the
breakthrough mechanism was being withheld from the public
pending the outcome of the legal proceedings and as a result,
thousands of people who could have been saved had already died,

and more would die needlessly. The Medibotics Corporation, a major medical supplier, initially filed a lawsuit in the United States District Court for the District of Central California against Roberta Seymour, the small business inventor of the CEM. The suit was based on the plaintiff's argument that the defendant was in the company's employ when she came up with the notion for the invention, and that she had filed fraudulently to receive the patent. The District Court found for the defendant as did the Court of Appeals for the Ninth Circuit. However, the team of Medibotics attorneys, seeking a reversal of the appeal ruling, was *somehow* able to convince the Supreme Court to hear the case.

Counselor Myles was confident despite the fact that the present court had been markedly unsympathetic to individual creative and discovery rights. In spite of this, even the most conservative of the justices was being swayed by her concise, restrained and unavoidably logical arguments. She asserted that though the defendant was indeed employed by the plaintiff as an accountant, her job description had nothing whatsoever to do with creating new products and that there was no contract, implied or otherwise to the contrary. She also claimed that the litigation was frivolous and should never have been heard by the highest court in the land. The justices of the Court advised that they would render a decision in due course.

It was hard to imagine that a formidable and self-assured woman like Leslee Myles had been, less than a decade earlier, a woefully insecure college student to whom mediocrity represented an upgrade. One who barely was earning a Bachelor of *Anything* degree and who dreaded the idea of pursuing a legal education. Her first Law School Admissions Test scores were a disaster. The sole chance she had for acceptance into law school after her fourth year at The University of Southern California was as a legacy when she graduated, hopefully, after her *fifth* year. However, senior year—part two, was still ahead of her, and it was at this juncture that her improbable journey began with rickety and uncertain steps.

A black SUV sat with a balcony view of the glimmering San Fernando Valley lights neatly spread out under a star-dusted Southern California sky. The gas-guzzling vehicle with the familiar cardinal and gold *USC* decal displayed prominently on the lower right corner of the rear window seemed out of place with the other, more environmentally-friendly hybrid and electric smooch-wagons parked at one of the highly picturesque *make-out* perches sprinkled along Mulholland Drive. There were a dozen or so motor chassis rockin' and rollin' to the strains of their teenaged occupants' passages through the various progressions of *contact amore*. Though most were still chugging for first base, a daring few were digging breathlessly for the apex of *home*.

Inside the cargo area of the charcoal sport-utility vehicle, at least one of the entwined was *whizzing* around the keystone sack and heading for third. The young man, Georgie Weiss, had already succeeded in unzipping and peeling open the frilly evening gown worn by his would-be pincushion, Leslee R. Myles. Tonight Georgie had a sure thing. It was the previously negoti-ated *quid* for his *quo*. He agreed to be Leslee's date for the Spring Formal if she agreed to come up *here* and let him get down *there*. Four years earlier when Leslee was a senior in high school she came to this very spot on one occasion to neck. That was limited to some light petting which didn't do much for her hormones or her self-image. It struck her that this was an odd memory to conjure, but as Georgie boorishly pawed at her breasts she was jarred into the realization that this was not at all how, where, and with whom her first '*go all the way*' sexual experience should take place. She expected a more conducive atmosphere; at least a three-star hotel room and a bed. However, as far as Georgie was concerned, the only *atmosphere* he desired would be provided by the heavy breathing which would generate a sufficient volume of *score-fog* to condense on and thereby obscure the outside view through the non-tinted windows.

Undeniably, things seemed to be going well from the *male* perspective. The auto glass was indeed beginning to steam up, although it was mainly due to Georgie panting like a Siberian snow dog in a Native American sweat lodge. On the other side of the pending penetration, Leslee was getting no joy from either the chest mauling or Georgie's frenching skills. His tongue darting in and out of her mouth reminded her of a rattlesnake she saw on a National Geographic cable show. It all came to a head the moment Georgie's roving hand slipped under her somewhat north of sized-sixteen custom-made frock. That's when Leslee's second thoughts about the price she was about to pay for a little male companionship began meandering to—*I don't think so.* "Uh-uh," she murmured, but Georgie was much too aroused to notice. His libido raging in maximum seduction mode and operating exclusively on orgasmic-overdrive, he slid his hand up past Leslee's knee and began kneading her upper leg as if he were an infomercial pitchman squeezing the water out of a Sham Wow. With Georgie's tongue jabbing at her teeth and gums and his hand creeping up her inner thigh, Leslee decided it was definitely time to bail—and so she turned up the volume. "Please, no." Once again Georgie missed the signal. By this point, Leslee's dissatis-faction was bubbling over and so to eliminate any uncertainty her oblivious suitor might have had she blurted out, "No!" as though she were reprimanding an untrained puppy that kept failing to hit the newspaper. Georgie hesitated and then continued on with his quest for her fire.

Recognizing that a more physical approach was needed, she grabbed his hand and forcefully bent his fingers back. "Yeow!" Georgie shrieked as Leslee removed his unwanted mitt from her reception area and leveraged it out from under her gown.

Wincing, Georgie pulled his over-torqued paw from his uncooperative date's grasp and began to shake, rub, and open and close his smarting digits in an attempt to relieve the pain. Leslee quickly took the opportunity to scramble to her knees, open the back hatch of the SUV and bolt out into the night air. Georgie continued to flex his throbbing fingers to make sure they were still functioning and then he jumped down from the tailgate behind his suddenly rebellious sex object.

"No? What do you mean no? That was our deal. Besides," he chided, "you'll only wind up hating yourself in the morning."

"Don't talk to me about hating myself. I've spent most of my life down that road."

Leslee put her left arm through the corresponding shoulder strap to keep the dress from sliding down too far. "Look, I'm sorry," she ventured, not that any apology was really warranted. "You're acting like some love-hungry teenager following his di... his libido and you ... you just can't be the first."

"First!" Georgie cried. His eyes lit up at the prospect. "You mean you're still a virgin?"

"That's not the issue," Leslee shot back. "Maybe I don't know how it's supposed to be but I do know that *this*," she swept her hand in a wide arc to emphasize the point, "a quickie in a car with a self-absorbed asshole ... is definitely not it. And besides, I thought the fluid-swapping part comes after the dance, not before."

"Why not on both ends?" Georgie posed. "I figured we'd go to the frat house later."

The increasing volume of Georgie and Leslee's verbal skirmish prompted some of the other aspiring young lovers to roll down their windows and check out the source of the commotion. Noticing this, Leslee defiantly thrust her right arm through the other shoulder strap, and indignantly marched away. There would be no legends made on this night, at least not with her name attached. As she high-heeled it past the other shake-and-bake chariots, Leslee turned her undone evening gown slightly to one side to make the zipper easier to reach. "I don't even like you," she tossed back over her shoulder and then refocused her attention on the balky zipper which was now caught on some frill or other. "I don't like you either," Georgie Weiss yapped and stepped around the rear of the vehicle in pursuit of his runaway tryst-ticket. "So what?"

In the interim, additional members of the Mulholland Climax Corps popped out of their autos to eyeball the spontaneous floor show. Leslee, now feeling embarrassment as well as humiliation, glared at Georgie.

"Actually, I think you really are a snake." She illustrated her point by blinking her eyes and poking holes in the evening air with a rapid in and out movement of her tongue. The lipstick-smeared crowd *howled* in approval.

Georgie's reaction to the obvious ridicule was predictable. "This is bullshit," he shouted in disgust then he opened the driver's side door, vaulted into the seat, slammed the door behind him, cranked the ignition key, jammed the stick into *R* and tromped down on the accelerator. The spinning wheels raised a swirl of dust as he backed up and then *screeched* to a stop. Next he popped the gearshift lever into 1st and *peeled* away in a cloud of burning rubber and floating grime.

Left flat in a billow of spewed-up road filth, surrounded by the applause, laughter and hoots from the mean-spirited onlookers, Leslee stood there mortified and wanted to crawl into a hole. She couldn't contain herself any longer and began sobbing as she continued to tug on the uncooperative zipper, eventually managing to get it halfway up before it quit again. Finally she started trudging down the hill in a tousled, coral-pink collection of chiffon and satin. Through her tears she dug into her bag, pulled out her cell phone and pressed the voice recognition key. "Home," she whimpered. "No, dammit, cancel." Then she forced herself to say, "Beverly Hills Cab." It hadn't yet occurred to her that for the first time in her *doormat* life Leslee drew a line in the sand and actually stood up for herself.

Sanford Myles, a high-priced corporate attorney and senior partner in Myles, Hornwood and Rubin, was waiting in his dark-oak, wainscoted study when Leslee arrived home. The instant she came through the door of the ten-thousand-square-foot estate in the north-side flats of Beverly Hills, she was summoned over the intercom to meet her father in his lair.

Sanford was seated at his large mahogany desk in an oversized leather chair, and Leslee's mother, Pinkie, was standing beside him when their daughter shuffled in and stopped near the doorway.

"Georgie Weiss called to see if you got home all right," Sanford announced.

"He was afraid that your father would have him arrested if anything happened to you," Pinkie added, then noticed the damage to the evening gown and rushed over to Leslee.

"Oh my, this is a Ms. Suzie Bren original! I thought you could wear it to your Cousin Rebecca's wedding." She tried to put one of the more severely out of place ruffles of fabric back where it belonged but it uncooperatively fluttered down to its previous dislocated position. Pinkie shook her head disapprovingly and sighed. "Now it's a wreck."

"I'm glad you're home early," Sanford said, not giving much thought to the fact that Leslee would have preferred *not* to be home so early. "I have good news. Your Uncle Mal got you a space on that Israel trip. You leave in two weeks. Oh, and by the way, I need some documents on the Lipman case proofread for tomorrow." He slid a bulky file toward the front edge of his desk, "Neither one of your brothers can do it. Jason isn't available and I don't know where Elliot is." He never knew where Elliot was—

no one did. Not even Elliot. Leslee, deflated, slumped against the hand-carved molding around the entrance to her father's sacred sanctum. Her body language was projecting the unmistakable signs of defeat and disappointment. *It wasn't new,* she thought. Sanford and Pinkie should have seen that she'd been crying. They should have seen the distress and tried to comfort their only daughter. They didn't—and worse, they never had. "Sure, dad, I'll proof the work. Let me clean up and get into something less scruffy," Leslee whispered softly, then looked back expectantly at Pinkie. "Be careful when you take the dress off," Pinkie cautioned. "I'll drop it by Ms. Suzie's in the morning. Maybe she can save it." Leslee opened her mouth as if to say something but instead sighed in resignation, bent her head down and with her shoulders drooping, moped away.

EPIƧODE TWO

"THE DAY THE WORLD ENDED"

Ahneevah settled into the StarStream's biotech flight seat, and as she ran through her pre-departure checklist she could feel the first penetrating surge of heat on the back of her neck from …

… the dragon-breath thermal gusts churned up by the primary blast-rays. Recognizing that the enemy spearhead had already advanced well inside the borders of the mainland, it crossed one of her profuse mental conduits that within the near day-part her entire planet would be saturated with lethal radiation, deadly poisons and the dank, hopeless smell of death. It was clear to her that the StarStream's onboard respiration system would serve as her final environment. Fully reconciled to her fate, she paused for a brief moment, slowly inhaled one last, long, deep breath of the yet uncontaminated morning air and opened her large, jade eyes to their optimum panoramic view to take a final look at a world she had no hope of ever seeing again. Then, with great resolve, the combat-hardened flight-leader brushed back her shining amber hair, set and secured her omni-vision helmet in place, activated the flexible-plasma visor and slid the palm-sized logic unit into its flight-dynamics interface slot in the starboard-side armrest.

As soon as the download-phase of her departure parameters were completed and fed into her Helmet-Mounted Display, immediate take-off authorization was granted by the Aero

Guidance Control Officer. Ahneevah activated the particle
sequencer which triggered the StarStream's muon-catalyzer and
initiated the low-temp fusion process. With an almost imperceptible *hum*, the craft's inner frozen-gas canopy slid forward and
sealed itself into the bio-magnetic capture system. In succession,
the outer clamshell slowly and silently lowered, locked down into
position and the ionized-plasma view-portal materialized in its
transparent mode. Upon reaching maximum thrust, Ahneevah
launched skyward to rendezvous with her battle section already
on station in orbit.

High above the planetary day-night terminator, Ahneevah joined
her Air Arm. She would lead them to intercept their enemy as they
had done so many times before, but this time their adversaries
would number in the millions—without soul and without con-
science. A force bent solely on terror and obliteration—instigated
by a malicious horde that had inexplicably and inexcusably lost its
sanity in a world that had now irretrievably lost its way. However,
Ahneevah also knew that her own people had not acted as they
should have to stem the wave of destruction before it grew to
uncontrollable proportions. On various occasions she tried to
convince her leadership of their intransigence. "We are becoming
our enemy." Ahneevah would warn. "Their tactics have become
our tactics. The land of my birth is no longer the land in which I
was born, it is no longer the bright beacon of hope that it had once
been. We must be better. We must find our way safely through the
maelstrom and cease our aimless march toward the end of time
itself. We can once again set an example and follow the guide
points of those who eons before began the journey on the Path of
Illumination—the earliest Time-Spanners—the First Prophets of
Integrity and Reason." But even with her status as a global hero,
her pleas fell on deaf ears and narrow minds.

The mission profile for Ahneevah's Air Arm was straightforward. Kill as many of their adversaries as possible despite the fact that there was no logical chance of a tactical or strategic gain or any hope of a positive outcome. Even though there was nothing left but mutual annihilation, she would carry out her assignment and heroically face her end knowing that she was keeping her oath.

Ahneevah's extraordinary and extremely gallant career was filled with missions that were considered to be of the *one-way* variety but somehow she always managed to turn them into round trips. Her heroism under fire during the previous two wars was legend. She flew against and destroyed more enemy craft on orbit than any other pilot in Air Wing history, and after the last war she was detached from her combat division, advanced in rank to Air Arm Commander and assigned to the Space Exploration Corps. As a flight-leader, test pilot and scientist, she made six glorious trips into the cosmos. Four of her missions took her to a series of lunar sites where she supervised the establishment of the initial Planetary Excursion Support Bases. Ahneevah almost perished on a daring and desperate mission to stop a double-barreled rogue comet from wiping out all life on her planet and its near space neighbor. No one in the Tactical Planning Authority of the Space Exploration Wing believed she would succeed and make it back home.

This time, however, she would not make it back home. Her extraordinary abilities would be unable to overcome the crushing destructive power she was about to face ... a power that was driven by the fearsome necessity for those with divergent views to exterminate their rivals rather than seek a compromise to resolve their differences.

The final confrontation raged vertically from the lower atmosphere to the orbital ellipses and horizontally over vast distances across the entire super continent. Wave after wave of the enemy's highly superior Flank Bombers came under the firepower of

Ahneevah's squadron, and wave after wave were decimated. But Ahneevah knew full well that her rapidly escalating air-kills were short-lived and hollow victories, and even with her battle group's extreme courageousness and sacrifice, she eventually found herself the last StarStream pilot left in the fight. An entire tactical wing of rival ships was spitting a relentless barrage of wide-beam pulse waves at her lone craft. Again and again, the supremely gifted and seasoned combat aviator masterfully darted out of harm's way. Each defensive shift brought a tactical advantage and each was used to counter-attack. Though she finally vanquished all those who challenged her, the countless detonations of her antagonist's aircraft and ordnance turned the air itself into a radiation-ridden inferno. Below, most of the surface of her planetary home had become a burgeoning sea of flame, dust and debris.

In the last agonizing stages of the battle, Ahneevah lost all on-board tracking data. She found herself at the top of her dying world fighting to hand-maneuver her stricken craft through the conflagration that was now amplified a thousand-fold in the wake of the chain-reaction of the exploding enemy air armada. Intense magno-thermic waves started to finger their way through the ionized titanium-silicate sections of the StarStream's organic composite skin, and the power immediately started falling off. In response, the fire suppression system robotically triggered to counter the ultra-high temperature acceleration by temporarily altering the subatomic matrix in selected sections of the ship's component parts. This action elevated their melting point and resulted in the hungry tentacles of superheated gas being forced to subside from their feeding frenzy. Nevertheless, the outside temperature was now spiking up toward stellar surface levels which were far beyond the maximum limit of the StarStream's heat-resistant molecular barrier. The onset of catastrophic structural failure was imminent in various sectors of the multi-carbonized and organic-composite materials forming the shell of the craft. This was an unusual situation for Ahneevah. She had never lost a single air vehicle in her entire military career. There was, however, little she could do to delay the inevitable. All that was left to her in this moment was to precisely follow her training which called for her to broadcast a distress call over the comlink. She did so even though a standby level of her varied layers of consciousness knew that the carrier wave would have only a minute chance of penetrating the pulse oscillations caused by the persistent salvo of the anti-particle based weaponry. The constant electromagnetic discharges emitted by the endless fusion-pod explosions had ionized the air surrounding the StarStream, further impeding the signal strength of the transponder pulses emitted by her onboard navigation and communications platforms. Worst of all, her intuition told her that there was no one left on the ground to receive her transmissions.

In spite of the critical reality, Ahneevah continued to follow procedure by recording her final thoughts into her logic unit and removing it from its slot. With a verbal command, the device separated into two sections and she jettisoned one of them along with the flat, circular Photonic Emergency Transducer location tracking module. Both pieces of equipment were whipped away in the fighting craft's slipstream and then caught in its wake.

The ancient swampland below stretched out over half of a hemisphere and almost into the last sunset. Over this most desolate region of the continent the air continued to be shattered by the massive chain-reaction explosions vaulting the outside air temperatures well beyond those found on a solar body. Subsequently, the tera-degree heat began generating severe turbulence of an unprecedented magnitude. Violent, vertical fire plumes and fierce wind-shear turned the StarStream into a superheated, out-of-control projectile plummeting from an altitude at the limit of the suborbital gravity effect down through a blazing hell-storm. Ahneevah was aware that she had only a negligible sliver of life remaining to her but simply giving in and waiting for the inevitable plunge into the nothingness of the roiling furnace below was not an option—not by any means. She deftly reduced the power and lowered her breathing rate to a barely perceptible level—just enough respiration function to allow her to stay alert and retain control. When her carbon dioxide recycling unit failed, she shut down her own active breathing system altogether—fully confident that the energy-oxidation components stored in her body would serve her through the completion of her final tasks.

As a result of the tornado-force convection currents, the cooler air that surrounded the virtually endless stretch of wetland vegetation was being vacuumed skyward. This action carried the oxygen-rich surface air to higher altitudes and gave the flames new life. The heat inside the StarStream's inner flight compartment had risen beyond the maximum operating limits of the reserve cooling unit. Finally, the scorching super-heated plasmic inferno won its battle against the fire-suppression system. The tentacles of scorching ionized gas began to crawl through the internal bio-structure of the teardrop air vehicle, making it impossible for the nucleonic regeneration process to continue. Although it was manufactured, the StarStream contained numerous biologic components and Ahneevah could, in a sense, feel her ship dying. The control-system initiators were destabilizing and the resultant thermic oscillations made the craft aerodynamically unstable causing its entry into a wildly gyratory downward spiral. The voice coming from her logic unit announced that the automatic abort sequence was in its final phase and that the *safe ejection* window was about to close. *Safe ejection to where?* She calmly deduced. *The whole world is burning.*

By this time, any thinking being would have been resigned to the inevitable and surrendered to it. But this particular aviator still refused to give in. Ahneevah was determined that she would not submit and simply give up her life-force—it would have to be taken from her.

"Terminate abort procedure … cancellation code XEL-EBR-09Z," she ordered and instinctively, in a last-ditch effort to reign in her runaway craft, overrode all of her automatic systems, opened the secondary weapons pod-bay doors and fired her remaining ordnance aft. Then she raised the outer clamshell slightly and deployed the rarely used auxiliary air brakes to add some aerodynamic drag. This action, plus the forward-aimed neutronic thrust from the missiles' power cores, effectively acted against the over-speed component and slowed the StarStream's velocity and rate of descent. The canopy remained intact and held solidly onto its central attach points, but she could hear and feel the grinding and tearing noises, shudder and scream throughout her flight vehicle as the extended air-brake panels and weapons pod-bay doors were blasted away from the main structure by the hypersonic slipstream. However, the structural sacrifices bought her an additional fraction of time before she would become the final casualty of a pointless, psychotically motivated war.

Gradually, as the StarStream's speed began to bleed off and drop below supersonic, Ahneevah stabilized it and regained some control. Though the ship was inverted, Ahneevah managed to lock down the outer canopy and, after descending through the escalating inferno, the huge, dark droplet—followed by the still-intact ejected data processors, corkscrewed in toward the expansive everglade below. The power automatically shut down when the flight vehicle crunched through the fiery crown of the bayou's flaming, moss-draped, giant trees. The hard contact with the thick, resilient foliage sufficiently decreased the teardrop craft's velocity so that when it finally impacted with the steaming, highly-irradiated sea of muck, it did not disintegrate. Due to its engineering and design qualities it immediately rolled upright.

With the power off, the superheated plasma rapidly cooled, but the slimy bog water poured in through the exposed air brake wells and pod bay. With the world collapsing around it, in a cacophony of bubbling and crackling reverberations, the normally buoyant StarStream sank down to the hypothermic depths of the marsh, with its undertow tugging the trailing ejecta behind it. The coming nuclear winter would permanently freeze the swampland and seal the legacy of the pilot. As her cognizance faded, her last sensory perception was of the vibrations and sounds of the convulsive, muffled explosions thundering relentlessly above the quagmire's surface. Then—nothing.

In a distant epoch, far beyond Ahneevah's comprehension, the choices she made and her inexorable heroic actions would have profound ramifications for a yet-unborn civilization—on a very different world.

EPISODE THREE

LESLEE AND DR. ISAAC CARVER
IN
"THE WHEELS OF CHANCE"

*S**wigging a malt brew, with a cigarette tucked above his right ear, Isaac L. Carver, Ph.D. was standing, up to his gray, sweat-stained, soft-wool fedora in …***

… an excavation pit scooped out of the Negev Desert floor. He was wearing a perspiration-soaked, non-logo tee-shirt because he totally rejected the idea of being a billboard for any 'goddamn corporation' without being duly compensated. A worn leather belt, with the words *Archeology<>Dig It!* inscribed on a round pewter buckle, was wrapped around his waist holding up a knee-holed pair of washed-out jeans. Carver took a long chug-a-lug and wiped his hand across his mouth. The beer provided a modicum of relief from the unrelenting heat of the desert sun. Zack never drank *real* booze on the job. It was his only hard and fast rule.

In his younger, more sober days, Isaac Carver was regarded as a prodigy and to his credit, at the age of twenty-two, he earned Harvard doctorates in both archeology and anthropology. Zack therefore considered himself an archeo-anthropologist or if the occasion required—an anthro-archeologist. However, most who knew him basically considered him an obnoxious prick in the extreme. Though he did have an intelligence quotient well in excess of one hundred and fifty, he unfortunately also had an intoxication quotient in excess of 150—proof.

A wiry and rugged-looking twenty-six, Zack had recently completed his second semester as a Professor of Archeology at Arizona State University and also completed his first stab at wedded bliss. His ex-doctorial thesis advisor, Alida Gray, also became his first ex-wife.

Included in Dr. Carver's teaching curriculum was an official archeological dig, and to lend a tone of authenticity to impress his latest entourage of Indiana Jones wannabes, Zack secured a position as a guest instructor at Tel Aviv University. The money was good and he needed the *additional funding* to pay part of the freight for his recent, self-induced marital train-wreck. In order to qualify for certain government grants, it was required that the program be open to a limited number of worthy students from other schools. And so it was that the Negev Desert would provide the summer playground wherein Carver's varied collection of rookie, relic-moles could gain some practical experience.

She walks like a penguin, Zack thought as he watched her shamble timidly past some of the other archeo-tyros and toward his hole in the desert sand. *It looks unnatural. Her arms don't swing at all. They just hang stationary at her sides, like a rag-doll's.* As she waddled along; her klutzy gait and almost waist-length hair made her seem out of touch and out of rhythm with everything around her—a classic misfit. If first impressions really mattered, this meeting had *false-start* written all over it. Therefore, neither one of the parties to this paradoxical encounter could have had the slightest inkling of the exceptionally significant role they would each play as shapers of destiny.

Clutching a crumple of paperwork with a trembling hand, Leslee R. Myles clumsily extended her arm toward Zack. He impatiently stared at her and waited—after a few pregnant seconds and a few self-conscious glances at some of the other young *'dig we must'* crewmembers, she managed to coax her voice up to a mumble and croak out in meek and barely audible tones, "Ummm, uhhh … hi, Dr. Carver, I … I'm Leslee Myles."

Following a few phlegmy, tuberculin-sounding cigarette coughs, Zack dragged himself out of the trench and stood up. Being six-feet tall, he was surprised to find that he was almost eye to eye with this uneasy, lumpish figure. Zack brusquely snatched the hodgepodge of documents from Leslee's outstretched hand, and began separating the pages. As he proceeded scanning through each wrinkled leaf, the bulk of his annoyance gurgled to the surface. "I didn't need this right now," he bristled, then drained the remaining amber liquid, crushed its container and tossed it on a recycle mini-mound where it clanked against a substantial heap of other dead aluminum players. He continued shuffling through Leslee's rumpled file, then removed the cigarette from behind his ear and lit it. "You're a week late!" he rasped through a mouthful of smoke. "And fuck! Archeology was only your goddamned minor … and you plan on going to law school!"

"Well … I'm gonna apply to … to …" Leslee stammered.

"I told those bastards, I wanted science majors … master and doctoral candidates only. Damned imbeciles!" he roared and then returned his attention to the papers. "Suck-hole grades as well. Pretty sorry-assed student, aren't you?" He said without looking up. "How the hell do you expect to be accepted into any law school with numbers like these?"

"Well, uh yes, Dr. Carver, I mean, I don't know but I …" Once more Leslee looked around and couldn't find anything to say that would be coherent, much less helpful, so she just stood blankly like a furloughed *Muppet*. Zack took another drag on his coffin-nail. "Look, Ms. Myles, you'll do us both a big favor if you cut the bullshit." With each fricative and plosive syllable Zack uttered, wisps of secondhand smoke came out in small bursts and swirled around Leslee who coughed several times and then took a step back. Zack took another puff and exhaled it to the side. "I know, I know, you thought it would be *way cool* to spend the summer at a real archeological dig."

"But I really like studying archeology, it's …"

"I couldn't tell by your transcript. You got a *C* in it … crappy grades … strike one! You're not a science major, Strike two!! And finally, you're gonna be a fifth-year student. Strike three!!! There it is." Zack made the baseball *out* sign with his thumb and simultaneously shouted "Yer out, not qualified for the program." Then realizing, "But how the hell did you get in?" Zack read a bit further and then a light bulb came on. "Oh, along came daddy Myles. He made a *donation* to buy you a slot."

Leslee knew that was not quite the case. "No … uhhh … it was Uncle Mal. He's on the board at Arizona State."

"Uncle Mal, daddy, whatever," Zack grumbled. "Okay, here it is. Don't even think that you're gonna get any preferred status here. You won't be digging in prime areas." Zack grabbed a broken chunk of pottery from a wooden sifter on the ground. "It's not like the Indiana Jones stuff. It's sweaty and dirty and grinding … and there's no Ark of the Covenant or Holy Grail at the end of it. There's mainly pottery, shards of pottery and if you're lucky … maybe a spearhead or two. Isn't that right, everybody?" The small company of amateur, artifact-baggers looked up from their ground-based chores, nodded vacantly and then carried on with their burrowing.

"And so Miss Rich-Girl," Carver went on, "you will work your ass off like everyone else, or you'll be home in time for the Fourth of July fireworks at the Beverly Hills Country Club."

"Uhhh … Malibu, Dr. Carver."

"Who in the fuck cares?"

In truth, Sanford Myles did not necessarily have Leslee's best interests at heart when asked his brother Mal to make the arrangements for her to go to Israel. He did it mainly because he saw the opportunity to ship his underachieving problem child off for someone else to deal with—someone else who would badger, bully and berate his only daughter who was toting around enough psychological baggage to fill the hole Zack had been standing in—and then some. Although Leslee's loose-fitting garments partially masked thirty-five plus pounds of *chunky*, there wasn't much she could do to hide the *clunky*. At the end of the day—any day—Leslee Myles was just a few weaves short of being a total basket case.

Zack quartered Leslee in a tent instead of one of the pre-fabricated aluminum lean-tos, and as the days plodded by he assigned her to every shit detail he could think of and some that broke entirely new fecal ground. She dug, sifted, stooped and scraped in the sweltering desert sun from before light until after dark. She would bruise, bleed, burn and ache until she welcomed *numb*. At times she felt as if she were excavating the entire Negev Desert on her own. But she never complained or showed the slightest sign of dissatisfaction in regard to the grueling work. She looked at it as a way of doing penance for all her frailties; inherent and acquired.

After several weeks, Leslee realized that something totally unexpected was happening. Because she was essentially being left alone with her labors, the incessant pressure and criticism that was so much a part of her life had mostly evaporated. This left her psyche free to be the Taoist un-carved block which made her receptive to a way forward—a way that might hopefully see her gain a sense of who she really was. To her great surprise, instead of feeling physically drained at the end of each day, Leslee was actually finding the work to be invigorating and she discovered that with each passing sunset she was anxiously anticipating the smell of the next morning's desert air. She was like an athlete getting a second wind, and no matter how early

Zack arrived at the site, she was already there digging and sifting. The harder and more drudgery-intensive the work got, the more Leslee wrapped herself in it. In her mind it was a form of redemption and she began to wear the toil like a protective veil which all at once seemed to shield her from her demons both within and without. Leslee had always been a half-a-tone flat and dissonant to the key of life's music, but now she was becoming attuned to the harmony of the natural concert playing all around her.

When Jewish boys and girls reach the age of thirteen they have Bar and Bat Mitzvahs. These are traditional religious ceremonies that commemorate their rite of passage into adulthood and its inherent responsibilities. Leslee's Hebrew name was Leah Rifka and in preparation for her Bat Mitzvah it was compulsory for her to read and speak Hebrew. Having acquired some familiarity with the Hebrew language, young Leah Rifka figured that it would be a breeze subject at Beverly Hills High—it wasn't. But now in the land of Israel, due to her constant exposure to it, she truly began picking up its cadence and pitch and was amazed that she was actually starting to *think* in the Hebrew tongue. She also began to stand taller, walk less gawkily and speak less haltingly. The need to eat became a practical matter as opposed to an obsession, and for both coolness and convenience she had her overly-long auburn hair cut short. Makeup became a trivial matter.

After nearly a month, Leslee's impromptu life-style adjustments began to provoke unforeseen side-effects. Some of the men on the project, who at first hardly even thought of Leslee as a female, began to pay attention to her and would vie to get assigned to the same dig site where she was working. Gary Layton, a USC senior, actually asked her out on a date, and they spent several evenings dining together—with no side deals.

In the fifth week of Leslee's Negev experience, while she was exploring a hillside cave, Gary slithered into the cramped area and began whispering warm-fuzzies, kissing her neck and nibbling her ear. This was dark territory for her and at first she didn't know how to handle the situation. So far Gary had been a gentleman.

"Gary, not now," Leslee objected but as her lips formed the *w* at the end of *now*, Gary's mouth was pressed against them and his tongue was heading toward her tonsils. Oddly, she didn't find herself put off by Gary's aggression. He certainly kissed a lot better than Georgie Weiss, and she found the experience some-what pleasant. However, before she knew it, Gary unbuttoned and unzipped her khaki cargos and his hand began creeping where no hand, other than her own and her OB/GYN's, had crept before. She tried to push him away, but he resisted. It was time to draw the line and Leslee's rich-girl terrorist training kicked in. Being less than three inches shy of six feet, she was easily able to force her right knee between Gary's legs. She could have driven her knee hard into his crotch, rung his bell and won a giant stuffed panda right then and there. Instead she decided on minimal action and chose to simply take a long step forward.

"That's enough," she bayed, as her move upset Gary's balance and slammed him hard against the opposite wall. After he smashed into and bounced off of the rock, Leslee grabbed his hand, spun him around, locked his arms and wrists up behind him and applied leverage to force him down and drive him like a wheelbarrow toward the daylight—with some serious attitude. "Yeow," Gary bellowed, in reaction to the intense pain.

Zack, alerted by the shrill expression of apparent discomfort, turned in the direction of the disquieting *yelp* just in time to see Gary come flying out of the cave entrance as if he were launched, and as a finale, *crash and burn* into a mound hot desert sand—face-first. Zack cringed at hearing the sound of the resulting muted *crunch*.

A few seconds later, Leslee, looking somewhat disheveled, stepped out through the cave opening. Zack was very quick to notice that she was buttoning her shorts. Gary in the meantime didn't notice much of anything. He was too busy spitting a generous helping of the gritty dune out of his mouth, riding out the dull pain in his groin area and fighting to hold down his lunch. Zack, however, immediately did the *math* and without a word he rushed over to Gary, grabbed a handful of his shirt, and pulled the would-be ladies' man nose to nose.

"Listen, you walking hard-on, this is not a goddamn singles bar. It's ARCHE-ology, not BI-ology. You wanna get laid, go to some pick-up joint or get yourself a pro. I catch your ass coming on to …" Zack turned in Leslee's direction …"what's your name again?"

"Leslee Rose Myles," she answered as she finished straightening her clothing.

"Right," Zack said and glared back at Gary. "If you make one more horned-toad move on … Rosy here, you're gonna be stateside before you can say 'what the fuck?' Got it?" Leslee never liked being called Rosy. There was a *Leslie* in her summer camp group and every year she would have to endure being called Rosy to distinguish her from the very popular Leslie Ginsberg.

After being read the *riot act* by Dr. Carver, Gary dolefully nodded in the affirmative and without another word dragged himself toward the hole in the hillside. Skulking away, he looked back over his shoulder at Leslee.

"Sorry, Ms. Myles, I was out of line," he acknowledged. "I know it's not an excuse, but you smell so nice and you stopped wearing all that gooey stuff on your face and your hair looks great." Leslee, not wanting to encourage Gary, just shrugged her shoulders. However, she gushed a bit inside and had to apply some serious *lip muscle* to fight off the satisfied grin that was threatening to creep onto her lips.

"Thanks, Dr. Carver, I'd like to get back to work now," she said and turned to follow Gary toward the cave.

Zack put out a hand to stop her. "No, uh … Rosy, you've had enough of that peckerhead. I think it would be better if you come over to the main dig and work with me. We're down near the 3000-BC level. I'll show you some of the more promising areas, and you can choose one of them to excavate on your own."

Zack didn't have the slightest idea why he did this. Maybe he saw something in her that was—no. Maybe he had a hunch—not likely. Maybe it was compassion—not possible. Whatever unexplained thought-train was rumbling through his mind, Isaac L. Carver, a man with no patience for anything or anyone but himself went out of his way to be kind to Leslee and even upgraded her living quarters.

In the next several weeks, the newfound reinforcement Leslee received from Zack so focused her that on her own she unearthed several rather substantial artifacts that dated back over five millennia. But her most important achievement happened very late in the summer. Zack became embroiled in a legal hassle with the local authorities when a dispute cropped up regarding the legitimacy of his dig. The landowner alleged that Leslee had picked out a site not within the dimensional dictates of the contract. That particular dig yielded an intact, circa 3000-B.C. Sumerian water jar probably from a passing ancient caravan. Leslee surprised herself by logically interpreting the written agreement and convincing the powers that be that Zack's actions fell within the dictates of the deal. Leslee, by now fairly conversant in Hebrew, introduced herself to the landlord Elon Margalite as Leah Rifka Millstein. Her original family name was Millstein before Sanford changed it to Myles. With some assistance from several of the local students on the dig, she explained to Mr. Margalite, in his native tongue, that he had misinterpreted the measurements.

"The contract terms were set forth in kilometers." Margalite sputtered in a rat-tat-tat burst of Sephardic Hebrew, fully expecting Leslee to be unable to interpret. Leslee was right with him, however, and her words came out with equal velocity as she displayed the contract.

"Mr. Margalite, with all due respects … if you will kindly look at the definitions page, it states in no uncertain terms that the excavation areas referred to are expressed in miles and not kilometers. Miles are two-fifths longer than kilometers. Thereby ten miles encompass more area than ten kilometers. I assure you that there was not a spade full of sand or an artifact taken outside the perimeters specified in the agreement."

Before they knew it they were all laughing, singing Israeli folk songs and drinking plum wine. They all became pals and Elon Margalite showed up at the dig after each day's work to hang out with the college professor and "that nice, tall, and very bright" Millstein girl.

For the good work she did, Zack rewarded Leslee with the first *A* of her collegiate life. Her hard labor in the scorching Middle Eastern desert sun also brought additional and unanticipated bonuses. By the end of the summer, the thirty-five pounds of *chunky* became less than ten; the *clunky* was barely evident; and the hint of *attractiveness* that Gary Layton spoke of was handing a *pink slip* to the old, misfit version of Leslee Myles.

On the night before they were to depart Tel Aviv, Leslee, draped only in the sheer curtain that hung in her room, slipped into Zack's hotel suite and served herself up on a platter to him. "Ms. Myles, you're a student, for God's sake!" Zack insisted, despite the fact that after his divorce his love-life was nonexistent.

"Uh-uh, I'm over twenty-one and school's out," Leslee purred as if it were an invitation and then held up her final grade card. "I got an *A*," she added as she walked over to the bed and planted herself on a corner near the headboard.

Zack considered all the people that he had hurt and disappointed through the years. "Look, I'm sorry, but you're just not my type," he said, knowing full well that he was lying through his teeth. Although not much outside of his work did turn him on these days, a selfish *quick dip* might have had its upside. *What the hell kind of perfume was she wearing? That Gary bastard was right… there was something about her.* Zack took a few measured steps toward this freshly minted sultress-in-training. She reached out to him, but then he stopped himself. Zack was mildly flabbergasted by the fact that he was actually considering someone else's feelings over his own. Ignoring his prurient interests, and somehow reasoning that carrying on with this particular student was on its face dishonest and selfish, he sheepishly backed away.

"What's the matter?" Leslee cooed and then lowered the sheet, exposing a wee bit more of her ampleness. "Gary's been practically begging to get in my pants all summer. Even after the cave thing when I almost made him a eunuch," she chuckled. "He said my power really turned him on. What do you say … Dr. Zack?"

"Ms. Myles …"

"Please, I liked it when you called me Rosy," she breathed demurely. Actually, the first male that ever called her Rosy got a black eye for his indiscretion.

Zack moved a step closer and then gently took her hand. He coaxed her up off the bed and for the first time looked directly into her hazel eyes. He read something that he found somehow extraordinary and yet elusive. Then Zack let go of her hand, put his arm around her waist and gently guided her over to the door. "Rosy, you deserve better than that … Gary," he said softly as he opened the door. "Christ, you deserve better than me! Have a safe trip home and a good life." This was an unprecedented display of restraint on Zack's part. He said, "Shalom," and tenderly eased

Leslee out into the hallway and began to close the door. Then he added, "You really did good work, thank you." Zack clicked the door shut and went directly for some vodka and—more vodka.

Leslee, the rejectee with her chin on her chest, sullenly shuffled along the hallway. Then something struck her and she stopped. A smile curled on her lips. The new and improved glass-half-full Leslee had unexpectedly arrived at another conclusion. Dr. Carver had acted quite chivalrously not to take advantage of her vulnerable state, and his stock rose even further in her mind. She turned toward Zack's room for a last symbolic look. "Well Dr. Carver, you're not really the son-of-a-bitch that everyone thinks you are. Are you?" As she moved on, Gary Layton came out of his room and stopped to admire Leslee's current *sheer* wardrobe selection. She raised her hands in a mock fighting position. Gary immediately got the message, waved and popped back into his room. Leslee's smile widened, she took a deep breath, pivoted around and headed resolutely down the corridor.

EPISODE FOUR

THE LAST CHANCE
"DESTINATION MOON"

In the precarious truce that existed before the final war erupted, Ahneevah was assigned to be the commander of the first expedition to ...

... explore the mysterious fourth planet where seas, lakes and gigantic underground glaciers were identified by advanced robotic probes. Unfortunately this was a mission that would never happen. During the final test phase of the newest variant StarGazer Trans-Stellar Explorer, a planetary extinction threat was discovered looming on the cosmic horizon. An undetected comet and a companion trailing fragment were on a direct-impact course with the lunar body circling Ahneevah's world. Sub-planetesimal objects such as asteroids and meteors were less difficult to pick up than comets because they traveled parallel to the solar orbital plane. Comets, on the other hand, came from the stellar debris sphere which completely encompassed the planetary system. This made them extremely difficult to track because they could approach from almost any angle. But even in the face of that scientific truth, under normal circumstances the path of the potential killer-masses of ice and rock might have been observed, plotted and their eventual contact point predicted when they were well beyond the Planetary Orbital Plane Debris Ribbon. However, due to the deteriorating geopolitical conditions

and global distrust, all major technology was being comman-
deered by the military. The orbiting science-gathering satellites
were re-tasked to scan the surface for any signs of an impending
enemy strike. Without the availability of the sophisticated long-
range detection systems, the ominous hazard was not recognized
until the invading space vagabonds were less than half of an
astronomical unit away. The collision would occur within three
lunar cycles and cause the highly-populated natural satellite to
de-orbit and crash into Ahneevah's planet, extinguishing all life
on both astral bodies.

Those in the Tactical Planning Authority of the Space
Exploration Wing knew that there were no options. With total
extinction hanging in the balance, Ahneevah was the only flight-
leader capable of effectively dealing with the enormous threat.
No other pilot possessed the requisite level of experience in the
StarGazer TSE, along with the expertise and instincts that would
offer any chance of successfully completing what was generally
regarded as a suicide mission.

The science and exploration flight profile for her planned excursion to the fourth planet was hastily revised. The new objective would be a desperate attempt to save her world; its near space
neighbor; and the twelve-billion souls living on both bodies. Even
if she ended the peril, no one expected her to return—at least no
one but herself and those who really knew her.

Her assignment dictated that she go out into the blackness to
an intersect coordinate of decimal three-three, line mark of the
distance to the fourth planet, the farthest point ever traveled by
other than robotic probes. Once there she would rendezvous and
fly in formation with the speeding two-fisted predator. That was
the easy part. Then, not unlike playing a mega-sized version of a
Spheres and Cubes game, Ahneevah would have to fire the
powerful magneto-plasma pulse cannon at the smaller chunk of
space flotsam. This in turn would accelerate it and drive it into the

one-hundred-mile-diameter comet nucleus. In theory, the contact would then alter the course of the dangerous larger celestial rock by enough of a margin to cause it to sail well beneath the orbit of its glowing, cratered target. Though the outbound trip was flawless, upon entering the dust veil of the comet, Ahneevah's immediate evaluation of the on-board telemetry data clearly indicated that she could not carry out the mission as planned. The trailing body was not simply a fragment that had separated from the comet. Rather, it was a young comet in the early stages of coalescing that somehow was swept up by the larger one. After careful analysis, Ahneevah determined that the newly forming comet's ice and rock center was far too fragile to be bombarded with the overwhelming potency of the magneto-plasma pulse waves. Even at the minimum setting, the crushing force would tear the core apart, and the reverberations and debris expelled from the explosion would shatter the larger projectile into a scattered discharge—a mountain of rubble substantial enough to be equally as devastating. Still, her planet and its orbiting companion, both teeming with life, depended on Ahneevah for their salvation. She calculated that the StarGazer had ample power to effect an almost imperceptible course change that would also accomplish her main objective which was to prevent the collision.

Drawing on her extraordinary aviating prowess she rendezvoused with the lesser object, flew nose to tail with it and then increased the speed of her craft so as to make contact with the smaller piece. Operating on multiple conscious levels, she then accelerated the StarGazer, propelling the baby chunk forward and closing the distance between it and the greater one. When the trailing fragment reached the velocity that assured impact with the main body, Ahneevah veered away at a reverse heading. She pushed the StarGazer to travel at extreme rates of speed while executing critical maneuvers well outside the trans-stellar ship's normal operating envelope. As a result of Ahneevah's action, the smaller fragment struck the menacing ice and rock bullet with enough force to destabilize its trajectory but not enough to destroy it. Once the course had been altered, Ahneevah patiently trailed the threatening ice and rock space debris until her instruments indicated it was no longer a danger to her world. Satisfied, and to alleviate the threat of any eventual course change, she fired the magneto-ion pulse waves to blast it to pieces. Then, at full thrust, she streaked away from the quadrant in order to avoid the stellar waves created by the explosive force of the comet and its companion.

However, like ripples moving outward in a pond the incipient gravitonic interstellar-fabric oscillations overtook the rapidly departing StarGazer. The celestial-mega tsunami buffeted the sub-light craft, causing a breech in the plasma-ionization chamber. A nano-span stood between deliverance and disaster.

Most commanders would have responded to the crisis by continuing to fly an already stricken craft at full plasmic power in an attempt to outrun the energy pulses and the hyper-speeding chunks of rock and ice. But Ahneevah's vast mental network flashed to another choice—a far better choice. She elected to reduce power, reverse her course and retreat toward the source of the *space-quake*. Using her extraordinary piloting skills to avoid colliding with the exploded comet's collateral debris, she found that the closer she moved to the center of the maelstrom, the more the high-energy shock waves began to subside. Additionally, the lower frequency waves carried ionic radiation which reacted with the StarGazer's magneto hydrodynamic buffer's nucleonic stream and formed a seal in the plasma core fissure. In a very real sense she fought fire with fire and won her bout with the cosmic interloper, thus sparing her home world and its proximate satellite from a scorching, horrific doom.

EPISODE FIVE

DR. ISAAC L. CARVER
IN
"WELCOME TO THE MONKEY HOUSE"

"I don't give a flea fuck's ass about dinosaurs ..."

... was Isaac Carver's initial strike, aimed at UCLA paleontology professor Ilias J. Solomon. Carver punctuated the verbal broadside by bolting down the last dregs of his ever-present glass of straight-up vodka. Like a flamed-out dragon he exhaled the intoxicant fumes in the direction of Dr. Solomon, who defensively waved his hand in an effort to disperse the foul puff of alcoholic air. A lit match would have probably ignited it.

It wasn't new news that Zack Carver had little use for dinosaur-fossil paleontologists. His career choices being anthropology and archeology, he classified Dr. Solomon and all those who pursued the study of the thunder-lizard geologic time scale as *monster groupies*.

"Come on, Carver, I'm a paleontologist and dinosaurs are what I do!" Solomon countered.

"For Christ's sake, I. J., those big uglies were dumb as a bag of hair. They had no damned IQ at all." Zack pulled at his scraggly beard. "I wanna know when the light bulb went on in mammals. Us! And I'm not interested in hearing about some bullshit evidence of rudimentary tool making either. Who cares if long ago some ancient chimpanzee picked up a twig and scratched its fuzzy monkey ass with it? That shows as much intelligence as early primates fucking. It was purely instinct … dealing with one *itch* or another."

The cocktail soiree was called for six o'clock at the Sportsmen's Lodge Hotel on Ventura Boulevard and Coldwater Canyon Avenue. Doctor Amelia Irwin Carle, the current chair of the Linguistics Department at USC, and her husband, Dr. Oliver Carle, Jet Propulsion Laboratory Senior Astronomer, were hosting the get-together. Amelia and Oliver, more familiarly known as Melli and Ollie, were Zack Carver's only remaining real friends in the world of academia … or anywhere else. It was through the Carle's recommendations and assistance that Dr. Carver was able to acquire his most recent professorship. However, obtaining gainful employment for Zack was far easier than ginning up a list of possible invitees to celebrate it. The Drs. Carle had to painstakingly arrange the evening's festivities by calling in years of favors and twisting a good deal of arms in order to round up a sufficient number of guests. The *shanghaied* attendees included USC and UCLA faculty members along with a light dusting of JPL rocket scientists. At first, the tone was mellow and genial but the tranquility and conviviality ended with the arrival of the guest of honor who came *roaring* in at 7:39— over an hour beyond the accepted, *so L.A,* fashionably late parameter. Although Zack knew he was tardy, he did exhibit a certain modicum of consideration for the rest of the gathering by being two *sheets in the wind* ahead of the crowd. Officially, Zack needed only one more *sheet* to fully qualify as a drunken sailor. The Carles, being well aware of his rant and rave potential, saw the storm brewing and discreetly tried to *crowbar* him away from Ilias Solomon.

Six years had passed since the Negev dig, and during that time a ceaseless maelstrom of controversy swirled around Dr. I. L. Carver. He had a lamentable inclination to pee in his own hand, which led to his dismissal from several major universities and a *second* marriage. Even worse, Zack's woeful life choices took a physical toll and, though actually in his early-thirties, he looked more like a man of fifty. Maybe that's okay if you want to take advantage of the early-bird Senior Specials at Denny's, but Zack wouldn't patronize clone restaurants—ever.

Much to their chagrin, Ollie and Melli's persistent efforts to distance Zack from Dr. Solomon were meeting resistance. Zack wasn't quite finished with the paleontologist.

"Dinosaurs ... shit! What a waste. In one-hundred and fifty million years those Jurassic farts didn't leave one fucking building nor a single scrap of writing or art that says 'we wuz here!' All they left was bone, dung and track fossils, and an ecology-busting supply of dino-petro-go-juice. Then, sixty-five million years ago," Zack made a *whooshing* sound through his clenched teeth and snapped his fingers, "*whisht* ... gone ... and I don't give a one rat pellet about exactly what caused their extinction. It doesn't matter to me if it was the freakin' Chicxulub, Yucatán asteroid or it turned out to be the goddamn beast's own flatulence that put 'em out of their misery. Fuck 'em!" Solomon tried to get in a word. "I think…"

"Yeah, yeah, I know. You think I'm out of line because you're only supposed to speak *good* of the dead. Okay, how's this? The dinosaurs are dead ... good ... if they weren't, we'd have surely ended up as fossilized dino-droppings."

Still armed with plenty of vitriol and alcohol, Zack decided it was time to fire his quiver of rancor-tipped vocal arrows at a new target. He turned away from Solomon and fixed his gaze on the chair of the UCLA Anthropology Department, Dr. Maxine Pearl.

"Dr. Pearl, maybe you can help me with something. I know you are aware that the Maya and the early Egyptians had the technology to build incredible pyramids and other stone structures to tolerances that would make contemporary architects consider blowing up their computers and burning their drafting tables. So how do you explain that while they were doing all this major construction work, they hadn't gotten around to inventing the wheel yet? The Maya resorted to sending runners down to the sea to pick up the catch of the day and the early Egyptians had to use enormous wooden sleds to drag the gigantic blocks of stone up huge ramps to their building sites because there was no damned wheel. And please don't give me any of that ancient astronaut crap."

Dr. Pearl shook her head and managed to force a polite smile. "Great steps take time."

"Time? Time?" Zack mocked. "It would seem to me that someone must've noticed that both the sun and the moon were round. Or that a Maya or two must have watched a rock or a melon or something roll down a hill or a mountainside. As a person of science aren't you the least bit curious about how both of these civilizations got a lot of the *Bob the Builder* crap but missed something as basic as the freaking wheel?"

Having properly offended Doctors Solomon and Pearl, Zack now turned his attention to the entire crowd. At that very moment Amelia thought it a good idea to shoo the other guests out of earshot. However, she was well aware that she would probably have to shoo them to the moon to accomplish that feat because Zack, now draining his fifth full glass of Slavic internal alcohol rub, was really ripped and pumping up the volume.

Zack's modus operandi was to seek out the most attractive and apparently unattached female in the group, then reel over to and lean against her for support. He studied his empty tumbler, narrowed his eyes to search through the throng and picked out Melli's friend from the Comparative Religion Department. *What wuzzer name?"* he thought ... *Ah yes ... Ruthie Becker.*

At this point the other partygoers began to treat the whole Zack experience as the entertainment portion of the evening. The Isaac

Ludlow Carver floor-show was chugging along at a full head of steam and guests were now collecting around him in the living room of the mid-sized suite. The main reason for the interest was the *pool* set up before Zack's arrival. Whoever guessed the precise moment that *the guest of honor* would pass out would win the pot, which was worth two hundred and fifty-nine bucks, and it was getting closer to crunch time.

Zack weaved over to the lovely Ruthie and inhaled her for a moment. "You smell delightful," he whispered in her ear with distilled-spud-soaked words. "Like the 3000-BC geological layer on a perfect Negev Desert morning." The perplexed Ms. Becker's nose crinkled at the remark and then Zack put his arm around shoulder—for support.

"You know, Ruthie, I once gave a seminar on 'Science and Organized Religion.' I can remember my opening remarks. "As a scientist I have seen no empirical evidence proving that there is some *guy in the sky* who runs the universe, punishes the wicked, and rewards the righteous. Far too few of the wicked get punished and far too few of the righteous get rewarded. But the human part of me has to be open to the possibility that the notion of a Supreme Being did have a reason and purpose."

In his mind's eye Zack visualized the crammed lecture hall at Arizona State. There he was, standing in front of an eager student body. "Remember, someone once said, 'An idea is more powerful than ideology.' The simple concept of a controlling force, the idea of God, might have helped bring our earliest ancestors down the bumpy road through the dark and foreboding night. All well and good, but then the psychos took over. Aristotle knew the drill thousands of years ago ....

'A tyrant must put on the appearance of uncommon devotion to religion. Subjects are less apprehensive of illegal treatment from a ruler whom they consider god-fearing and pious.'

Given Zack's dubious personality it was no Herculean leap to conclude that most of Melli and Ollie's guests were not seeking membership in an Isaac Carver fan club. There were also a copious number of Zack detractors in the scientific community. Like—most of the scientific community. At best, Dr. Carver was considered off-center, but the majority thought he was a full-blown crackpot—and they didn't like him much either.

Zack was about to slosh into a new topic. But before he was able to continue, his eyelids fluttered. Knowing what was on tap, he quickly wrapped his arms around Ruthie's most prominent parts and slid down the length of her body. An instant before things got dark; he couldn't help being the scientist. "If someone cops a feel but was too numb to actually *feel* the feel, did he really cop a feel at all?" The blitzed-out Zack would have fallen on his face if his friend Oliver wasn't waiting to catch him before he hit the floor. Then Ollie, with Amelia's help, carried Zack to the room they had reserved across the hall for him to sleep it off.

So it was that Zack's often erratic social behavior reduced him to pariah standing. Without the intervention of Amelia and Oliver Carle, Zack would have found it impossible to secure any academic position at all. The Carles cajoled the University of Alaska in Anchorage to hire Carver to beef up their Department of Archeology. However it was no secret that this would be his last stop before becoming a tour guide at an igloo village in Deadhorse. Yet it was in Alaska that Zack believed he could find evidence to help prove his theories and perhaps provide him with some measure of vindication. He speculated that he might uncover proof of indigenous intelligent hominoid life dating back over a hundred thousand years. Life that was able to do much more than scratch its ass with a twig.

EPISODE SIX

DAX WOLF
IN
"SOMETHING WICKED THIS WAY COMES"

Enola Wolf's biological clock was winding down and gobbling up the time remaining to her ...

... for child bearing. Enola was an extensively published and accomplished microbiologist, and her dedication to science took up the greater part of her life. She never had the time or the inclination to get married. Further, Enola did not know anyone that she considered to have any of the necessary qualifications to father her child and was well aware that finding a suitable male and going through the *mating* act would be time consuming, inelegant and could very well prove futile. However, as a woman of science she knew that the statistical probability of her successfully conceiving and carrying a child to full-term was swiftly dwindling leading her to conclude that it would be some-what of a failure on her part if she did not at least try to pass on her genetic gifts to another generation. It wasn't ego but rather a logical observation. And so, at forty-three years of age, Enola Wolf decided that she would pursue the only viable option for her—in vitro-fertilization. She began checking out the inventory of various sperm banks, reasoning that as long as she had the opportunity to pick a donor, she would choose the best that was available. Armed with graphs and charts, she scientifically went about her quest for motherhood. A highly accredited biological father was found, and within a year Enola had a son. She named him Dax Exeter Wolf. Dax was born six weeks premature, and due to his early arrival he weighed in at a mere three pounds nine ounces. He also weighed in with a life-threatening complication, respiratory distress syndrome. This disease is brought on by a shortage of a substance, surfactant, which is normally produced in adequate amounts by cells in the airways and found in the amniotic fluid by the 35th week of gestation. The surfactant is released into the pulmonary tissues to aid in keeping the air sacs or *lung alveoli* open. With the lack of a sufficient quantity of surfactant, the tiny air sacs in Dax's lungs collapsed. The damaged cells, called hyaline membranes, then collected in his air passages, causing increased blockage which made normal respiration extremely difficult. The newborn had to fight for every breath and was immediately placed in a hyper-oxygenated environment. During the first seventy-two critical hours, Enola was informed on three separate occasions that due to her son's negative reaction to the surfactant replacement protocol his chance of survival ran from barely possible to bleak—but he inexplicably endured and was thereafter referred to by Enola as her miracle baby.

The real miracle, however, came several years later. Enola and a cadre of child psychologists and pediatricians feared that as a consequence of initial oxygen deprivation resulting from his early battle to stay alive, baby Dax most probably suffered some subsidiary brain damage and might be intellectually disabled. The evidence was compelling. Dax had reached his second birthday and the child had yet to utter his first words or take his first step. Enola kept this lack of development as much to herself as possible and swore, as a woman of science, that she was seeing an indescribable cognizance in her baby son's eyes. Many rejected the notion as wishful thinking and insisted that she was in denial.

The amazing turnaround occurred at local toy store when Dax was two and a half-years-old. While Enola was pushing him along in a shopping basket down row after row of games, dolls and various other playthings, he suddenly became fascinated with an advanced Lego set. Dax kept reaching for it but Enola quickly dismissed the idea because it was recommended for children within the age group of seven to fourteen. She thought it was simply color attraction, and even with all her positive feelings about her only child she just couldn't wrap her mind around the idea that he could be capable of constructing anything with the tiny plastic pieces.

In truth, Enola's early intuition about her son was right on the mark. Baby Dax only *seemed* to be slow off the blocks because he had been keenly observing and absorbing absolutely everything going on around him. He was engorging inestimable amounts of knowledge into the giant vessel that was his mind. Then, right there among the plethora of bright, multi-hued child-friendly items in Toys "R" Us, Dax Wolf finally uttered his first long-overdue words.

"Mother, I would like to have that Lego set," he said in a clear voice. "It really interests me." The stunned Enola could hardly believe what she was hearing and began to laugh uproariously. With great joy and paying no attention to the strange looks she was getting from those around her, she picked up Dax and hugged him tightly. She also complied with her son's request, and then some, by purchasing every Lego set in the store.

Dax was highly motivated by the building toy and created a multitude of unique and intricate objects that were giant leaps beyond the complexity of those pictured in the instruction book and far above the aptitude of any average toddler. Dax continued speaking in full sentences and then paragraphs—on every subject. Enola decided that public education was out of the question, and dedicated herself to home-schooling her young genius. Very soon his distinctive, high-level genetics kicked into overdrive. He retained everything he heard, saw and read. Dax finally decided to walk only after his manual dexterity was greatly developed. His eye-hand coordination was so extraordinary that at seven years of age he was a top video gamer and also competed in and won the World Sport Cup Stacking Championship—first in his particular age group and then in the overall open competition.

As Dax was growing up, he never mentioned or asked about his biological father, though he knew full well that he had one. Money in the Wolf household was never a problem. Several of the patents Enola held on her microbiological breakthroughs provided a small fortune in royalties.

By the time he reached high school age, Dax was a gangly whiz-kid with no particular interest in any kind of social life. When he wasn't at Enola's side learning many of the scientific disciplines and the methods used in pursuing them, he was being tutored by some of his mother's colleagues in their particular area of study. Dax finished the entire four-year high school curriculum in less than a year, and after perfect Scholastic Achievement Test scores he was accepted to the Massachusetts Institute of Technology several months before his thirteenth birthday.

At this juncture, Dax Wolf appeared on the radar screen of the U.S. government. Specifically, he was being eyed by the recruitment department within the Special Technologies Division at DARPA, the Defense Advanced Research Projects Agency. MIT was advised by DARPA management in no uncertain terms to keep Dax Wolf's attendance there as low-profile as possible. Dax breezed through his MIT courses and even had time to make improvements on his mother's discoveries, which increased their wealth even further.

At fifteen, Dax was devastated when Enola was diagnosed with pancreatic cancer and died within a few months. He was bitterly disillusioned and this prompted within him a great enmity toward medical science for being unable to save his mother or at least to somehow prolong her life and reduce her suffering. He was furious that short-sighted political expediency trumped certain avenues of critical research that might have made a difference.

A year after Enola's death, Dax graduated from MIT with doctorates in Biological Fragmentary Molecular Sciences and Quantum Physics. His papers on quasars, dark matter, black holes and hyper-gravity and their relationship to electro-magnetic particle waves were of special interest to the Department of Defense. The higher-ups at the DOD were particularly intrigued with his theory that through the use of an anti-matter matrix created in a super high-speed particle accelerator, unique hybrid micro-miniature black holes could be formed. Unlike normal black holes, these crossbred mini dark-stars could be tuned to absorb all surrounding subatomic energy, which would in turn have the ultimate effect of neutralizing radioactivity. The theory alone was stunning and, if true, could reduce the half-life decay of radioactive materials from thousands and millions of years to minutes or even seconds. To neutralize any form of fission/fusion weaponry almost in an instant would be the Defense Department coup of the millennium.

The fortune Dax had inherited could have easily put him into business in the private sector. But he realized that the research he was doing was truly cosmic in nature and required funding of interstellar proportions. What better sponsor could there be than the Department of Defense? Wolf knew that the he would have numerous opportunities in the future to start his own company. He also found that the DOD wanted him so desperately they acquiesced to his every demand. Since salary was a minor consideration for him, he instead negotiated for almost unlimited funding, minimal oversight and unrestrained access to the world's most advanced research facilities.

Dax Exeter Wolf spent the workdays of the next two years commuting on a special Boeing 727 from McCarran International Airport in Las Vegas to various undisclosed black project locations. His main base of operations was the Nevada desert in the proximity of the legendary Area 51. But sometimes he would be flown in a military supersonic jet to other exotic research facilities, such as the Center for Advanced Microstructures and Devices, located at Louisiana State University: or even across the world the Large Hadron Collider outside of Geneva, Switzerland. Aside from working on his own research he was occasionally asked to consult in the development of various covert weapon technologies. One of these projects was the creation of a functioning Electro Magnetic Pulse generator which was small enough for deployment on various air, land and sea-based weapons platforms.

Although he added his expertise to many fields of development, Dax Wolf was unswervingly intrigued with Einstein's theories of space and time and Schrödinger's quantum mechanics. He was deeply dedicated to researching the relationship of the work of those scientific masters to the eventual navigation and control of the temporal streams and the galactic continuum. "The fact that one speck of light or a low-frequency radio wave can infinitely travel the endless reaches of the cosmos demonstrates the possibility that time itself could be no less a dimension than any other in the continuum scale and can be a transport means." Dax would postulate. "The particular method of transversal exists and is waiting to be revealed."

The prevailing DOD assessment held that the possibility of developing a time exploration mechanism was light-years beyond the realm of current science. Even Dr. Schrödinger's cat failed to shed any new illumination on the subject. Nonetheless, the military higher-ups at the DOD's "Dreamland" division, where *let's make believe* was the rule rather than the exception, couldn't help but salivate over the strategic potential if jumping around the continuum ever became a reality.

Dax Wolf's persuasiveness gave the Defense Advanced Research Projects Agency's search for chronotempic pathways a new emphasis. After all, how far of a leap was it to go from synthetically engineered nano-black holes to ESP psychics to psycho kinesis to quantum leaping and time hopping? At the very least, with top-secret access to much of the existing particle accelerators and other sophisticated space-age apparatus, courtesy of DARPA, Dr. Wolf was like a child in a nano-particle Legoland.

However, unlike the legendary Albert Einstein or men like Dr. Robert Oppenheimer, the father of the atomic bomb, Dax Wolf felt absolutely no compunction about creating more effective methods of destruction for use by the military. Wolf's pursuit of science was purely for science's sake and certainly not for the improvement of the human condition. "It would amount to a waste of time." he always argued. "Why bother?" Dax Exeter Wolf was incontrovertibly convinced that humankind was obstinately headed in the wrong direction to a dead end—although it didn't exactly take a genius to recognize that.

Wolf also sensed an inexplicable presence in the universal order—a presence that he could not quite get into proper focus. Had anyone been aware at this point of exactly what lurked in the darkest recesses of his mind, they would have been wise to suggest to Wolf that he *get a life*. Unfortunately, that specific concept was the furthest thing from his consciousness. As far as he was concerned, he had a life. It was separate and distinct from all other lives but it was his life—his and his alone. And the cauldron of contempt that churned deep within him was blacker than any project he had undertaken and was as vile as anyone, even he himself, could ever have imagined—and Dax Exeter Wolf's imagination was unbounded.

EPIJODE JEVEN

ALBERT BARRGRAVE II
IN
"THE CREATURE FROM THE BLACK
LAGOON"

"*Nathan Barrgrave was a cold son of a bitch in business and he'd cut your nuts off ...*

... if you stuck 'em out too far. But like his father Albert, he loved and respected the land and never took from it without paying it back." These final words of the eulogy at the funeral of Nate Barrgrave were spoken with great respect by lifelong competitor and friend, Andrew Russell Tate of Tate World Wide Enterprises.

Since the middle 1800s, the Barrgrave family owned most of everything that made money, including power companies, steel manufacturing, and large holdings in the aircraft and armament industries. Nathan Barrgraves' great-grandfather, Nikita Bargranoff, came to the United States in 1825 from the city of Kiev in the Ukraine. He was a woodsman by trade and began to amass the family fortune harvesting pine trees in the northern woods of the Oregon territory. When Oregon became a state in 1859, Nikita Bargranoff celebrated the event by changing his name to Nathan Barrgrave. Nate's son, Albert, showed great financial expertise as well by setting up new company headquarters in Texas where he expanded the family interests into oil, coal and holdings in steel. Albert also had the foresight to acquire millions of acres in Alaska containing timber and petroleum reserves. Sensing the outbreak of the Second World War, Nathan Barrgrave II, Albert's progeny, added an armament business, bringing the Barrgraves' thriving spheres of financial influence into the lucrative military-industrial complex.

Isaac Carver's dedicated research had finally put him on the trail of possible archeological proof that an ancient nomadic people crossed the Bering Strait land bridge into North America millennia before the generally accepted time frame dating back some twelve-thousand years. The information also implied that tactile evidence of these earliest migrations might be found in the western coastal region of Kodiak Island.

Through the university, Zack received written consent from Nathan Barrgrave II himself to excavate the unspoiled tundra area owned and controlled by Barrgrave International Industries. Finally, after a massive amount of research and several years of chipping, poking and digging through geological layers, the seemingly unyielding permafrost ground had at last relinquished one of its prizes. Dr. Carver unearthed the cambered section of what appeared to be a spherical granite marker. It contained a series of petroglyphs possibly designating the location of a nearby pre-Columbian sacred burial site. Some of the etchings seemed to indicate that the tomb might well be that of a Paleoamerican tribal chief. However, Zack was mildly perplexed by the surrounding geology, which had no formations similar to the unusual granite marker. Where could it have come from?

In any case, the curious finding enabled Zack to get permission to continue his excavation for an additional two years. But then, barely two months into the contract extension period, old Nate died and the family-owned controlling shares of the corporation and its holdings, including millions of acres of valuable oil deposits in

Alaska, came into the stewardship of Albert Barrgrave II.

Now that the old guard was gone, Albert II could finally run things as he always desired. It was well known that this newest Barrgrave-in-charge never gave much thought to the environment except for the resources it provided. He always believed that the *climate-change* issue was a ploy used by the left-wing tree-huggers to scare the public. Even if it were true, Albert was a businessman, not a nature lover and he now had control of millions of acres of petroleum reserves to drill for millions, maybe billions, of gallons of oil.

Summoned to a powwow with Albert Barrgrave II, Dr. Carver found himself bouncing along in the bumpy air on the relatively short flight from Kodiak Airport to Anchorage International. The flight arrived on time and the dizzy and nauseous Zack was greeted by a pair of three-hundred-pound Barrgrave security staffers and driven in a stretch Humvee limousine to a Gulfstream VII corporate jet parked on the tarmac at the executive terminal.

One of the last ancient-growth rosewood trees from the Brazilian rain forest provided the bulkhead decor for the walls of the airplane's executive suite. The opulence was mind-numbing. Several Silk Kashan Persian carpets, a desk that once belonged to Thomas Jefferson, and original Monet and van Gogh paintings were hanging on the paneled walls of the luxury jet.

Zack was *positioned* about a yard from the desk. He was offered no handshake and no pleasantries. Not even a chair or an invitation to sit. It was all business.

Barrgrave fired the first shot. "I'm canceling our deal. There are more urgent considerations."

"But we have a contract."

"We do not. *You* had one with Nate, but he's gone and I no longer choose to recognize or contend with his mistakes." Zack tried reason. "The agreement was with the Barrgrave Industries Foundation."

"Yes, the Foundation," Albert growled, "another one of father's bad ideas, a haven for social do-gooders and environmentalists. The Foundation has been dissolved, and you have sixty days to finish your work and clear out of the dig site."

"Sixty days? It'll take a lifetime to explore that find. This is unacceptable … illegal."

"You'd never win in court. But you can't even afford litigation can you?" Albert II wouldn't have asked the question unless he already had the answer. "Not a chance. You have no resources," Barrgrave sneered, then opened a file folder on his desk, snatched a single sheet paper from it and held it up for Zack to see. "This represents your entire financial picture … there are homeless people in better fiscal shape. You're swimming in debt. Alimony payments to a pair of ex-wives, you don't own a home or anything else, and your charge cards are maxed out. With your current credit score and restricted earning potential no decent attorney would even consider taking your case."

It was true, and Zack was deflated. He pissed away everything and couldn't even ante up the fee necessary to undertake an action in small claims court, much less come up with the tens or hundreds of thousands of dollars necessary to wage a protracted legal battle against a multinational conglomerate such as Barrgrave Industries.

With brimming condescension, the powerful magnate picked up the folder, opened it, grabbed a smaller file from the top and unceremoniously tossed it in Zack's direction. It landed on the floor in front of Zack and he kneeled down to pick it up. It contained a two-page agreement with a cashier's check stapled to it. Barrgrave stood as Zack glanced at both. "The check will cover all your debts plus a sizable sum for your next project," the corporate Goliath said. "Sign the attached release and it's yours,"

"That's it? Pay me off and send me slinking away? Money? It's about money?"

Barrgrave shook his head. "Please," he said impassively, "You say that like it's a revelation … it's always about money … "money breeds power." Then the tycoon closed the file folder and dropped it back on his desk for accent. It landed with a loud *thwink*. "Oh yes, the meek shall inherit the Earth," Albert II pontificated and made a pompous, sweeping gesture with his hand indicating the collection of finery around him. "The meek shall inherit the Earth only when the powerful are through with it." Then he brushed his hands together as a sign of sheer dismissal and sat back in his chair.

"You mean after you and the other bastards like you turn this planet into a complete slime pit." Without taking his eyes off Barrgrave, Zack stood up, took several steps forward and stopped when his thighs bumped up against the priceless desk. He felt his cool slipping away and closed his eyes in an effort to grab hold of it. He failed, spread his hands on the Jeffersonian sample of Americana and leaned in slowly toward Barrgrave to get more in his face. "You greedy corporate sons of bitches are all alike. Who cares about a few prehistoric trinkets and some land basically undisturbed since the beginning of time as long as you can harvest your oil and keep your creepy hands around the throats of the people? Who gives a damn that the criminally negligent actions of the BP bandits and the rest of the fossil-fuel pimps turned the Gulf of Mexico into a giant, toxic vat of dinosaur ooze?"

Zack removed his hands from the desk, rose to his full height, and staring at Barrgrave eyeball to eyeball, the archeologist crushed the release along with the accompanying check.

"I take it that we have no deal," the industrialist said coolly, barely glancing up. "So be it. Our interview is over, Dr. Carver." The magnate then motioned his two super-sized underlings into action. They flanked Zack, grabbed him under his arms and dragged him away from his tormentor. But as they were man-handling him toward the aircraft entryway, Zack broke loose, turned and seethed back at Barrgrave over his shoulder.

"There are better ways to produce energy. And you and your international gang of petroleum thugs know damn well what they are. You can get four times the amount of ethanol per acre from the hemp plant than you get from corn and you can grow hemp almost anywhere. Christ, it's like a goddamn weed! And the Sun … it shines down on half of the world every single day."

One of the security men bent over and grabbed Zack by his feet. The other took him by the arms and they lugged him in the direction of the cabin door.

"When are people like you going to learn that it's useless to resist," the mogul scoffed, "utterly hopeless?"

"Right … so you're saying that if I complain no further things will get better? Well then … fuck OPEC, fuck Exxon/Mobile and fuck you, too!" Zack punctuated his remark by throwing the crumpled wad of the release and check back at Barrgrave. It bounced off the big shot's forehead and landed on one of the ancient Persian rugs. The two mammoth *bearers* quickly regained control of Zack and were hauling him out of the cabin door when Barrgrave shouted out as a reminder,

"Sixty days, Carver, sixty days!"

Then Albert II picked up the phone. "Still there, Bix? Right, you heard? Carver's done. We're ready to move. Have the President sign the order to nullify Carver's contract with the Foundation on the grounds that it is in the national interest." Barrgrave listened for a beat. "Absolutely … that's why we keep the dumb son-of-a-bitch in power."

EPISODE EIGHT

THE COMPONENTS IN "CLOSE ENCOUNTERS OF THE THIRD KIND"

With a sixty day 'Sword of Damocles' hanging over the proceedings ...

... the activity at the dig site began moving at a frantic pace. Heavy equipment was brought in and the semi-frozen earth was carefully removed from around the spherical boulder, which turned out to be the size of a mail delivery truck. Several smaller bulldozers carved out an incline leading down to the unusual discovery which Zack believed had been keeping its monumental secrets buried in the earth for untold millennia. It was nearly ten feet high and had hundreds of petroglyphs pecked all over it. A system of lasers calculated the precise dimensions of the giant globe and indicated that it was close to being perfectly round which summarily discounted any possibility that it was a natural formation.

Snow Smith had jet-black hair, deep brown eyes and looked great in a faux-fur parka. As a dedicated environmental and animal rights activist, she would never wear real fur. Snow might have made a fine ski-bunny. She even looked good in ear muffs, and no one looks good in ear muffs. But most of all, Professor Smith was a scholar and a widely published expert in the field of primitive cave art. Although Snow Smith was her *nom de voyage*, her ancient native name was Aput Omak. In her Aleut language Aput meant snow. When Zack first discovered the petroglyphs, he contacted Dr. Smith at the University Southeast at Juneau. Although the etchings were worn, they were highly decipherable. Almost immediately, a new slice of history leaped off the huge granite ball.

"They tell the story of a prehistoric race that migrated across the land bridge from the Asian continent to North America," was Dr. Smith's first revelation.

As the days went by, Snow painstakingly studied, photographed, videoed and continued to translate the pictorial messages from the dawn of civilized history. Additional assessment of the ancient rock drawings led Zack and Snow to postulate that the large orb might be a granite gatekeeper possibly put in place countless millennia ago to seal off a hidden burial cave entrance or conceal other unique markers.

When some of the project workers leaked word of the find and its associated theories to the locals, a sea of indigenous people flooded into the area and immediately began demonstrating. They protested against the drilling that was to begin in several days and they objected to any further excavation by Dr. Carver of what they were convinced was a sacred ancient tomb.

In an effort to mollify the churning controversy, Zack borrowed a bullhorn from the crew foreman, motioned Snow to step forward and raised the bullhorn to his mouth.

"You all know me," he said. As expected, the crowd erupted in catcalls and boos. Zack then raised his hand.

"This is Aput Omak. She's an archeology professor as well as a representative from the Afognak Native Corporation. Aput is here to see that the native people's interests—your interests—are protected. I promise you that I have no intention of desecrating your sacred heritage."

Zack then handed the bullhorn to Aput. "I am here to make sure that we all work in harmony to investigate questions of common interest," she pledged. "I believe that it will enhance our culture to know its true history. It is the sacred right of every one of us to know how we became who we are."

The crowd murmured and nodded their agreement, and settled down.

When Aput returned the bullhorn to the foreman he barked the order for a custom woven, wide-circumference, nylon thread harness to be secured around the sphere and then motioned the green John Deere caterpillar tractor to inch forward. The chain was pulled taut and the heavy granite guardian began to slide ever so slowly away from its long-standing post.

Zack was surprised to find that the entrance revealed was not much more than a crawl space skillfully chipped into the shale boundary layer. He turned his 10 TB, holographic, pod-corder on and handed it to Joshua Dov Benjamin, one of his teaching assistants. At heart, Josh was pretty much a basic geek. His IQ was well in the 160s and he hung out mainly with other geeks. However, Joshua was in reality a semi-geek at most. He didn't really look very geekish, dressed with more than a slice of style and never had a vinyl pen and pencil holder in his shirt pocket. Actually he always wore golf shirts which had no pockets at all. Joshua could also throw a football over sixty yards in the air. It would sail like an artillery round, but he declined every football scholarship that was offered to him. He was first and foremost an academician.

The trio donned their hard hats, switched on the lights, wriggled into the opening and entered the cave. The first observation was that the area inside was amazingly dry. No dankness or musty odors whatsoever. It was also quite cramped. Shell, bone, ivory tools and decorative objects were scattered about. These were quite different from those linked with the Alutiiq people, who had left evidence of their presence dating back from two to ten millennia. The drawings carved into and painted on the stone walls indicated that the journey of the individuals that created them occurred well before the Alutiiq or any other ancient nomads crossed the Bearing Sea. This provided Zack with an internal *Ah ha!*

The etchings depicted hunting rituals and expeditions, a man and a woman at the moment of childbirth and images of primitive deities. Though similar pictorials had been uncovered in other areas of Alaska, Zack was awestruck at the level of detail and preservation in this new find. Also, unlike the weathered appearance of ancient illustrations on the outside of the cave, the petroglyphic art inside gave him the strangest feeling that he was looking at sophisticated work that could have been created in the not too distant past by someone with a keen, artistic eye. The colors were bright, showed no signs of wear, and the figures were anatomically accurate and to scale. Zack continued moving slowly along the wall and after several steps he came upon another almost perfect sphere. It was the about twice the size of a large beach ball and had a drawing of an evil-looking ancient deity. Zack instantly interpreted it as a "Keep Out" sign. All it needed was a red circle and diagonal line.

"What on earth did the priests have to hide?" Zack muttered.

Though the mini-boulder was round, it was expertly fitted into a rut chiseled out of the cave floor and it took all of Zack's strength combined with that of Snow and Joshua to push it free and roll it aside. This revealed a DVD-sized drawing on the adjacent wall of what at first glance appeared to be a spaceship. It was shown spitting fire and was engulfed by a white cloud-like object. Zack smacked his forehead. Snow and Josh knew what was coming and retreated several steps.

"No … no … we're off again, Area 51 the prequel. A flying saucer! Here comes more of that Plane of Jars Peruvian ancient astronaut bullshit; more of Ezekiel's flying chariot of fire.

Joshua, who was carefully studying the cave wall etching, perked up. "Dr. Carver, if I may say so, it looks to me like it could be the depiction of a comet and not necessarily a UFO."

"Say what?" Zack mumbled. "A comet?" Zack scrutinized the primeval artwork more closely, then let fly a Cheshire cat grin. "Yes, a comet … of course … it does look more like a comet, doesn't it?" Snow and Josh smiled and nodded their agreement— happy to have nipped a rant-in-the-bud. Several yards farther along the prehistoric archeological treasure-trail, Zack spotted another smaller globe, which when rolled away revealed another *comet*. It was a foot or so lower on the wall and smaller than the first. Then he found another sphere and another comet etching. Each primitive scratching and stone globe was getting lower and lower and smaller and smaller until the last sphere was the size of a marble and the last *comet drawing* was at ground level, maintained the same detail as the previous ones and was no bigger than a pea. Zack scraped away some of the soil near the tiny symbol and after a few scoops uncovered a perfectly straight seam in the solid rock of the cave floor. He motioned for Snow and Josh to help him move the dirt and the three uncovered a six foot by three foot stone slab. Zack ran his finger along the full length and width of the rectangular groove. He looked at the others and spoke in a near whisper. "It's like an ancient trap door cut by a prehistoric tool of some kind to fit perfectly in the granite. Go up top and bring back some picks, shovels and heavy-duty crowbars and don't say anything to anybody." Josh and Snow hustled out of the cave to do as Zack requested.

There was a *scraping* sound of steel *grinding* against stone as Zack and Josh, using a pick axe and a crowbar, carefully pried the heavy tabletop granite slab up from the position it had no doubt been in for many thousands of years. When it disengaged there was a *whoosh* of air comparable to the sound of a vacuum-seal being broken, followed by a chilling draft as if the trio had just opened a meat-locker door. Zack's flashlight beam played on the rectangular hole, and spread down an intimidating and perfectly proportioned stairwell carved into it. Zack was about to become the first human being to trod this antediluvian set of steps in perhaps countless eons. Like a curtain rising, this was the opening scene on a series of unexpected discoveries in an astounding chain of events.

In reverent silence, with only the echoes of their footfalls reverberating sharply off the granite walls, Zack and his companions descended the stone flight of stairs. As they continued down, the air became more frigid and yet the frosty air did not smell like it was musty underground air. Strangely, it was slightly dizzying as if it contained an abundance of oxygen. They also noticed that as they headed further down, the petroglyphs became sparser. When the three reached the lower landing, the etchings disappeared altogether. Josh counted the steps observing that they fell one short of an even hundred.

At the bottom, Zack and the others found themselves in an unexpectedly massive chamber. It was at approximately the size of a baseball diamond with rocky walls and an abnormally smooth seventy-five foot high ceiling.

"The air seems to be fresher down here than it was up top," Zack observed with surprise. Then the beam of his flashlight caught a wall of blue ice roughly one-hundred feet away at the far end, and Zack's eyes widened. When Snow and Josh also pointed their lights in that direction, a frozen mound about three meters high that protruded some fifteen meters out onto the cavern floor also became visible.

"I'm not a climatologist, but that looks like a corrie glacier." Zack ventured.

Dr. Smith nodded. "I think you're right but how could this little toddler of a glacier be born *inside* a cavern like this?"

"Glaciers are formed outside from snow," Josh added. "Millennia upon millennia of snow."

"Unless it snowed inside or this cave wasn't always ... a cave," Zack said and approached the bus-sized, mass of ice. Then he caught sight of something that stopped him dead in his tracks. Greenish shafts popping through the icy surface—plant stalks! Taking care not to touch the shoots, he moved in for a closer inspection.

"This looks like swamp pricklegrass similar to the type normally found in California—and what the hell—why is it still green with no sunlight for who knows how long? How could photosynthesis even take place? And look at the geology. The different levels of sediments and permafrost show no evidence that a wetland ever existed anywhere near here. How could swamp grass in any condition be explained? What in the name of Gene Shoemaker is going on here?"

After a few more paces, Zack spotted the head of an unrecognizable species of animal visible through the ancient, icy wall. He held the lens of his flashlight directly against the surface to improve the illumination on the creature and to permit its overall shape and size to be determined. "It seems to be in one piece and it looks like some kind of water reptile—except that it has fur. This is like the damned Twilight Zone. What's next—a woolly freakin' mammoth?"

A complete visual record was shot while Zack supervised the careful cutting of the ice sections containing the creature and the grass shoots, into blocks. These highly prized specimens were swiftly and safely transported back to the school to be stored in a special freezer unit.

Zack could have e-mailed the video and photos, but he wasn't comfortable with Internet security. Therefore, UCLA paleon-

tology professor Ilias J. Solomon, Ph.D. was considerably surprised to receive the FEDEX package sent by I. L. C. Ph.D. of the
University of Alaska Southeast.

After reading the preliminary report that accompanied the
digital images of the exceptional flora and fauna, Solomon went
completely gaga. He wished he had programmed Zack's cell
number on his auto dial because in his excitement his fingers
were tripping all over themselves trying to punch in the ten
numerals that followed the one.

"I think it's a new genus," Zack said as he used the camera
feature on his cell phone to shoot a live image of the ancient
animal. "Snow named it a Zackosaurus in honor of my seeing it
first."

"Did you photo-document the exact spot where you found it?
Is there any evidence of other specimens? Where are the ..."

"Stop jabbering, Ilias, and listen. I need you to send me two of
the large *Keep Frozen* containers from the college hospital. You
know—the special ones they use to transport bio-medical
materials, and also put a bunch of those *'Radioactive Material'*
warning stickers on them." When Solomon protested the idea
Zack cut him off. "Just do it and get the proper clearances and I'll
send a couple of blocks of ice that'll keep your department
buzzing for years. Shit ... maybe decades. Oh, and even though
the creature is hairy, I'm fairly sure that it's somewhat reptilian.
Also, it's female, and the portable MRI indicated that it is in an
initial embryonic phase—and it also showed that the baby
Zackosaurus would have been born live and not hatched. Kind of
like a duckbill platypus in reverse. One more thing I J, there'll be
some interesting specimens in the second block of ice for your
botany department. And for God's sake ... keep it quiet."

Nineteen days before the court-ordered end of Zack's access to
the dig, a fleet of Barrgrave Industries giant earth-movers,

bulldozers and drilling equipment was assembled and poised to violate and ransack the virgin land.

Zack decided it was of the utmost importance to keep the interior environment as stable as possible, and opted to avoid the high-heat-producing incandescent or halogen floods. Therefore, the inside of the cavern was bathed in cool fluorescent lights powered by several portable, high-efficiency, *Sun Station 1*, photovoltaic generators that were set up outside.

Zack, Snow Smith and Josh had just begun ferreting around the mini ice field when the cave area was suffused by a soft light-red aura emanating from inside the frozen mass of otherwise undisturbed ancient geological history. It almost seemed to be calling out to Zack and when a section of ice, containing rocks and assorted vegetation was painstakingly removed, it revealed the pointed tip of a larger object buried deeper in the glacier. Additional clearing resulted in the apex flaring out in a funnel-like protrusion extending a meter beyond the bluish ice. Zack slowly reached out until his gloved hand made contact with it. "Whatever this thing is, it's no natural formation. It reminds me of a rocket nose cone." Snow and Josh moved in for a closer look. "I agree," Josh said.

"Maybe those petroglyphs weren't comets after all." Zack said reluctantly as he slowly took off his gloves. "This could be a research probe or a transportation module manufactured by some high form of prehistoric intelligence." Zack tentatively stretched out with his arm and carefully rubbed his bare fingers along the surface. "It feels warm and there's not one detectable rivet or any evidence of bonding, and it's perfectly smooth but doesn't feel at all like a metal of any kind."

Joshua began to chip away at the ice, but as he proceeded he miscalculated a hammer blow and accidentally struck the conical enigma.

"Careful, dammit!" Dr. Carver grumbled and then he and his

assistant quickly scrutinized the spot where the wayward blow landed. To their amazement they recognized that there was absolutely no sign of a scratch or a dent on the surface of the unique, highly reflective material.

Then, unexpectedly, seconds after being struck, the tip of the cone became semi-transparent and illuminated. The additional light source revealed a teardrop-shaped silhouette which extended back about forty-feet to the cavern wall. The exposed section began to generate waves similar to those which rise from a sun-baked street on a sizzling summer day and at a glacial pace the wall of ice began to liquefy one drip at a time.

Suddenly, a rainbow of pulse waves beamed out from the top of the cone, shot up the ninety-nine step stairwell, out through the cave opening and disabled every piece of rolling excavation equipment outside the cave.

The crews were baffled but no matter what was tried, none of the electric-powered machinery within a mile of the dig would work. The foreman had to consult with the higher-ups to see what could be done. Zack took this break in the action to have a 10 by 20 foot pole tent pitched in front of the cave entrance and ordered most of the crew to another location to dig.

Feverishly and secretly, a small group was gathered. Due to the thawing action, the pace of the operation was quickened. Zack found two small pieces of material that matched the exposed section of the icebound teardrop in its makeup. One was thin, flat, rectangular and roughly the size of a cell phone or PDA. The other was round and approximately the size and thickness of a silver dollar. Zack examined and hefted the items and was amazed to find that neither one gave the slightest physical indication that gravity exerted any force over it.

"I can't say for sure, but I'd bet that if you put these on a scale they would register zip. I think they're virtually weightless.

Either separately or together," Zack announced and gave the pair of exceptional articles to Joshua to handle.

"This stuff is unparalleled," observed Josh, duly flabbergasted. "Mass without weight … unreal, whatever these things are made of seems to exert an inherent force that negates gravity … with no perceptible power source. Einstein would flip."

Not only were the materials weightless, they also turned out to be virtually indestructible. Blows, pressure, heat and obviously cold had no impact. "We could be in the presence of the most startling find in the history of the world," Zack postulated. "It could virtually relegate the Dead Sea Scrolls, the Rosetta stone and even Lucy or Ardi, the hypothesized *mothers of our race,* to footnote status."

EPIƩODE NINE

THE FIND
"THE THING"

If it was a transport vehicle, who built it and why was it buried there where it was, in a baby glacier that ...

... itself should not have been *there* where *it* was? Isaac Carver Ph.D. fiercely resisted his first impression even though he was well aware that a teardrop was considered to be the perfect aerodynamic shape. Could he really have found what might actually be an ancient rocket or some other kind of air vehicle? Snow and Josh remained at the site while Zack rushed by helicopter to the university in Anchorage. The science department had recently acquired a Potassium-Argon Ion Probe system capable of molecular analysis and dating of the extraordinary samples.

After the initial testing was completed Zack met with the head of the Geochronology Laboratory, Dr. Lawrence Sloan. "The flat, round and rectangular samples are indeed weightless and seem to be inert but further analysis was impossible because their molecular and atomic structures couldn't be identified," Sloan reported.

Zack raised his eyebrows. "I don't understand, Larry. What do you mean, they couldn't be identified? Everything in the universe is made out of the same stuff." Dr. Sloan picked up one of the artifacts in each hand and waved them for emphasis.

"True, but there are an infinite number of elementary particle recipes, I'm telling you that the atomic oven that cooked-up these objects used a concoction of elements that have no equal at any stop on our current periodic table." He took a deep breath and continued. "As far as we can tell there is absolutely nothing like these on Earth. Well ... nothing before these."

"Weird," Zack said as he scratched his beard then pulled out a cigarette and prepared to light it. Sloan shook his head, quickly reached out and stopped Zack from igniting the noxious, death-fuse. Zack shrugged, tucked it behind his ear and took back the two items.

"It gets weirder," Sloan went on. "Most of the strata samples that were taken in close proximity to the craft date back about forty-thousand years. But some of the core samples that were extracted a foot or so below the surface from the same period went back nearly a billion years."

"A jump from forty-thousand years to a billion within one geological layer ... that never ... it's ... it's like a goddamn time warp. Unimaginable, unthinkable, how can it be explained?" Zack bellowed.

"Maybe antediluvian visits from time-traveling alien races," the geochronologist offered.

"No, Larry, don't dare tell me that," Zack fired back, exasperated. "If this gets out we'll have the tabloids, the History Channel, the Discovery Channel. They'll pull out all the old tried and true film clips and assorted other bullshit. UFO this and UFO that ..." To Lawrence Sloan's great relief, Zack's *Wimoweh* ring-tone sounded and he pulled his cell phone from his Spare Pocket adjustable carry pouch. It was a breathless I. J. Solomon on the other end. Zack slipped his phone into a PDA slot in the nearby computer and Solomon's live image popped up on the screen. "Zack, as far as we can tell, your ... uh ... Zackosaurus has no equal anywhere on this world ... now or ever. It's like it was left behind on a visit by some interplanetary ark."

Zack jumped right on the reference. "Jeez, just like in *ET*. "Uhhh … Ilias, did the animal hold together when the ice melted away?"

"Are you kidding? It looked like it could have stuck out its tongue."

"Did it have any weight?" Zack blurted out, not knowing for sure if he really wanted an answer.

"Of course Isaac, everything has weight." Zack picked up the two unclassifiable pieces of high-tech antiquity and hefted them in his hand. "Don't bet on it I J, we're heading into new territory," he said, and placed the two unearthly samples in his pocket.

"Zack, you were right on the money about the Zackosaurus being pregnant. She was in the early stages of delivery before whatever event took place to preserve her. Also, we found the DNA was totally intact. We could probably clone another one if it were legal. And get this … the lab report says the air bubbles trapped in the ice didn't match any of the other air samples taken in prior studies from that period. The electron spectrometer indicated that the isotopes of oxygen show a content of O_2 much lower than that contained in the air of the other specimens from forty millennia back and even the air at present. Also the carbon-dioxide content was fifty percent less than expected, and the nitrogen was twice as high as what had been considered normal."

Zack was now pacing the lab, "Normal? Forget normal! You got any theories Ilias?"

"The maximum resolution DNA scan indicated that when the Zackosaurus became … uhhh … inanimate it was over a hundred and fifty years-old. Now it has long been suspected that although we depend upon oxygen to live, those who live on less O_2 might live longer. The hypothesis is that oxygen causes us to physically rust."

"Are you saying that less oxygen can mean a longer life? What about that guy from high in the Ural Mountains in Russia—what was his name—Bagrid Tapagua? He was in his eighties and his mother was a hundred and two. Is that why they lived so long— the thinner air with less oxygen?"

"Perhaps, though there's no real proof yet. It was either that or possibly the yogurt."

Zack felt some of the tension seep out of him and he chuckled at Ilias' joke. "I'll go out and buy some immediately. What about the carbon dating on our animal friend?"

"Couldn't do it."

"Potassium-argon"?

"No go, too much ambient radiation And before you ask, Abbie Diamond over at Paleo-Botany said the plant has no match here either—and that's only the half of it!"

Zack was already on a fast track to Dumbfoundedville. "I don't know if I'm ready for part two."

"No, you're gonna love this. Dr. Diamond said she couldn't understand why the grass was still green since it showed no other signs of photosynthetic activity. I suggested that it might have been *mummified,* but she disagreed and said that she leaned more toward paralyzed—but then thought better of it and went completely science-fiction on me. She told me outright that the best way to accurately describe the specimen's state was … *suspended animation."*

"Suspended animation? That's just one small theoretical step before still alive! Is that why you used the words *when it became inanimate* to describe the Zackosaurus' final state instead of *when it died?*"

"I think we may have to look for some new words, Zack. Dr. Diamond has the grass samples under a battery of sunlamps. We'll keep you posted."

"Good, Ilias. But take care not to overheat our little suspended Zacko-friend or she may bite you in the ass when you're not looking … and Ilias, don't mention any of this to anyone. I still want this whole business kept under wraps. Keep everyone quiet. No papers, no announcements and no interviews." Zack took a quick glance at Dr. Sloan. "Oh, one more thing, I J—Make sure you speak with Larry here at Geochronology about the billion-year-old core samples." Zack lifted his phone from the PDA slot and the computer screen went to standby. "I need a good stiff drink. No, make that drinks."

When he returned to the dig site Zack became a force of nature; an immovable object remaining awake for days on end while ingesting a river of coffee and smoking incessantly. The excavation work preceded one scoop-full of ice, dirt and rock at a time, and as more of the craft was uncovered, it incredibly showed no outward signs of damage. The spaceship, or whatever it was, seemed to be as intact as the Zackosaurus. Geiger counter readings and spectrometric wavelength analyses registered substantial signs of an unfamiliar form of radiation on the exterior and the other matching pieces. How could there be any radiation at all? It was nearly a million millennia old and any radioactivity would have long since decayed. Even more bewildering was the fact that except for traces of Carbon 14 there was absolutely no evidence of radioactivity in the surrounding soil.

Inevitably, the story of a startling find somewhere in the frozen north was mysteriously leaked to the press. CNN covered it first. What was it that was discovered in the Alaskan tundra? What makes it so newsworthy? How long will it remain under wraps? Why is it a so closely guarded secret? These questions were setting the table for Dr. Isaac Ludlow Carver to become one of the most sought-after talk show guests and lecture circuit speakers in history. But in fact, the only sliver of integrity Zack still possessed was bound up in his work. Above all else he considered himself a scientist and not an opportunist. In spite of the magnitude of what he had come upon, he said nothing and refused to go public even though it could have represented an instant salvation of his career.

However, principle didn't stop others. In the University of Alaska at Anchorage geochronology lab, Lawrence Sloan was intently studying Dr. Abbie Diamond's Paleo-botany report. Something caught his eye; he picked up the telephone and punched in a set of numbers.

"Hello, this is Dr. Sloan. I need to speak with him. It's urgent. I have some valuable information." The geochronologist listened for a moment, "Yes sir, and tell him the terms we discussed will do nicely."

EPISODE TEN

WADE BIXLER
IN
"PLANET OF THE APES"

*W*ade T. Bixler had been a career senator for five terms, thirty years "Bix," as his friends called him, seeped ...

... like an oil slick through the inner sanctums of Capitol Hill. Now he was oozing all over the White House itself as the Vice President in an administration headed by President Garth Trelane—an administration that had no problem seeing that less and less got more and more while more and more got less and less. Worse, the President used the world terrorism crisis and other global unrest to issue an executive order which put the nation under martial law. Trelane and Bixler cancelled two elections, claiming that any transition of power during critical times could endanger our national security. The media failed miserably in its obligation to demand accountability, and though there were pockets of protest, the majority of the people were too concerned with their day-to-day struggle for survival to organize any meaningful resistance.

Albert Barrgrave II was sitting across the desk from the Vice President. When Bixler spoke he had the idiosyncratic habit of putting the finger and thumb tips of his hands together and moving them in synch with his speech. "Alright, Albert, what's all this nonsense I'm hearing about the discovery of a UFO in Alaska?"

"It's not nonsense, Wade. One of my most reliable people in Anchorage told me that the Carver find on Kodiak Island could yield a goldmine based on the technology we can pull from it through reverse engineering. There are materials that might be stronger than anything we've ever seen or imagined and have absolutely no measurable weight. My man swears that the unidentified object might actually be a spacecraft of alien origin. The magnitude of what Zack Carver unearthed is nothing short of world shaking," Barrgrave declared. "It could usher our military industrial complex into an entirely new paradigm of power and cutting-edge weaponry."

Bixler rummaged through various folders on his desk and began to thumb through a very thick one. From this file he pulled out some paperwork and an accompanying photo of Dr. Isaac Carver. The picture was not very flattering. It was a mug shot of his last DUI arrest. Bixler flipped the photo across the desk and scanned through the papers.

"This Carver's a wack job," the Vice-President said, "No one of his low moral character should exert control over what could turn out to be the most important and most lucrative discovery in history. It's just not going to happen. Besides," Bixler went on, brightening, "it's a matter of national security."

"Always," Barrgrave said flatly.

Bixler subsequently ordered his Justice Department *stooges* to, as swiftly as possible, have Dr. Carver's contract with the Barrgrave Foundation vacated and also make certain that he was relieved of his post at the university. "We must ratchet up a heavy smear campaign against Carver," Bixler demanded of the toady Attorney General. "We've got to control the press and all media, including the remaining progressives. Our main talking point should be that we can't afford to allow what is potentially one of the greatest discoveries in history to be under the auspices of a drunken, drug-addicted crackpot and fool like Isaac Carver.

That's the message I want drummed into the public forum by all our media *water carriers* until it becomes conventional wisdom."

When the U.S. marshals came to escort Zack from the dig, he tore up the court order and threw the pieces at them—then he was forcibly removed. A string of gut-wrenching jabs to his stomach supplied the initial *forcing* and then for good measure the officers slammed him to the ground and bound his wrists behind him with plastic restraints. "Bastards like Barrgrave won't be satisfied until they've sold us every last drop of that slimy, liquid monkey they have on our backs," Zack screamed over the pain as the two marshals dragged him away from his startling find.

Zack Carver was out of a job, out of money, and out of hope. His DUI mug shot was plastered all over television and the print media. Leslee Myles looked at the unfortunate photo and knew that while Dr. I. L. Carver was indeed a drunk, he was neither a crackpot nor a drug addict. And though he frequently acted foolish, everything within her being told her he was no fool. She knew this because she had seen Zack's genius and dedication to his work. She knew this because of the compassion he had shown her over nine years before in the Negev. She knew this because after all that time she was unable to get him out of her psyche or her soul. These reflections impelled Leslee to book an Alaska Airlines flight for the next day out of Bob Hope Airport in Burbank, one-way, nonstop to Eskimo country.

After picking up a Ford Focus Extended Range EV at Anchorage International, she headed the rarely available for rental, battery-powered electric vehicle to the Anchorage address she pried out of the University of Alaska Human Resources Department. It was nearly eleven o'clock at night when Leslee rolled through a particularly depressed neighborhood and pulled into one of the many available spaces in an icy, potholed parking lot. When she got out of the car she found herself bathed in the tenacious twilight of a Yukon winter, standing in front of the fleabag Aurora B. Motor Lodge and being pelted by the freezing rain and sleet that was the *Alaskan dew*. The lifelong Southern California-girl *thin-blood* that pumped through Leslee's veins was no match for the bone-chilling cold. *"Brr… this place must have been the real-life inspiration for Frostbite Falls,"* she spit out through chattering teeth, recalling the cartoon home of Rocky J. Squirrel and Bullwinkle the Moose as she trudged shivering in the damp, sub-zero weather through the courtyard of the seedy-looking motel. With no elevator in sight, she plodded up the stairs to Room 306, took a deep breath and knocked on the door … nothing. Once again … still nada. Finally, after she hammered on it assertively with the side of her fist, it slowly opened to reveal an unshaven, unsteady figure smelling like a booze-saturated strip joint. His personal scent was slightly less unsavory than the general odor of the room itself. Leslee forced a smile.

"Hi, Dr. Carver, I'm Leslee Myles. Remember me?"

Zack just stood there in the doorway like a zombie, totally toasted and looking even more run-down than his shabby, depressed, surroundings.

"If you're seeking to achieve artifact status on those rags you're wearing, I think you're there," Leslee cracked.

Zack blinked then stared vacantly as if someone popped his escape key. In the inebriated blur of his adult life he hardly remembered anyone. Yet this apparition from nearly a decade ago, now poised before him, sprang out of his memory like a blast of pure oxygen. He was at once struck with the fact that she no longer looked needy and paradoxically—he read in her eyes a reflection and amplification of his own neediness.

Leslee Myles had changed—big time. Now in her late twenties, she looked confident, graceful and delicious.

As opposed to their first meeting, when Leslee struggled to put words together, it was now Zack who stood there dumbstruck. Finally he managed to blurt out, "Rosy?"

Leslee's smile widened and warmed. "You remembered ... encouraging. I've got some things to say and I want to say them now. Dr. Carver, I'm reasonably certain that you have no idea how much our Negev experience affected me. My life did a complete one-eighty degree turn thanks to you. When I came home from Israel with my *A*, I sat my parents down and told them that I'd taken enough from them, both bad and good. I said I was going to earn my own way in life and that I wasn't going to accept any legacy admittance to law school. I decided to use my fifth year at USC to turn my long parade of C's and D's into straight A's, and to a great extent because of my work with you in the Negev, I was able to earn a master's degree in archeology. Mom and Dad were tickled pink. Then I stunned everyone in the law firm by getting a 179 on the law boards. That's out of a possible 180. Dad's L-SATs were nowhere near that. I was accepted with a scholarship at UC Berkeley Law School. Law schools like high LSAT scores and science majors. I think it has something to do with the scientific method and deductive reasoning. Anyway, after graduation I worked with my father and my brother J J and became the firm's intellectual property maven. I won a major case before the Supreme Court involving the Cardiac Event Monitor ... and if you don't start thinking about changing your lifestyle in a hurry, you ought to consider getting one," She added with overt disapproval. "I can get you a good deal."

Zack's brow puckered and he hung his head. Leslee continued. "I also prevailed in a class action suit against the recording industry which finally gave the artists the right to legal fee recovery and punitive damages... up to three times in cases where they were forced to sue or audit major corporations to get a legitimate count on their contracted royalty payments. It set a precedent for the entire entertainment business and I wrote a textbook on the subject, *Intellectual Propers.* They use it in most law schools—even Harvard and Yale."

Through all her schooling and success in the years that passed since Leslee last saw Zack, and in spite of the constant parade of highly eligible young men that pursued her, the feelings she had for him always seemed to intrude.

"Look," she said through her still chattering teeth as the numbing wind and rain stepped up a notch or two. "I'd love to continue this conversation, but this rain is like super-cooled BBs … so in the interest of my comfort and safety and in consideration of the fact that I am a California girl, how's about inviting me in to this *palace* you've got here? I promise … no seduction attempts." Leslie unbuttoned her parka and *mock* flashed Zack. "See! I'm fully dressed. Not a sheer curtain in sight."

Zack dumbly nodded and gestured for her to come in. Leslee looked around and got the full brunt of the disastrous condition of her former mentor's digs. Gingerly traversing the room, she also caught an even *fuller brunt* of the stench, and recoiled. "This place was probably borderline toilet to begin with but now you've managed to bring it down to complete port-a-john status." Then the sole of her Ugg boot struck a discarded aluminum beverage container which clinked against another. She looked down. The cans had more friends—lots of them.

"Correct me if I'm wrong but isn't 'kick the can' usually played outdoors?" she asked. "I've gotta be honest, Dr. Carver … I've never been in one of the old sports stadium men's rooms but now I know what they must have smelled like." She shuddered and pulled her outerwear tight around her. "But that's not the worst of it. You look like pure shit. Now, I'm okay with that, but judges don't like it. I've filed a motion to put you back in the archeology business and we have a court appearance in ten days. That means we've got a week to get you looking somewhat human again. I suspect that you once did…look human, I mean. Though I wouldn't know for sure, I have no real reference. I never actually saw you sober, shaved or dressed in normal people clothes. Oh … and by the way, I'm your new lawyer, although I prefer 'counselor'… we'll discuss fees later."

Before Zack could answer, Leslee spotted his shabby coat on the floor and threw her hands up. "Where else?" she picked up the coat, sniffed it and rolled her eyes. "We'll burn it later." Then she tossed the unsavory garment to Zack—and handed him his hat. "You know, hiding behind fermented grain isn't the answer to every problem."

"It isn't?" Zack squeezed out in a scratchy mumble. Leslee Rose crossed her arms in front of her chest and patted her left foot impatiently. Her mouth and eyes showed her displeasure. She shook her head, grabbed Zack's arm, yanked him out of the room and *mushed* him down the stairs.

Leslee took Zack in hand both literally and figuratively. Within three days she cleaned him up, had his wardrobe taken out and burned—and then took him shopping. She also upgraded their living quarters to a motel that not only had shampoo, conditioner and lotion in the bathroom but also provided mouthwash and even a sewing kit.

A week later at nine o'clock on a Thursday morning, Leslee and Zack went before Judge Sylvia Feit at the U.S. District Court in Anchorage. When the judge noticed Leslee's signature L. R. Myles on the papers she smiled at Leslee. "Counselor Myles … are you the L R Myles who authored *Intellectual Propers?* I teach law at the university and use the textbook in my classes." At once, the pack of high-priced attorneys representing Barrgrave Industries paled as the blood drained from their argument.

"Yes your honor." Leslee answered. "Good to have you here, Counselor Myles, and congratulations on the 5-4 Medibotics v.

Seymour Supreme Court decision in that CEM case."

Not surprisingly, the judge agreed with Leslee's pleading but also held that the writ that she was about to issue would permit Dr. Carver access to the site for an unspecified number of days while the legal wheels lumbered toward a conclusion. "I could delay the process with oceans of motions, Leslee whispered to Zack, "and the judge knows it." The U.S. Marshals Office also agreed to drop the attempted assault charges against Zack for throwing the torn shreds of the court order at the officers if Leslee would agree to drop the lawsuit she was going to file for excessive force. Leslee and Zack celebrated their victory that night at dinner.

Back at the motel, as Leslee was about to drift off into dreamland, Zack trundled in from his adjoining room wearing a bathrobe and nothing else. He had drastically reduced his alcoholic consumption was starting to lose the numbness that had invaded his groin area. Though he would have liked to pick up the unfinished business from their Negev adventure, Leslee was humming a different tune. "Not yet," she whispered. "This is not the time," she took a deep breath and looked around, "and definitely not the place. Besides, I'm saving myself,"

Zack was perplexed. "Saving yourself? For marriage?" Leslee shook her head and crinkled her nose. "No way, I'm … uhhh … almost thirty for God's sake. It's like this …we're only a week in and we're gonna wait until you're really off the sauce and you get to know me again. For now … why don't you think of me … as the light at the end of your drunk?

EPISODE ELEVEN

THE ENIGMA
"STAR TREK"

Spawned in primeval space, of carbon and silicon ejecta, amid the chaos of a multi-galaxy collision ...

... the Nine came into being within the core-collapse of a supernova. Their arrival on Kodiak Island was marked by extra-spectral particles of starlight which showered the ice cavern dig. It would have been literally breathtaking to behold their coming if anyone present and working in the cave at the time could have actually seen it. However, that would have been impossible because it happened outside the boundaries of the existing temporal envelope and the cosmic standard plane. But if the star-borne newcomers were observed or their extra-sensory communications in some way perceived, the main topic of the discussion among these unearthly super-beings was centered on why *it* still existed and what specific action was to be taken. Several drifted over to the section of the corrie glacier where it had been chipped away and commenced a photonic fragmental-trace, making it possible to recapture the recent image of Zack and the others taking possession of the small, rectangular and circular pieces and exposing the conical end of the craft.

"It is possible that the items in question were somehow immune to the neutralization process?" One of the Nine commented.

Another offered, "The craft's composition might in some way

be resistant to our reboot-cycle."

"It should be destroyed along with its contents," voiced a third, "destroyed without a trace, and then we must commence the necessary cleansing procedure."

"No," said another. "Such a choice is clearly in violation of our temporal purpose. Furthermore, this time the circumstances are very different. There have been unexpected consequences, and before we take further action we must learn exactly how much, if anything, were these beings able to deduce."

Sitting in front of a computer at the Center for Advanced Microstructures and Devices on the campus of Louisiana State University, Dax Wolf was reviewing results of the last series of runs in the particle accelerator. Suddenly he began to shiver as if he'd been hit by a chilling arctic wind. Then he sensed something odd.

Something ancient—no, beyond ancient, he thought—*something more like ... always.*

A wave of status quo-twisting data inexplicably swept through his mind like a tsunami. Revealing itself was a mathematical highway to a method of accomplishing the annihilation of weak-force particles and leaving strong-force particles to multiply unfettered—the subatomic super-highway to the eventual harnessing of unlimited nuclear fusion power.

Back in the ice cavern, one of the ephemeral beings interrupted the chrono-spectral replay of Zack and the others removing the alien objects. "The acquisition and scrutiny of these instruments could effectively disclose their origination and functionality to the inhabitants who found them. This circumstance might provide those native entities with a logical channel to our planetary sterilization measures. If so, it would be the first time since ever began, almost a universe ago, that a sentient life-form had any cognizance of the Null Quotient. For the present we must leave the air transport vehicle alone and carefully observe those who have taken possession of the missing mechanisms."

The Nine departed as they arrived, unnoticed and in silence. Unnoticed, that is, by those within the standard temporal envelope.

EPISODE TWELVE

THE PILOT
IN
"ALIEN"

At the crack of dawn, with the court order in hand, Leslee and Zack, accompanied by Snow Smith and Josh Benjamin, charged through the cordoned-off area, whipped past the cave entrance ...

... and down into the inscrutable Kodiak Island cavern. They were dressed in hooded parkas and various other warm and fuzzies. Though Zack had been away from the dig for less than three weeks, most curiously, everything was exactly as it had been when Zack, Snow and Joshua first saw it. The progress had shifted into reverse. The drip, drip stopped and the craft was again buried deep inside the baby glacier. Zack clutched the *silver dollar* artifact and Leslee carried the cell phone-sized piece as the four approached the huge frozen mass.

It was at this moment that the series of astonishing events vaulted into mega-high gear. The mysterious weightless rectangle in Leslee's hand suddenly unleashed a series of wide-arc, full-spectrum beams toward the ice-imprisoned vehicle. In answer, a narrow, multi-hued ribbon of light shot from the craft and the two intersected within the glacier. "These trinkets are not simply trinkets," Zack exclaimed. "They must be some sort of high-tech alien electronics." Immediately after Zack spoke, the craft began to radiate and pulsate rapidly, bathing the group in a fiery scarlet glow, and the drip, drip from the glacier recommenced. Then the quartet was thunderstruck when, without warning, the vehicle began to uncover *itself*. The defrosting process jumped to warp speed with a shattering roar and in an almost instantaneous meltdown the frozen veil became liquefied, sending a surge of raging water which quickly inundated the cavern. The ice-cold torrent swept up Zack, Leslee, Snow and Joshua and heaved them with bone jarring force against the chamber walls. In a matter of seconds the flood level rose halfway up the twenty-five-meter height of the cavern. After being slammed several times against an outcropping of rocks, Zack lost his grip on the circular device in his hand, and it was whisked away in the foaming tempest. The four were barely remaining afloat. They bobbed up and down violently and were smashed unrelentingly against the cave sides while they struggled to tread water. As they continued to fight the treacherous, swirling current their bodies were being battered to the point of exhaustion.

"Rosy," Zack shouted as he reached out for Leslee's hand. But Leslee knew from her training that grabbing someone hand to hand provided the weakest grip. She dropped the rectangular alien item, slid her hand up between Zack's wrist and elbow and secured it. Zack responded by doing the same and tightening his hold on her arm.

"Maybe we can we get back to the stairs," Leslee hollered over the thundering cascade as the water level continued to swiftly rise.

"No," Zack shouted back. "It's too late for that. The stairway must be ten to twenty meters beneath us … and even if we could make it there, it's got to be swamped already as well."

They were now floating near the top of the grotto with just a scant few minutes worth of air. Snow and Josh were holding onto each other for dear life and all were utterly oblivious to the supernatural reddish glimmer wavering beneath them.

Meanwhile, up on the surface at the excavation site, all hell broke loose. The small cave entry was suddenly blasted away by the raging surge of melted ancient ice. Panicked, the entire crew and the onlookers began scrambling to get to higher ground.

Dax Wolf had been covertly flown by DARPA to Switzerland to run some experiments using the Large Hadron Collider particle-accelerator near Geneva. He was intensely involved in highly advanced experimentation with the tiniest building blocks in nature when once again he became intolerably cold and he began to shiver, and instantly recognized that it was the same eerie chill that he had experienced previously. He began shaking uncontrollably and as he was losing consciousness, he became curiously aware of the fact that the other lab technicians seemed perfectly comfortable in this same environment in which he was now freezing.

Inside the underground cavern, the water level rose to a mere two finger widths from the top. Zack, Leslee, Snow and Josh, straining to keep their faces above the surface, were gasping for air and beginning to feel the numbing effects of first-stage hypothermia. Then, suddenly, numerous streams of bubbles began to erupt in eddies all around them and the deathly cold temperature of the water started to rise. It was as if they were floating inside of a giant can of warm soda pop. As the frothing pockets ascended they began to inflate, becoming as big as king-sized fitness balls. The introduction of the unusually significant volumes of the gaseous matter substantially reduced the buoyancy of the surrounding water. Zack was the first to sink beneath the surface, followed by Snow, Joshua and finally Leslee. Water began filling their lungs and a drowning death was lurking only a few short moments away.

On the ground above, the rumbling surge of water was pummeling the derricks, vehicles and drilling machinery; pounding and rolling them over and over and reducing them into a junkyard heap of twisted scrap metal. The dozers and other vehicles were overturned and wrecked beyond any salvage efforts. Supply tents were washed away entirely. When the crashing flood water began to diminish, the extensive damage to the Barrgrave Company resources was apparent.

When Dax Wolf awoke, he was still at the console. No one else in the lab seemed to notice that anything unusual had occurred. As he did following his previous seizure, Dax looked older, and felt more worn and haggard. In spite of this, like a ball dropping on a winning number slot on a roulette wheel, Wolf clicked into another astounding epiphany. Incredibly, the secret mini-universe he was studying had suddenly become no more difficult to perceive than the advanced aptitude he had for spatial relations when he was a child building with Legos. In a blinding flash he acquired the ability to, in his mind's eye, actually *be* one of the minute fragments of matter and energy and visualize their positions and movements. He could see them in the accelerator, a feat no one else could even approach. Was it just his imagination, or had his relationship with the subatomic world become an up close and personal experience?

Dying was odd, Zack thought as exhaustion forced him to give up fighting and he tumbled through the bubbling maelstrom, finally thumping down on the cavern floor. He was somehow consciously aware that he had ingested vast amounts of water and clearly remembered that at one point he was choking and sensed he was blacking out. With those impressions in mind, his deductive reasoning led him to the conclusion that he must certainly be—dead. But if that were true, how was it that he was now sitting comfortably at the bottom of a warm effervescent pool, breathing in and out with great ease?

Holy shit, he mused as a bell rang in his head, *so there really is an afterlife. I guess I should've prayed more.*

Zack's religious inner conversation trail was cut off at the pass when he saw Leslee paddling over to him through the streams of rising bubbles. She was smiling like some diaphanous water sprite.

And you get to take those you love with you. I do love Rosy, he thought. *I wish I could have found a way to tell her when I was alive.* Then the other shoe dropped. *Oh no, Zack* moaned internally, *No! Rosy must be dead too and it's my fault!*

Leslee swam up face to face with Zack and kept pointing to her nose and mouth but Zack couldn't concentrate enough to understand what she was trying to communicate to him. He was too flushed with guilt about Leslee and the revelation of his being among the deceased.

Then he caught a glimpse of Josh and Snow. *Wow, you even get to see your friends in the hereafter. Hey, I wonder if secondhand smoke is a problem when you're dead. Shit, I wonder if firsthand smoke is a problem when you're dead. Jeez, I wonder if it's okay to even say "shit" if you're dead.* The questions, as it turned out, were moot.

The choking was caused by the initial influx of the super-oxygenated plasma that was introduced into the water. It was *inhaled* through Zack's air passages and taken into his lungs. When he temporarily lost consciousness his body relaxed and his lungs ingested the oxygen that saturated the liquid plasma. This in turn established a normal respiration pattern, and the same unique phenomenon occurred with Leslee, Josh and Snow as well. They were all still quite present in the *here-before.*

The deluge of water drained away as abruptly as it had filled the cavern. Zack, Leslee, Joshua and Snow found themselves on the floor of the cave lying near the now totally exposed, teardrop-shaped craft. They began gagging and coughing up the residual fluid in their lungs as their bodies started readjusting to normal breathing. Then another oddity—they realized that in spite of the giant flood, the entire cave area as well as their clothing and they themselves were thoroughly dry. Moreover, none of their equipment showed any hint of exposure to water. But most curious of all, there didn't seem to be any residual effects from the physical pounding they each took.

Leslee was the first to notice the soft hum and pale red pulsating glow emanating from the enigmatic round and rectangular pieces of electronic equipment that she and Zack had dropped. When she picked up the instruments, they immediately stopped glowing. Leslee studied them, handed the circular item to Zack who examined it for a split-second, then slipped it in behind the round *Archeology<>Dig It!* emblem on his belt buckle. The four turned their attention to the exotic vehicle and were surprised to find that it looked to be a dark, slate-colored, completely unmarked and oversized droplet. It showed no outward evidence of a command deck or power source: and no visible control surface seams, apertures, vents or openings of any kind. As they drew nearer to undertake a more detailed inspection, the cell phone-sized device in Leslee's hand began to radiate again with great intensity and emitted a wavering multi-spectral beam which fell on the mysterious conveyance and scanned its length. Then the unpredictable ultra-tech, gravity-defying rectangle stopped humming and switched off. Dr. Carver walked around the ancient object to search for an indication of flight-control surfaces or any other information that would provide a clue to help explain the astonishing events that were taking place. He found none. "This thing might be an unmanned probe. Maybe we can get an idea of where it came from if we can get inside."

That notion was dead on arrival because there seemed to be no way to *get inside*. Then another beam from the instrument in

Leslee's hand shot out laser-straight and became a wide shaft of blue light that played on the rounded end of the large, murky-shaded craft, instantly initiating a slightly fluctuating, opaque windscreen to deploy.

"I can't see through it," Zack said as he and the others advanced closer, "maybe this is a viewing port and if it is, there could be a pilot."

"The surface around the *cockpit* area looks smooth like the rest of the craft and seems relatively intact." Snow added. "There's a chance that we'll find some evidence of whatever creature or being flew this machine if we could get aboard." Joshua suggested.

"There might even be some alien … or whatever … organic remains … an articulated skeleton … skin … hair … if they had any," Leslee said.

Then she stepped right up to the remarkable aerial artifact to get a tactile fix on it. She cautiously stretched out her hand and the instant her fingertip made contact with the body of the vehicle, the seamless clamshell canopy lifted, revealing an inner flight deck bubble which also opened almost as if it were an invitation.

Zack was blown away. "Holy shit, the thing still works? What the hell could be the power source?"

Zack, Leslee and the others were overwhelmed by the mind-numbing possibilities of what this discovery might portend. Holding their breath, hoping to see some kind of weird extra-terrestrial collection of bones, Zack and Leslee gingerly leaned in, anticipating at least one solid clue that would shed some light on the ever-growing plethora of incredible mysteries.

Their stunned gazes fell on a gloved, booted and helmeted figure wearing a one-piece, azure flight-suit. The uniform was remarkably preserved and was adorned with undecipherable military-style insignia bearing characters that indicated some form of a written language. There were no visible pockets or fastening mechanisms of any kind and though the garment was neither worn nor torn, it exhibited a significant amount of what seemed to be scorch marks, some of which inexplicably vanished after a few seconds. Though they could not see the pilot's features through the wrap-around face-plate that was identical in color and state to the windscreen, they could clearly discern that the flight-suit itself was solidly filled out with two arms and two legs attached to a torso.

"This is no bundle of bones." Zack observed. "Who or … whatever this alien astronaut is … it looks like he could have died last week and he looks humanoid." However, being well aware that he was treading on unfamiliar ground, it was hard for Zack to be sure—of anything. Then Leslee noticed that the chest area was amply convex-shaped. "Look!" Leslee declared with enthusiasm, pointing to the pilot's upper torso. "Breasts … this first alien astronaut isn't a he … but a *she* … a female … a … me!"

"An us," Snow added and shared a high five with Leslee.

Joshua got busy shooting digital video of the craft's exterior while Snow took a battery of high-resolution, three dimensional stills of the cockpit area and the expired humanoid pilot within. Upon closer inspection Leslee noticed that clutched in the alien flier's right hand was a shimmering object that appeared identical to the glowing piece that she was holding. Using great care, Leslee gently tugged the palm-sized rectangle free from the pilot's gloved grasp. The second she did so it stopped radiating. "This has no apparent weight either," she said and handed the second rectangular instrument to Zack. He slipped it into his pocket and then attempted to locate some sort of release mechanism on the helmet. However, as soon as he made physical contact with the headgear, the canopies started to close and he was barely able to get out of the way. Leslee started to reach out, hoping that touching the same spot she touched before would reopen them but Zack stopped her. "This may be the best way for the moment, to protect whatever is able to be preserved. This space ship seems to know much more than we do. It gave us a quick peek and now it just told us ... *that's all folks*."

When Zack, Leslee, Snow and Joshua reached the outside entrance to the cave the four were shocked when confronted by the devastation to the site and the equipment. However, they were relieved to hear that in spite of the evident destruction, by some unknown miracle no one was seriously hurt. But the fact that there would be no oil drilling until new equipment could be brought in was met with muted appreciation.

Before Zack and the others were allowed to leave, several security operatives insisted on searching them. Leslee immediately raised the rectangular piece she had in her hand up in front of her face and began looking into it and sliding her pinky finger over her lower lip as if she were looking in a mirror and applying lip balm. After also mock-treating her upper lip she placed the *mirror* in her pocket. When Zack took the other piece from his pocket he whipped out a pen and began *writing* on it as if it were a notepad then quickly slipped it into his Spare Pocket behind his cell phone. The guard, having no real idea what he was looking for, saw nothing suspicious and allowed them all to leave without further incident.

As soon as the four archeologists were gone, one of the members of the security detail placed a call to corporate headquarters. By dawn, word of the mini-flood reached the powers that be, and a legion of Barrgrave International technicians and additional security personnel arrived at the dig.

EPIſODE THIRTEEN

THE VOICE
"CONTACT"

Back at the motel room, Zack was sitting on the bed nervously fondling the dark, rectangular scrap of cutting edge, antediluvian science which ...

... was indeed an exact match to the piece he found outside the craft—whatever *that* was. Leslee held the original object in one hand while channel-surfing with the TV remote in the other. She stopped at a news report.

"Based on new information," the commentator declared, "it turns out that the whole *miracle* in the tundra was nothing but an old B-25 bomber that crashed in the late forties and lay buried in the ice for over three quarters of a century."

Zack went ballistic. "Fuck you," he shouted, then charged off the bed toward the TV screen and held up the weightless rectangle. "I'd like to see a World War II airplane made out of this!" He plopped back down on the bed out of sheer disgust, snatched a fresh pack of smokes from the night stand and started to open it. "The fucking Foxtica Nitwork ... spin 'til ya puke. Where the hell's the truth when you need it? Don't they get Keith and Rachel here?" Leslee switched the television off, "We'll catch them later," she said, then dropped the remote on the bed, grabbed Zack's hand and took the box of cigarettes from him. "Look at me," she demanded and pointed to her eyes with the middle and index fingers of her right hand. Zack turned his head toward her and she held up the pack with the side right in his face. "Smoking causes cancer, heart disease, emphysema; that's you." Leslee admonished somewhat flintily. "Cigarette smoke contains carbon monoxide; that's from secondhand smoke and that's me! If you're so hell-bent on ignoring the Surgeon General's warnings and slowly killing yourself that's your prerogative, but you're not gonna take me with you and … no … you know what? I won't let you kill yourself either." She crushed the *crushproof* cigarette box in one hand and looped it over Zack's head across the room into the trash can—nothin' but—*swishhh*.

"You want me to quit drinking *and* smoking at the same time?" In response, Leslee slid over close to Zack, and put her free hand on his cheek and kissed him softly. "I promise you, it will be much better and deeper without the tobacco breath," Leslee half-whispered, "Look, I'm only asking for two out of three. I don't mind your locker room language. You can curse like a drunken sailor for all I care. As a matter of fact I think it's kind of cute."

"Okay," Zack conceded, "I'll try."

"No, young Jedi," Leslee countered. "Remember what Yoda said. 'Try not. *Do* or do not. There is no try.'" Then Leslee dropped her hand and took the PDA-sized piece of alien material from Zack. She began to idly compare it to the one she was holding by turning them over and placing one on top of the other like she was shuffling cards. "Amazing … mass without weight. It feels even lighter than aerogel."

At the very instant the two pieces were lined up a particular way, they morphed and re-morphed through a rapid succession of different shapes until they combined as one unit and commenced emitting a steady, high-frequency tone. Then the pitch started sliding lower and lower, began to waver, and a series of sounds that seemed to mimic a spoken language gradually became audible. Although not intelligible, the solitary voice was calm, soothing and deliberate. How could Zack and Leslee have possibly realized that they were listening to the pilot recording her last words before she was to meet her destiny after an epic but fruitless battle on a doomed world?

Zack tried to take the instrument from Leslee, but the voice became silent the instant he touched it. It wasn't until he released the device from his grasp that it resumed speaking again. Zack realized this was similar to what occurred when Leslee touched the space craft. "It must be an intergalactic chick thing," He offered flippantly. Leslee punched him in the arm—hard.

Leslee continued to hold the instrument while Zack listened. He found that although it could be phonetically evaluated, the language had no commonality with any tongue he had ever known to be spoken on this planet.

Oliver and Amelia Carle were in deep alpha when the phone *warbled* them awake. Ollie picked it up, but before he could say anything, the voice at the other end stopped him. He listened for a moment.

"Zack, are you crazy? It's two o'clock in the morning here, and I …" Ollie tried to continue but Zack was in high gear. Ollie took another stab.

"Zack … Zack."

"Zack!" Amelia said. "He's got to be drunk." She covered her head with the pillow.

Oliver was pissed. "You're drunk!"

Then Ollie pulled the phone a foot away from his ear but Zack's voice was loud enough for him to hear it even at that distance. Ollie listened for a moment, and then he spoke into the phone.

"Talk to who … your lawyer? " He nodded his head several times. "She prefers counselor. Okay, wait a sec."

Ollie turned to Amelia. "He's putting someone else on the phone ... a woman." Amelia lifted the pillow. "A woman? Jesus, not again—and it's talk to *whom* not who," she added, then reburied her head in the pillow.

Ollie listened some more. "Melli, an attorney named Leslee Myles swears that Zack is not drunk, and I don't think he sounded drunk. I know when he's drunk and right now, he's not drunk."

Amelia let go of the sides of the pillow that were covering her ears and lifted her head. Ollie was nodding in the affirmative.

"Right, Zack, we'll do it as soon as we can."

"We," Amelia rasped in an effort to try to press her consciousness to brush away her Tempur-Pedic miracle-mattress-induced sleep cobwebs. "We," answered Ollie. Then he switched on the lamp on the night table and Amelia raised herself up on her hands.

"Oliver, what exactly are *we* going to do as soon as we can?"

"Pack your flannels, your thermals and your mukluks, we're going ..." Ollie started to sing the late Johnny Horton's song, "Way up North ... Way up North ... North to Alaska, we go North the rush is on." Then he hopped out of bed, reached over and in time with the tune began gently nudging his wife into *fully awake.*

The Alaska Airlines flight departed Los Angeles International at 8:00 a.m. and the captain greased the Boeing 737-900 onto runway two-six at Juneau International Airport at 1:31 p.m. for an on-time arrival. Zack and Leslee met the Carles, and in the car on the way to the college, Leslee demonstrated the behavior of the rectangular shaped electronic instruments that had been gathered from in and around the craft. Ollie reacted as a scientist would, but Amelia's mind was more than fifty percent on the road to *boggle.*

"I couldn't bring them to you because they might have set off the alarms when I went through security at the airport," Zack said. "Uhhh they're radioactive … slightly. I don't think they're detectable, but it wasn't worth the risk."

The foursome went directly to the university to fire up the super-computers. Amelia and Oliver were seated in front of the computer screen. Zack was too nervous to sit, and paced back and forth behind them. Leslee was standing near Ollie. Using the digital photos of the printed placards found inside the aircraft cockpit, Amelia tried but was unable to even begin to translate the unique utterances from the joined mini-monoliths into English.

Zack couldn't keep from opening his mouth. "Can this craft and its dead pilot be from an alien world long ago in a galaxy far, far away? If that's true, then the UFO hoopla might not be bullshit after all." Zack flopped down into a chair.

"Jesus, Zack," Ollie said agreeing. "Maybe, at the end of the day, the Roswell, Hanger 18 and Area 51 wackos aren't wackos." Zack leaped up and started to pace again. "Don't tell me that, Ollie," he bristled. "Fuck! I don't wanna hear that."

Zack's dread was short-lived, however. The mysterious device suddenly emitted a rainbow of plasma waves that interfaced with the super-computer. These beams also scanned Zack, Leslee, Oliver and Amelia. The other Mega-Macs in the room inexplicably came to life without being touched. Their displays filled with blurred, imperceptible flows of picture and dissonant sound. The surge of the input was too strong for the existing circuitry, and geysers of sparks spewed from the majority of the hi-tech equipment and cascaded into the room.

Amelia shielded her eyes from the shower of fireworks and shouted over the cacophonous din. "The download is coming too fast! It's impossible for these machines to absorb the data. The memory-chips will burn out, and the electronics will fry from the overload." Within a split second after Amelia's words, the artificial intelligence which was instantaneously imbued into the super-computer by the alien instrument had recognized that the information was indeed being presented much too quickly to be safely processed and downloaded by such primitive hardware. The pace was also far beyond the sensory ability of the unclassified life forms present to assimilate the torrent of data.

Consequently, the whirring display began to slow and exhibited a pictorial essay that conveyed an amazing story about a ten-bodied heliosphere including nine planetesimal objects and a central star around which they orbited. One of the nine worlds had a bluish-green tint and a single moon. Then a pleasant sounding male voice came on and began to speak in English, explaining that the star was known as Lano Sokyam which was also the expression for alive or living. The pictures on the screen switched to views of the inside of the familiar teardrop aircraft. The pilot was adorned in the recognizable navy flying gear and was identified as Ahneevah, a high-ranking officer in the air and space command. Visuals flashed by showing highlights of her multiple expeditions to the *near satellite*, at first to explore, and then oversee the construction of bases and colonies.

Oliver thought he saw something familiar in the depictions of the lustrous planetoid that was the destination of Ahneevah's missions. Then a series of starry celestial navigation charts flew past on the monitor. One particular stellar view prompted Ollie to shoot up out of his chair. After it went by, out of sheer frustration he instinctively shouted, "Pause!"

Zack, Leslee and Amelia were as surprised as Ollie when the display froze. "Back slow," Ollie semi-whispered, and the video-stream slowly shuttled back to the chart image that piqued his curiosity. "Freeze," Ollie requested and the machines complied. Then he walked up to the LED monitor, carefully studied it, sat back in the chair, did some quick inputs on his hand-held computer, and then shot to his feet again.

"Unbelievable!"

The stunned expression on Doctor Oliver Carl's face matched

the astonishment in his voice.

Zack leaped to his feet. "What? What??"

Ollie signaled a *timeout* like a referee style by forming a T with his hands and then plopped down and took several deep breaths to gather his wits before he continued.

"This lineup ... this astronomical lineup dates back ..." Ollie tapped a few more keys. "It dates back over nine-hundred and ninety-six million years."

"So?" Zack said. "The Sagan Space Telescope can look back practically to the "Big Bang" itself. An alien race capable of this advanced technology we're seeing can certainly make those kinds of observations. What's the big deal?"

"Isaac, that's just it. It's not from an alien point of view. This particular celestial configuration would have only been visible nearly a billion years ago from one single place ... here ... on Earth!"

Leslee's eyes owled-up at the implication. "Our Earth? You mean old blue-and-green Mother Earth?"

Then Ollie locked into something else, "Rewind, please." The display once again started running in reverse until an image of a planet peeping over the horizon of the near satellite was visible on a small area of the screen. "Stop," commanded Oliver. "Now zoom in on the background object."

The computer enlarged the item of Ollie's interest and it became clear that the planet was indeed blue and green like the Earth. However, there were several continental bodies evident in the northern and southern hemispheres and another much larger land-mass centered on the equator that was rotating into view. A full latitudinal image revealed that the third continent extended across the equator and covered almost two-thirds of the face of the planet.

"Ollie, that can't be the Earth. It's showing only three land masses aside from the poles. That geography is nothing like ours."

"But take a look at the size of the coastline of the one on the western edge, Ollie pointed out."

Leslee's brow furrowed in thought as she studied the visual. Then her eyes widened with clarity, "Incredible, I can't believe it. That's Rodinia … Rodinia, the super continent … it goes back on the time scale over a million millennia; hundreds of millions of years before Pangea. Though the assumption has always been that Rodinia was a single body of land until around 750 million years ago, this depiction shows that it started breaking up much sooner … and then, 500 million years later, Pangea itself … broke into pieces which drifted apart to eventually form the continents as we know them today."

Oliver was in astronomic Shangri-La. "A billion-year-old image, shot from space, that could be illustrative proof of the theory that the movements of super continents like Rodinia, Pannotia and Pangea were cyclical … and … that these mega land masses have and will continue to ride the tectonic plates, be split into pieces that float away from each other, and then recombine as one super continent. In any case … the bottom line here is that for damn certain … whether this particular continental depiction looks like the Earth or not, I would stake my reputation on the fact that it most definitely is. Consider the data overlay on the right side of the screen. Those numbers don't lie. They corroborate that this body is the same diameter, circumference, has the same molten inner core composition, is roughly the same distance from its sun and has one moon that's twenty-five percent its size. Further, it's located exactly where the Earth would have been in the celestial scheme of things a billion years ago. The one curious thing is that the Moon's orbit around this world is nearly the same as it is today. Given that we know the Moon is receding from Earth at a rate of thirty-eight millimeters per year it should have been twenty three thousand miles closer. I don't know … maybe there were some other forces at work."

"Yeah," Leslee said. "Other forces ... you could say that."

Zack plunked down in a chair and all could manage was a subdued "Holy shit!"

Then the views of the planet crossed the day/night terminator and twinkling lights became visible throughout much of the land areas. This caused Ollie to take another deep breath and exhale slowly. "Those lights must be cities ... an organized society. I can't believe I'm about to say this but although I'd have to do more investigation about the Moon thing, for now I can draw only one rational conclusion. This woman ... or whatever she is ... represents a highly advanced civilization that either visited but more likely existed here on our very own planet nearly a billion years ago."

Flabbergasted, Zack vaulted out of his seat and began to move back and forth like a caged animal. "Are you suggesting that a form of intelligent life evolved on our little lump of primordial matter and was here hundreds of millions of years before the goddamned dinosaurs and then somehow disappeared without a trace? How could that be? There's no evidence of that."

"There is now," Amelia declared. "Holy shit!" she then uncharacteristically exclaimed. "Look at the screen."

In additional support of Ollie's contention, the recording, made almost a million millennia in the past, switched to a life-sized holographic image replaying Ahneevah's final moments. Due to her headgear, her face was not visible but her actions in air-to-air combat were swift and sure. Then, through the forward view port, they saw the true extent of the brave warrior's piloting skills as she regained some control of her aircraft during its wild plunge through the fiery skies. Finally, they watched in awe as the flight vehicle smashed into the vegetation canopy, then crashed and sank in the deep, slimy waters of the swamp.

The four had just witnessed, in terrifying flashes of doom, the end of a world. The complete destruction of a civilization on a planet referred to as Lano Pahntri. Breathless and with nothing to say, Leslee slid the chair behind the pacing Zack, separated the two segments of the weightless piece of *ancient* technology and, with a deep reverence, handed one of them to Zack who solemnly bowed his head and slowly sat down ... drained.

EPISODE FOURTEEN

"A BRIEF HISTORY OF TIME"

A hneevah was born to fly ...

... and all those within her near circle considered it a birth right. They recognized that everything about her physical and mental being said *airborne*. Her specific physiognomy allowed her to *wear* her primary training aircraft almost as if it were an extension of her life shell. Her intellectual capacity was at the very highest percentile on the Cerebral Assessment Scale. Even during her earliest educational period she showed a remarkable aptitude in practically all academic disciplines. Later on in her intermediate cycle, she excelled at every one of her advanced study modules, including aero-engineering, flight dynamics, photonic propulsion systems, virtually all other sciences, and most of her planet's history and languages.

One reason for her exceptional learning prowess was that in her formative phase she was able to develop and put into practice the technique of lucid dreaming. This skill allowed her to pre-select and program specific dream subject matter before her sleep periods began. As a consequence, she was able to review and assimilate each day's curriculum during the nights as she slept. Later on at the Air and Space Tactical Flight Center she used her highly perfected conscious dreaming ability to create a varied selection of mental flight simulators so that during her REM sleep phase she could *fly* almost any aircraft within the Air Arm inventory. All aerial control inputs, emergency procedures and combat maneuvers were performed over and over again and became auto-reflex actions ingrained in her subconscious-to-conscious memory nexus, making it possible for her to consistently perform every flight-related task instinctively and flawlessly. She also utilized her self-activated dusk-'til-dawn sleep seminars to rehearse actual mission profiles, which prepared her to execute her duties and handle crisis situations with amazing fluidity, alacrity and perfection.

Though Ahneevah's mastery of the lucid dreaming technique was indeed amazing, it represented merely a small fraction of her extraordinary natural arsenal. The most incomprehensible of all her abilities was her omniscient consciousness. She had the uncanny power to simultaneously hold and individually track a multiplicity of active thoughts. Even within her highly advanced race this was considered a one in a hundred-million phenomenon.

Ahneevah's life mate, also a combat pilot, was a casualty of war. Although great honors were conferred upon him, Ahneevah was never able to reconcile the circumstances surrounding his untimely death. She always believed that the civilian leadership had failed in their oversight duties. Their dereliction resulted in the military being forced to overuse and overextend its forces and all other strategic assets until it had broken down. Ahneevah always maintained that her mate was an unnecessary sacrifice to the gross ineptness and negligence of those in power.

With the exception of the loss of her mate, the intrepid Ahneevah had never faced a difficulty she was unable to completely overcome. However, all of her mental focus could not conquer the unbearable sorrow deep inside her—the profound regret that her highly advanced race had been unable to avoid annihilation.

EPIJODE FIFTEEN

REVERSAL
"MENACE FROM EARTH"

A lbert Barrgrave wanted to take unhindered possession of the astounding discovery and ...

... in a *shadow* session, his lawyers brought the case to the Supreme Court seeking a ruling to nationalize the finds and to forcibly remove Carver and his meddlesome attorney from the site—and the equation. With special assistance from the Department of Justice, Barrgrave prevailed in setting aside Judge Feit's Anchorage U.S. District Court decision. Additionally, no one was to be permitted to go into the cavern until proper security and science teams could be sent in; *proper,* meaning hand-picked by Barrgrave and Bixler from the private sector—*their* private sector. Barrgrave Industries was also granted the exclusive right to oversee a full pathological examination of the nearly billion-year-old mummified pilot and initiate an immediate effort to reverse-engineer the craft's system to learn what technologies could be adapted.

Leslee Myles clearly had the facts and the law on her side, but she was prevented at every turn from arguing her case. The Attorney General's office provided a number of *trumped up* legal precedents, and two of the Supreme Court Justices were originally appointed through the efforts of Vice President Bixler, so their decidedly biased decision was of no particular surprise to anyone.

"It is a matter of executive privilege and national security," they ruled exactly as they were supposed to in 6-3 decision.

Leslee framed a written objection which was noted and ignored. She and Zack had summarily been given their walking papers and ordered to turn everything over to the government. Moreover, they were warned that if they even showed up at the site, given the national security aspect of the situation, they would be met with deadly force.

Zack, fearing for Snow and Joshua's safety, ordered them to return to the university and run tests on all the items that he and Leslee managed to *appropriate* from the excavation area. At first they objected strenuously but eventually they complied. It seemed that Zack's tenure with the life-on-Earth altering project was ended—but it only *seemed* that way.

When the urgent directive came to DARPA from the Vice President's office seeking one of its best and brightest, Dax Wolf was immediately recalled from Geneva.

Furious, Dax resisted. He asserted that he was at a crossroads in his research on matter and energy fragments. "Why are you taking me away from my experiments?" he fumed. That information was strictly *need to know*, he was told, and as yet he had no need to know. So without any further explanation he found himself flying well above 40,000 feet in an FA-35 two-seat Joint Strike Fighter/Trainer bound for Elmendorf Air Force Base, north of Anchorage. Dax seethed for the entire Mach 2 flight over the North Pole and was still simmering when he boarded a revving Sikorsky X2 advanced coaxial-rotor helicopter and was whisked from Elmendorf and touched down at Kodiak Airport, a joint civil and military facility.

To his complete surprise, upon his arrival at the cave site on the island where the Gulf of Alaska meets the Pacific Ocean, Wolf was met by none other than Vice President Bixler himself, along with Albert Barrgrave and General Ethan Mitchell. When he was briefed on the situation, his skepticism bubbled over into disdain.

"A billion-year-old alien spacecraft? Intelligent life existing before the first hominids on Earth slapped their handprints on cave walls?" he said frostily. "What, no crop circles? How long has this nonsense been going on? If it is real, then it could throw everything we think about this world … no, I take that back … it could throw everything we think about the Universe into complete chaos."

Dax Wolf and the entire security and science contingent assembled by Bixler and Barrgrave were placed under the command of General Mitchell.

Wolf was torn between his scientific need to see the prize on the one hand and another sudden onset of twitching, chattering and quaking on the other. It made no sense. First of all, it wasn't that cold, and second, he was wearing thermal undergarments, several layers of clothing and a military-issue extreme cold weather parka. Then he grabbed onto something that stunned him. He realized that he was freezing from the *inside* out and not the *outside* in. Wolf was also vaguely aware of a mysterious omnipresence that even his enormous intellect could not begin to comprehend. Maybe there really was something worth investigating.

When Dax and the group crawled through the small access tunnel and descended the long flight of stone stairs into the cavern, they found that the craft was once again encased solidly in the corrie glacier and its silhouette was barely discernable. How could this have happened in only a few days? General Mitchell ordered that the object be chopped free but each time a piece was chipped away, the blue ice would regenerate in seconds. This didn't simply impede progress, it completely thwarted it. It also forced Bixler and Barrgrave into considering an action that caused them to ingest increased doses of Mylanta, and Dax Wolf's earlier sharp cynicism had at once turned to acute scientific curiosity.

The apartment multiplex was in a pleasant Anchorage neighborhood. The month-to-month two-bedroom, third-floor rental, number 315, in Building 9 was a far cry from Zack's previous, squalid Aurora B. Motor Lodge roach-pit in its having the requisite acceptable furniture and clean floors. A fresh blanket of snowfall added an eerie silence to the frosty arctic twilight as Leslee, bundled in an oversized and very faux-furry parka, opened the sliding glass door and stepped out onto the balcony. Her hazel eyes glimmered in the reflection of the dancing beams produced by the spellbinding aurora borealis light-show. She leaned on the railing and took a deep breath and as she exhaled into the freezing air, a swirl of vapor appeared and quickly dissipated. Being a California girl she was amused by this phenomenon and started taking a rapid series of deeper breaths which produced increasingly larger mini-clouds.

Leslee was getting a bit woozy from hyperventilation and if Zack didn't have the Tokens' *Wimoweh* ring tone on his cell phone set at an extremely high volume, she never would have heard it through the insulated, double-paned glass. She was tickled by this. Much of what Zack did tickled her. Leslee steadied herself and after a moment, Zack, in basic bathrobe, whipped the door open and burst out into the night's chill. He took hold of her hands and began dancing her around. The jumping and skipping made Zack breathe heavier, and the frosty breath-mist coming from Zack and Leslee's mouths combined with haunting hue of the flickering northern lights made their movements seem like a part of some primitive ritual.

"They're picking us up in two hours at Elmendorf. We're back in the game; we're back in the game!" Zack shouted euphorically.

Leslee was caught up in his enthusiasm and began to laugh but then shrugged her shoulders and raised her eyebrows indicating she didn't quite understand what the party was about. Zack caught this. "General Mitchell ... the cavern," he gurgled. "No progress. No drip, drip. Not without us. The craft was resealed again in the corrie glacier, and every time they tried to melt or chip the ice away, it came right back."

When Zack and Leslee arrived at the bustling dig site in the mysterious cavern, Zack immediately began belting out orders.

"I want this place cleared. Counselor Myles and me will remain down here. Everyone else please relocate yourselves up and out." Zack indicated *up and out* with exaggerated hand signals as a flight attendant would. "Also, make sure you all stay beyond a mile radius from here. That goes for everyone, including you, General Mitchell."

The general, being a general, wasn't buying. "I'm in charge here, Carver, not you. I'll send the support staff out, but I'm staying right here—and Dr. Wolf as well."

Leslee pulled the hood of her parka back and stood nose to nose with Mitchell. "General, this is not about who's the boss. You hit a wall here—a big, blue, icy wall, and you asked for our help. Our plan is to re-create the same set of circumstances that made the craft uncover itself in the first place. Dr. Carver and I were here for that. You and Dr. Wolf were not. Do you want *us* to leave?" The general was about to respond, but thought better and stopped himself. He knew full well that Leslee had him, checkmate. Game over.

A short while after Mitchell and everyone else left, Zack handed his section of the rectangular *gizmo* to Leslee. She quickly removed its twin from her parka, lined them up and the rainbow of spectral colors shot out from the combined devices and bathed the corrie glacier in its vibrating hues. The ancient frozen mound began to melt. This time they knew the drill and sat comfortably on the cavern floor waiting to make like fish again.

EPIJODE JIHTEEN

THE POSTMORTEM
"ROSWELL"

*I*t *was truly a scene out of Close Encounters as …*

… a swarm of aircraft, bulging with cadres of medical and mercenary personnel and masses of equipment, descended upon an undisclosed, deserted military installation deep in the Arizona desert. A flight of Apache, Blackhawk and Cobra firebirds led by the state-of-the-art Sikorsky high-speed X2 Coaxial helicopter touched down in front of the airport tower. The facility had been abandoned for twenty-seven years and due to the barren region's creeping, physical encroachment, the flock of spinning rotor blades churned up a grainy haze of grit and grime through which scores of Barrgrave's security forces spilled out onto the tarmac. Several C-17 cargo planes and a C-130J Hercules touched down on runway Two-Five Right and quickly disgorged their payloads of trucks; Humvees and other vehicles; advanced weaponry; meals ready to eat and high-tech generators that would pour new electric life into the weather-worn complex. The wheels of the last arrival, a special C-5A, gently squeaked onto and re-inaugurated Two–Five-Left, the longest landing strip which stretched out nearly three miles. The Lockheed Galaxy heavy airlift transport was laden with an additional assortment of vehicles, hospital equipment and an extraordinary hominid specimen. The autopsy was scheduled for early morning and so the base hospital hummed throughout the night in a hive-like cluster of activity connected with the rapid installation of the most advanced medical and laboratory apparatus available.

At 0700, the scene in the operating theater was reminiscent of a Roswellian publicity stunt except that there were no little gray aliens. Dax Wolf, in surgical garb, blended in with the dozen or so masked and scrubbed doctors and technicians buzzing around the surgical table. His ID badge identified him as *Dr. Wolfson, M.D.* Zack stood near the left corner of the head end of the operating table and the visitor's name tag which adorned the left breast pocket of his white laboratory coat, read: Isaac Ludlow Carver, Ph.D. Having refused to go completely military, Zack was wearing standard desert fatigues under the lab coat which was partially open, revealing the '*Archeology<>Dig it!*' belt buckle. Though he declined putting on the obligatory operating room scrubs, he did wear a surgical mask. Leslee, with the appropriate identification, was also wearing military fatigues and was observing from an adjacent viewing area as the procedure began.

Colonel Avery Thompson, the lead pathologist, prepared to zip the plastic morgue bag open. "There may be some foul odors," the doctor cautioned as he slid the zipper down the length of the body bag. Unnoticed, the weightless rectangular alien device in Zack's breast pocket behind the vinyl pen holder began to emit a barely discernable infra-red glow. Several of the medical personnel struggled to raise the corpse slightly so that the body bag could be slid out of the way. They ultimately had to accomplish the task in small increments and in spite of Dr. Thompson's warning, there were no offensive smells. The five-foot nine-inch, 250-pound corpse of Ahneevah was now stretched out on the operating table. Her weight was puzzling because of the assumed absence of body fluids and also that her frame was rather willowy and did not seem to possess an ounce of fat. A human female of her proportions would weigh no more than 140 pounds. How could the additional 110 pounds be explained? The anxious, highly-paid Barrgrave team of pathologists was drooling at the prospect of cutting into the incredible assemblage of protoplasm that was spread in front of them.

A technician carefully detached the flight-helmet and lifted it. He was surprised to find that it took hardly any effort and at the precise moment he began to move it clear of the subject's head, the opaque 270 degree wrap-around face-shield dematerialized and a cascade of translucent, honey-colored hair spilled out onto her shoulders and over her face. The procedure was halted for a moment so that everyone could catch their breath. Surprisingly, the exposed hair gave off a familiar sweet fragrance which seemed to counter the strong medicinal odors in the austere, anti-septic surroundings. The framework of the helmet, without the frozen plasma face-shield, folded itself into a single thin strand. When the technician gave it to Thompson, the doctor hefted it a few times and his face registered a curious surprise.

"It has mass but doesn't seem to have any weight," he reported and put the object on an instrument table. Zack eyed Leslee knowingly. Leslee pointed back in a *message received* gesture.

One of the nurses, Lieutenant Marla Fredericks, carefully brushed the amber strands aside and all in attendance stood in further amazement as the pilot's face was revealed. They ex-pected to see bone or perhaps a dried out, leathery, mummy-like visage. Incredibly, their eyes fell on a stunning combination of finely sculpted and smooth textured feminine features. The nose was small and seemed to almost melt into high cheekbones. Her skin tone resembled the pastel lavender hue of summer lilacs and her lips were full and approximately the shade of pale violets. Zack sniffed the air several times. It was a familiar aroma.

"I swear I can pick up a sweet honey-like scent," he said as he leaned closer to the alien and then took a few sniffs. "Jeez ... she smells like a ... a vanilla bean."

The flight suit had no discernible fastening system. No buttons, zippers or hooks of any sort. "Let's get in there for a closer look," Colonel Thompson ordered. "We'll just cut the jump suit away."

That step turned out to be more problematic than the colonel anticipated. Nothing that was attempted would completely penetrate the multi-layered material. The titanium scalpels, dissecting scissors and even a surgical bone-saw were not up to the task. The instant the blades touched the surface layer of the garment, the fabric separated and moved out of their way. Then the material recombined immediately after the cutting edge broke contact with it.

Zack shot a quick look at Leslee and motioned with his head and eyes for her to join him. When she rose to do so, Dr. Thompson raised some objections but Leslee, nonetheless, glided toward Zack. As she approached, Zack could see that her segment of the dual rectangular mechanism in Leslee's fatigue pants pocket also took on the barely perceptible infra-red glow.

"I think it might need a woman's touch," he whispered.

Leslee remembered the way the teardrop craft and the pair of mini-monolithic objects reacted to her presence and nodded her concurrence. She carefully placed her hand near the aviator's chin and ran it down the front of the flight suit which to everyone's surprise, peeled apart. Then a chorus of mild gasps was raised when the opened flying uniform revealed that the subject wore no underclothes whatsoever and her light-lavender body was strikingly perfect.

It took almost all of the OR supporting staff to actually raise the heavy corpse so that the garment could be removed. The doctor observed that the flight suit also had no discernable weight, and then everyone in the operating theater watched in amazement as the open flaps re-engaged.

When one of the support staff tried over and over to fold it, the unique article of clothing kept returning to the shape that it had when it was being worn. Finally the befuddled tech leaned the uniform against the MRI console where it initiated a self-cleaning process. Every vestige of heat damage quickly vanished, making the billion year old item appear brand-new. In the meantime, Leslee had already removed the gloves and boots from the remarkable specimen and all agreed that except for her unusual coloring the entity certainly could pass as a contemporary female. Along with the fine features were graceful arms and shoulders, hands with four long fingers and an opposable thumb, two legs with musculature and bone structure similar to their human counterpart and feet containing five toes. The subject also had mammary glands and a vaginal opening. An X-ray was attempted, but when it was switched on, the machine shut down instantly due to an inexplicable power malfunction. Despite the efforts by the group of well-trained technicians, the hi-tech device refused to light up again.

Next, an MRI examination was tried. At the outset, it revealed that Ahneevah was made of the same stardust that all humans were made of, albeit designed quite differently. Though female, this specimen bore striking differences to the physical make-up of contemporary women. She had no discernible uterus but there were some small, unrecognizable vestigial organs located where a reproductive system might have been. This led to the initial theory that the females of this alien race nursed their young but did not bear them. But that was it for the MRI.

Suddenly, the costly state-of-the-art piece of equipment shorted out and shut down along with all the lights, security cameras and the digital video cameras recording the procedure. The stand-by generator kicked in almost immediately and the emergency lighting system snapped on, but not one of the pieces of advanced medical apparatus issued another beep or blip. Nurse Fredericks turned to Colonel Thompson. "Colonel, I could swear that I saw a red, flashing glow on the skin surface of the subject's left arm right before everything went dead." Dr. Thompson quickly disabused her of that notion. "No," he corrected her. "It was just a reflection of one of the various illuminated panels." Zack and Leslee knew that something unusual certainly did occur on Ahneevah's arm. "The only way we are certain to find out anything more about this alien creature is to start cutting," Thompson declared.

"Doctor, I think you should consider the possibility that nothing pertaining to *this creature* can be *certain*." Leslee cautioned.

"No, not a damned thing," Zack added.

Had the MRI examination been able to continue, the entire medical team would have been astounded by the organic intricacies that were inherent within the extraordinary molecular miracle that was stretched out before them. She was an extremely efficient physical machine. Her respiration system required the absorption of oxy-nitrogen compounds only about once every ten minutes. Having no specific pulmonary organs, her entire upper body served as a storage reservoir where measured quantities of the required biological combustion elements passed osmotically through microscopic valve-like apertures in her torso. Pollutants and other extraneous gases were completely filtered out by these respiratory gateways as well as by a unique array of nasal passage barriers. The O_2 and N_2 permeated her chest area and dissolved in her plasmodic fluid through every organ and every cell within the wall of her chest. Her circulatory system was peristaltic and structured with muscled artery and vein-like vessels. These vascular channels were capable of thousands of micro-contractions per minute and efficiently moved *blood* throughout her system with minimal or no use of the central cardio-impeller. Unlike a human heart, Ahneevah's main circulating pump had a standard rate of only three pulses per minute and was basically held in reserve except for extreme circumstances. Her brain, though smaller than a human brain, was twice as dense and protected from most traumas by a series of three inner skull structures. The cerebral mass was used mainly for thought but also served as a backup to her motor processes. She was not hard-wired and had no direct-connection neural-pathways. Messages that stimulated body motion and responses were sent at light speed via biologically induced nano-wave transmissions with billions of variable coded frequencies. They emanated from an auxiliary cerebral substation in the spinal area and skipped along a sequence of interspersed silicon flecks that served as relays which sent signals that induced action—that is, the chosen voluntary or automatic response. Each fleck served as part of micro-broadcast network. In the event that one or a number of these stand-alone beacons were damaged or ceased to function, others picked up and dispatched the neural signals until replacements were reproduced by her body. These nano-wave signals could also be transmitted in an extra-corporeal manner by electrostatic projection and touch. This allowed her to effect certain ambient electronic impulses within a limited range. Her hearing adjusted to the volume, tone and pitch of sounds and her visual receptors compensated for bright and reduced light conditions in milliseconds. The two concentric pupils in each of her emerald irises had distinct functions. One served as a zoom lens and the other took in the general landscape. Also her two extra-wide, almost wrap-around eye sockets allowed her to expand her angle of view through a panoramic arc encompassing three-quarters of a circumference, in excess of a 270-degree peripheral vision. Finally, due to her extensive conscious levels, she was able to override almost all of her involuntary bodily functions such as plasmodic flow, peristaltic rate and glandular secretion, and bring them under voluntary control.

When the scalpel was placed at the top of Ahneevah's sternum and was about to bite into the *Sharpie* dotted line drawn down the center of her rib cage, her hand seemed to twitch. Nurse Fredericks dropped a bone cutter and *shrieked*.

The others tried to reassure the spooked nurse that nothing was amiss. However, that attempt went down in flames when the autopsy subject's arm rose and her long and powerful fingers wrapped around the hand wielding the surgical tool and in one swift motion twisted it away from her breast bone, turned it up, and raised the cutting edge of the stainless steel blade to less than a centimeter from Colonel Thompson's throat. The pathologist released the instrument and it *clinked* and *clanked* on the concrete floor after which the *alien's* arm dropped back on to the table and the already highly-agitated Nurse Fredericks promptly fainted.

Zack pulled his mask down and shouted, "Get some new monitoring instruments and life support over here." Like the proverbial deer caught in the headlights, almost everyone froze where they stood. Finally, Zack screamed out, "STAT!" This shook the medical group out of their iced-up state and they hurriedly scattered in all directions to comply with Zack's order.

Dax Wolf used the commotion to snatch a strand of Ahneevah's hair which was clinging to the table near her head. He stashed it in the thumb of a surgical glove while his mind was conjuring breakthrough theories about how to identify and categorize this alien female.

As quickly as the new battery of high-end medical electronics Zack had demanded were put in place, it became apparent that this second round of apparatus could survive no better than the first group. Every piece of radiological equipment within her aura suffered an instant meltdown and was reduced to a pile of electronic junk. No readouts were possible. Stethoscopes and manual examination revealed no discernible heartbeat, pulse, or breathing.

Then the debate began. General Mitchell asked stoically, "Is she alive?"

One of the doctors shrugged his shoulders, baffled.

Mitchell continued, "If she isn't living, how in the hell could she defend herself?"

"What caused her hand to move and stop the scalpel?" The still unsteady Nurse Fredericks said hazily as she was being helped to her feet. "It could have been an automatic response," offered another doctor.

It was impossible for any of those present to suspect that Ahneevah's self-defense action was totally disconnected from any kind of known consciousness. It had occurred on a secondary, quasi-cellular level, a level at which their current understanding of anatomical neural science did not reach. The two rectangular instruments in Leslee's and Zack's possession digitally stimulated one or more of Ahneevah's multiple mind tracks to induce animation and then reversed the intruding particles from the X-ray and MRI and concentrated their force to short out the highly advanced medical equipment. Leslee sidled toward Zack. Without taking her eyes off Ahneevah's inanimate form she cleared her throat and spoke in subdued tones out of the corner of her mouth.

"I have to tell you. I always wondered what it would feel like to be Alice ... now I know."

Zack inched over to her. "Alice?" Leslee's focus continued to remain locked on Ahneevah. "Yeah, you know—Alice ... as in Wonderland. I mean the stuff that's going on here makes the Mad Tea Party look like a milk and cookie minute at a nursery school." Zack was still not completely on the page and Leslee motioned for him to lean in closer. "Did I ever mention that in my second year at Berkeley Law I got a summer job at the Los Angeles County District Attorney's office?" Leslee whispered. "I called it my season of the deceased. I saw nineteen dead bodies, and believe me; I know what a dead body looks like ... and I have a nagging suspicion that this," she said as she waved her arm down the length of the exquisite figure on the table, "isn't one of them. I mean … look at her color. She's light lavender for God's sake. Now, if she were Barney the Dinosaur, I'd think she was a tad pale. But at this point in time she certainly doesn't look like a corpse. And that bit with the hand coming up to put the kibosh on the autopsy—she definitely doesn't act like a corpse. And corpses don't usually smell like—" Leslee sniffed the air several times— "like the Shalimar counter at Neiman's. You do know where I'm going with this?" Zack blew out some air. "Where no one has gone before," he said.

At forty-five thousand feet above the desert floor the otherwise placid morning sky was traumatized by the shrill whine, brilliant flash and thunderous roar of the explosive General Electric GE - F414 400 afterburners being sprayed by JP-10 jet fuel. An F/A-18F Hornet Trainer was carrying Dax Wolf as the back-seater to Columbus, Ohio. Wolf hated to leave the base but with the Hornet he knew he could get to Columbus, do his research and return within twenty-four hours. He was positive that only some solo time with the powerful Titan Transmission Electron microscope at Ohio State University would permit him to conduct a proper analysis of the honey strand of the female alien's hair.

EPIJODE JEVENTEEN

"BLOWUPS HAPPEN"

The two vials of agony and certain death had originally arrived at ...

... the Port of Los Angeles via the Republic of China. The consignment was shipped inside a container that was identified on the cargo manifest as computer hardware and software. It was addressed to the Saudi Arabian Mission.

The end recipient was Mohammed Ibrahim Najar, the mastermind and leader of a terrorist unit that planned to unleash a wave of fanatical horror commencing in the Southwest. Najar knew to strike during the daytime because his comprehensive surveillance had taught him that was when the most people would be at the medical center in the heart of Albuquerque, New Mexico. There were nearly four-hundred beds and a staff of over four-thousand. This included doctors, nurses, medical assistants, therapists, administrators, security and janitorial personnel. They worked in three shifts to keep the sprawling medical facility running in an efficient groove.

The EMS rescue chopper that Najar and his men had hijacked landed on the rooftop helipad of the newest and largest structure at the University of New Mexico Hospital complex. Najar finished checking the vials of bio-toxins and snapped the metal case shut. Two of his hooded underlings had their firearms trained on the pilot. A third got out and was lugging two cumbersome yellow cases bearing the familiar *Radioactive Materials* symbol. The extremist leader stepped out onto the roof, turned back to his men and barked orders at them in Arabic. Then he and the third man headed toward the door to the stairway. When the pair reached the door, Najar took out a remote device and pressed one of the buttons on it with his thumb.

At that instant, the high explosives concealed in a stolen FedEx van that was parked near the maintenance and ventilation systems building were detonated. The force released was powerful enough to demolish the structure and shake the entire university like it was hit by an earthquake measuring in the high sixes on the Richter scale.

The chaos resulting from the explosion and the ensuing burst of automatic weapons fire sent Nurse Lynne Daniels racing toward the entrance of the pediatric wing. She knew that it was filled to capacity, as was almost every other ward in the hospital.

Many workers were killed and dozens more were injured but the initial blast was merely the diversion in an expertly organized strike. Najar's sixty-three member raiding party had already placed themselves in strategic positions in and around the complex, which enabled them to assume almost immediate control of the entire medical center. Any of the security guards that attempted to return fire were summarily mowed down. The rest surrendered. Najar was grateful to once again be on the prowl and in direct combat action as opposed to his former role in tactical planning.

Nurse Daniels reached the children's ward at the same time as Najar and several of his men. When she tried to prevent them from entering the ward, Najar beat her mercilessly, screaming at her with each blow and leaving her unconscious, clinging tenuously to life.

Mohammed Najar's hatred for Americans was initially provoked during the middle years of the bloody and futile war in

Iraq. When barely in his teens Najar watched panic stricken as his entire family was slaughtered when they were caught between the warring Shiite and Sunni factions in western Baghdad. Like many other young men in his situation he was irretrievably set on a path of hate and destruction. The Al Qaeda higher echelon took notice of the fact that he survived the deadly crossfire. They quickly attributed this to some kind of divine intervention and recruited him. However, Najar was spared the homicide bomber route and was sent to the Syrian Desert for advanced training.

Najar fully understood that the attacks on 9/11 reverberated in a series of devastating negative effects on the American way of life, from the economy to civil liberties. And although he knew that the main object of terrorism was to terrorize, his loathing of America and anyone or thing that was American drove him to his personal participation in multiple acts of violence that resulted in death and destruction. He was involved in the assaults on several embassies and bombings in five major cities. Najar moved up in the ranks and was eventually put in charge of creating false terror plots against the United States to create fear and disruption. Due to his efforts, liquids were banned from passenger carry-on baggage, shoes had to be removed at all the Transportation Security Administration checkpoints, embarrassing full body scans were instituted, and the airport lines became longer and the system much more difficult to navigate for the average citizen. But this was not satisfactory to Najar. He became obsessed with making sure that the nation which began the Iraq War and was in support of Israel would pay dearly in blood and treasure as well as fear and disruption. He decided to create his own splinter network and left the main organization.

In the lab at Ohio State, Dax Wolf was operating the advanced Titan Transmission Electron Microscope. He shoved a one-petabyte memory stick into the data-storage receiving slot and began focusing on the strand of Ahneevah's hair. Wolf was totally rocked when he saw the image that came up on the viewing screen. Did he actually see what he thought he was seeing? If so, then there was nothing else like it—certainly not on this Earth. Before he could thoroughly digest any visual input, Wolf shouted, "No. No. Please," and began to shiver violently as he was once again inexplicably thrust into a freezing status. He flew out of his chair to check the room thermostat and found that it was properly set at 72 degrees. He raised it to its maximum and began pacing back and forth in an attempt to counter the extreme cold and then instinctively headed toward the area in back of the instrument array to seek some relief from the numbing chill. Fearing loss of control of his wildly convulsing body, he fell to his knees and crawled part way down the narrow space behind the giant microscope. Then Wolf ripped the wires from the auxiliary ventilation unit so as to allow the heat being generated by the Titan's considerable circuitry to build up and provide him with additional warmth. At this point a new dread descended upon him. He suddenly felt as if his head was exploding and became aware that there was a liquid trickling over his earlobe and down his neck. When he raised his hand to the spot, dabbed at it and brought his hand in front of his eyes—his bloodstained fingers said it all. Dax Wolf crumpled to the floor and continued to drag himself, face down, further behind the console and began screaming, "I don't know who you are. I don't know who you are. Please … no more … no more …" Mercifully, he became oblivious as his mind faded to darkness and crimson rivulets of blood continued to flow out of his ears and track across his cheeks.

After securing the hospital compound, Najar assembled the doctors, hospital workers and whichever patients could be dragged, wheeled or rolled to the main quad. At first Najar had to discourage any interference with his operation and so to demonstrate his cold-bloodedness he demanded that the hospital administrator be brought to him. When she arrived, he ordered a video camera to be turned on and callously shot her through the head for the entire world to see.

An army of dust-tumbleweeds surrounded the unconscious Dax Wolf as he lay curled in a fetal position on the floor between the wall and the Titan. He was breathing heavily then coughed several times. He rubbed his cheek and felt the crusted blood which had dried in the heat that continued to pour from the back of the ultra high resolution imaging device. Suddenly, his entire body convulsed if jolted by a heart defibrillator. Being unable to focus his eyes, Wolf blindly reached out for some of the protruding metal struts at the rear of the apparatus and tugged himself upright. Trancelike and looking older and more haggard than before, he managed a few wobbly steps and using the console for support he worked his way to the side of the large machine. He staggered around to the front of the Titan and with a trembling, almost out-of-control hand, Wolf missed at several tries to pull the memory stick from its slot. On his fourth attempt he finally succeeded in tugging it free and raced out of the laboratory.

EPISODE EIGHTEEN

THE AWAKENING
"THE END OF ETERNITY"

In sharp contrast to a light, westerly breeze and the generous spattering of stars across the grand celestial easel provided by the clear midnight sky, the perimeter surrounding the newly rehabilitated covert Nevada desert base …

… buzzed incessantly with security patrols mounted on a raucous herd of all-terrain vehicles and Humvees, adorned in desert-camo. The rolling growl of these monster-wheeled machines and the droning swarm of Self-Propelled Mobile Assessment & Response Systems rudely interrupted the routine nocturnal activities of the native creatures. After a brief sniff of the brisk night air, the disoriented and agitated denizens were forced to scamper about in an urgent search for a new niche in their hastily transformed environs.

Leslee and Zack also were also *finding* their new niche. They were jarred awake and plucked from their rooms in the Bachelor Officer's Quarters while still in their underwear—"You're being transferred to the base detention facility," bellowed an ogre-like sergeant. A stunned and incensed Zack moved toward the soldier. "Who the f...oof," Zack was unceremoniously silenced and doubled-up when a rifle butt pounded into his abdomen. "General Mitchell's orders," the non-com barked.

Under *aggressive* escort, Leslee and Zack were forced to dress, one article of clothing at a time, while negotiating a series of long, shadowy, underground corridors and several pitch-black stairways. Ultimately, they arrived at the base detention wing and were manhandled up to an entranceway with a coded electronic locking system. The sergeant punched the succession of numbers which opened the steel door and the rest of the guard contingent brutishly tossed the two detainees into an austere, clammy, dimly lit interrogation room. "Bullshit," roared Zack. "This order came from somewhere higher up." The sergeant set and checked the electric locking mechanism and without another word he and the other members of the small detachment tramped out and secured the door. As the unit made their way down the corridor, the last man peeled off and remained behind to stand watch outside the entrance.

Zack took in his current surroundings. "This is outrageous. This is where they grill bad guys."

"They prefer the term *interview*," Leslee said.

"But we haven't been charged with anything. How can they lock us up like this?"

"Patriot Act VI, the sequel. They can hold us incommunicado … essentially until we rot."

"Rosy, while I was drunk for the past ten years what the hell happened to our free country?"

"Don't blame yourself. I couldn't do anything about it either. And we'll only have a free country again when we stop being afraid and when we start remembering that the words *inalienable rights* refer to rights and not privileges—rights which are guaranteed by our Constitution … rights which are n-e-v-e-r to be alienated."

The Super Hornet was cleared for an approach and landing on runway Two-Five Left on its return flight from Ohio. Dax was anxious to get to his lab. Things were stirring around in his head that he was having a great deal of problems amalgamating into reasonable thought. During the earlier part of the flight he began to feel better but now he was once again in freefall. His scientific logic told him that he was clearly in the process of some kind of incredible metamorphosis—but what was he becoming? What were the fleeting images and scraps of imperceptible telepathic contact? Was it the foundation of an exponentially advanced reasoning network; a harbinger of some awesome power? Or could it be that he was simply going insane?

Ahneevah's body was moved to the base maternity ward and locked in one of the delivery rooms. The sole illumination penetrating the murky, improvised holding cell was a negligible sliver of light dribbling in through the razor-thin slit at the bottom of the door. The chamber was sealed inside by an inflated plastic bubble containing a zippered panel which was lined up with the entrance. Filtered and refrigerated air was being pumped in by a *whining* portable compressor outside. Since no electronic monitoring device could survive in the presence of the volatile cadaver, the Barrgrave security team figured they'd contain her the old-fashioned way. She was placed unclothed in a prone position on a bare metal obstetric examination table using plastic shackles to keep her arms and legs secured to the stirrups. However, a great deal of twitter was being raised within the facility re why a *corpse* had to be confined and restrained in the first place.

When the tandem-seat F/A-18 jet aircraft touched down, Dax ordered the pilot to taxi directly to the science center. He needed to get to his lab as soon as possible to learn what he could from the data on the memory stick generated by the Titan. Although the frightening cold continued to envelop Dax and the uncontrollable shivering infected his entire being, there was now an added nightmare. The numbing chill was accompanied by the sounds of

massive explosions at such a paralyzing level that Wolf instinctively began to bring his hands to his ears to escape the mind-
shattering cacophony. However, his hands merely cupped the
sides of his flight-helmet. He quickly concluded that his action
was useless. The cataclysmic blasts were emanating from within
his aural network. It was as though Armageddon were taking
place inside his head. But Dax Wolf was unaware that at that
same instant, the identical sounds of the Apocalypse were also
echoing in the make-shift confinement area where the lilac space
woman was lying—dead still.

   Suddenly, Ahneevah's wide, green eyes popped open and, like
a wall of television monitors with different displays, various
segments of her expandable mind tracks began to come on line.
Her abundant neural clusters brought her up to consciousness and
provided a functional, though significantly incomplete situational
awareness. Immediately, her pupils expanded to exploit the
miniscule wafer of light bleeding in under the door and vastly
increase its intensity sufficient to allow her full visual perception
in the dark room. As several of her cognitive trails were debating
the possibility that maybe the world had not destroyed itself,
others considered the alternative circumstances.
   After analyzing every scrap of sensory and mental information
available to her, Ahneevah theorized that she must have somehow
survived the downing of her aircraft and had been taken captive.
But then she clearly remembered that her world *was* undeniably
ending. While she attempted to explore the question of how
much, if any, of the world still existed, certain selected tiers of her
multi-layered consciousness began spilling uncontrollably into
others and she could not settle on a logical assumption. *If any of
my squadron survived, it is well known that the enemy summarily
executed all prisoners. But then ... why am I still alive ... or am
I in fact still alive?* While this internal debate was transpiring, a

scarlet glow about five strides away on magnetic bearing nine-six caught her attention. She focused her telescopic pupils in that direction and through the translucent plastic insulation she was able to see a flashing red dot of light which seemed to indicate an electronic instrument of some kind. The device was affixed to a portal and had an illuminated panel on its face which was imprinted with four rows of unfamiliar symbols. She also detected a curious living presence on the other side of the entryway. However, Ahneevah's ability to mentally coordinate the information felt unusually imprecise. The input signal wavered but then appeared to register as a biped whose electric emissions were nothing like the electrostatic signature of her enemy but rather a life-form that was entirely unfamiliar to her. In any case she knew that her first duty was to escape captivity and attempt to free others who may also be confined.

In the fraction of a second that these coterminous thought processes were percolating, Ahneevah had already torn off her shackles, arose from the obstetrics table and taken a few rocky steps in the direction of the entry way. She studied the zippered seal, unzipped it and placed her hand on the automatic mechanism.

The guard at the door never heard the *whir* of the lock being disengaged, nor did he perceive the infinitesimal change in pressure as the detention room door opened slowly behind him. He barely felt the slight tingle as a purple hand brushed the back of his neck but before he was able to give it any further thought his reality became inky and silent. When he fell back into Ahneevah's arms, she handled the dead weight of the over two-hundred pound sentry with ease, then quickly removed his belt and used it to secure him upright—on his feet—at his post.

Unexpectedly, as Dax Wolf climbed out of the back seat of the Hornet, for what seemed a hiccup in time, all of his senses were projected to the obstetric ward where the alien was being held. He was startled to be able to *see* the entire section. The guard was still standing outside the door of the room but inside it was empty. He also saw that the plastic *handcuffs* which had been confining the remarkable specimen were ripped apart and scattered on the floor. Wolf was also able to feel the cool air, pick up the scent of vanilla, and could even hear the *whine* of the compressor. *Had someone released the subject? If not,* he reasoned, *she must have escaped on her own. If true*—and he tended to believe it was—*then she must be alive.*

While stealthily making her way through the installation's labyrinthine underground passages, Ahneevah locked in on the already familiar digital output frequency. As she approached an intersecting corridor she sensed the presence of another living biped. Peering around the corner, she spotted a uniformed officer stationed at a security checkpoint and casually glided toward him. When she caught his attention, it was clearly a scenario that his training did not cover. How could it have? The sentry became too stupefied to function when he saw the lissome, light-purple, nude figure, and even if he had reacted, it wouldn't have made any difference. He was abruptly switched off. But before he hit the floor, an electric cart with a three-man detail pulled up and the occupants charged at Ahneevah. One of them was actually able to get a hand on her shoulder, which surprised her because she knew that these beings moved and thought at a far slower rate than she did. In spite of this slight glitch the outcome was the same; the three guards were barely fractions of a second behind the first sentry in generating their own floor-contact *thuds*.

Ahneevah moved along the corridor and arrived at an intersection where light was visible at the far end—then something stopped her in her tracks. It was as if a dark shadow had crossed her entire consciousness. The spell passed in a split second, and she dismissed the incident as a residual effect from the combat action and the subsequent crash of her flight vehicle.

Continuing to noiselessly negotiate the maze of subterranean tunnels, Ahneevah reached the well lit main junction area where the network of detention center cell bay corridors converged. She hesitated for a split second as she caught some sounds from a room nearby that seemed to be a focal point of activity. Drawing closer, she became cognizant of voices and flickering light pulsing through a partially opened door. She continued advancing silently in that direction.

Six guards were busy at their consoles when Ahneevah stepped into the area. They were stunned at the vision of the bare, lavender creature that was standing in front of them, alive and entrancing. As the aroma of vanilla wafted through the room she spoke a sentence in a language they found unfathomable and then she quickly sent the sextet of security men off to dreamland. Reasoning that this area was dedicated to communications, she shorted out the control panel, which included the circuitry for the central alarm system and a host of other tactical instrumentation. As she approached the television monitor and was about to void its warranty, she became intrigued by an advertisement that was running on the screen. It was for a deodorant and showed sweat-stained underarms and strawberries. *These beings seem completely alien, like an entirely new life-form,* she reasoned. *Where in the world am I?*

When the commercial spot ended there was an urgent sounding background noise indicating a breaking news story. Ahneevah was unable to understand the language spoken, but the pictures clearly indicated that an entire hospital was under siege. She winced as the broadcast displayed an edited version of a female being viciously murdered and then the scene switched to another area to reveal a group of frightened children. Ahneevah recognized in the extremists' eyes the same willful hatred and wanton desire to extinguish life that she had seen in the face of her enemy, and uttered a few empathetic sounds in response to the horror. *Wherever I am,* she thought, *it seems that chaos and terror are still prevalent.* Ahneevah closed her eyes and sighed ruefully.

EPIJODE NINETEEN

THE ALLIANCE
"STRANGER IN A STRANGE LAND"

The wafer-thin, rectangular logic unit sections behind Zack's vinyl pen holder and in Leslee's fatigues lit up the dank interrogation room with the ...

... same rainbow of plasma wave emissions as they did during the interface with the University of Alaska supercomputers. Zack and Leslee quickly removed the devices from their pockets and the spectrums of light widened and painted the entire steel door. After a split second, the primary color waves in the beam began shifting their spectral order and then tapered down to a single blue beam which narrowed on the electronic security lock.

Simultaneously, Zack and Leslee heard a thump outside the portal and a *whirring* noise followed by a *click*. Then the door popped open and the security guard that was stationed outside it sprawled limply into the room and directly following on the sentry's heels stood the incontestably alive and sartorially-challenged Ahneevah. Initially, Leslee and Zack suffered sense paralysis. Their logic froze as they attempted to come to terms with the concept of exactly what was standing in front of them. Zack flashed on the vision of her in the flight-suit, helmet and gloves when they first saw her in the cockpit of the teardrop air vehicle. Leslee was the first to recover a crumb of composure. "Do I know dead or don't I?" she ventured with somewhat less than full conviction. Though Leslee had a notion that Ahneevah was somehow not *exactly* dead, she never imagined that the billion-year-old being would be quite *this* not dead! It was almost too overwhelming to assimilate. But undeniably there was this creature—this horseless Lady Godiva in mauve, and at that precise moment, in the twinkling of a pair of wide, entrancing, sea-green eyes, Zack and Leslee's previous concepts of time and existence became substantially irrelevant.

Before Zack could blurt out the first of the fifty-million questions teetering at the tip of his scientist brainpan, the blue plasma beam emanating from the instrument in his hand became rainbow again and shifted its focus to the unclad figure's forehead. Ahneevah exhibited a look of muted surprise then she extended her right hand toward Zack and Leslee and turned her palm upward. Zack, not quite sure of what to do, reached out and took her outstretched hand in his as if to shake it in greeting. But as he held it, Zack found it to be warm, soft and comforting and was in no particular hurry to let it go. He was also immensely surprised to find that he had no desire to say anything. After a moment, Ahneevah reached out with her other hand to Leslee. When they touched, Leslee smiled and completely understood why Zack continued to maintain his grip on this captivating being's hand.

Ahneevah looked at their clasped hands and her eyes paled slightly. Surprisingly, she did not immediately withdraw her hand either and a trace of understanding appeared on her face almost as if she was aware of the unfamiliar ritual. She spoke a phrase in her language and the multi-hued beams emanating from the rectangular devices shifted to Zack and Leslee and bathed the two from head-to-toe. *These life forms were not the enemy,* Ahneevah thought. Then, with a slight shift of her saucer eyes, Ahneevah indicated the pair of instruments, and after puzzled looks, Leslee and Zack understood what Ahneevah was trying to communicate and reluctantly disengaged their hands from hers. "Oh, right. Sorry, this must belong to you … and I gotta tell you … its freakin' amazing," Zack announced as he and Leslee handed the two sections of the weightless instrument to Ahneevah who joined them together and made a few adjustments. At first, the logic unit projected holographic images of her circle and her progeny. After a deeply melancholy look followed by a long sigh, she held the device between the thumb and forefinger of both hands and spoke a phrase of her mellifluous, indecipherable tongue into it. All at once, due to the instrument's earlier interface with the university super-computer in Anchorage, a holographic history of intelligent life on the planet known as Earth was displayed. The exotic stranger's vast cognitive network absorbed and stored the information as the millennia whizzed by in a blur.

Leslee and Zack stared transfixed as the process slowed a bit and more recent events appeared. They noticed Ahneevah grimace as a series of mushroom clouds from Hiroshima, Nagasaki and then progressively more powerful thermonuclear explosions flashed by. Finally, Leslee couldn't wait any longer and let the name slowly and deliberately work its way out through her lips, "Ah…nee…vah?"

At hearing her name spoken, Ahneevah turned to Leslee and her face revealed a Mona Lisa smile. "That is almost right, Leslee R. Myles." She said after a quick glance at the name tags. "However, the correct pronunciation of my name is …" When Ahneevah articulated her name in her tongue, the mere sound of it evoked an inexplicable sense of reassurance, calm and acceptance in Leslee and Zack.

"That's incredible," Zack said. "You … you picked up our language in a hairsbreadth."

"Amazing," Leslee crowed. "It'd make it so much easier for all of us if everyone could learn each other's languages as fast as you learned ours."

"It is possible, with this," Ahneevah said softly as she indicated the rectangular mechanism. Leslee nodded her head in recognition and said, "Of course, we've seen it in action ... I'm not at all surprised."

"It is a Neuronal Logic Unit." Ahneevah explained.

"An NLU ... got it," Leslee responded. Ahneevah smiled at the acronymic simplification and bowed her head once in the affirmative. "Yes, an NLU," she repeated and then continued to receive and corroborate the depictions of Earth event chronology and other information via the World Wide Web. Her broader-vision optics were concentrating on the download while her close-vision pupils were zeroed in on Zack, who was mesmerized by the imaging procedure. "Dr. Isaac Ludlow Carver, my mind channels will require an uncertain time-span to process all of the information I am inputting. So I need you to tell me, exactly when in time am I?" The open-mouthed Zack slightly closed one eye. "You don't need to use *all* of my names; my first name is enough. My ... uhhh ... friends call me Zack. You are my friend, aren't you? I mean I'd hate to think otherwise." Ahneevah contemplated Zack's words for a split second and waved the NLU in Zack and Leslee's direction, Zack flinched.

"Don't worry Zack; it senses no danger from either of you. We shall start as friends and we will see. Now please tell me when I am? Your recorded history indicated that the earliest ancestors of the intelligent species now existing on your ... Earth had their genesis at some point during the last few million years of the Cenozoic era."

"That may be so but I think *you* are close to a billion years from where you might have come from. Give or take millennia or two."

Ahneevah weighed the information. "A billion years?"

Zack continued, "A calculated guess. Potassium Argon dating is not as exact as ... ooof ..."

Zack's train of thought was driven off track by a polite elbow nudge in the side from Leslee.

"A year is one orbit around the Sun ... your ... Lano Sokyam." Leslee said.

The holographic projections ceased and Ahneevah turned to Leslee and nodded her head.

"Your capacity for sounds is well developed Leslee R. Myles."

"They called me Leslee R. Myles at Berkeley Law. Let's keep it simple and go with Leslee."

"Very well...Leslee. It appears that I have been dormant for almost a billion planetary orbits of the daystar ... the Sun ... and now, once again, I have conscious life," Ahneevah said as she mentally shut down the NLU. "Where is the StarStream? My craft?"

"Kodiak Island, Alaska," Leslee answered. "It's still in the cavern buried in the glacier where we found it."

Zack jumped in. "The ice melted and we took you out of it ... then the ... StarStream sealed itself in the ice again and started to generate a force field or something. No one could get near it."

Ahneevah shook her head. "It was not a force field. You were fortunate to have been in possession of both ... NLU segments when you removed me from my craft."

Leslee shrugged her shoulders. "I don't understand."

"The logic unit scanned your cerebral networks and read your intentions as not being hostile. These results were relayed to my craft as they were just conveyed to me. If the StarStream detected any threat, it would have perceived you as the enemy and neutralized you the instant you tried to extract me."

"Neutralized?" Zack gulped as he tried but failed to avoid doing a visual *up and down* of the stark-naked Ahneevah.

"The StarStream can restrict all surrounding electron flow both biological and mechanical either on a temporary or permanent basis. The great majority of organic life, most certainly yours ... and mine, depends on natural electrical impulses."

"Wow," Zack whispered hoarsely. "We could have been short-circuited?"

"Permanently," Leslee added.

"Yes, but fortunately the StarStream knew better." Ahneevah said.

During the whole initial exchange, Leslee caught Zack slyly grabbing eyefuls of the striking vision nonchalantly standing naked before them. However, the *quick peeks* had finally grown into an obvious trance-like stare. Leslee gave him a subtle elbow in his side and whispered, "You're ogling."

"Only as a man of science," he countered.

"Never mind … it's okay." Leslee said and gestured for Zack to give Ahneevah his lab coat. "Oh … right." Zack muttered. Without taking his eyes off Ahneevah, Zack slowly removed the garment. Leslee smiled. "She is quite a specimen. Actually, I think she's dazzling too."

Zack's eyes widened. "You do?"

"Yes," Leslee responded and sniffed in Ahneevah's direction. "And I believe it's more like vanilla than honey."

Zack sheepishly draped the coat around Ahneevah's shoulders.

"Thank you," she said as she slid her arms into the sleeves. "It is undeniable that there was a point where my world ended and then your world began, but there's no knowing at this juncture exactly what took place and why and how it is that I am here." She looked down, skeptically as she experimented with the hook and loop closures on the lab coat. Leslee smiled. "It's Velcro."

"Yes, Velcro," Ahneevah echoed. "Noisy. We use Tiered Molecular Adhesion to perform the same task. It's based on a concept similar to your Johannes van der Waals interaction of attractive or repulsive forces between atoms and molecules, with a measure of a … highly advanced type of … artificial intelligence in the mix. The molecules of fabric act like gears meshing." She demonstrated the concept by bending her fingers on both hands at the medial and end joints to approximate the cogs. Then she rotated her fingers of both hands within each other to simulate the gears in motion. "However, as you can see, Tiered Molecular Adhesion ... TMA," she gave a quick nod to Leslee and continued, "is a silent operation and leaves no observable junction sites." Then Ahneevah took a quick glance at the NLU, smiled and then winced slightly. "I must report that the logic unit did a comprehensive physiological scan of both of you. Leslee, you are in perfect homeostasis but Zack," Ahneevah shook her head. "The examination indicated that you have a fairly significant amount of calcium build-up in your plasmodic vessels, especially those associated with your cardio-impeller."

"Artery *schmutz* ... I'm not surprised," Leslee said, hands on hips. "Smoking, drinking, not exercising and eating mostly crap will do that."

"I stopped doing all the bad stuff," Zack said guiltily. "I guess it was too late."

"It isn't ... too late. The NLU initiated a hybrid combination of secretions from your endocrine glandular system that will flush away the clogging," Ahneevah said clinically and then closed the lab coat. "However, I must caution you that for the next few days your liquid wastes will have an orange tinge."

"I'm going to pee in orange?"

"A minor side-effect from the breaking down of your arterial plaque," Ahneevah replied.

Leslee smiled at Zack. "Keep me posted," she said. "I think Roberta Seymour will recognize a positive synergy between the NLU and her CEM."

Suddenly, the NLU in the lab coat pocket became illuminated again and the amiable male voice came on. "Alert, security forces magnetic ninety-five, two hundred and seventy-nine ... meters. Single entity ... fifty meters bearing ... nine zero."

"Understood," Ahneevah responded and then directed Zack and

Leslee to the entryway. "I'll tell you about other intermolecular applications at a more opportune moment … right now we must leave this place." The three dashed out of the cell and sprinted down a haphazardly lit corridor.

A short while later, as they raced through the subterranean catacombs, they rounded a corner and found themselves face to face with Dax Wolf. Before he could react, Ahneevah grabbed his arm and cast a deep passing blackness on his world. But as she guided Dax to the ground, she unexpectedly became weak and unsteady. When she tried to step forward she lost her balance, staggered and fell to one knee. Leslee and Zack, together, and with a great deal more effort than they anticipated, helped her back to her feet. Ahneevah regained her balance and was once again upright but recognized that she had just experienced an encounter with a mysterious and bewildering force. She glanced curiously at her hand and flexed her fingers several times, then shook her head. "Strange." Ahneevah commented, and began rubbing her hand, "I am all right," she reassured her newfound friends. Then the trio continued along cautiously down the long and dank underground corridors.

In truth, Ahneevah was far from all right—at least not by any measurement familiar to her. She had always been able to dig deep into her myriad channels of intellect for any answer to any problem. At this moment, however, she was stymied—totally unable to access the hidden reaches of her subconscious to obtain any understanding of what had just happened to her.

Neither she nor Dax Wolf had any awareness that they had just crossed mental swords in the opening round of an epic battle of wills. Neither of them imagined that the outcome of their upcoming conflict would decide the destiny of each and every Galactic Quadrant in both the known and the unknown Universe. The result of their war would determine the fate of every sentient life form in existence.

Zack and Leslee watched in amazement as Ahneevah used the NLU to locate the positions of the security squads. After a series of decoying and backtracking moves, the three arrived at the science lab.

Ahneevah stepped up to the door to check for any life signs inside. She discovered one being but seemed unconcerned and quickly disabled the locking mechanism. But as she cracked the door open, a Taser prong hit Leslee behind and below her left shoulder. Fortunately, Leslee felt only a slight tingle because a nano-tic after the dart struck; Ahneevah removed it, spotted the shooter and with blurring speed dispatched the electric mini-arrow back to its launch point. The barbed projectile easily penetrated the uniform and the skin of the security guard who fired it and in half a heartbeat, the 200,000 volt shock buckled his legs, and he collapsed in a pile of twitching desert camouflage. The high velocity at which Ahneevah was able to send the small metal object back at the shooter made Zack's jaw drop. "You know you sure don't throw at all like a girl" he whispered. "With a Major League arm like that all you need is a good curveball and I think you could have a pro career."

"Curveball, I'll have to research that." Ahneevah noted in a barely audible tone as she steadied Leslee, took her hand and neutralized the electrical impact of the Taser weapon.

"Forgive me Leslee; I should have been ahead of that. It seems that my down time has resulted in some adverse physical and mental consequences."

"*Down time* is a bit of an understatement." Zack pointed out.

"That sounds logical and logic requires a search for all possible explanations," Ahneevah responded. "There is one technician inside, give me a minute." Ahneevah pushed into the lab and startled a technician who was at a well-stocked testing station, holding the wire-like substance that morphed from Ahneevah's flight helmet with a clamp and preparing to heat it over a Bunsen burner.

"Don't hurt me. Please. I am a friend. I mean you no harm," the lab-tech babbled upon seeing the *alien*. "We will not harm you," Leslee assured her as she and Zack entered the room. "But it *is* time for a nap," Ahneevah added, then touched the technician lightly and guided the woman's limp frame to the floor. Leslee recognized the thin strand of material that was the retracted flight-helmet now resting on the table and disengaged it from the clamp. When she picked the sliver up, it morphed back into its functional state. Ahneevah showed a hint of surprise that Leslee's touch was able to accomplish that. Zack picked up on the opening. "It's a chick thing," he put in and indicated Ahneevah's flight gear, which was sitting on a nearby work bench. She ditched the lab coat and stood the one-piece uniform up in front of her, turned around and backed into it. The tunic opened and draped itself around Ahneevah and closed. Then she slipped into the boots which fastened themselves and seamlessly meshed with the uniform. The gloves went into a pocket that appeared and then disappeared.

"I wish I could get dressed like that. It's like wearing an imaginary friend," Leslee said with a degree of envy. "Tiered Molecular Adhesion," Zack observed.

Ahneevah nodded in the affirmative. "Partly … also …it remembers me."

"Smart clothes," Zack observed. "Yes, memory fabric," Ahneevah corrected.

"How come you don't wear any uhhh … under … thingies?" Leslee asked.

"Under thingies? Oh yes … they are not necessary. I'll show you later."

Zack chuckled, "I can't wait. I bet you don't wear pajamas either."

"Security forces intersect … these coordinates." The logic unit voice interrupted. "Heading, magnetic two three zero," Ahneevah cast a quick glance at the instrument. "We must find some form of air transport," she insisted and stashed the NLU into the instantly materializing compartment in her flight suit. Leslee and Zack had already gotten the memo. "Molecular adhesion and memory fabric," they said in unison and then high-fived.

Suddenly, alarms began to *blare* and lights snapped on all over the base. "They must have repaired the circuitry in the communications room. I'll need my hands free to deal with any resistance," Ahneevah said and took her helmet from Leslee. "The face-plate's display will indicate and track proximate life forms." She slipped the headgear on and the frozen-plasma shield dropped down in its transparent mode. Then Ahneevah eyed Zack. "Oh, and by the way, we did have nightclothes—but they were not for sleeping." With that, she sprinted out the lab door.

"Rosy, did she just wink when she said that?"

Leslee smiled. "Did you see a wink? I didn't see a wink." Then she sped out after Ahneevah. With the back-up alarm system sirens wailing, Zack shook his head and followed. "Maybe it's time we turn the tables on those oppressive, son-of-a-bitch government goons," he muttered.

EPISODE TWENTY

AHNEEVA, LESLEE AND ZACK
IN
"AGAINST THE FALL OF NIGHT"

*B*eing *rudely awakened at 2:00 am by shrieking alarms was bad enough, but …*

… it got worse when General Ethan Mitchell vaulted out of bed and saw two of the detainees, who were supposed to be incarcerated, standing in the open doorway of his quarters. Still in his Skivvies, the general thought about snatching his fifteen-shot M-9 semi-automatic sidearm from the drawer in his metal nightstand. But before he could translate that impulse into action, a figure in the dimness wearing a strange flight suit and helmet was already holding the Beretta in one hand and the ammo clip in the other. The 9mm shell that had been chambered was bouncing and tapping harmlessly on the Spartan concrete floor. The general switched the night light on and Ahneevah stepped out of the shadows and removed her headgear. Being a combat-tested veteran who spent five years in Iraq and Afghanistan receiving Purple Hearts for wounds inflicted by rocket-propelled grenades and improvised explosive devices, Mitchell quickly connected the dots.

"So, you *are* alive," he said almost offhandedly, as if being confronted by a reanimated billion-year-old corpse was a routine part of any CO's day. His calm continued as he eyed Ahneevah.

"Are you a soldier?"

"I was an Air Arm Commander," Ahneevah replied, "equivalent to your four-star general."

"There ya go," Zack needled. "She outranks you by two stars. Maybe you should salute her."

"We have need of a three-passenger flight vehicle capable of at least transonic speeds," Ahneevah said firmly. "There is little time and many innocents are in grave danger."

"There are no aircraft of that type here," Mitchell said as he assertively took a step toward Ahneevah.

Zack gingerly inserted himself between the *alien* and the officer. "Look, you don't want to do this unless you feel like getting a face full of floor. Our friend here has moves that the *Crouching Tiger* and *Hidden Dragon* can only dream about."

Ahneevah shoved the Beretta between them and angled the gun butt toward the general's hand. Mitchell took the now harmless weapon and backed off a step.

"The flight vehicle," Ahneevah insisted.

"I don't know how you got this far, but you can't simply go and take one of my aircraft. Even if I gave you permission, which I would never do, and even if you forced me to go with you, my soldiers have their orders."

"General, I assure you she is capable of downsizing your available manpower without as much as breaking a sweat. And also …" Zack stopped as his train of thought found another track. "Come to think of it maybe she doesn't even actually sweat." He turned in Ahneevah's direction, his expression trawling for an answer. Ahneevah got the gist. "I need water the same as you, and I do perspire," she responded. "My hair strands function as part of the system that maintains nominal body temperatures." Leslee was teetering on impatience. "Look, I hate to interrupt this seminar on personal hygiene, but we do have pressing issues."

"I realize that but I *am* half anthropologist," Zack pointed out turning up his palms in a *begging your pardon* gesture.

Reaching across her body, Ahneevah took Mitchell's empty hand. The tough officer instantly lost his belligerent edge. A touch of a smile, an expression that hadn't appeared on his face in decades, pried his lips into a slight crescent.

"General, tell me, which is the swiftest single pilot, multiple-seat craft you do have?"

"The fighter jets are mostly single seat with a few two-seat training variants. The Sikorsky X2 Helicopter ... parked in the big hangar is a prototype but it's a four seater and can travel over five-hundred kilometers per hour."

Leslee shot a knowing smile at Zack. "That's better than three hundred miles per hour," she said.

When Ahneevah let go of his hand, Mitchell tried to recall why he mentioned anything about the X2. "But I'm not giving you a pilot," he insisted, trying to recover.

Before the general could think or say anything else, Ahneevah waved him off.

"We will have no need of a pilot," she said, and then her eyes softened to the warm turquoise shade of the Caribbean Sea. "General Mitchell, please notify your flight-line personnel to fuel the Sikorsky bird and make it ready to fly."

"There are set operations to deal with this kind of scenario," Mitchell declared, "You'll never make it to the flight-line, much less fly the thing out of here."

"Fine," Ahneevah replied. "Then what are you worried about? Get air ops and order it."

Mitchell was about to respond but then Ahneevah looked him in the eye. "General, you are being deceived by your leadership. It is all madness. You will figure that out on your own much sooner than you expect." Ahneevah put her helmet back on and secured it in place, then tossed the Beretta ammo clip to the general; he caught it, turned around to his nightstand and picked up the phone. "This is General Mitchell. Prep the X2 and input the start code sequence." He looked back over his shoulder and the three were gone. "Also, get the Vice President." The CO listened for a beat. "I don't care what time it is in DC: call Bixler and tell him I said to get here ASAP. That's an order." Mitchell, shaking his head, stooped and picked up the 9 millimeter bullet from the floor, put it back into the clip, shoved the clip into his weapon and chambered a round.

Ahneevah loped effortlessly along one of the underground corridors. Leslee was in a sprint mode to keep pace. Zack was running a distant third and had to push himself one gasp at a time to catch up to Leslee and Ahneevah, who looked back and slowed to a medium jog. Zack, after all, was an educator and there were things to be learned. His words came between huffs and puffs.

"Ahneevah, I'm guessing that your hair strands act as cooling conduits and disperse excess body heat into the air, like the vanes on an air conditioner. True?"

"That is correct, and before you ask I do not use deodorant."

"Well, neither would I if I dripped honey and vanilla."

"Honey and vanilla?" Ahneevah mused. "Is that comparable to smelling like a strawberry?" Zack grinned. "Close enough," he said still clomping along and gulping air. "Now can we discuss some of your other bodily functions?"

Leslee interrupted, "Zack is this really necessary?"

"Look, I'm not sure of what'll happen to us even in the next ten minutes, but I am sure that right now is a once-in-a-billion-year opportunity for this person of science." Zack rasped between labored breaths. "I've got to find out as much as I can. It's what I am." Ahneevah nodded her head and blinked her eyes in appreciation of Zack's dedication to his work. "I understand," she said. "Which particular bodily functions are you most interested in?"

"All of them, but let's begin with digestion. Do you eat food?"

"Yes, I need nourishment like you. But my digestive tract almost completely absorbs whatever I ingest for use in sustaining the various physical networks, or stores it for later use as reserve energy. Also, I have a strong mental governing system which rules that I eat only when I require sustenance and prohibits my consumption of more food than I actually need."

"No shit?" blurted Zack.

Ahneevah's eyes widened. "That would not be entirely correct. There *is* an elimination process for solid and liquid wastes, but they are of such negligible amounts that their purging occurs very infrequently."

"Ahneevah, I spent most of my life consuming more than I needed," Leslee confessed. "Are you saying that in your world … or time … there was no obesity and every woman looked … like you?"

"No, Leslee. Like the inhabitants here we had varying physical manifestations. Different shapes, different sizes and different colors. Like in your population, each individual had their own specific nature and the body systems basically operated to maintain whatever that particular nature was. The idea was to respect each other for our diversity. Sadly, it was a standard that we eventually failed to live up to."

Leslee sighed. "We're not living up to that standard all too well here either."

Zack tried to keep the talk on his track. "Are all your bodily functions similar to ours?"

"In principle many of them are. And before you ask, that does include what you call sex. Mmm … I guess I call it sex now as well. As you can see, we are built in similar fashion."

"Yes, I know," Zack coughed, then stumbled and lost some ground to Leslee and Ahneevah. "Kind of mysterious when you consider the billion years in between."

"Not really. The infinitesimal, terameter microbes that are the essence of life are all the same, and the conditions that existed here for development were also similar. Especially the prime ingredient—the water."

"How do you like that?" Leslee popped in, "there really *is* something in the water."

Zack was not to be denied though. "Now, you know I'm a big fan of evolutionary science but let's get back to the sex thing for a minute."

"Let's not," Leslee insisted as she and Ahneevah ended the brief interview by accelerating their pace a notch and opening the gap between them and Zack. Ahneevah was the first to pick up the sound of a patrol clopping down a hallway. The helmet-mounted-display face plate shifted from transparent to a reddish hue. "They will enter this corridor from the second access tunnel about fifty meters up on the right. I can identify twelve sets of boots."

Ahneevah motioned for Zack and Leslee to remain behind in relative safety as the security force detachment approached. When the patrol marched into the passageway Ahneevah revealed herself. The phalanx of guards hesitated for a split-second at the sight of the *alien* creature, which gave Ahneevah ample time to dash in among their ranks.

The martial art form she utilized initially looked to be exclusively defensive. To Leslee it appeared similar to the ancient style she learned that was practiced sixteen centuries ago in the Shaolin and Quang Yen monasteries in the Hunan Province of China. But Leslee was somewhat surprised to observe that none of the moves Ahneevah used resulted in deadly strikes. She simply avoided getting hit and followed-up by using her unexpected mass to disorient her opponents.

In rapid order she touched one after another behind the neck. Their spinal columns then served as wiring and sent the disruptive pulses directly to their brains. The guards staggered, and found that there was nowhere to go but down.

After seeing their fellow security force members dropping all around them, several of the guards realized that they had better bypass the tall and powerful alien. The human female and male might make for easier prey.

"Come on," Leslee snarled at one of the charging sentries, "It's time to find out if all that stuff I learned from Kung Fu Masters Hecht and Meza, really works. I'm ready to rumble."

Leslee stood relaxed as a challenger came at her. She casually stepped back with her left foot and down-blocked the left punch thrown by her oncoming opponent. Then she secured his left wrist with her left hand and held the arm out perpendicular to the ground. Shifting around 180 degrees, she put her right hand in back of her rival's left elbow and locked it up. In a whiz she spun him around and smashed him flat into another security guard. Both attackers collapsed like unstrung marionettes to the floor.

"That's my girl," Zack proudly announced and Leslee smiled.

Ahneevah shouted. "You don't have to hurt them," as she dropped five others within a matter of seconds.

"I'd like to help," Zack offered, "but you guys are doing so well."

"Don't worry, I think we've got it covered," Leslee shouted between strikes.

When the last guard was short-circuited out of action, Zack's curiosity required a feeding. "How long will they be ... uhhh ... neutralized?"

"I'm still not in full control. It could be anywhere from an hour to a full solar day," Ahneevah said, "but there will be minimal side effects—maybe some pain due to cerebral blood vessel contraction.

"You mean a headache?" Leslee posed. Ahneevah nodded her head in the affirmative.

Zack smiled. "Good. I hope it's a freakin' migraine."

Ahneevah used the logic unit in conjunction with tactical display in her helmet to locate the positions of other patrols and saw that the corridors of the research wing were now flooded with security personnel. There were many more headaches waiting for the armed guards as the fleeing trio could not avoid running into several roving units of them before reaching and entering the giant aircraft hangar.

By the time Ahneevah's senses locked onto the sniper perched in the cross-beams above, it was a fraction of a second too late. The sniper had dissolved into the shadows of one of the girder assemblies supporting the roof of the hangar. At the instant her amazing eyesight picked up the precise angle of fire, she selflessly leaped in front of Zack and Leslee to protect them. While in mid-air she felt the stinging heat where the bullet entered, and clutched the left side of her chest. The impact of the high-velocity, 9 millimeter projectile spun her around and slammed her hard against the corrugated tin wall, but somehow she managed to remain on her feet—sort of—by hanging onto a greasy, rusty oil drum.

Leslee reached Ahneevah first and was greatly relieved to see that she was conscious and upright—more or less. "How bad?"

"Bad enough," Ahneevah said through increasing discomfort.

Zack moved Ahneevah's hand away from the wound to take a closer look. His face went ashen. "It's your heart! It could be fatal."

"Not exactly," Ahneevah responded. "My heart doesn't work like yours. I can do without it for extended periods of time and still have an ample blood flow."

With that slight reassurance, Zack noticed blood oozing out and soaking the top left side of Ahneevah's flight suit, prompting yet another *eureka*. "Your blood… it's red. It looks much darker than ours and has a trace of purple, but red just the same!"

"What did you think … it would be green?" Leslee said.

"It's the iron," Ahneevah explained. "As I told you, we are basically quite similar in many respects. Now I need your help. We have to get moving."

Zack and Leslee stood on either side of Ahneevah and she put her arms around their shoulders. Zack noticed that her dark emerald eyes had faded to the color of an apple-green opal and that she was gritting her teeth as she leveraged herself up to a full standing position.

"Before you ask, yes it does hurt," Ahneevah grunted. With her left arm still draped on Leslee's shoulder, Ahneevah reached around and placed her hand over her heart about an inch or so above the wound. Her hand emitted a blue electric discharge and she recoiled slightly from the pain.

"I've cauterized the injury to stem the plasmodic flow."

Zack's mouth hung wide open. "You're like your own ER."

"To a certain extent, but the projectile is still lodged in my chest and will have to be dealt with."

When Ahneevah moved her hand away from the wound, Leslee and Zack watched in amazement as the hole in the flight suit made by the 9mm slug, repaired itself.

Zack made the connection. "Just like in the operating room … it remembers."

"Yes, and it shall also remember what it was struck by and will now be able to defend itself against it. I wish it were that easy for *my* epidermal layer to regenerate and remember." Ahneevah was wobbly and she whispered hoarsely, "I'm having a problem shutting down the active pain receptors in the injured area. We must get to the X2."

Several more squads of security men entered the hangar and Ahneevah quickly looked around. She zeroed in on something ahead and to the right of them. "There, the main circuit junction box." While still leaning on Zack for support and with bullets pinging all around, Ahneevah took Leslee's hand, picked out a safe route, and as fast as possible the three dodged between assorted vehicles and aircraft and arrived in front of the breaker panel.

"Leslee, a good deal of my inner electrical reserves are dealing with this injury. I'm going to need some of yours." Leslee threw Ahneevah a quizzical glance. "Bring your free hand near the cable leading into the junction box but don't touch it." Ahneevah encouraged, "I'll do the rest."

Leslee did so and she felt a strong jolt of electric current run through her body. She instinctively drew her hand away from Ahneevah and shook it. "Leslee, it won't harm you. It will only take a short time. You can do this." Leslee nodded her head, took a deep breath and took Ahneevah's hand. After ten seconds or so, a mini aurora borealis display radiated around both of them and then a solid blue shaft of voltage leaped from Leslee's fingers to the wiring which erupted in a geyser of sparks. In an instant, the hangar went pitch-black except for the persistent muzzle flashes from the various firearms and the smoldering flames from the electrical outlets and plugged-in devices.

"Now *that's* what I call a *buzz*," Leslee said as she brushed her open palms together in a *took care of that* gesture, which generated additional blue discharges.

As the three escapees slowly made their way through the hangar and advanced toward the Sikorsky chopper, the shooting continued. Many of the weapons were equipped with infra-red scopes and could *see* in the dark. But the high-tech assault arms could not *see* clearly through the billows of smoke precipitated by the ceaseless waves of gunfire and fried circuitry, and as a result most of the bullets were hitting parked trucks, forklifts, Humvees, and other vehicles and equipment. This produced even more of the coalescing particulates, which gathered over the action like a threatening storm cloud.

The pungent odor of cordite was a completely new sensory experience to Ahneevah. Her civilization had gotten past the exploding shell stage long before she came to be. She used the infrared setting on her helmet's frozen plasma face-plate in combination with her natural optics to see through the shrouded, vaporous hangar in order to locate the X2.

When they reached the prototype rotor-wing craft, Leslee and Zack helped Ahneevah into the pilot's seat. She focused her attention on the instrument array and frowned. "This craft has no bio-link. I'll have to try to create a conduit through the fly-by-wire and navigation systems."

She clicked the master switch of the highly-advanced air vehicle on, and the rainbow beam from the NLU instantly painted the uploading connectors of the flight computer. Incoming rounds began kicking up chunks of tarmac near the helicopter, and even though Ahneevah was not entirely satisfied with the results of the teletronic scanning and interface process, she engaged the starter switch, pushed the throttles forward a bit and the engine *whined* to life. More of their pursuers were now pouring into the hangar and heading in their direction. Bursts of gunfire sent bullets ricocheting off the composite hull of the twin-rotor chopper.

Leslee read a hint of doubt on Ahneevah's face and asked, "Can you really fly this thing?" Ahneevah continued to study the glass instrument display. "It reminds me of a species of bio-photonic hopping and blinking marshland creatures that I was fascinated with in my very early span-time. They were furry and grew as big as a fist. I kept one as a pet."

"Fascinating, I had a pet tarantula once. His name was Sparky. But seriously, you *can* fly this whirlybird, can't you?"

"I certainly hope so, but there is only one sure way to find out."

Still in significant physical distress and trying to shake off the pain, Ahneevah flinched as she advanced the throttles and the X2's rotors began biting into the air. The craft lifted off erratically and as she guided it through the hangar, barely avoiding collisions with some of the parked aircraft, the emergency generator kicked in, the hangar lights came back on and the huge steel doors began to roll together.

The coaxial bird barely cleared the immense doors before they *clanged* shut, and at full throttle, the unique chopper clawed skyward under a massive barrage of gunfire. A squad of mercenaries were stationed at the outside of the hanger and one of them launched a Stinger surface-to-air missile which exploded loudly near the X2's pusher propeller tearing two of the six blades away from the shaft. The chopper became unstable and began buffeting. Ahneevah immediately disengaged the integrated auxiliary propulsion system. She fought desperately to regain control. It was critical that she put some distance and altitude between them and their assailants. Just as the helicopter was getting out of range of the hostile fire, another Stinger missile exploded aft and destroyed a section of the port-side dorsal fin. The buffeting became more severe, and the body of the crippled craft began spinning horizontally. Warning lights on the enunciator panel flashed an incipient transmission-linkage failure alert, and the X2 computer voice advised, "Pull up. Pull up."

The wounded bird was out of control and descending rapidly, and the fuselage was shaking and gyrating starboard almost as if it were a third rotor. The irony murmured through Ahneevah's multi-mind tracks. *Two flights in a row, nearly a billion years apart, both ending in a plunge toward the ground.* In her present debilitated condition, even with all her exceptional skills, Ahneevah felt weak, powerless and unable to handle the crisis.

EPIJODE TWENTY-ONE

"PROJECT NIGHTMARE"

Inspector Clayton C. Reed had loyally and superbly served in ...

... the Federal Bureau of Investigation for nearly a decade. Before he joined the Bureau, he spent nine years with the New York City Police Department. Having been raised in Upper Manhattan, he opted to work in his former neighborhood. Within several years he made the Detective Bureau and soon became regarded as the top homicide investigator in the street gangs unit. He also managed to start a family, attain a law degree and rise to the rank of lieutenant.

Reed attended a counter-terrorism seminar given by the FBI and showed remarkable promise in that arena. This turned some heads at higher levels, and Reed was recruited by the Bureau. Within a short five years his instincts and expertise helped him to achieve the rank of inspector and he became the head of the Federal Bureau of Investigation's Counter-Terrorism Unit. Since the siege at the hospital was clearly an act of terrorism, Inspector Reed was alerted and dispatched to the Albuquerque battleground in a special FBI Gulfstream V.

En route to the scene, Reed received a secure satellite transmission via video phone from on-site Special Agent Zoe Reese. Zoe, in her late twenties with shaggy, blond hair, blue eyes and a freckled complexion, looked more like a high school student than a seasoned veteran of the Bureau. "Sir, aside from the almost four hundred patients, the shift staff numbers well over fifteen hundred. If you add the out-patients and visitors, we have in nearly three thousand lives hanging in the balance," Agent Reese declared.

"Any shots being fired at this moment?"

"Negative, sir, we have the Albuquerque PD SWAT team in position with most of the agents from our local office, and it's relatively quiet now. But it is a highly fluid situation and all indications are that it's a Mohammed Najar operation.

"Najar? I thought he was in Afghanistan."

"No more. And apparently he's gone freelance. He's demanding that a stockpile of spare-parts for seventy-nine F-14 Tomcat fighters be shipped to the Iranian Air Force. If we don't agree, he's threatening to release bio-toxins and contaminate the entire area."

"That's insanity. Those F-14s were sent to Iran when the Shah was still in power. They must be forty years old … at least."

"That's true sir. But it's also true that our navy retired the Tomcats only a few decades ago and we have B-52's that are being flown by some of the grandchildren of the original pilots. Those birds in Iran probably have minimal flight time and it's pretty well known throughout intel that the Iranian government would love to get them back in the air."

"Maybe, but the whole thing still doesn't quite fit together. In any case, at least for the moment … we'd better take him seriously. What about casualties?"

"It's difficult to be precise, but as near as we can figure we're looking at thirty dead and several dozen seriously injured. And Inspector, Najar threatened to kill others the way he shot the hospital administrator. It's going to be long, long night."

Reed recoiled and shook his head at hearing the morose casualty report. "Well then, Agent Reese, I'll see if I can make it shorter. Our ETA is two hours."

"Yes sir. We'll have a chopper standing by at Kirtland."

EPISODE TWENTY-TWO

THE CUSTODIANS
IN
"HITCHHIKERS GUIDE TO THE
GALAXY"

The Sikorsky coaxial whirlybird was seconds from a catastrophic rendezvous with terra firma ...

... when the logic unit voice came to life. "This craft incorporates a torque and vibration-compensator," it announced. "With activation it will automatically readjust the rotation speeds of the coaxial rotors to bring them into a mode that will counterbalance the spin of the fuselage."

Leslee spotted the dampener switch first and punched it. The onboard computer decreased the RPM rate of the starboard-turning rotor and allowed the faster port-spinning rotor to offset the loss of directional stability caused by the damage to the port-side dorsal fin. The intensity of the life-threatening oscillations gradually diminished and as Ahneevah regained control of the dysfunctional helicopter she turned to Leslee and gave her a single nod of approval for her crucial and timely action.

Just as the X2 reentered stable flight, a number of Ahneevah's multiple mind tracks detected a slight drizzle of minuscule golden globules on the windscreen and the outside skin of the craft. Leslee and Zack were oblivious to the shimmering phenomena and by the time they finally noticed, the sparkling beads had substantially enshrouded the X2. When the helicopter was completely enveloped in the glowing dew, all became silent and Ahneevah found that she no longer was flying it. The control of the air vehicle was under some other unknown influence, a circumstance that was baffling to Ahneevah and for which no clarification immediately presented itself within any branch of her vast reasoning network.

As was subsequently explained, time, in all its complexities, though it remains a relatively incomprehensible dimension, is still in essence a component of nature and conforms to specific natural laws, as do matter and energy. Although most of these laws have yet to be discovered, they do exist. And as chaotic as all of nature seems to be, there *is* a prevailing celestial balance. In the same way that positive and negative atomic particles are separated from the nucleus by proportionally infinite distances, the time continuum is divided into an inestimable number of standard temporal planes and null-fragment stanchions. The standard planes are those that are readily perceived and on which the conventional flow of time occurs—the continuum sector where time moves ever forward. The null-fragment stanchions, on the other hand, are imperceptible dimensions where the chronometric-stream is pliable. The Custodians inhabit the chronostasic interface; the boundary between the fragmental and the standard where time can flow omni-directionally and can even be totally suspended.

Abruptly, in what seemed like an infinitesimal blip after the splashes of radiant droplets inundated the X2, Ahneevah was once again at the controls of a flying machine, but it was no longer the Sikorsky bird she was flying. It was the StarStream. Ahneevah was the first to comprehend what had happened.

Leslee came to it next and finally Zack. All three had the same recollections dancing in their minds as a blur of images and words that passed between and across the minute fragments of the temporal band itself. The extrasensory exchange that was about to transpire had already happened in a time and place that was part of an alternate but nonetheless existing reality which was neither a time nor a place.

Ahneevah, Leslee and Zack saw themselves standing—indeed, they *were* standing—before a perfectly intact X2 in the cavern at the Kodiak Island excavation site. They were encircled by nine phantasmic figures that constantly alternated between the colors of the spectrum. The StarStream was somehow free of its icy bonds and hovering several feet above the cave floor. No palpable stimulus acted to stir any of the five senses. Therefore, Zack, Leslee and Ahneevah weren't quite sure whether they were actually *there* or not. This was expressly due to the fact that all ordinary sensory signals were irrelevant and everything that was happening was occurring from the inside out rather than from the outside in.

Zack unsuccessfully tried to wrap his already over-saturated brainpan around the inexplicability of the present moment. He knew Ahneevah had been wounded and was in distress, but now she showed no signs of trauma whatsoever. One of the Nine glided in toward Ahneevah and the fluctuating, spectral glow stabilized at a pulsating red. Then a voice that no carbon-based living creature had ever heard, surrounded them—a voice both male and female that seemed to come from everywhere and nowhere.

"You are where you do not belong."

Zack was never much for intimidation and after everything that had happened, including being just about *dead,* what else could anyone or anything do to him? Besides, he never was fond of the way Dorothy Gale handled herself when she first met the Wizard of Oz. It was his opinion that she was much too meek. So Zack stepped confidently toward the ruby specter that seemed to be the source of the declaration. "And what about you ... where exactly do *you* belong?" Zack said, sending the ball right back into the mystery being's court.

Another of the strange visitors sailed forward, shifting to an orange hue, and declared:

"We are where we should be."

Leslee jumped in. "We? Exactly who are *we*?"

"We are that which is before," interjected the wispy crimson figure who *spoke* first.

"Before? Before what?" Zack pressed.

"Before ... ever," was the reply.

Zack swallowed hard, trying to find a handle. Leslee found it first. It was shaped like a question mark. A big one.

"Before ... ever? God?"

"No, merely a before," announced a third ethereal wraith, alternating slowly between orange and yellow.

"A before? A before to ... our ever?" Leslee mumbled softly trying to grope for some clarity.

"A before to many evers."

"If you are really a before to many evers—then you must be some type of deity," Zack ventured.

"There are no simple explanations for the inexplicable," stated the fourth of the gossamer entities reflecting the translucent tint of a yellow sapphire. "Why must it always be deemed that assigning some mysterious, cosmic, ether-dwelling, all-powerful hand as the creator of everything justifies and explains sentient existence? We assure you that scientific reality is no less a miracle than the myths and superstitions."

"After the first Terran System Configuration was terminated," a fifth, dark-emerald-green, ghost-like being advised as it floated closer to Zack, "certain prerequisites had to exist to allow for subsequent forms of intelligent life to once again emerge from the primordial soup."

"The slime?" Zack postulated.

"If you prefer," a sixth, creature cloaked in a flickering, cobalt, replied, "but keep in mind that whether it is called a singularity, the primordial soup, or even the slime … it is nonetheless the beginning! We are simply one of the preexisting conditions that are necessary before there can be beginnings."

Ahneevah's green eyes widened and deepened. "You are the creators of the very beginning?"

"No," asserted an indigo, seventh form, "we are *a* before, not *the* before and were not present at the first beginning—only those thereafter."

"We do not initiate new life. It must issue forth and evolve on its own," offered an eighth, barely visible, violet phantom. "We merely manage that which has already been. We are what you might call caretakers of that which is before the beginning and after the end. We are approaching the beginning yet again."

Zack's scientific deductive reasoning kicked into overdrive. "Since you are here and this is clearly not the beginning, it follows that we must be near an end."

Flashing with alternating rainbow spectral hues, the ninth constituent of the now almost humanoid-shaped group of dappled lights responded, "There is no beginning without an end and no end without a beginning."

"Look, I appreciate all the poetry, but I'm a scientist," Zack offered in a slightly louder tone.

Ahneevah moved closer to the first apparition who *spoke* to them and was who or what she perceived as the leader. She tried to find eyes within the radiating, scarlet manifestation to make contact with. Despite finding none, she addressed the luminous entity. "What is your origination point?"

"Yeah," Zack jumped in. "Where do you come from?"

"Our conception was initiated deep within the Pillars of

Creation … the womb of stars. We were born out of the chaos and cataclysm of colliding galaxies and have been navigating the universes for many billions of your millennia. This marks the first time we have made direct contact with any form of responsive living matter."

Zack's eyes widened. "Well, this particular form of *responsive living matter* would be curious to know exactly what do you mean by univers*es*?"

"There were, are, and will be again," was the reply.

"How do you …" Zack was cut off by the Lead Entity's raising of an arm-like appendage.

"Your science is not yet aware that Spectrons are the building blocks of photonic light particles and are the most infinitesimal fragments of matter and energy. They are the main foundation of the universe and the framework of the essential astrophysical constants—dark matter, dark energy and gravity. They are present in everything that exists whether organic or inorganic. The nano-orbs that transported you back here are the Spectron's footprint. We navigate through the countless highways in the cosmos by breaking our energy particles down into streams of Spectrons. This allows us to travel on the infinite interstellar winds and waves of starlight in our extra-temporal search for intelligent life. We are unaware of time and can spend millions, even billions of years in transit, only to feel like it was, in your terminology, a good night's sleep."

"That's it?" Zack intoned. "We're just another Motel 6 on your celestial star tour?"

The Custodians regarded each other for a nano-second. One of them moved closer to Zack who at first backed away a step but then held his ground.

"Not so," was the reply. "It is certainly not just another stop. This marks our twenty-ninth visit to this body and its near satellite over the past thirty-nine billion years."

In no way could Zack let this pass. "Thirty-nine billion? That's ridiculous … impossible! Hubble's spectral red-shift application to the expansion rate indicates that the entire Universe itself is no older than thirteen and a half billion years."

"That is true only if you presume that the Universe has been expanding evenly and at a constant rate. We can state unequivocally that the expansion velocity has varied greatly in the diverse celestial quadrants and will continue to do so. This erratic outward movement is the result of time and dimensional shifts and anomalies in combination with the opposing forces contained in dark matter, dark energy and the reciprocal effects of concentrated gravity."

Zack's mind was bending. "What exactly are you saying?"

"Your current suppositions regarding the immutability of time are deeply flawed. In truth, the temporal order is highly flexible. Factors such as the instability of wormholes, the collapse and regeneration of the space-foam itself, and the intense pockets of mega-gravity throughout the Universe, serve to destabilize the time-stream flow. Trillions of black holes of various dimensions exist everywhere, including giant ones in the center of most galaxies. They constantly ingest gravity, space matter and other ambient energies. The byproducts of this process are dark matter and dark energy, which as well as being forces unto themselves, represent the main components of the Universe and create barriers that also act to decelerate and resist Universal expansion. Drop one stone in a pond and its ripples will expand outward, but drop additional stones in an opposite proximity and their ripples, depending on the intensity of course, will decrease or even cancel the outward moment of the ripples generated by the first stone."

"Speed bumps?" Leslee chimed in.

"This is conceptually accurate," the green-hued apparition advised as it glided in her direction. "And … time bumps as well. Although your contemporary astronomical research tells you that

that the light-horizon is thirteen and a half billion light years away, it is actually well over forty billion light years deep in the cosmos. The stellar-radiance beyond the light horizon is not yet visible to your investigations but nonetheless it does exist."

For Zack, this revelation represented one more stunner to add to the growing list. "Wait a minute. Then what about the geological radiometric dating evidence that shows the Earth itself to be only four and one-half billion years old?"

"The nulling protocol is nucleonic, and each time it is introduced it resets the radioactive half-life signature back to its pre-decay state."

Zack's mental choo-choo was stopped dead in its tracks. "Wow! It's getting so you can't count on anything anymore. Wait … what exactly is the nulling protocol?"

"When a civilization reaches its *doom point,* it is our province to erase all evidence of that succession's history so as to allow the evolution of life to once again get a fresh start," the crimson figure said. "It is the Null Quotient."

Zack cringed. "You're here to take out the garbage? You're like intergalactic janitors?"

"We are … Custodians. And we do not *take out* the garbage ... we restore it to its pure essence … as it was at its beginning," countered the blue, spectronal-energy ghost.

Leslee shuddered, "Like pressing the delete key." Zack glanced in Ahneevah's direction, "Well, don't look now but I think you missed something on your last scheduled trash pickup."

"That is why we have brought you here."

"Hold on a second. If everything from the past primordial soup generated configurations has been … *deleted,* what about unexplained discoveries that have been made, and the mysterious giant leaps forward in technology like ancient batteries or the ability to build the pyramids?" Zack asked.

The Custodians again regarded each other as if in a brief

telepathic consultation, then the Lead Entity offered: "Your perception is accurate. The leaps forward are part of the timeless formula that allows one configuration to build on some of the discoveries from those that came before."

Zack massaged his temples. "How can a completely nulled-out civilization pass anything along?"

"Brainwaves emitted by all sentient living matter are electric impulses, not unlike all other radio and interstellar transmission signals," replied the Lead Entity. "Just as this world continually receives various signal impulses from the entire Universe, it has ever been sending measurable electronic bursts, many of which have been echoed back to this quadrant. You have to remember that any broadcast or thought stream remains constant and as an indisputable energy form which must comply with universal physical laws of matter and energy." Zack lit up. "Right, high school physics first law of energy ... it cannot be created or destroyed." The Custodian continued, "Precisely, and unless otherwise altered, thoughts, ideas and all else that originated as electronic pulses are not affected by the Null Quotient. Even we cannot blot out the entire contents of space and time. All transmitted signals, whether sent by electronic devices or registered by any conscious or subconscious thought process, will forever remain intact within the vast continuum. On certain occasions under conditions still not completely known even to us, there is an involuntary cerebral synchronism between existing brain frequencies and those of one or more of the infinite thought or radio projections suspended in this universal cyber-matrix. This phenomenon enables the ambient thought or image to be perceived by the senses as if it were occurring in real time."

"Holy shit!" Zack croaked. Leslee quickly grabbed him by the arm.

"Isaac, ix-nay on the four-letter word ing-thay," she whispered.

Zack shrugged, "Well, they said they're not God."

Leslee wasn't dancing to that tune quite yet. "They're not God, huh? Excuse me. I hate to be a drag, but let's take a peek at their resume. They are children of the stars, born out of chaos and galactic cataclysm, so we don't have a clue what their sign is. They travel as photonic fragments on beams of starlight, and they've been hopping around the ..." Leslee made air quotes with the index and middle fingers, "*universes,* for maybe ... oh ... tens of billions of years. If they were a baseball team, they'd be the starting lineup for the 1927 New York Yankees. And there's more. In a heartbeat, they could, and I'm paraphrasing here, 'restore us to our essence ... like *we* never were.' You know ... back to the slime and all. And when I say *us* I mean the *whole Earth* us. Call me dippy, but I think that it's fair to say we are exceedingly mortal by comparison. Don't you?"

"Okay, you sold me," Zack said and then turned his attention back to the Nine.

"So what you are telling us is that there is a humongous, perpetual cosmic archive out there waiting to be researched?"

"If one has the right library card," Leslee proposed.

"That is true, but there is no real knowing," the lead Custodian added. "The neural, psychic interface can occur on singular or multiple levels, and is quite random."

Zack shot a quick look at Ahneevah. "Imagine if we could somehow tune into those signals ... those brainstorms," he speculated. "A wheel here, a pyramid there, $E=mc^2$, it could give us a window on untold billions of years of ... what was and can be!" Then Zack paused for a moment and peered directly at the Lead Entity. "Do you have a name? Or should we call you Custodian Number One, Two and so on?"

"We exist, that is enough," was the response, and the Nine figures faded away. Leslee peered philosophically at the empty space. "I really hope it isn't something we said. This is one minority group we truly don't want to piss off."

"I'd like to see the Science Channel tackle this one," Zack muttered under his breath.

The StarStream was still hovering and Ahneevah spoke a command in her language. The opaque frozen-plasma canopy opened and a beam of rainbow-colored light emitted from the cockpit area and scanned Leslee and Zack.

"Great. I can't wait to see what color I'm gonna pee now?" Zack said, half jokingly.

"Still orange for the next several days. The StarStream is merely taking your specific measurements so it can accommodate you," Ahneevah said as the spectrum pattern of the scan steadied at an indigo color. Then Ahneevah nodded affirmatively and gestured for Zack and Leslee move toward the craft.

Zack couldn't help but notice that there was only a single seat. "Am I going solo?" Ahneevah answered the question by aligning the NLU at the apex of an equilateral triangle formed by the device and Zack's eyes. She took a quick reading and repeated the process with Leslee. Then she motioned again for Zack to get aboard. He shrugged his shoulders and climbed into the pilot's seat. To his amazement, the seat contoured perfectly to his anatomy and a second flight-couch seemed to rise from the floor of the craft. Having seen the drill, Leslee waved Ahneevah off and jumped into the empty seat next to Zack. It conformed exactly to her physique and then the commander's chair appeared and glided forward as the two passenger seats slid behind to either side.

Zack got a kick out of this and smiled, "Wow, when you say *accommodate* you're not just *blowing smoke.*"

"The StarStream is capable of making adjustments from millisecond to millisecond and is in a real sense alive," Ahneevah said.

Leslee went straight to irony and whimsy. "Terrific, now we're gonna fly in Christine."

Ahneevah grappled with the reference for a split second and

then found it. She smiled. "Oh yes ... Christine, the Stephen King novel about an evil automobile possessed by supernatural powers. Correct concept but I assure you, the StarStream is no Christine."

Leslee looked around at the sides of her flight seat. "There aren't any safety-harnesses."

"Right." agreed Zack. Then he turned to Ahneevah, "What gives?"

"No need for belt-retention devices," She responded. Zack immediately made the jump, "Another case of Molecular Adhesion." Ahneevah looked at Zack and smiled. "Are you sure you never lived in my configuration? You'll find that you can move around freely at subsonic speeds unless there is an emergency that requires the neutralization of hazardous motion. If that should occur, the flight-couches will form an instantaneous subatomic particle-to-particle bond with the elements that make up your clothing. You will in effect become part of the seat itself."

"Wow, an invisible, artificially-intelligent restraint-system. The geniuses in Detroit would pony up for that in a New York minute," Leslee speculated.

"It *would* be an upgrade but the truth is that even with your current technology, much more can be done to make all vehicular transportation cleaner, faster and safer," Ahneevah said and then climbed into the cockpit of the StarStream, as she did on that *final* morning nearly a billion years in the past. She couldn't help thinking that although she should be dust, for some as yet incomprehensible reason she has survived a billion years to fly her craft another day. Ahneevah slid into her command-chair, slipped the NLU into its armrest interface and activated the frozen-plasma canopy closure system. The opaque clamshell windscreen silently locked down in place. As the StarStream lifted off, the entire cavern dematerialized and all that remained was a huge dusty crater with a pristine Sikorsky X2 sitting in its center.

EPISODE TWENTY-THREE

"THE FUTURE IN QUESTION"

The wheels of the Barrgrave Industries Gulfstream Seven had barely stopped rolling when the cabin door was hastily opened and ...

... Barrgrave the mogul and Bixler the VP dashed down the steps as a Humvee *screeched* up to the aircraft. The vehicle was carrying the significantly less-than-swaggering security force commander, General Ethan Mitchell, and a dazed and disheveled Dax Wolf. Barrgrave went right after the general. "How in the hell could you let them escape? He hissed. "What am I paying you idiots for?"

The mercenary leader groped for words as Bixler and Barrgrave boarded the Hummer. "I never saw anything like it outside ... *Star Trek*. It was like a Vulcan nerve pinch except there was no pinch! She barely touched people and they went down."

Barrgrave leaned in Mitchell's direction. "Dead?"

"No, unconscious," Wolf declared before the general could answer. "And that's not a conjecture," he continued as he rubbed his neck. "I assure you it's a scientific fact drawn from actual observation and personal experience."

"Wolf, you look like shit." Bixler snarled. "What the hell happened to you?"

"I don't know, sir. I can't explain it. I was out for nearly twelve hours. I finally regained consciousness less than an hour ago.

Some of the men are still semi-comatose, and those that have awakened are dealing with mild to major headaches."

"I had forty-six casualties total at various locations," Mitchell added as the Hummer pulled away from the jet. "Ten of my best men had the woman cornered and she neutralized the whole squad. I believe she easily could have killed them but for some reason she chose to merely put them to sleep."

"General, you said *she*. Who? The lawyer?"

As the king-sized Hummer rumbled toward the main facility, the general stepped into the breach once more.

"Sir, you don't understand. It wasn't the lawyer … I mean, she escaped as well, but it was the other one … the, uhhh, dead one."

"The dead one?" Bixler cried. "The corpse? What the hell are you saying? She's ambulatory? Like some alien zombie?"

"Mr. Vice President, begging your pardon but she's no zombie. She's one of the most beautiful creatures I've ever seen," the general mused, almost dreamily. "She was wearing the flight suit when she came to my … uhhh when I … confronted her, but some of the men reported that she was naked when she fought them and they said that she was able to take on any number of attackers at once. Like she could simultaneously keep track of every one of them and every move they made, even those who weren't in her direct line of sight!"

"One of my snipers was absolutely certain that he hit her with a kill-shot. The impact of the bullet slammed her against the wall but then she was somehow able to straighten up and keep going like the … Energizer Bunny."

"So maybe your sniper was wrong. Maybe he missed." Barrgrave lashed back.

"No, Mr. Barrgrave. The shooter said he saw her in the night scope and was sure he hit her in the area of the heart … if she has one."

Dax Wolf perked up and turned toward the general. "In the

heart? Precisely where did the shooting take place?"

"The main hangar … the report said that after she was hit, the other two helped her to get over to the circuit breaker panels and then somehow, she shorted out the main power supply junction box and everything went dark," Mitchell replied.

"General, I'd like permission to question that sniper," Wolf requested. "Maybe he can show me the exact location where she was when he shot her. I've already done some preliminary work and any tissue or blood samples could be extremely helpful. Based on what she can obviously do with her electrics, I have a theory that it was the involuntary actions of her nervous system that turned the emissions from the X-ray and MRI machines back on themselves and shorted them out during the … uhhh … autopsy."

"I'll have the soldier report directly to you, Dr. Wolf,"

"Well, general," Barrgrave said, "the alien is wounded and the three of them are on foot. They can't get very far."

"They're not on foot, Mr. Barrgrave. They took the X2."

"The X2?" Barrgrave exploded. "How could they take the X2? It's a prototype." He waved his hand as if to chop away that notion. "There is a special code needed to even start it, and there are only a handful of pilots qualified to fly the damned thing."

"Well, you can add the alien woman to the list. And I provided the activation sequence," Mitchell admitted.

An outraged Bixler shouted, "You provided it? You turned over a state-of-the-art piece of technology to enemy combatants without a fight?"

"I still don't know why or how," the general said, deeply puzzled. "She asked me for the X2 and I just … called the codes into the flight-line."

"Did you track it and at least get some kind of probable destination?" the mogul probed.

As cool as the general was trying to be, the events of the past hours caused a sizeable stress crack in his otherwise solid military constitution.

"Mr. Barrgrave, we got a clean signature when it first took off. Then they ... she must have done something to the bird to reduce its radar cross section."

"What do you mean ... reduced its cross section? Barrgrave shot back. What are we taking about?"

Mitchell coughed, "It was less than the F-22."

Barrgrave looked at him like he was daffy. "The F-22? General, may I remind you that the Raptor is a stealth fighter and the X2 is a helicopter with twin rotors on top that spin in opposite directions and—a six-bladed pusher-prop in its ass. It should be like a neon sign up there. How in the hell could it have a return the size of a goddamn sparrow?"

"I said its radar cross section was *less* than the F-22's," Mitchell reminded him. "It was smaller than that of a humming-bird, sir. We tracked it for a few minutes and then lost it completely in the ground-clutter. That woman ... or being ... or whatever she is must have been flying at an altitude of less than fifty feet. I thought we hit the chopper with two shoulder-launched Stinger missiles but there was no significant debris located. All that the search team could recover was a few sections of composite material that check out as being part of the port-side dorsal-fin and a piece of one of the rear propeller blades."

Albert Barrgrave II shook his head in disbelief as the Humvee arrived at the main hangar where scores of technicians were attempting to restore power. While Bixler and Mitchell were getting out, an aide rushed over and saluted the general.

"Sir, the Communications Officer asked me to bring you directly to the Situation Room."

"Why did he send *you*? He could have contacted me over the network."

"We're still having, uh, power problems sir."

EPIƧODE TWENTY-FOUR

"TUNNEL IN THE SKY"

Although they were once again in the air and back on the standard temporal plane ...

... Zack's mind was still spinning. "Ahneevah, you had a lead slug in your chest. You were wounded ... in pain. What happened?"

Ahneevah pursed her lips and shook her head slightly. "Perhaps the healing was an auxiliary benefit of the matter-displacement shift that brought us to our encounter with the Custodians. If they read our basic DNA alignment in order to transport us, then the bullet, having no relevance, must have been deleted in the reassembly and any other physical anomaly was corrected. The same could be the case with the molecular structure of the X2 ... and the ... plaque in Zack's arteries."

"Right, if the schmutz had no place in my natural DNA pattern, it would have been eliminated as well."

"And ..." Leslee added with a wisp of a smile, "You won't have to feel like you're an orange-paint spray-can." Then Leslee tilted her head up and gazed with wonder at the dazzling view of the night sky through the top of the canopy bubble. "Wow, look how bright the stars are ... and I can see so many of them. Amazing ... we're here at the very threshold of space."

Zack gazed at the spectacle above. "So now I'm an archeo-anthropological-astronaut." Then, out of the corner of his eye he picked up the terrain below whizzing by in a blur. "Ahneevah, I can tell we're traveling at a very high velocity but I have no sensation of motion and I don't feel any acceleration force whatsoever. Like sometimes when I'm in an elevator and I know it's moving but it seems like it's standing still. Precisely how fast are we going?"

"Yeah," Leslee said. And what's our altitude? Maybe we're entitled to astronaut wings."

Ahneevah scanned the control panel. "We are flying straight and level at one-hundred-thousand feet … slightly less than twenty miles. I believe astronaut wings are awarded for flights at altitudes of fifty miles or higher. And Zack, we are cruising at five-thousand six-hundred and seventy-nine point nine-six-three-five-eight-seven-two miles an hour."

"Point nine-six-three-five-eight-seven-two?" Zack mimicked.

Leslee raised her eyebrows. "Well, you did say precisely."

Zack grinned and nodded his head in agreement. "Okay, okay. But fifty-six-hundred plus miles per hour is well in the neighborhood of eight times the speed of sound. Our hyper-sonic shock wave must be leaving a fifty mile wide *boom carpet* and a thousand mile swath of shattered windows behind us. "Not likely," Ahneevah said. The propulsion system emits sub-atomic particles that ionize the air molecules and restricts their build-up prohibiting their compression and the formation of shock wave cones on the leading and trailing edges of the craft."

"I get it," Leslee acknowledged. "It's like we have an aerodynamic non-stick Teflon coating. With no shock wave cones to spread to the ground beneath the flightpath, there's no sonic boom."

"True," Zack added. "But what about the severe *G* forces at speeds beyond Mach 8? They should be crushing. The instant *peel out* from zero to over five-thousand MPH alone should have squeezed the crap out of us." Ahneevah nodded her head twice.

"Crushed you flat as a … pancake. It's the instant acceleration more than the speed, but there's an inertia-canceling component built into the StarStream's propulsion system. The inside cabin section is not connected directly to the outer shell. It is suspended within the main body in a synthesized bio-plasma material which acts similar to the inter-vertebral discs in your spinal column." Zack slapped his forehead with his palm. "Jeez, like we're in here floating on cartilage. The whole system is like an organic airbag." "Correct," Ahneevah replied, then continued. "This prevents the inner compartment from being subject to any external forces. The laws of motion are universal. During the first millisecond of extreme accelerations, decelerations or abrupt changes in pitch, yaw or heading, a fly-by-wire system with an independent power train automatically shifts the inner cabin in an equal and opposite reaction to the direction and degree of the change in the flight path and continues that pattern seamlessly from nano-tic to nano-tic until another change in direction is detected. This constant opposing motion absorbs the inertial and gravitational moments, effectively canceling them."

"The ultimate shock absorber," Leslee reasoned.

Zack and Ahneevah smiled. "Look who's a physicist now," Zack said.

Leslee shrugged. "Just basic logic, but what if the inertia-canceling system somehow becomes inoperative?"

"If the system goes off line, the StarStream will detect it, and the capability for achieving excessive velocities and severe directional changes will be temporarily suspended."

Ahneevah went on to explain that the inertial compensating system was only one feature in the extraordinary group of components within the craft that was now carrying them. "The outer shell of the StarStream is biologically engineered using a composite titanium-silica atomic bond," she added. "The surface is permeated with a redundant power supply system composed of trillions of nanobotic fusion reactors created from inert substances and living DNA." The scientist in Zack was intrigued. "What ... like stem cell materials?"

"Negative. Actually, each StarStream is constructed specifically for the pilot who will be assigned to it, and that pilot's life-ladder is used in the construction."

Leslee got it. "Whoa," she said. "That means that the StarStream is like your ... sibling."

"Incredible. Then each cell is, in a sense, a living micro-nuclear power plant," Zack added.

"Not in a sense," Ahneevah clarified. "It is a micro-organic reactor with every individual cell being fully capable of regeneration. When the particle sequencer is engaged, ambient radiation is attracted and bathed in cool plasma which in turn activates the muon-catalyzer which triggers the fusion of two atmospheric and cosmic forms of hydrogen: deuterium and tritium. In that billionth of a second, the H_2 and H_3 atoms are separated, and the electrons are stripped from the atomic nuclei. Since the stripped electrons are negatively charged and have a natural repulsion, the ionic conversion system serves to balance the negative ions by creating positrons, or positively charged ions. This creates the condition for the plus and minus ions of the two hydrogen derivatives to fuse and break apart to form a helium nucleus."

Zack was right on the page. "And just like basic stellar mechanics, two protons and two neutrons and an uncharged or free neutron are released. Trillions of liberated neutrons, moving at light speed in one chosen direction or another ... providing propulsion energy similar to that of a rocket engine ... action and an equal and opposite reaction ... and it all happens without the extreme star-surface temperatures. Cold fusion ... the reality!"

"I thought you were an archeo-anthropologist," Leslee said through a slight smile.

Zack placed his hands on the side of Leslee's face. "Hey, I did read between binges."

Leslee put her hand on Zack's cheek, softly narrowed her eyes and nodded in understanding. Her smile grew a bit wider. Then Zack turned to Ahneevah. "How are these trillions of separate reactors kept in synch with each other? I mean, there's no computer in the world that could manage that."

"That's true. Not even back in my world. But actually it isn't necessary. The power pods are linked biologically through the guidance network to control the StarStream's velocity and tracking. The *fly-by-wire system* receives one input and instantly relays it to the entire directional control network."

Leslee felt the rays of enlightenment. "I get it. Like our brain. It gives one command to raise an arm, but the millions of cells that accomplish the action automatically communicate with each other and work together."

"I thought you were just an attorney," Ahneevah chided.

"I do have a master's degree in archeology," Leslee volleyed back.

"She does indeed. I gave her an *A*," Zack boasted.

"And since the propulsion neutron can emanate at light-speed from every nano-speck of the StarStream's hull," Ahneevah said, "its response is instant and directional control is virtually unlimited."

"I bet this baby can really corner," Zack declared. "Even make right-angle turns and instant reversals in direction."

Ahneevah reset the translucent frozen plasma windscreen to clear, then demonstrated exactly what Zack said—right-angle turns, hard stops and instant reversals in speed and direction. Zack's reaction was less than joyous. He started feeling queasy and spoke haltingly with his hand covering his mouth. "Uhh … this ultra modern flying machine wouldn't happen to have any puke-sacs on board, would it?"

Leslee was surprised. "Zack, how could you be getting sick?

We're equipped with an inertia canceling component. There's no feeling of motion."

"Tell that to my visual perception ... you know those theme park projection rides like *The Simpsons, Superhero School* and *Star Tours*? Well, I get nauseous on those unless I close my eyes. I even get woozy at roller coaster movies."

"I'll try to keep that in mind," Ahneevah said, then continued her seminar. "The StarStream's entire power system is based on nuclear mechanics of the most advanced nature and a technology that is not even a glimmer in the eyes of your most cutting-edge atomic particle research. Prevailing scientific theories consider that metals and silicate elements can be combined molecularly but not atomically. In the StarStream's fusion process the titanium silicate material becomes a reservoir for proximate radiation, much like a sponge absorbs water. It utilizes the radiation as a basic fuel and the isotopes as regenerative building blocks. This formation of the new material releases energy that not only supplies power to continue the fusion process but also can be used for practical everyday needs. In effect, it is a perpetual-motion system that is fueled by any radiation that surrounds it. It can process atomic particles from solar winds, cosmic and gamma rays or any other stop on the entire spectrum of existing radioactivity. There is nothing lost because the energy created leaves its own fuel as a by-product." Zack was right on the page. "Shit, Big Oil would put a hit out on you."

"Wait a minute. I'm beginning to understand something, Ahneevah said, "Try this. Since radiation exists in many forms and is ever present ... and this craft went down in the middle of a radioactive cataclysm ... perhaps it was the combination of the varied and overwhelming radioactive emissions inside and outside the StarStream combined with an unidentified random factor like the initiation of the Null Quotient that somehow induced a form of subatomic-microbial embalming."

"And your *ride* here could have served as a kind of long-term DNA bank," Leslee ventured.

"Good theory," Ahneevah said. "On the other hand, I probably did the same for my *ride*, and the reciprocal genetic flow resulted in a constant regeneration and preservation of my biological elements as well as those of my, mmm … sibling."

"I understand," Zack blurted out in an eyebrow-raising, mini-brainstorm moment. "It's almost like you nurtured and gave birth to each other. But consider this hypothetical … the reason you survived through nearly a billion years might also be because you didn't actually have to survive for nearly a billion years."

Both Leslee and Ahneevah looked at Zack as if he suddenly went blooey. Zack raised his both hands in a *wait a minute* gesture. "Look-it, when I first entered the cave on Kodiak Island and looked at the drawings, it struck me that the paint seemed like it was still wet. After our little meet 'n greet with the Custodians and their cluing us in about how time is not constant, it occurred to me that … well … in that particular environment, time might have stopped. It stood still for you and the StarStream, the designs on the cave walls, the Zackosaurus and the swamp grass. Everything in that immediate space was in chronological suspension." Ahneevah jumped right on board. "That's good, Dr. Carver. Excellent! Although the world was taking a billion years to get from *there* to *here*, if time wasn't moving forward in my immediate surroundings, I might have, in a quasi-reality, only been *there* for a relatively short temporal duration, certainly not a billion years."

"Right," Zack concurred. "Your existence could have been mainly on the null fragments and therefore … non-standard temporal as we know it. What nags at me though is that when we exited the cave, everyone outside was aware that we were gone for a few hours. If time wasn't passing inside the cave, then we should have been perceived as exiting at almost the instant we entered."

"Maybe not," Leslee suggested. "It's possible that whenever we were present beyond the entrance, the clock of our reality could've somehow superseded the suspension and we and everything from the ... *sphere and comet room* down through the cavern was ticking and tocking again. Like the Universe expanding much more slowly than we were able to perceive. The relationship between *where* we were and *when* we were may also have been inconsistent."

"Yes," Ahneevah said. "You reinstated the standard temporal plane when you entered the cavern area and everything inside was freed from the overall null-fragment chronomic hold."

Zack was really getting stoked. "It's Einstein, Hawking and Carl Sagan all wrapped up in one package. But how come when Bixler, Barrgrave and company went into the chamber everything remained frozen."

"It was the StarStream simply acting to protect itself." Ahneevah replied. However, as she was speaking she was also deliberating a different problem reverberating in another level of her consciousness. A look of concern brewed on her face as the shade of her emerald-green eyes slowly deepened. "There are innocents, including many children, who are in great danger. We have little time. All right, Zack, I recommend that you close your eyes, we'll be accelerating at ten-thousand."

"Ten thousand what?" Zack gulped.

"Ten thousand miles per hour," Ahneevah answered. "It is imperative that we get to Albuquerque in less than nine minutes."

The StarStream became an imperceptible blur as it streaked southeast across the Gulf of Alaska toward New Mexico.

EPISODE TWENTY-FIVE

CLAYTON REED AND ZOE
IN
"A GRAVEYARD FOR LUNATICS"

*W*hen the FBI Bell JetRanger arrived over the scene, it was
the telltale muzzle flashes Inspector Clayton Reed observed on
the ground below immediately told him ...

... that Zoe Reese's *fluid* situation had once again swerved into
the tempestuous white waters of violence. As the chopper
descended, Reed could clearly see the letters F-B-I stenciled on
the backs of the nylon windbreakers that his response team was
wearing. Also, due to the illumination provided by a string of
powerful explosions, Reed was able to quickly pinpoint the
strategic positions of both sides in the conflict. Any way he
looked at it, the odds weren't good.

Down on the ground; job one for the band of law enforcement
personnel was avoiding the hypersonic, envoys of mayhem and
death that were biting through the air all around them. The result
of the alloy-jacketed bullets' impacts was shattered windshields,
flattened tires and the eruption of several FBI vehicles into
distended fireballs which summarily spit out the former vans and
autos as flaming chunks of scrap-metal.

It was 4:05 am Mountain Time and a high overcast reduced
the moonlight to a single, pasty-white smudge in a charcoal sky.

The StarStream floated down soundlessly and swooped over the treetops undetected. Then it settled into a motionless hover inches above the ground in a small glade near the picturesque Duck Pond within the University of New Mexico campus. Ahneevah took the NLU from its slot, did a quick sweep with it, climbed out of the cockpit before the canopy completely opened and then turned to Leslee and Zack, who were still seated inside. All three were able to clearly hear the hammering *blasts* of the automatic weapons-fire occasionally punctuated with loud, shuddering explosions.

"Stay here," Ahneevah stated emphatically. "I'll lock everything down and the StarStream will carry you out of harm's way. Maybe up in a low orbit where it will be safe ... then you would certainly be entitled to astronaut wings."

Leslee wasn't quite ready to cut and run. "Tempting, but I'll take a rain check on that kind offer." Then to further indicate her displeasure with Ahneevah's plan, Leslee quickly sprang out of the StarStream and Zack jumped out right behind her.

"Yeah, remember, after you went missing for a billion ... or whatever years we were the ones who found you, and we're not letting you out of our sight now," he said, emphatically.

Ahneevah drew a step closer to Zack and Leslee and pointed towards the gunfire. "Those fanatical men have already taken many innocent lives. Lives that meant no harm to them ... lives that included the young and the infirm. They do this out of hate to serve a fringe belief that has no evidentiary basis, and the killing will continue whether their demands are met or not. These are the same seeds of insanity, terror and destruction that were sown and reaped in my time on this world."

Leslee was adamant. "But in *our time* on *this world* you might be our only hope. So ...we go where you go."

"Absolutely," Zack added, we're stickin' with you. No ifs, ands or buts."

Ahneevah smiled and nodded her head ever so slightly in acquiescence as a sliver of her vast consciousness noted the courage and integrity of these two beings—these two—friends.

"Very well," she responded, "but there is little time to explain and few options. You must do exactly as I say." Leslee read her loud and clear. "Done ... it's your call."

"Yep, you sing, we dance." Zack added.

Ahneevah pondered this for a snapshot and then began absorbing information from the logic unit. "Go now and seek out those in command of the forces opposing the invaders. Tell them that there are sixty-three male entities, forty-three inside and twenty outside. They have nuclear materials, extremely virulent bio-toxins, high explosives and armor-piercing ammunition. The fissionable and biological weapons pose a major peril to one-third of your nation. I will temporarily disable most of the power grid. As soon as the electron flow in the structure is discontinued and the armed ones outside have been neutralized and are no longer a threat, it is of the utmost necessity that the law enforce-ment personnel move in with the greatest speed. You must impress that upon them. Seconds can make the difference. I will deal with any of the assailants that might evade capture."

Leslee started to ask, "Why are you risking ...?"

Ahneevah silenced Leslee by gently placing her left hand on Leslee's shoulder and softly touching Leslee's lips with the index finger of her right hand. Her alluring eyes softened to an aqua-blue as their penetrating gaze answered Leslee's question without another word. Then Ahneevah started toward the fire-fight. After a few steps she stopped and looked back. "It is crucial that you make the gravity of the situation I have described clear to the authorities ... and stay low." The crackling sound of the gunshots began intensifying. "We must act swiftly ... we are down to minutes," Ahneevah said, then separated the two sections of the NLU, handed one to Leslee and dashed toward the combat zone.

At first, Leslee and Zack were prohibited from entering into the cordoned-off area. Special Agent Zoe Reese insisted, "You have no reason to be here."

"I am an attorney," Leslee told the FBI officer.

"But she prefers *counselor*," Zack interjected.

While the special agent was searching for any relevance in Zack's remark, Leslee took a deep breath, inched closer to Agent Reese and in a firm but quiet voice continued.

"Please listen to me. We know this is not simply a hostage situation and you must believe it when I tell you that we know that you have a code-red nuclear and biological weapons threat here." Reese stiffened. "How can you know that?" Zack came over to Leslee. "Take my word; we have it from a very reliable source." Then Leslee picked up the ball. "And the cost can be far worse than you realize. If the WMD are released there will be an immeasurable loss of life and an area of five-hundred-thousand to a million square miles will be uninhabitable for decades. We can help to stop it." The agent hesitated. Leslee relaxed her stance, looked directly in the Special Agent's eyes and didn't have to shift her view to read her name tag. She caught it at check-in.

"Tell me Zoe, what if we are right and you are wrong?"

Agent Reese loosened up ever so slightly. The change in posture was almost imperceptible, but Leslee somehow picked up on it and then continued. "I don't want to see the hostages, you, or any of your FBI brothers and sisters get killed or injured because the proper information was not relayed to where it was needed. Would you want that?" Agent Reese sighed. "No, I wouldn't."

"Bullshit," snorted Reed. "I've got a local nightmare on my hands and I know who you two are. You two were part of that big hoax in Alaska with that *alien*. How am I supposed to believe you can do what Reese here told me you can do?"

Leslee stepped nose to nose with Reed, "Sir, you are gravely underestimating the danger here. The threat to release bio-toxins is not just intimidation. These bastards have them and they won't hesitate to use them." Reed took in some air and was about to speak but Leslee got there first. "Never mind how we know but this *nightmare* is far from being exclusively local" she warned. "You have a potential national emergency right here … right now." Then Leslee pulled back a step to allow her words to sink in and after a beat continued in a softer tone. "Look, what exactly do you have to lose? Get your people ready to move within the next five minutes. If all the power doesn't go out and the bad guys don't begin to fall like dominoes … arrest us."

"That's right, arrest us," Zack reiterated. "And FYI, contrary to the propaganda you might have heard on the Foxtica Nitwork, the incident in Alaska was no hoax."

Ahneevah, meanwhile, had cautiously made her way to the hospital complex maintenance building. As she peeked around a corner of the totally collapsed and still smoldering structure she spotted a four-man detachment guarding the emergency-wing entrance. Casually, she strode out of the shadows and into the sallow moonlight. At the sight of this unexpected figure in the unusual flight gear, the quartet of terrorists hurriedly raised their machine pistols and aimed them. However, their 29th Configuration *quick* was purely slow-mo to the 28th Configuration pilot. It was no contest. Not even close. By the time they fired, their target had already moved behind them and could have easily ended their tenure on Earth. But Ahneevah held to her precepts. Remaining adamant about taking a life as evil as it might be, she chose to simply douse their brains in midnight.

Najar entered the hospital's nuclear medicine facility on the lowest level of the research wing. Five of his men were already there. Several were opening the cases containing radioactive material and the others were setting the explosive charges. In Najar's mind, the lab was the perfect place for the blast to occur. The two-story building would certainly be leveled and the heat produced would serve to enhance the virulence of the murderous poisons and special viruses contained in the vials. The force of the explosions would send the toxins tens of thousands of feet skyward and the jet stream would transport the horrible death they carried, far and wide.

Ahneevah darted to the side of the main building, adjusted the logic unit and touched it to the surface of the hospital wall. Softly, she gave a verbal command in her native tongue.

"It would be more appropriate to use the language of where we are rather that where we were," prompted the male NLU voice.

Ahneevah smiled. "Okay ... Wilco," she replied. "Scan the life forms within the building coordinates and modify the transponder ranging frequency emitted by the StarStream's guidance system into a wave-form that will cancel out all electric stimulation to the cardiac muscles and prevent their contractions. Make absolutely certain that the myocardium pulse intervention signal strength is set to minimum intensity. We are seeking temporary immobility not termination."

The logic unit voice responded, "Roger that. Also be advised that the biological weapons are in a sector 090 mark at thirty meters and ten down."

Inside the subterranean lab, Najar checked the detonator and made some final modifications on the small control panel of blinking lights. He raised his eyes skyward and clicked the main arming switch. The digital timer display read 30:00 … 29:59 … 29:58. With a grunt of satisfaction and then a wave of his hand, Najar dismissed the others. When he was alone, the terror mastermind reached into his waistband, grabbed the metal case and opened it. Then he carefully removed the bio-toxin vials, which he placed on top of the package of explosives, looked toward the heavens and shouted, "God is great."

Leslee did not have it quite right. The terrorists didn't drop like dominoes. Most of them went down like mosquitoes caught in the noxious mist of a DEET pesticide fogger. When the FBI and local SWAT teams charged into what they presumed a besieged objective, they encountered bodies strewn around like dead leaves on a blustery, late autumn day. Terrorists were flattened with their firearms scattered on the ground. Up on the roof, the two raiders guarding the helicopter were sprawled out on the landing struts and the pilot folded over unconscious in his seat. Most of the hospital personnel were lying inanimate as well.

Ahneevah cautiously approached the nuclear medicine lab door with only three and one half minutes to go before the affects of the cardio-pulse intervention waves would result in termination. Suddenly, she was confronted by the quintet of Najar men exiting the research facility. This was an unexpected turn and Ahneevah was not close enough to any of the terrorists to act immediately. Her *captors* growled in Baghdadi Arabic motioning in an upward direction with their guns to indicate that she should raise her hands. Ahneevah responded in the same dialect that she understood and lifted her arms. With their machine pistols trained on her, the enemy combatants began to bark at each other about what exactly to do with their prisoner. Through the jabbering, Ahneevah reasoned that the heart-stopping electronic jamming frequencies she called for could not penetrate the lab area due to the specialized insulation associated with the MRI equipment and the nuclear devices and materials.

Although Ahneevah was as yet unaware of precisely what the terrorists were after, aside from terrorism, she was painfully cognizant that all of the souls, bad and good, that were the victims of her electronic cardiac assault were running out of time. One of the men moved closer and reached out, attempting to remove her helmet. For a fraction of a second before his mind went blank he swore that he was rolling over and over in an unconscious heap with the four other rats. He was right. Ahneevah's inner clock told her she had less than two minutes.

A puzzled look wiped across Ahneevah's face as she made her way toward the radiological lab. One of her numerous mind levels picked up a seemingly out-of-context phrase. *Seventy-two virgins?* But in a flash it made sense. *Oh yes, seventy-two virgins.*

Najar was staggered to hear the words *seventy-two virgins* in perfect Arabic. The voice seemed to come from inside his head and the intonation sounded so angelic he thought he was receiving a response to his previous supplication directly from heaven. His rapture, however, was cut short by several crunching noises coming from the corridor outside. The sounds were followed by *thuds* and he instinctively reached for his weapon. To his dismay, he found himself grasping only a handful of air. Then he located the missing firearm partially sticking out of the far cinderblock wall as if it were an arrow buried in a straw-backed target. As the timer *beeped* down toward detonation, Najar became painfully aware that he was no longer alone in the room and for the first time in his many years of wanton murder and fanaticism, he felt fear.

He jerked his head around and saw the figure in the unique helmet and flight suit, at which point the angelic voice in his head became harsh. "Is that why you blow yourselves up?" Ahneevah bristled, "Because someone once said you get seventy-two virgins? And you believe that?" Najar was too stunned to even contemplate the question, let alone come up with an answer.

"Actually the truth is that when you get blown up, you get blown up, period. And even if there were seventy-two virgins waiting for you, you couldn't actually satisfy them—but why don't I arrange a bit of a preview just to demonstrate that too much of anything is not good? I'm going to give you eighteen minutes in heaven right now. And you won't even have to die to get there."

"But the bomb is set to go off in ten minutes." Najar protested in Arabic.

"No problem. We have plenty of time. Besides I thought you looked forward to death." The terrorist leader became rigid. "No, I do not die. I must avenge ... it is the soldiers who die."

"Spoken like a true coward. Of course you don't die. You and your psychotic cabal brainwash others to die for you ... you teach death instead of life ... a billion years and nothing's changed." With that Ahneevah leveraged Najar's arms behind his back and brought her hand close to his groin area. He was bewildered and in considerable pain when a crimson tendril of energy jumped from Ahneevah's forefinger to his crotch. His eyelids fluttered and he started to bleat out uncontrollable groans of pleasure.

Ahneevah smiled to herself and turned her attention to the real elephant in the room. The digital clock on the rigged up explosive package read less than nine minutes and counting. She studied the device for a split second and determined that there was no fail-safe mechanism. Her next move was to cancel the detonation profile by turning off the arming switch and tearing out the wires running to the fusing assembly and ignition sequencer. As Ahneevah dashed out of the lab, she relayed new orders through the NLU.

"Cancel myocardial hold."

Ahneevah found Nurse Daniels unconscious on the floor in front of the children's ward and immediately went to work on her. In hardly no time at all, the both of them were in the cardiac unit moving from one patient to another. Ahneevah was electrically jump-starting their hearts by touch as if she was a living defibrillator, and Lynne Daniels was checking them over as they were being revived.

Meanwhile, Inspector Reed, Special Agent Reese and Company entered the hospital and set about flushing any residual terrorist roaches from out of their dark corners. Leslee and Zack were escorted over to Reed. "We have fifty-one in custody. Dr. Carver, how many suspects did your friend say there were?"

"Sixty-three, that would leave twelve." Then Ahneevah's voice chimed in over the NLU. "Meet me ASAP in the nuclear medicine laboratory in the research wing."

Zack and Leslee brought Clayton Reed and Zoe Reese into the lab where the now defanged nuclear device was located. At the entrance they saw the two cases of the radioactive plunder stacked by the door. Ahneevah was facing away from them when they came into the lab. She was tending to the group of six slack-jawed, motionless terrorists sitting quietly on the floor. They had no visible restraints and their backs were against the wall where the machine-pistol was partially buried.

"Make that *six* more bad guys to go." Leslee announced. Zack picked up the digital countdown timer. It was frozen at eight minutes and one second.

He showed the explosive package to Leslee, Reed and Reese. "My God," Reed said as he studied the device and then took it from Zack. "If we'd waited out there, this entire set of buildings would have been toast, and everyone in the surrounding area … ashes. Thanks for making me listen." Then the FBI inspector looked toward Ahneevah. "And thank you for…"

"You are welcome, but there's much more," Ahneevah said and slowly turned to face the group. "The low yield nuclear explosion was primarily intended as the means to most effectively spread the deadly bacterial cocktail of substances. Casualties would have numbered in the millions. Every living thing in the city of Albuquerque, except for a few scattered types of fungal growth, would have died within hours, and the preponderance of animal and plant life in the surrounding thousands of square miles would have been dead within weeks." She eased closer to Reed and Reese and opened her hand to reveal the pair of lethal vials of biological weapons. "I believe you call them BWs," she added and closed her hand around them. "They are heinous."

Leslee, ever polite, made the proper introductions, "Special Agent Reese and Inspector Reed, meet the hoax from Alaska."

Ahneevah removed her headgear and now it was Reed and Reese's turn to be slack-jawed. "I am ..." Ahneevah recited her name and the two FBI agents relaxed. Smiles edged onto their lips. Almost reflexively they reached out, and Ahneevah shook each of their hands. As they touched her, their smiles broadened into the happy face realm. "That's better. As you can see, I was part of a chain of command as you are, so I will do a condensed debrief for you."

Reed barely managed to respond; "Mr. Carver and Ms. Myles said that ..." Ahneevah put up her hand and then gestured to Leslee and Zack. "For the record, that would be Dr. Carver and Counselor Myles."

"Of course," Reed replied. "Dr. Carver and Counselor Myles said that you were like a reverse pacemaker and stopped the terrorists' hearts."

"Affirmative, at least most of them; the only way to achieve immobilization over that wide an area was to jam the electric pulses that drove the pumping action in their hearts. But I was unable to neutralize all sixty-three of them as some were at locations deeper underground that were shielded by various materials that our blocking signals could not penetrate. Also, because I am still somewhat unstable and could not relate the entire sequence of information, there was not enough time to distinguish one human bio-electrical impulse from another. Since time was of the essence, I unfortunately had to interrupt circulatory muscle function in the captives as well." Ahneevah then turned to Leslee and Zack. "If within five to six minutes I failed to rescind the order it was necessary for me to give, the result would have been irreversible brain damage. If the hostages' hearts remained inactive much beyond the six minutes it would have been fatal," she said, horrified at the possibility. "I am relieved to report that there was no further loss of life and no permanent damage, although I was down to bare nano-tics on some of the good people my tactics affected. And ... oh ... be careful with these," she cautioned, as she handed the two deadly glass containers to Reed. "As you may have already figured out, the demand for aircraft parts was just a ploy to give the terrorists time to remove the radioactive materials. Their solitary interest was in death and destruction and not the maintenance of the Iranian Air Force." Ahneevah took the detonator from Zack and continued. "This wing would have been blown to dust, with not a shred of evidence remaining to indicate that any of the radioactive materials had been removed. Geiger counter readings would have given the impression that the elements in question were destroyed, leaving no more than a residual trace of radioactivity. Najar would be free to use the stolen nuclear resources in those yellow containers to build a full-sized dirty bomb for his next phase of chaos and murder. "These beings are as evil as any I ever faced in my world."

Agent Reese was not about to let that remark slide by. "*Your* world? Exactly what are we talking about here?"

"I'm sorry, but we have no time to get into that now,"

Ahneevah said as she glided over to area on the floor where Mohammed Najar and his five underlings were sitting. Najar was still feeling the after-effects of his *heavenly* experience. Ahneevah effortlessly lifted him to his feet. "He is the leader of this group."

Leslee couldn't help but noticing the uncharacteristic expression on the terrorist's face. "A smiling defeated terrorist? That's new."

"Weird. What the devil did you do to him?" Zack asked.

Ahneevah's face melted into an uncharacteristic and very mischievous expression. "What I did to him had nothing to do with the Devil at all ... quite the opposite. Actually, he was in *heaven*. I introduced him to the practical application of a concept you had here in the sixties ... *make love, not war*. I'll explain later," she informed the others over their puzzled looks. "I can't wait," Zack said as Ahneevah turned to the FBI agents. "I also *gently* assisted him in finding a change of outlook. He knows the location of every cell in his network and will now be willing to share that information. Some of those in the other cells have knowledge of even more units." She directed the subdued terrorist toward Reese and Reed and continued. "If you act fast, you can begin a purge that may ultimately lead to the dismantling and defeat of worldwide terrorist operations."

Najar began to spit out a deluge of Iraqi Arabic. Ahneevah stopped him—in Iraqi Arabic. Suddenly, Ahneevah's attention was drawn to the NLU. "There is a new immediate concern," the logic unit voice announced. Ahneevah hesitated briefly to absorb the digital information then glanced at Zack and Leslee. "Our Nine photonic friends are requesting our presence. Inspector Reed, we unfortunately cannot remain here any longer. You'll find four of the missing six members of the raiding force on the north side of the maintenance building. They are lying unconscious, but otherwise uninjured. The last two are up on the roof with the captured helicopter pilot. We must go now."

Reed quickly pulled out his card and handed it to Leslee. "I'm available 24/7. Anything you want." As the three turned to leave, Agent Reese added, "How can we reach you?"

Ahneevah glanced at Leslee who smiled back at her to let her know she got the message. Leslee took her section of the logic unit out of her pocket and handed it to Agent Reese, who hefted the weightless item, turned it over several times to inspect it and shrugged her shoulders. "I don't understand. What do I do?"

"It's a Neuronal Logic Unit, NLU for short. Hold it between the thumb and forefinger of both hands, give it a second or so to scan you, and then ask any question in any language," Leslee said and then pointed to the flat rectangular device. "I know it doesn't look like much but trust me … it's mind-blowing."

"You got that right," Zack added, "it's like an iPhone … on steroids." The three rushed out the door, then Leslee looked back and shouted, "We'll be in touch … and good hunting."

"Okay," said Reed as he handcuffed the terrorist leader, with grim satisfaction. "Now we know where to start."

Although Inspector Reed and Special Agent Reese were well trained in the art of stoicism, they had to take deep breaths when they got their first glimpse of the StarStream and then watched it silently rise, zoom away and disappear into the lightening sky. Reed looked at Reese, all business. "Not a word about this yet. We might have a credibility problem with the Director."

"Are you kidding? I have a credibility problem with it myself and I saw it!" Zoe replied.

"Let's see if this … NLU works as advertised so we can find out the locations of the other cells and perhaps really start winning the war on terror."

"Yes, sir, Inspector," Zoe said and held the logic unit as per

Leslee's instructions.

As they turned back toward the hospital, they didn't notice the broad smiles on each other's faces ... smiles of knowing.

Inspector Clayton Reed and Special Agent Zoe Reese stood at a podium in front of the University of New Mexico Medical Center. A crush of media was in attendance.

"They rigged an explosive device in the nuclear medicine laboratory and planned to detonate it right here." Reed announced. "Had they succeeded, the blast would have spread a virulent and highly aggressive strain of bio-toxins over hundreds and maybe even thousands of square miles. The samples are being analyzed but we believe their release would have precipitated a national public health disaster on the level of the Black Plague with a death toll reaching tens of millions."

When the reporters continued to press for information regarding exactly how the threat was dealt with, Agent Reese stepped to the podium. "For security purposes we can't reveal any of our newest tactics. Sorry, but you can understand that if we made those methods available to the press and they became general knowledge, then those with criminal intent might come up with counter measures. All we can tell you is that we had some highly advanced weaponry and some, uh, extremely proficient ... uhhh ... local assistance."

"Was that local assistance personnel from the Albuquerque Police or Sheriff's Department or the New Mexico State Police?" one of the members of the press corps hollered out.

Reed and Reese looked at each other. "Yes," Reed replied ambiguously, "but that's all the information we can share for the moment,"

"How was it that a terrorist cell of that size was able to avoid earlier detection?" Another correspondent shouted. "We are very interested in finding the answer to that question and have already undertaken an investigation into the matter. I assure you, when we know, you will know."

EPIƧODE TWENTY-ƧIX

"TIME BANDITS"

In his lab, Dax Wolf had already prepared a slide with Ahneevah's ...

... blood samples that he collected at the aircraft hangar. He also managed to cut a one-millimeter cross section of her unique strand of hair and was readying a second slide. Wolf placed the blood-slide on the view bay of the electron microscope, adjusted the LED screen, and raised the magnification: as the genetic material came into focus, his face took on an expression of disbelief, and then became more and more intense. He hurriedly switched to the hair-slide to confirm what he had been observing. His reaction was a rare experience for him: utter bewilderment.

"In the annals of all space and time, what in hell are you?"

A pall of smoke was still hanging in the air bearing the acrid odor of fried circuitry, and sparks continued to discharge intermittently from the main systems console and in the walls of high-tech electronic instrumentation throughout the Situation Room. The Communications Officer handed Mitchell a high-priority dispatch. The general quickly scanned it and shook his head.

"Mr. Vice President, it's from your people at the dig site in Kodiak. They're reporting that a little over three hours ago the entire excavation area disappeared."

Bixler's eyes goggled, "What do you mean, *disappeared*? How could millions of tons of earth just vanish?"

"It could vanish if it were never really there," Dax Wolf suggested as he stood in the doorway of the Sit-Room. The others shot puzzled looks at him. "You have to ask yourself," Wolf continued, "was it indeed *really there* as we understand *there*?"

Dax wheedled the communiqué out of the general's hand and skimmed it. "They say that the entire excavation area seemed to *dissolve* into the cavern … and when the dust settled they found the X2 at the bottom of the open pit, partially buried in a fine, gray, powdery substance." Then Wolf got bug-eyed. "Get this … chemical analysis showed that the residual dust contained excessive amounts of iridium. Iridium is comet stuff. There was no known comet or meteor impact in that area." He shook his head in disbelief and handed the message back to the general. "It's really bizarre."

"*That's* bizarre?" Bixler spat, checking his watch. "Kodiak is over three thousand miles from here. At full throttle the best the co-ax rotor bird can do is three hundred miles per hour. They would have had to be traveling at more than a thousand MPH to cover that distance in three hours."

"It didn't take them three hours," Mitchell responded, shaking his head. "According to this message, they were there over three hours *ago*."

"Impossible," the Vice President blared, "nothing can move that fast.

General Mitchell cleared his throat. "Begging your pardon sir, apparently *something* can."

Bixler glared at the general and growled, "If the X2 has in fact been there for three hours, what the hell took our people at Kodiak so long to report it?"

Mitchell glanced at the communiqué. "Apparently they had a complete power outage and it took time to get the auxiliary Nav-com network up and running."

Bixler's mind was reeling as he snatched the paper out of Mitchell's hand and studied it.

"It says here that the Sikorsky coaxial ship was undamaged and flyable. You," he said accusingly to the general, "reported a missile strike."

"Yes, sir … we had two confirmed hits."

Bixler peered at Barrgrave. His cock-sure attitude was starting to exhibit some cracks. Strident was giving way to subdued.

"General Mitchell," a Com Specialist broke in, "we've established direct contact with the Kodiak unit on one of the scrambled satellite frequencies."

A subdued voice came over the speaker: "General Mitchell, this is Lieutenant Skip Anthony."

"Roger, Lieutenant, the report we received said nothing about the spacecraft that was sealed in the glacier. Do you have any further information?"

"They think it … it flew away, sir," the Lieutenant responded.

"They think?" Mitchell said. "Didn't they see it fly away?"

"Negative," replied Anthony. "The field report says that the craft was frozen in the ice one minute and gone the next. It must have moved too fast for anyone to track with the naked eye. No one even saw it lift off. It just sort of …" they heard Lieutenant Anthony snap his fingers, "… disappeared."

"Nonsense," Bixler groused. "To do that it would have had to accelerate instantly to thousands of miles an hour."

"We don't have any machine that can do that," added Barrgrave.

"Someone evidently does," offered Dax Wolf in a measured tone, and for the first time in Albert Barrgrave II's adult life, a patina of fear became evident on his face. The sole surviving heir to an American dynasty was at last experiencing something to be afraid *of*. He could feel his scrotum sac tightening as if he had been suddenly dumped into a vat of ice water.

Bixler caught Barrgrave's chill of apprehension, and his heart began pounding in his ears like the thud of the bass notes on an over-stoked automobile woofer. "Albert, how far along is that Pulse Wave cannon project?"

Barrgrave had to think for a minute. "Wolf?"

"There's a working prototype mounted in the weapons bay of a specially modified B-2 Stealth Bomber, but there's a lot more here to consider. We are dealing with potential solid evidence that could shed light on some of the hypotheses advanced by the greatest minds in physics. A billion-year-old alien corpse has risen from the dead and taken off with two humans in a prototype chopper. Then the bird winds up over three-thousand miles away in a matter of minutes, maybe even seconds, and they could be, at this very moment, tooling around in a billion-year-old spacecraft that moves faster than the human eye can see. It brings up the intriguing prospect that they've found some means of traveling inter-dimensionally ... outside our temporal envelope. Incredible! The theories of Einstein, Schrödinger and Hawking, which seemed far beyond our current realities, are now moving at light speed toward the possible ... maybe even the probable."

Bixler and Barrgrave paused to digest Dax Wolf's words, which continued to remain suspended forebodingly in the air. It occurred to them that they were now facing a problem they couldn't simply squash under their thumb. Finally, Bixler spoke. "Albert, we could be stomping around in deeper shit than we ever imagined. Dr. Wolf, you'd better get on those blood samples and find something extraordinary."

"I already have," Dax replied. "I mean something that can help us fight the alien," Bixler rattled. "For Christ sakes, we're going to need it."

EPIƧODE TWENTY-ƧEVEN

"REPORT ON PLANET THREE"

"*We were alerted when the current configuration detonated its first nuclear device and ...*

... entered its Atomic Age in your year of 1945," the Custodian Lead Entity explained to Zack, Leslee and Ahneevah as they all stood somewhere between coterminous realities. "However, we are not here now due to the imminent dangers of nuclear, biological or weapons of mass destruction of any kind. We have come because the current Configuration is both suffocating and bleeding the planet to death. The Brazilian rain forest is this body's heart and lungs. Aside from being a haven for fifty percent of all living species on this world, it serves as a global ventilator and air conditioner, constantly moving the weather and the air. The influence of its demise on the Earth's environment is critical. It affects everything from fresh water to food to oxygen production on an overwhelming scale. At a given juncture in the very near future there will be a tipping point and the remaining southern hemispherical rain forest will not be able to sustain itself. Also, the atmospheric saturation of greenhouse gasses due to the burning of fossil fuels is causing an unabated meltdown of the Arctic and Antarctic ice caps. Without the vast expanses of North and South Polar snow, the sunlight can no longer be reflected back into space, thus exacerbating the climate change problem.

"Fucking big oil," Zack snarled.

"That is not an appropriate word," Ahneevah advised softly and the Custodian went on.

"The grievous paradox is that had this civilization decided to urgently pursue the development of manned space travel, the danger would have become evident on the first trip to your fourth planet, strangely named for one of your icons of war, and the 29th Configuration could have been saved. Your destiny was to reach the planet ... Mars, successfully terra-form it so it would support your life-mode, and then continue moving outward to the stars. But that is not to be. Of the previous 28 incarnations of civilizations this world has had, the 18 that developed advanced technologies destroyed themselves and only a fraction of those were able to reach the Moon. The first configuration never even made it past their hunter-gatherer phase before they annihilated each other. The rest were ended by random extraterrestrial and planetary misfortune ... asteroid and meteor strikes, gamma ray bursts, severe coronal activity and two mega-volcanoes. This 29th Configuration is lurching toward the same destiny as the preceding twenty-eight and is almost unalterably close to its doom point. But this is the first sentient civilization to kill its ecosystem before a thermonuclear war or other more natural global ending events could take place."

"Great," Leslee interjected. "The 28th picked door number one and the 29th picked door number two." Ahneevah bowed her head. "Ending all life through conflict or wrecking the place where you live are both equally insane," she declared.

"You got that right," Zack added. "You don't shit where you eat." Leslee reacted by rolling her eyes and punching Zack in the arm. "Ouch," Zack spit out. "Okay, it may be a bit crass but it's still the fu... freakin' truth."

The Custodian Lead Entity drifted over Ahneevah. "A billion years in the past we were also here to monitor your configuration's pending destruction. But the ebb and flow of space and time also afforded us the opportunity of bearing witness to your uncommon bravery and considerable abilities. We observed as you intercepted and destroyed the two comets that would have struck the near satellite, causing it to de-orbit and collide with this world. The obvious result would have been total obliteration of all life contained on both bodies. However, you could not have known at that time exactly how significant your action was ... that it precluded an even greater universal catastrophe."

A puzzled look swept across Ahneevah's face. "What could be worse than the end of all living things?"

"Though the severe angle of the collision would have been indeed catastrophic," the ethereal figure continued, "through natural celestial mechanics a large section of the main body would have been spun out into space and a new moon would have been formed with approximately the same mass and properties and exerting the same influences as the original lunar body."

"Just like Theia did for our Earth somewhere around forty-five million years after the formation of the solar system," Leslee interjected. "It was struck by another planetesimal that the scientific community calls Theia. It was about the size of Mars ... I learned that on the Science Channel ... but based on new information," Leslee threw a quizzical look at the Custodian, "their timeframe may be erroneous."

"Actually the figure is reasonably accurate," the Custodian replied. "However, Theia's contact was more of a glancing blow than a direct hit, but nonetheless it succeeded in throwing enough material into orbit to form the young, proto-planet's moon."

"But that suggests that intelligent life would have re-emerged in any case, so what difference did my mission really make in the overall scheme of things?" Ahneevah asked.

"The comet's force would have generated massive electric storms, mega-tsunamis and rampant moonquakes," the Lead Entity advised. "These disturbances would have unquestionably triggered widespread power outages which in turn would have caused fissures in the electromagnetic buffer fields surrounding the massive arsenals of antiparticle weapons in the storage depots concealed beneath the Terran and Luna surfaces."

Ahneevah was stunned by this information. "We did develop passive-antihydrogen triggers for the fusion-pod warheads, and there were rumors about the development of positron and antiproton military hardware, but the leadership never would admit its existence. Stockpiling antimatter arms was banned by treaty—worldwide."

"Nevertheless, the treaty was violated even before it was ratified," the Lead Custodian responded. "Fully active antihydrogen missiles were being surreptitiously developed, manufactured and placed in multiple holding facilities where any breach in the electromagnetic buffer fields would have allowed the excessive amounts of antimatter contained in the warheads to be exposed to the surrounding normal matter. As a direct consequence, particle/antiparticle annihilation would have occurred on a stellar scale and in the fraction of time that it took for the Big Bang to occur, Lano Pahntri, its moon, and the entire surrounding solar system would have become immense, heliospheric *puffs of light*— then dust. However, most fortunately, before the final war, the scientists from the opposing forces recognized the inherent threat of particle annihilation. They somehow convinced the leadership that as a tactical measure they must store the armaments in deep underground bunkers to protect the antimatter weaponry, its shielding and the power sources for the buffer fields from being compromised. In the end, when we nulled the 28th Configuration, all existing positron and antiproton particles were neutralized as well."

Zack spoke ahead of the curve. "Incredible. If this planet got blown to pieces then there would have been no 29th Configuration … no planet *Earth* at all, and no Sol-3 system."

"Ahneevah, you saved our entire solar system including the Sun," Leslee said.

Ahneevah's saucer eyes paled to a very light green and she turned, closed her eyes and nodded to the Lead Entity and then to Zack and Leslee. "So you do not have the power to create new celestial bodies," she said to the Custodian.

"We do not," the Custodian responded. "Those are random actions of the continuum and the temporal stream. We are restricted to setting certain conditions. The probability of the reoccurrence of the circumstances that made this world … so … special is far too remote to calculate. This Universe would most surely collapse once more into a singularity before that came to pass again." The enigmatic consciousness glided up to Ahneevah. "So you see, in giving your Configuration an undeserved and regrettably unredeemed second chance, you were also responsible for the continued existence of this unique physical world. Thanks to your supreme heroism you have enhanced the possibility of a positive outcome for extended universal intelligent life. However, we must warn you again that no previous civilization that has reached an advanced technological stage has been able to survive it. Ultimately, the discovery of nuclear, biological and chemical weaponry and the pollution that accompanies advanced societies ultimately took its toll on every avenue of intelligent life. Only the eighth, nineteenth, twenty-seventh and twenty-eighth Configurations were even able to reach and colonize the lunar sphere. Therefore, once we were alerted, we began to introduce a nulling process that would return this most extraordinary world back to its beginnings."

"But you're here on spec. We haven't actually exterminated ourselves … yet," Zack argued.

"You are close enough," the Lead Entity responded.

"Maybe you could take one more spin around the Galaxy?" Zack proposed.

The Custodian moved on. "We initiate the Null Quotient by the controlled introduction of Spectrons into the nuclei of all existing matter, altering the atomic structure. Once the procedure is completed, the evolutionary clock is set back to the *primordial slime* phase to set the stage for an entirely new manifestation of life to emerge."

The RPM of the legal wheels in Leslee's mind was revving up to flank speed. "If I were a higher form like you seem to be, I would think that after these untold billions of years you might be getting a bit weary of one after another up and out, up and out, up and out. I mean, how much of the constant negative repetition of history can any supreme being stand? Maybe in your heart of hearts … or whatever … you yourselves might have a desire to finally see a positive outcome. It's like when a crime suspect seems to purposely make a major blunder so that they will get caught … like … with all due respects … you did with Ahneevah and the StarStream. Tell me—was this the first time in all of your travels throughout time and the Universe that you made this kind of mistake?" They answered in the affirmative and then Leslee made the next jump. "Are you saying before your uhhh … miscalculation, no physical element from one Configuration has ever found its way into another? And in all the other countless worlds with intelligent life this is the first time that you missed something?" The Custodians regarded each other in thought and then the other *shoe* was slammed to the ground. For the first time the entire group of Nine spoke as one.

"No other planets in this *Era of the Stars* have ever produced sentient life with the high level of intelligence that developed here!"

Gasps! Even with all that had already transpired, Zack, Leslee and Ahneevah were totally rocked by this daunting revelation. Zack, dumfounded, drew closer to the Lead Custodian and spoke in a disbelieving whisper. "Are you saying that among all the unending billions and trillions of galaxies we... humankind... who... trudge along on this pale blue speck in an unimpressive galactic spiral backwater called the Milky Way, we are the best and the brightest? The exclusive example of intelligent beings in the entire vast ocean of known universes? No other cognitive aliens exist anywhere out there in the void?"

Leslee and Zack moved closer to each other as the astonishing answer was revealed by the Custodians. "We have roamed the cosmos for untold billions of your years. We have beheld giant gas planets with moons of acrid, steaming ammonia and unending rivers of molten lava. There are frozen, desolate, carbon dioxide worlds, arid, airless masses and bodies which inexplicably orbit their stars in the opposite direction from the star's spin. Throughout, we searched for any sign of imminent biologicality capable of advanced thought processes. The varying conditions do bring about unique molecular signatures of life. Most are the primitive microorganisms that exist and have existed throughout all the cosmos almost from the beginning. Other forms are present below the surface of frozen worlds and are contained in the exterior crust on rocky planets and within the pond scum on liquid worlds. Yes, it is life, but in further need of precise conditions to evolve and flourish into a more advanced state. There are fewer planetary bodies than you would suspect that demonstrate even the hint of a promise to generate any order of intelligent life at all within the next several billion years. To this point in almost all of time we have observed nothing on the more clement worlds that would allow us to conclude that there will ever be any species as advanced as the humanoids that evolved here over the past forty-billion years. Here on this third planet in a minor solar system within this *galactic backwater;* the planet now called Earth … an appropriate name. Thus, the answer to your question regarding your uniqueness in the entire known Universe is in the affirmative. Yes, you are all there is to offer in the dark void. Why else do you suppose we have judged Ahneevah's action in the past as a deed of such enormous magnitude?"

Leslee shook her head. "That's incomprehensible."

"We really are alone?" Zack muttered. "That would mean that all the UFO and alien crap is bullshi ... excuse me ... B-S-, after all. There were no flying saucers from outer space!"

"Your words are true but not entirely accurate," said the Custodian Lead Entity. "Those who have claimed to see those unidentified objects really did see them ... but they were not physically from outer space. They were holographic visual outputs emitted by trillions of organic and non-organic sources from various earlier configurations that had developed those exotic machines. Radio waves that due to anomalies in the Universal fiber were reflected back to their original source ... here, on this body."

Zack was about to burst. "Holy crap ... like you said ... I think. All that thought energy forever remaining intact in the continuum and returning as digital flashbacks. You've just explained the creation of half the shows on cable TV; the ancient cave drawings and carvings of helmeted spacemen and winged aircraft and the flying saucer mania; ghost sightings; ESP; visions of the future and everything else in the supernatural genre. Perhaps even the remarkable insights present in the futuristic visions of Jules Verne, H.G. Wells and Gene Roddenberry. Ha! They're all playbacks of brainwave and radio transmissions still swirling in the air. No less amazing but it seems impossible to me that out of the googolplex of stars and galaxies there are no other planets that have developed intelligent life forms."

"You must understand," the Custodian replied, "though it is true that all the basic ingredients for analytic existence ... thought and such ... are present throughout the Universe, the exact conditions that nurtured the evolution of your level of intelligent life are a miraculous confluence of coincidences that occurred only here in this galactic backwater. Take into account how the ever-fiery furnace within the bowels of this amazing chunk of spinning rock supports the generation of gravity and radiates heat to the surface. Then there is the fact that as an inner planet, Earth, to a great degree, has been shielded by the outer gas giant worlds from a constant bombardment of asteroids and comets."

"There ya go," Zack said. "It's location, location, location."

Also, consider this planet's proximity to its perfectly-sized central star. If your star were larger or smaller or Earth's distance from it were lesser or greater, this body would not sustain your particular niche of life."

"That's right ... *the Sun*. It should have run out of fuel long ago. How come it's still burning? It's only supposed to spend 10 billion years as a main sequence star then become a red giant and incinerate the rest of the solar system including Earth. Eventually, it will eject its outer layers leaving only a hot stellar core to cool and fade as a white dwarf."

"Impressive," Ahneevah said, and gave a slight nod of approval to Zack.

"But at the age of 39 billion," Zack offered, "what is the explanation for good old Sol living thirty-billion years beyond its expected lifespan?"

"Good observation," the Custodian said. "It's a matter of elementary particle physics. Every nine-billion years or so ... utilizing ambient celestial radiation, we have the capability of Spectronically transfusing liquid hydrogen fuel elements into the solar core where your sun ... *the Sun's* energy-producing nuclear fusion process takes place."

"You can do that? Wow, talk about your mid-flight refueling," Zack uttered in a restrained voice.

"We chose to do so because of this world's matchlessness within the space-time continuum. Its molten core which provides gravity and radiates heat: its distance from a medium sized star, the Sun, and its protected location and finally the formation of the Moon which exercised regulation over the tides and the oceans on the post-collision body. These factors shaped the destiny for the eventual inhabitants of this world to become citizens of the Universe if they could ever learn to rise above their deficiencies."

This awesome reality hit Ahneevah, Leslee and Zack like an ocean wave knocking them down, taking their breath away and rolling and twisting them violently around. But waves subside and after a few moments Zack, the man of science, gathered his thoughts.

"So you Nine are responsible for keeping the Sun fueled up, and Ahneevah's bravery and resourcefulness preserved the hope of the spread of intelligent life. Then why not, out of respect for her bravery ... and in consideration of your own actions ... why not grant us a reprieve?" Zack proposed. "Without her actions and your intervention, this planet would be gone and the development of virtually all intelligent life in the Universe would have hit a brick wall. Since, by your own acknowledgment, our Earth is so unique, there's no telling how long it would have taken, if ever, for another world like it to come into existence. With nothing in the wings to take *ole' blue and green's* place, the Universe would have no other rock capable of developing a new crop of sentient beings. Therefore, I have to ask … if there were no thinking creatures to contemplate it, would the Universe be here at all?" Zack opened his mouth to put his next thought into words, but the encounter with the Custodians had already ended. Ahneevah's section of the NLU began to chirp, and a missile hurtled past them and exploded. The three had been transported back to the StarStream, and were now taking fire.

Ahneevah quickly removed the logic unit from the compart-ment in her sleeve and slipped into its armrest interface slot. "Evasive maneuvers," she said calmly. "Close your eyes, Zack."

EPISODE TWENTY-EIGHT

THE STARSTREAM
IN
"FANTASTIC VOYAGE"

"They're shooting at us," an agitated Zack blurted out ...

... as the StarStream, appearing to move faster than time, veered ninety degrees to port enabling it to evade a Sparrow air-to-air missile fired by an F-15 Strike Eagle.

Ahneevah glanced at the instrument panel. "Our nine new friends have sent us back to the chase in the Arizona desert."

Leslee checked her pocket. "I don't think so. I don't have the NLU section you gave me, which means that our bout at the hospital actually happened. This must be a new chase."

Zack was trying to wrap his mind around something but it was like a sneeze that couldn't quite make it all the way out of the nose. "Was that all of it? I'm almost certain I remember more."

"Not now," Ahneevah stressed. "Leslee is correct. We must finish this later. There are new and urgent priorities."

"How the hell can a private mercenary army get high-level military jets and advanced weapons systems?" Leslee pondered out loud.

"I don't think that we've encountered a private army at all," Zack added. "I'd bet anything that we are dealing with covertly detached U.S. Forces."

"Detached from where and by whom?" Leslee asked as another missile zoomed by.

"Not a clue, but just the same, the sons of bitches are trying their best to kill us," Zack grumbled.

"The StarStream knows. It will not be struck by those projectiles," Ahneevah calmly said.

Leslee wrinkled her brow. "Why doesn't the StarStream … uhh … shoot back?"

Ahneevah replied to Leslee on one conscious level while navigating and acquiring the strategic positions of the various enemy air combat assets on others.

"They are your own people … and the countermeasures inherent in the StarStream are not primarily defensive. They are ingrained to be predominantly offensive."

"Like they say," Zack offered, "The best defense is a good offense."

Ahneevah nodded in agreement. "The super-ionized residue from the StarStream's power core is redirected through bio-cybric plasma ejectors which condense it into waves that neutralize any attacking component whether particle rays, bullets, cannon shells or computer-guided missiles."

"Way to go, StarStream!" Leslee cheered.

"However," Ahneevah continued, "Special tracer frequencies embedded in the ion-ripple will seek the aerodynamic trail of the incoming ordinance through the displaced air molecules in its wake. If magno-plasmic pulse waves are detected, elementary particle tracking rays will use the specific alignments of the subatomic particles to locate the initial firing source. Either way, the unit of aggression will be incinerated."

"The same as Kung Fu," Leslee said. "Use their force against them."

It would have been that easy. Ahneevah could have simply turned the StarStream loose and exterminated all of them in a human heartbeat if she wanted to. The Apache, Blackhawk and Cobra choppers, the F-15 Eagle fighter jets and the C130J Hercules, all of them blown to pieces, every living soul in the hostile craft—dead, including the passenger in the Herk's jump seat, Dax Wolf. However, Ahneevah had seen enough death and destruction to last her—more than a billion years.

"I cannot allow the StarStream to proceed unchecked. Its auto-defense systems will annihilate every aggressor. This act is against my precepts. I will not unnecessarily risk the safety of those who represent no real threat. The armaments on the hostile air vehicles are of limited performance and cannot harm us." As if to demonstrate Ahneevah's point, another Sparrow missile exploded near the StarStream with no apparent physical effect.

"I'm surprised that the 28th Configuration didn't survive. You had the right idea," Leslee said.

"Yes, but we abandoned it," Ahneevah responded, her words shaded with palpable anger, an emotion that Zack and Leslee had yet to see in her. "We could have chosen a different path, but we were ordered to resort to our enemies' tactics. We had to kill because over half of our population believed and followed the lies of an inept and arrogant leadership. Those in power wanted to conduct everything their way without regard for other ways, and sadly, too few of our population had the courage to speak out, and far too many were deceived and mindlessly accepted the faulty leadership's deeply flawed views."

"There ya go! Once again, the divisive, intolerant, moron majority with their ultimate pissing contest," Zack bristled. "They'll do it every time ..."

"A dose of live and let live might have been in order," Leslee reasoned.

"Yeah, just like us," Zack added, cynically.

Ahneevah nodded her head wistfully. "Even I, myself, knowing what I knew, made the mistake of choosing duty before honor. Our world was left with no higher example to follow, no one in authority who ever said words like your former Senator John McCain." The NLU generated a hologram of these words:

"The enemy we fight has no respect for human rights or human life. They don't deserve our sympathy. But this is not about who they are. It is about who we are."

"I think that comes under the *do as I say, not as I do,* caveat," Leslee responded.

Ahneevah shook her head. "It does not matter," she said. "The words themselves stand on their own, even if the person who said them failed for political purposes to live up to them."

The 28th Configuration supreme aviator was about to show her pursuers exactly who she was. Instead of completely annihilating the opposing forces, she decided to hold a seminar on sky-tech and aerial aggression flight techniques.

"I must change the StarStream's mind-set." In a nano-tic, Ahneevah telepathically initiated the manual-override procedure for the craft's auto-flight system. "I am synchronizing one of my neural streams with the tactical and navigation elements of the logic unit." Almost simultaneously, a set of manual *stick and throttle* controls bloomed out of the console.

"Elementary," Zack proudly said.

Ahneevah grabbed the stick and slammed the throttle full forward.

The other aircraft commanders could only gawk as the *bogey* wove in and out of their formations and gun sights at will and actually out-flew the ordnance launched against it. The 30mm penetrator depleted uranium Gattling shells and 30mm DU cannon fire from the C130 traveled in slow motion compared to the StarStream. All the air-to-air smart missiles suddenly developed major *brain cell* drippage. Strategically, the helicopters were the easiest to deal with. "The way these machines operate, it's amazing that they don't tear themselves apart by their own actions," Ahneevah remarked. "With technology like this, it's a wonder that you ever landed on the Moon? Neil Armstrong and the other astronauts who were chosen to undertake those journeys must have been exceptionally brave."

Even as Ahneevah spoke she was positioning the StarStream inches above the *whooshing* rotors of the lead whirlybird. Imperceptibly the radionic variants within the structure of the StarStream began to ionize the air above and around the Apache's whizzing blades. This action interrupted the electron flow that powered the helicopter's engines.

The StarStream then darted away and the pilot of another chopper reported the teardrop craft's abrupt maneuver.

"Red Charlie One, this is Red Charlie Two. Looks like our bogey disengaged."

"Red Charlie Two, Red Charlie One, disengaged? Maybe, but I've been shut down … flame outs on both turbines and total navigation and tactical electric systems failure. All I've got is the backup com circuit. Switching manually to auto-rotation mode and heading for the deck."

Inside the other choppers, the mystified pilots were also forced to instantly shift over to the flight system's emergency auto-rotation mode, an operating condition that permitted the rotors to spin freely and generate enough lift to allow for a controlled descent. Once on the ground, without electric power, they were unable to lift off again.

Negating the fighter jets was more of a challenge. Out of the box, Ahneevah swiftly jammed the F-15s' avionics and target acquisition radar. She knew that by their design these flying machines could not hover or descend vertically under control. They needed long strips to land on. Her firepower could destroy them completely and not allow them time enough to employ their primitive and dangerous ejection systems.

"If I decoy them into chasing us, it will lead them out of their normal flight envelopes and into catastrophic structural failure. This would most likely result in all the pilots' deaths."

Ahneevah decided that the simplest way to handle them was to shut their power plants down by fusing the fuel nozzles in their Pratt and Whitney engines. This caused the jets to flame out. Since the electric currents were unimpeded, the F-15 Eagles' onboard computers continued to operate the fly-by-wire system and allowed the pilots to maintain normal control. With this action taken, the 28th Configuration ace reversed the procedure which restricted the build-up of air molecules, causing them to form and coalesce on the trailing edge of the StarStream. This in turn provided the necessary lift to keep the F-15 aircraft aloft long enough for the *teardrop* to *tow* them back to the base.

The commander in the C-130J Herk executed the wisest maneuver of all. He made a one-eighty-degree turn and got the hell out of there, happy to make a landing under his own power.

All the while, Dax Wolf was furiously making notes on his hand-held, voice-responsive computer link. "The green-eyed space woman could have easily wiped out all of us, but she didn't … useful."

The C-130 returned to the base and the aircraft commander along with Dax Wolf reported to Bixler and Barrgrave. "The entire battle group was neutralized … our ordinance was no match for that *little rocket* and its pilot," the Hercules aircraft commander spat out. "There is nothing it can't do. Every move it made seemed to defy another law of physics. By comparison, our so-called high-tech weaponry is Wiley Coyote Acme cartoon crap and she's the Roadrunner."

The VP and the mogul would hear none of it. After all, Barrgrave manufactured most of that *Acme cartoon crap* and Bixler influenced the military to purchase it.

However, when Dax Wolf confirmed the C-130 commander's

observations, Bixler and Barrgrave began to experience a reality check—a wake up call that came home full force when they saw the StarStream circling overhead at ten-thousand feet. It was being trailed by a flock of flamed-out F-15s, which began to descend one-at-a-time in lazy spirals. With the completion of each circuit, another F-15 broke off and proceeded to glide gently in to a safe *dead stick* landing.

"How the hell are we supposed to kill that?" The Herk commander said in frustration.

A puffed-up Bixler shot Dax Wolf a penetrating glance. "Wolf."

EPISODE TWENTY-NINE

THE VICE PRESIDENT AND THE MOGUL
IN
"ORPHANS OF THE SKY"

As Ahneevah approached the base, the defenses let loose with a massive barrage of …

… surface-to-air Patriot V's against the StarStream. She evaded them by performing sharp ninety-degree maneuvers in all three dimensions—moves she used to practice a world ago in her sleep. While Ahneevah was tending to the armaments being hurled against her, she noticed some data on her panel which indicated that one of the Humvees was unoccupied. She fired a low-power, sub-particle ionizer at the vehicle and it instantly transitioned through the states of matter, from solid to liquid to gas, and was literally blown away.

Zack and Leslee began to applaud but the NLU voice interrupted them. "Scanning detects a fluctuating propulsion flare in a Patriot missile; target bearing zero nine six mark elevation nine hundred meters. Self destruct command inoperative and the over-temp status will reach burn-through in onboard power train in two, one, now."

The Patriot V rocket's aft section suddenly became engulfed in flames and the missile plunged earthward out of control toward the Central Command Bunker from where Barrgrave and Bixler were directing the attack.

As the out-of-control bird plummeted down, the Centcom crew began to disperse amid the shattering bleats of the emergency warning system. Barrgrave, Dax Wolf and Bixler raced for the exits as well.

Ahneevah determined that none of those trying to escape the danger had enough time to succeed. Always true to herself, she positioned the StarStream in a hover between the front of the command bunker and the errant Patriot V.

Zack picked up on this move. "You're in the runaway's precise track."

"I've established an intercept," Ahneevah said coolly.

"An intercept? You mean … you *want* to get hit? Why don't you just vaporize the thing?"

"The defense regime is one of the few functions of the StarStream that cannot be totally overridden. It has a mind of its own. When I disintegrated the Humvee it was a one-step attack and no further action by the StarStream was necessary.

"Got it, like a shark to blood," Leslee offered. "If you destroy the rogue missile, the StarStream's defensive system will automatically sense it, track the weapon back to its firing source and obliterate it."

"But its source is a mobile launch battery," Zack said.

Ahneevah shook her head. "Negative, Zack, that's the firing *point* and it would most certainly be destroyed, but the original source is where the initial command input occurred. In this case it was the main control room which would be obliterated and most, if not all of the personnel inside would be killed even though they are there through no real fault of their own. They are merely the victims of an incompetent, corrupt chain of command and should not die because of it."

"Boo-hoo," Zack sniffed. "They're still pretty serious about killing *us*. Who cares?"

"I do," Ahneevah countered in a more elevated volume than

usual. "Remember, it is about us, not them. The greatest error my people made was to sink to our enemy's level." Her gaze settled on him. "We must always be better. We must set an example. We must be true to what we say because if we are not, then like your Senator McCain, *my* words ... will remain just words and stand for nothing."

Ahneevah's selfless act resulted in the wayward rocket hitting the StarStream instead of the Centcom Bunker. Though the StarStream was rocked, it instantly began to absorb the energy of the explosion and the amazing air vehicle's biological components restored the titanium-silicon skin on the outer hull. The maneuver saved the structure and more importantly the lives of those inside or anywhere near it.

Suddenly, the craft was jolted by another powerful blast. This impact, however, was different from that of the Patriot missile. Ahneevah felt an immediate loss of control as warning lights and audio alarms flashed and blared. The StarStream crackled as millions of mini-lightning-bolts began skipping on its atomically-fused, organic outer fuselage. Then Ahneevah's multiple consciousness became aware of the presence of another aircraft. Again, because she had less than the full range of her mental facilities, she did not pick up the B-2 Stealth Bomber when it entered the conflict. Her cheeks paled slightly and as she scanned the instrument array, a look of concern appeared on her face. She immediately recognized the full extent of the jeopardy they now faced. In stopping the Patriot strike, Ahneevah had to keep the StarStream in one place. This provided the B-2 Spirit Aircraft Commander, Lieutenant Colonel Noah Jax, a brief window in which to track and lock onto the StarStream with the highly experimental, Dax Wolf-designed, Electro Magnetic Pulse cannon tucked into one of the flying wing's internal weapons bays.

"We've been hit by an EMP wave from that B-2 Spirit," Ahneevah said without modulating her voice. Her delivery made the current circumstance sound as if it were a minor inconvenience, which it definitely was not.

Leslee wasn't fooled. "That doesn't sound like such a good thing," she said with more than a small helping of anxiety.

Zack scratched his head, trying to understand. "I read that the military was investigating the pulse wave concept, but I had no idea they had reached a prototype phase."

"Apparently they have," Ahneevah said wryly.

"It must be one of those black projects. My tax dollars went to have that damn thing designed and built, and now it's being fired at *me*."

"I've encountered magno-plasmic pulse waves before," Ahneevah added, "but this technology is surprising. EMP waves reduced to a pinpoint laser-type beam. Your 29th Configuration research has somehow managed to solve the problems that our 28th Configuration science could not. It seems that your weaponry experts have discovered how to narrow a wide plasma wave down to the width of a micron to enable a neutronic concentration of force.

A bell rung in Zack's brainpan. "Don't let it bother you. The ancient Egyptians and Mayans were able to build pyramids before they invented the wheel."

"Yeah, and maybe the EMP technology came via a blast from the past," Leslee suggested. "You know, one of those leaps forward provided by thought waves perhaps left over by one of the other twenty-seven configurations."

Ahneevah then sensed a curious phenomenon. The bulk of her immense thought web registered a highly elevated bio-electronic output similar to one she had encountered after her awakening. She found it unnerving, perhaps even startling.

"No," Ahneevah said. "This is something ... someone who exists in the present time. I believe I encountered this manifestation before but was unable to analyze it. Now it's reading loud and clear." But before she could go on, the StarStream was rocked by another light-speed burst from the pulse-wave cannon. This blast provoked an aura of complete astonishment to sweep across Ahneevah's face. Since her science was never able to develop a concentrated EMP wave, she could not remotely imagine that the StarStream, being essentially biological, did have vulnerability in its exterior cell strata. It was susceptible to the EMP on a bio-mechanical level. The electrostatic charges in the pulse waves somehow opened fissures in the cellular membrane structure of the billions of micro-fusion reactors. The biologically engineered DNA plasma contained in the inner cell chamber bled out through the breach like a runny egg yolk. This in turn led to total nucleonic collapse.

"We've lost the fusion propulsion train," Ahneevah reported.

Leslee stiffened. "That doesn't sound like a positive development."

"Can't the StarStream compensate?" Zack asked.

"Negative." Most of Ahneevah's consciousness was now considering alternative actions. "The reactors have been neutralized. They are completely off-line, and at this low altitude there isn't ample time to recycle, regenerate and restart."

Like a giant raindrop, the stricken StarStream began to fall toward the desert floor. "We are stripped of power and there's no way to avoid the impending contact with the surface." With terra-firma rushing up at them, Ahneevah, showing no agitation, simply stated, "Time to eject."

"Eject? Abandon ship? How? I don't see any parachutes," Zack shouted.

"Trust me," Ahneevah replied softly as if she were referring to a day at the beach.

"Yes, trust her," Leslee echoed.

Zack relaxed a bit. "Okay, okay. I'm trusting, I'm trusting."

With the StarStream plummeting earthward, Ahneevah

removed the NLU from its slot, uttered a few unintelligible commands in her 28th Configuration tongue and slid the instrument back into the armrest.

An instant later the three were outside the StarStream and floating in—something, at an altitude somewhere around ten thousand feet. Zack studied the unusual conveyance, then clarity. "I'll be damned, a frozen-plasma bubble. How in the world can plasma be directed to flow spherically?"

"Under certain magnetic influences, plasma can be made to bend as desired," Ahneevah explained.

"Of course, just the same as light waves," Zack concluded. "This is not much different from the ride Glenda the Good Witch used to get around Oz," Leslee quipped, and Ahneevah nodded in agreement. Then Leslee reached for her iPhone. "Maybe I can contact Agent Reed."

"Good idea," Ahneevah said, "but not workable. The EMP wave most certainly drained your cell phone's battery and fried its circuits."

Leslee, Zack and Ahneevah watched as the StarStream erupted in a huge fireball on impact beneath them.

"We've just witnessed the world's future go up in flames," a deflated Zack moaned and then looked solemnly at Ahneevah. "What happened? I thought the StarStream knew everything."

Before Ahneevah could answer, Leslee jumped in.

"Zack, no entity knows everything. Not even the Spectron Custodian gang ... and they have *really* seen it all."

Back in the lab, the powerful photonic particle-laser was easily beginning to burn through the three-inch thick titanium plate as if it were an ant under a magnifying glass. Dax Wolf smiled to himself and made a few adjustments on his console.

Then once more the penetrating chill descended on Wolf and he winked out.

EPISODE THIRTY

CAPTIVITY
"THE CAVES OF STEEL"

The Flight Compartment Ejection Pod ...

... gently floated earthward. Powered by a neutrino-ion solar battery, the escape capsule was designed to bring the pilot and crew safely to the ground in an emergency situation. There was no manual override and its approach profile was similar to that of the six Apollo lunar modules as they prepared to touchdown on the surface of the moon. Ahneevah turned her attention to the military complex below, and though the sun was a barely visible reddish arc on the horizon, her long-range pupils could clearly pick up Mitchell's troops assembling in the vanishing twilight. The slow descent would give General Mitchell's patrols more than enough time to be there in force to *greet* their *soon-to-be* prisoners at their landing point. When the pod settled on the hot sand it dematerialized around Ahneevah, Zack and Leslee almost as the general himself strode up to *welcome* his three *fugitives* back into captivity.

Ahneevah moved forward and was about to swing into action when Mitchell motioned to several gargantuan members of the security team. They quickly moved in, secured Zack and Leslee and dragged them over to their commander. The general narrowed his eyes and stared icily at Ahneevah, then pulled his Beretta sidearm out of its holster and pressed the barrel hard against

Zack's head. Zack shut his eyes tightly preparing for the *big bang*.

"These two will survive only as long as you cooperate," the general barked, punctuating his warning with the intimidating *click* made by the M-9 automatic's hammer as it was *thumbed* back. Ahneevah gave a slight nod of her head and retreated a step. Then she became aware of a penetrating and unsettling conscious-ness in close proximity and her attention was pulled to a speeding Humvee bearing down on the crash site. As she watched the vehicle vault over the crest of a nearby sand dune, the nagging sensations she experienced during the EMP attack returned with greater ferocity. When the *Hummer* slid to a stop in front of General Mitchell and Dax Wolf got out, Ahneevah felt as if an arctic wind was permeating her entire being. Wolf, still trembling slightly, was wearing a heavy parka—in the desert. After receiving a few of looks of incredulity, he casually linked the cold weather gear to an experiment he was working on and, given his idiosyncratic behavior, his answer quelled any further attention.

"Put sentries around this site in four-hour shifts," Mitchell demanded of a bulky sergeant. "I want lights brought out here immediately so that we can commence a full investigation of the impact area. Dr. Wolf here will be in charge. Now take these prisoners to the brig until further notice. And I don't want there to be so much as a scratch on the … foreigner."

Mitchell ordered that the security crew wear non-conducting Butyl rubber elbow length gloves and Navy Seal neoprene wet suits to protect them from Ahneevah's electric sting. The general also instructed that the alien be put in a full chemical protection suit to keep her at bay and to neutralize any aggressive action on her part. To restrict her mobility, thick steel chains were wrapped around her legs and arms and secured with titanium alloy locks.

The three were brought to the detention center, which contained two sets of holding cells facing each other across a cracked, cement walkway about six feet wide. Ahneevah was gruffly dumped on the floor of one and Zack and Leslee were manhandled into the brig diagonally across from it. Being a relatively old military base, the confinement sections had vertical steel bars. The floors were cold, bare cement and though there were no chairs or cots, a television monitoring system was hurriedly rigged and activated. Mitchell wanted his prisoners' every action and every word observed and recorded.

Throughout the incarceration process, each time Dax Wolf began moving closer to Ahneevah, waves of chills began slicing through him and he therefore decided to keep his distance from this alien being. Although he knew full well he would have preferred to confront her, he needed to know more about the risk. He believed that anything he might salvage from the crash site of the remarkable aircraft could hold the key that would unlock the flood-tide of mystery surrounding this unique creature. Wolf quickly busied himself with the task of an initial forensic investigation of the impact area. He was stunned when he found no physical evidence of the flight vehicle whatsoever. His Geiger counter registered nothing more than nominal, ambient radiation. However, still sensing *something,* he began collecting soil and rock samples. After a satisfactory amount was gathered, Wolf rushed back to the lab eager to see if his efforts might yield something useful. Perhaps the full investigative team would do better in the daylight.

The Bureau higher-ups vigorously refused Inspector Reed's request to form and lead a strike component against the desert base. They insisted that the facility had been closed for years and that it was a waste of time. Of course, Clay Reed knew better, but he had no way of knowing that FBI Director Paul Runyon himself was a Bixler-Barrgrave confederate and even though Runyon was stymied as to precisely what charges he might bring against his two meddlesome and publicly acclaimed subordinates, both Reed and Reese were well aware that politically at the very least, their days at the Bureau were numbered. In response, they took on the task of covertly putting together a small force recruited from the growing list of other disenchanted and disillusioned operatives from Central Intelligence, National Security and the FBI.

In the middle of the night, one of Reed's contacts at the CIA informed him that Bixler had been picked up at a private airfield in Maryland and was en route to an undisclosed location in the Arizona desert.

With the sun's first smattering of light, Dax Wolf's main recovery unit arrived at the location where the StarStream went down. They painstakingly searched the cordoned-off area, but like Wolf, were unable to find a single solid fragment of the mind-boggling craft. It was almost as if the bird dematerialized rather than crashed and burned.

Bixler and Barrgrave were watching the live video feed from the crash site on one of the row of television monitors inside the main security room. Barrgrave fired first.

"Wade, what were you thinking when you brought in that goddamn pulse wave? Can you imagine the incredible power and control that the technological breakthroughs inherent in that spaceship might have brought us? Now all we have to reverse-engineer is a pile of sand?"

"How the hell could I know that the EMP wave would obliterate the infernal thing?" Bixler steamed. "It looked as if there was nothing that could destroy it."

"At least we still have the alien, but you'd better make sure no harm comes to her," Barrgrave demanded. "She has too much to offer."

"For right now," Bixler said.

"What about the archeologist and the lawyer?"

The VP put the spread fingers of his hands together. "I don't care what you do, short of killing them. As long as they remain alive, we can use them to keep the space-woman under control and possibly convince her to ... cooperate with us." Suddenly the lights began to flicker.

Dax Wolf was running his mini-particle acceleration unit at full capacity. He was using an enormous amount of energy. He had to. Wolf was driven and absolutely certain that an undiscovered paradigm was within his reach. The power of the stars was about to stretch out before him. But even *he* was filled with great humility when the first analysis was complete and he saw the results.

A sly smile crept slowly onto his face, and he began to laugh uncontrollably. He realized that he would now see the dynamics of the Universe and all that was part of it in a completely new light.

EPISODE THIRTY-ONE

"THE FLY"

Several of the bank of video screens on the wall of the base main security room displayed views of the three detainees ...

... imprisoned in the confinement center lock-up. Leslee was curled in a fetal position leaning against the wall near the bars; her arms wrapped around her legs and her hands clasped in front of her knees. She was rocking slightly and gazing intently at Ahneevah, who was stretched out prone on the concrete floor of her cell on the opposite side of the containment area. Zack ... being Zack, was pacing like the caged animal he indeed was. Ahneevah was still bound in chains and wearing a chemical protection suit and hood. Her visage, which was visible through a double-layered face shield, projected a serene *dreamland* expression.

"Look at her." Zack indicated Ahneevah and then turned his palms up in frustration. "It's been almost two hours. How can she sleep so peacefully at a time like this?"

Leslee took on a reflective air, nodded her head and stopped rocking. "Well ... let's reconsider what happened to her between yesterday and today," she posited, then half-smiled, unlocked her fingers and waved her right hand toward Ahneevah with a *there she is* motion. "For openers, she saw her world destroyed, lost everything and everyone she knew and loved, yet still did all that was human-oidly possible to forestall her own inevitable end.

Then, after being *basically* dead for almost a billion years, came back to life again on an alien world … so to speak. Since her awakening, in just the past few hours … she fought her way out of captivity, made some new friends, took a bullet to the heart, was *Spectroned* away by nine super beings that travel the *universes* at the speed of light and call for timeouts that are really *time*-outs. Next, there was another round of hand-to-hand fighting, followed by air-to-air combat which resulted in the complete loss of her aircraft. Finally … she was recaptured and wound up behind bars," Leslee again indicated Ahneevah and continued, "dressed in that second-hand, ventilated, pus-yellow, what-not-to-wear Hazmat suit. Maybe she's sleeping because she needs the rest."

Zack stopped, turned and looked down at Leslee. "Okay, Rosy. But I don't understand why she didn't paralyze the military people here like she did the terrorists at the hospital. She could have just stopped all of their hearts … permanently."

Ahneevah opened her verdant eyes. "It was not possible. I cannot achieve that kind of broad-range effect without the aid of the StarStream, and, more importantly, deadly force would have been inappropriate," Zack heard her say in a surprisingly unimpeded tone.

"I thought you were asleep."

"Not all of me, Zack. Several of my neural pathways remain awake while the rest are in a REM state."

"I'll try to remember that." Leslee said, and then jumped to her feet. "Wait a second. How come we can hear you so clearly through that hood? Why doesn't your voice sound muffled? Is it like mental telepathy … woo-woo stuff?"

"Similar, but I assure you it's not woo-woo stuff," Ahneevah responded, "not at all. The process is grounded squarely in physical science. In ordinary *analog* speech, vocal impulses vibrate the surrounding air molecules and create sound patterns that the auditory system picks up and sends to the brain for interpretation. However, because we also *think* the words as we speak them; our left cerebral hemisphere simultaneously broadcasts those thoughts as a series of short-duration digital transmissions."

Surprises had become so commonplace that Leslee simply exhaled slowly and softly breathed out a question. "Are you saying that what we're hearing is being received directly by *our* brains like my iPhone receives wireless transmissions?"

"Yes," Ahneevah replied, "it occurs as long as we are all on the same wavelength. It's due to spectrum-frequency-hopping discovered here by your beautiful, brilliant and famous actress, Hedy Lamarr. Just as your iPhone constantly seeks a clear channel to enable it to send or receive information without interference from thousands of other cell phones, your brain scans for, locates and automatically locks on to my particular broadcast frequency."

Zack slapped his hand on his forehead. "Wow, I didn't know we could do that."

"Neither did I," Ahneevah said offhandedly.

"So how *did* we do it? I mean I wasn't exactly thinking about tuning you in."

"I'm not quite sure. It could be that *my* signals are somehow seeking your wave lengths."

"Go know … we've got our own wireless network," Leslee said.

"That's right. You see, in the 28th Configuration we were able to hear each other even when there was excessive background noise and especially if someone had auditory network damage," Ahneevah explained. "But even though we always heard each other it didn't follow that we always *listened* to each other."

Leslee opened her mouth to continue when she suddenly spotted something at Zack's mid section. She quickly stood up and placed herself in front of Zack to serve as a shield from the peering lenses of the security cameras.

"Don't look now Zack, but I think that Tinkerbelle just arrived," Leslee whispered. "And she's going right for your belt … the little slut."

Zack glimpsed down and saw a faint, pinkish glow and threadlike shafts leaping out from behind his pewter *"Dig it!"* belt buckle.

"I almost forgot. I've been carrying this thing around since the first flood in the Kodiak cavern."

One of the rosy veins zigzagged like a lightning bolt from the buckle directly into the lenses of the obtrusive video cameras. Simultaneously, in the Security Center, the images on the wall of monitors rolled for a second and then stabilized. The subtlety was lost on the guards in the room. They never knew that every pixel contained in the video of the pinkish mini-lightning had been instantly altered to blend in with the background. Nothing seemed wrong.

Then the belt buckle began to hum softly and vibrate. This prompted Zack to immediately turn away from the television camera. He opened the front of the buckle and hidden in a small circular compartment beneath the *Archeology<>Dig It!* inscription was the silver dollar-sized object that Zack originally found near the StarStream. He removed it, and the device sent a rainbow of light to the lenses of all the mini surveillance cameras. Ahneevah's eyes now began to sparkle behind the face plate of the radiation-proof hood.

In the Security Center, the audio from the observation system in the brig became intermittent and scratchy and the video started to break up and waver. When the guard attempted to make some adjustments the sound and pictures settled down and the screen showed everything in the detention area to be status quo, but that's only what it *showed.*

Ahneevah, wrapped in chains, stood up and shuffled her way over to the door of her cell. "I can't believe it, the P-E-T. I ejected it into the holocaust near the end and thought it was lost forever. I forgot all about it and never even thought to ask you."

Zack threw a puzzled look at Ahneevah. "You forgot to ask me? You mean there was no memory of this ... P-E-T on any of those unlimited thought trails you have?"

"Well actually there might have been but you know ... uhhh," Ahneevah exhaled. "Yes ... I believe I forgot. But what would be the chances that you would find the NLU component ... and the P-E-T? The odds are incalculable."

Zack shook his head ironically and then his lips formed a very slight smile. "The odds on everything since Kodiak Island have been incalculable and ... what's a P-E ...?"

As he was asking the question, Zack was interrupted by something that zipped by his ear. He tried to squash it by clapping his hands together. "Damn mosquito."

"Don't hurt it. It may have friends," Ahneevah cautioned. "Isaac, I'm curious. What made you think to keep the PET with you?"

"PET?"

Ahneevah pointed at the circular instrument, "Photonic Emergency Transducer ... P-E-T."

Zack made a subtle motion indicating the quartet of spying video eyes. "Are you sure we should be talking about this?"

"No problem. Our words are being altered as we speak them and those watching us think everything is as it was before the PET reactivated. Now ... how did you know that the PET was important?"

Zack held up the device. "It was my find, uh, like you. And any find should be protected and preserved as if it were the Rosetta stone. But I am still surprised that you didn't know I had it."

"There's no way I would know. The PET activates when a crisis situation exists and is set on a single-link, stand-alone frequency."

"A single-link frequency to where?"

"To the StarStream."

Leslee turned her palms upward. "But there is no StarStream."

"It's gone," Zack whistled from a high to a low pitch and with his right hand Zack made a motion suggesting a dying duck which he punctuated by mimicking the sound of an explosion in his throat. "I mean ... poof ... we saw it."

"Well ... the PET doesn't know that the StarStream crashed. It's trying to locate it," Ahneevah said.

Zack felt another mosquito whiz by his ear and tried to shoo it away by waving his right hand in front of his face.

"Oh, great, now I got mama mosquito after me."

"Never mind the insect," Ahneevah urged. "The Emergency Transducer can get us out of here. It has the same mini-fusion reactor power train as the epidermal surface of the StarStream, except the PET's reactors have a built-in baffle that reduces the initial force of the free neutrons that are released."

"And I bet that baffle protected it from the EMP waves," Zack conjectured.

"No," Ahneevah said and indicated Zack's belt buckle. "It was an element contained in the *Archeology<>Dig It!* emblem."

Zack was right on the page. "Don't tell me. It's the lead ... pewter is made with lead."

"Symbol Pb, number 82 on your ...no ... that would be *our* Periodic Table of Elements," Ahneevah said. "It was the lead that prevented the NLU from *seeing* the PET."

"I love it. I knew I had to have this buckle. But who knew how major ... talk about the little things making a big difference, and don't worry, Superman's X-ray vision couldn't penetrate lead either." Zack smiled and Leslee high-fived him.

"Superman?" Ahneevah whizzed through her memory banks for an instant, and then she found the reference. "Yes, disguised as mild-mannered reporter Clark Kent. *My* secret identity would probably be … Barney the Dinosaur."

Leslee smiled. "Hey, I loved Barney. He was my pal. And while we are on TV trivia, I am also a major Trekkie you know. Is the PET anything like a mini phaser pistol? Can it really get us out of here?

"Phaser … Trekkie … Oh, the hand-weapon that Captain James T. Kirk used on the *Starship Enterprise*. Space is indeed the final frontier and yes, the PET has a similar function to the phaser but operates under an entirely different principle. The PET doesn't require photonic energy. It's more nucleonic than laser. The process is virtually instantaneous. Captured free neutrons are pooled until they build into a strong force and then are discharged to bombard and freeze the motion of the atomic particles within the more stable elements."

Zack's eyes widened with realization and he glanced downward. "More stable elements like people and perhaps these cell door locks and those chains?"

"Exactly, but for right now we should go with the locks and chains," Ahneevah answered. "All it takes is one weak link … so let's weaken one."

"I think I'm having a déjà-vu moment," Zack observed. "We already escaped from this base. Didn't we?"

Ahneevah smiled impishly and nodded. "Yeah, talk about ironic."

The pithy remark and hearing Ahneevah use the word *yeah* tickled and drew smiles from Leslee and Zack. Ahneevah flashed them a close-lipped, mini-Mona Lisa and continued. "Hold the PET between the thumb and forefinger of each hand and lightly touch the lock with it."

Zack complied and in an instant the inner workings disintegrated atomically in a white-hot flash. As the cell door swung open, alarms began to sound. Zack shook his head in wonder. "Boy, am I good or what? But how did I do it?"

"The PET was able to read the molecular composition and overload the particle tracks," Ahneevah said.

The monitors in the main security room still showed everything to be normal. Nonetheless, the alarms alerted waves of security personnel who began flooding the base corridors and streaming toward the detention area.

One of the guards outside the cell complex whirled around and tried opening the main entrance to check the status of the prisoners. Suddenly, an intense streak of blood red light shot out from the lock, blew the sentry across the corridor, liquefied the locking system and then solidified it into a single blob.

Zack, now with the program, *fried* Ahneevah's cell door open and then casually touched the PET to the padlock securing the chains that were enveloping her. The crimson beam instantly dissolved the lock and several key links, and the metal bonds *clattered* to the cement floor.

Ahneevah took the device from Zack. "Nice shootin,' partner," she noted, and dashed toward the detention area entrance, tapped the metal edging around the door with the PET and then by means of the scarlet shaft of light melted the frame and sealed off the entrance.

"Awesome," Leslee cheered "The PET read the molecular composition of the steel around the door and used it as a welding material."

Abruptly, the *sputtering pops* of automatic weapons erupted in the outer corridor and bullets *zinged* and *pinged* as they pummeled the steel brig door. Ahneevah quickly ripped the Hazmat and the neoprene Navy Seal wet suits off in pieces, and tossed the shredded remnants aside.

"Is it getting a bit too hot to stay in here ... or is it just me?"

Leslee asked with an edge in her voice.

Ahneevah took a quick glance at the PET and looked around. "We'll get out as soon as there's a viable exit," she responded.

"Is that a *soon*, soon or a later soon?" Zack yelled.

"Imminent," Ahneevah advised as she slipped the PET into her sleeve. "Get to the back of the cells ... now."

Outside the detention room, most of the demolition team retreated to safety in the intersecting corridor while General Mitchell and his second in command Major Sheridan Trent checked the placement of the C-7 explosive packs around the door and moved back with the others. Once out of harms way, the general gave the order to ignite the charge.

The detonation sounded far more powerful than it appeared as the entire building shuddered. The main door was blasted inward and the small collection of military personnel washed in through the blown-out opening.

Slides on machine pistols and automatic pistols began chattering. No less than fifty separate gun barrels were aimed in the direction of Ahneevah, Zack and Leslee. However, when the smoke cleared, the mercenaries found that they were merely pointing their armaments at a smooth, two-meter, laser-made hole burned through the back wall, and the prisoners were nowhere in sight. Within the next few seconds the entire building shook, rattled, and disassembled around them. Though it looked as if it shattered into a zillion pieces, for some unknown reason, not one combatant was injured. Even more curiously, the wreckage from the buckled structure formed a crater around the Security Force, delaying their pursuit of the *alien* and her accomplices.

Mitchell turned to Major Trent. "I'm going back to Central Command. Call in all available air and ground support."

"What the hell happened in there? What made the place blow like that?" Zack asked Ahneevah as they were sliding and stumbling down the slope of debris outside the crumbled detention center.

"*We* did," Ahneevah answered.

"How in the world did *we* do that?"

As Ahneevah was about to answer, a line of automatic weapons fire ripped up funnels of sand in front of them.

"We've got a Humvee bearing down on us," Leslee cried out.

The approaching armored vehicle appeared to be fifty yards from their position and was continuing to rain fire on them. Four security squad members in full battle gear were blasting away with a mounted .50-caliber machine gun and 9mm Micro-Uzi machine pistols. Incoming shells were whistling all around and kicking up dirt and rock.

"I'll explain about the explosion and everything else later," Ahneevah shouted and quickly hauled Zack and Leslee back behind some of the debris for cover.

"That should be some seminar," Zack said, ducking down. By this time, additional ATVs and other Humvees that were patrolling the perimeter had joined the battle, producing a fierce thunderstorm of multiple-caliber lead-alloy hail.

Ahneevah, Leslee and Zack were pinned down on the outside of the crater of rubble that moments before was the base detention center. At their rear, some of Mitchell's men who had been trapped on the inside of the wall-wreckage were beginning to dribble over the peak. The rest were slowly crawling behind them. Ahneevah became aware of this and started to climb the heaps of dirt, twisted steel and ragged cement blocks.

Leslee wrapped her fingers around Ahneevah's forearm. "Do we have a plan?" she shouted over the *chattering* barrage.

Ahneevah quickly steered Leslee and Zack farther behind the protection of the debris-strewn mound. "I want you both to wait here."

"Wait here? While you ...?"

"I have to go alone. They can only harm me by hurting you."

"That's your plan? Well, excuse me," Leslee shot back with a palpable dash of frustration while simultaneously making circles in the air with her index finger. "Do we have to go 'round and 'round like this every time? You *are* good, but let's do a brief recap. It seems like only yesterday that I saw you bleeding reddish-purple blood, thanks to a chunk of hot lead buried in your chest. Oh … come to think of it, it *was* only yesterday, and I don't believe we can always rely on our sparkly friends doing a temporal switcheroo to save your 28th Configuration … pale-lavender ass."

Ahneevah looked at Zack for help. He shrugged and said, "No dice, you know she's right ... 28th Configuration pale-lavender ass and all." Though the piercing shrill of another onslaught shrieked around them and drowned him out, his facial expression clearly indicated that Zack wasn't buying. Then he placed his open hands on each side of his mouth as a megaphone and hollered over the screaming incoming ordnance.

"Excuse me, Rosy is a hundred percent on the money."

Ahneevah smiled slightly. "There's no reason to shout, Zack. I can hear you just fine," she replied.

"Oh … right … sorry," Zack pointed to his head. "I forgot … Hedy Lamarr. Look, you may be amazing, but you're not invulnerable. Even Superman had to deal with Kryptonite ya know."

Ahneevah nodded her head. "Yes, I guess we all have our frailties."

"Right, no matter how good you are there is always something that can ice your puck," echoed Leslee as she tugged Ahneevah back toward her and Zack. "And some of those things they keep pointing and shooting at us spit out hunks of metal that'll make even bigger holes in you than the last one you had … less than twenty-four hours ago … give or take a few continuum ticks in the twilight zone with the uhhh … rainbow gang." Then Leslee took both of Ahneevah's hands in hers and spoke softly. "And we don't want to lose you."

"Believe me, Leslee, I'm in no danger," Ahneevah said reassuringly. "I have seen their voracious greed and hunger for power before. It cost me everything and it is not new to me. As far as the present evil is concerned, I'm well aware that I'm a crucial key in their pursuit of absolute control, and at least for the present they need me to remain … intact. Now you must stay here where it is safer." With that said, the incredible refugee from another world sailed up toward the crest of crater.

As an unmistakable reminder of how relative the concept of *safer* actually is in a battle zone, another fusillade of hot-metal rounds ricocheted off a concrete block near Leslee. Part of the resultant exploding plume of razor-edged cement shrapnel caught her on the side of her face. She recoiled from the pain and instinctively brought her hand up to check the wound. Her fingertips seemed to pulsate slightly as she felt the blood oozing from the multiple pockmarks dug out of her left cheek and jaw. Leslee wiped the crimson streams away with her sleeve.

Then something peculiar happened. The bleeding stopped almost instantly and Leslee was overcome by a unique and strengthening sensation. The feeling lasted for less than a heartbeat, but it gave her an intriguing sense of power that she had never felt before.

"To hell with safer," she exclaimed, and then took off after Ahneevah. Racing up the incline, Leslee looked back at Zack, "You comin' or what?"

Zack exhaled and shook his head. "Oh, Rosy … shit," he rasped. Somehow emboldened by Leslee's bravery, Zack started to scamper after the two women who were being followed up the slope by the torrent of incoming projectiles. However, when Zack saw several security force mercenaries climbing over the debris ridge that were unseen by Ahneevah and Leslee, he stopped mid-stride and began waving his arms and shouting at the soldiers in an effort to draw their fire. Zack succeeded and their machine pistols' discharges trailed after him and he was forced to dive behind a partially buried, twisted chunk of steel to avoid getting hit. As the bullets peppered the metal slab, Zack realized that his *shield* was a section of the main cell bay door that Ahneevah welded to the doorframe with the PET. Zack shrugged his shoulders. "Talk about ironic," he mumbled to himself then hesitantly peeked above the ruins to be greeted by Ahneevah giving him a thumbs-up while sliding behind a large, mangled I-beam. Then Ahneevah motioned for Leslee to duck into a crevice outlined by a blown out window frame. At the same moment that Leslee dashed for cover, Zack once again started to scramble up the mound. "I must be fucking nuts."

Meanwhile, the leading edge of the pursuit squad began to flood down the incline. As they swept past Ahneevah and Leslee, the pair pounced on them from their concealed positions. Ahneevah used short circuits and Leslee fired swift hammer-blows that literally put some noses way out of joint. Ahneevah could hear the cartilage crunch.

"Don't hurt them any worse than that," Ahneevah said as she carefully lowered one of her victims to the ground. "It's not entirely their fault."

"Not entirely? Then exactly how much of their fault is it? Can I break bones or limit myself to contusions and bruises? Let me respectfully remind you," Leslee continued as she knocked down vicious strikes from multiple assailants, "they seem to be trying real hard to hurt us as much as they can."

Leslee then slickly blocked a left punch with a blurring down windmill of her right arm and proceeded to double her opponent over with a side kick to the groin. Following that, she smoothly sent several other aggressors back to the bottom of the slope with sweeping high kicks that reminded her of the floating action sequences in the new-era kung fu films. *That's weird, I don't ever remember learning those moves,* her inner voice echoed. In the next split-second Leslee leaped nearly six feet in the air and effortlessly used a scissor move, wrapping her legs around her opponent's neck and flipping him to the outside of the crater.

"What the hell? Master Meza couldn't even do that," Leslee thought out loud as she secured the back of another opponent's neck, bent him over and drove her knee sharply up into his solar plexus. This blow knocked the wind out of him and sent him toppling over backward. Ahneevah gave a slight nod of approval as the ineffective attacker rapidly tumbled down the crater in a race to the bottom with Leslee's previous victim.

Looking up, Leslee noticed that most of the patrol vehicles were converging from the base perimeter onto the combat sector. "We're becoming very popular."

Ahneevah glanced at the oncoming vehicles. "Don't worry. The soldiers manning the motorized units will have to limit their blanket of fire to a containment approach. Otherwise they'd risk inflicting casualties on their own forces; we'll be all right for now."

"Tell me, exactly how long is *for now?*"

"It depends on which *now* you're talking about. We have learned there's more than one," Ahneevah responded.

Instead of trying to rush up the crater mound, Major Trent painstakingly crawled up, using the heaps of partially melted and deformed metal girders and concrete blocks as cover. Zack, who had been clambering up the incline, reached the action a split second before the major aimed his sidearm directly at Leslee and was about to squeeze the trigger.

"Rosy, look out," Zack shouted and dove headfirst toward the major.

Leslee whipped her head around and then everything seemed

to slow down the split second she heard the crack of the 9mm pistol which had already discharged its mutilating round point-blank in Zack's direction.

"No!" Leslee screamed and could only watch in horror as blood splattered from Zack's head, and he toppled face first onto the slope. As Zack began to tumble over and over down the crater wall of debris, Major Trent drew a bead on him and attempted to get off another shot but this time the outcome was a soft *click* followed by the barrel of the Beretta semi-automatic blowing apart. Trent was stunned by the sudden explosion of his pistol but he had no time to think about it because his thought process was shut down by Leslee's multiple strikes that crunched into both sides of his head. After dealing with Major Trent, Leslee took a step toward Zack but was stopped in her tracks when she spotted four Unmanned Aerial Vehicles approaching. Ahneevah took a quick glance at them. "They're Predator UAVs. They carry Hellfire missiles with pinpoint accuracy."

"Not good, I can't be a damn pinpoint right now," Leslee said with escalating apprehension. "I've got to get over to Zack." Ahneevah's enhanced optics zoomed in on the oncoming threats for a split-second. "Don't worry. You won't be a pinpoint, at least not just yet." Suddenly the four Predators began to wobble and at once veered sharply toward each other and converged at the same location in the air. This clearly violated the *two things cannot occupy the same space at the same time* rule and the result was a bright flash and a shower of shattered Predator and Hellfire composite materials.

EPIƆODE THIRTY-TWO

RESSURECTION
"THE WINDS OF CHANGE"

General Ethan Mitchell returned to the command center just as Bixler and Barrgrave were coming to the realization that ...

... the current situation was *tight roping* on the ragged edge of spiraling completely out of control.

"Albert, we've got to end this now," the Vice President declared as he leaned forward in his chair, his fingers pressed together doing *spider push-ups* in rhythm with his words. "There's too much at stake. I can't risk my office."

"You should have thought of that before we got in this deep," Barrgrave snapped.

"I'm telling you, those three must be disposed of," Bixler fired back.

"Not the alien," Barrgrave argued. "With the spacecraft already blasted to smithereens the loss of that female creature and her knowledge would be incalculable, unthinkable."

Bixler thought about this for a second, but an added sight on the monitor caught his attention. "Who the hell is that?" Bixler snorted as he pointed to the LED display which showed a real-time satellite image of a small contingent of Blackhawk choppers approaching the conflict.

"They look like FBI and CIA strike force gun-ships," General Mitchell said. "We deploy them in Mexico for covert operations support in the war on drugs."

Bixler slammed his fist on the security console. "The FBI and CIA? Together? How in hell did Reed and Reese pull that off?"

Barrgrave was indignant. "I thought you ordered your lapdog attorney general to kill that request."

"Is that so?" Mitchell said dryly. "Well, those birds are east of here, about twenty clicks. It seems the AG didn't quite come up to your specs."

Bixler hastily connected the dots. "No, I'm sure he did. Inspector Reed and Special Agent Reese must be acting on their own volition—it's insubordination and that's how it'll be noted officially. This incursion is being carried out by a group of renegade FBI and CIA operatives."

Barrgrave stood up. "Maybe we should scramble some of our remaining air assets."

Mitchell jumped to his feet and shook his head. "We have no remaining tactical air assets. The alien saw to that. They're all grounded except for the B-2 and the Herk and we're going to need those ships to fly cover for the Gulfstream in case a strategic retreat becomes necessary. We seem to be short on options."

Bixler brightened and waved a finger. "No. We always have options." A scowl percolated on the CO's face, "I belong out there with my troops," he sputtered through clenched teeth. He punctuated his words with a dismissive salute, turned sharply on his heels, and strode out of the command center.

As it turned out, the attorney general did follow orders and denied Inspector Clayton Reed's request to organize a mission to investigate reports of a siege in the desert. The fact that Reed's presence at the conflict was unsanctioned, and was outside the jurisdiction of the Bureau and the Department of Justice, made it illegal and unpredictable. There was also no backup for the cobbled-together, joint operations aerial strike force that was flying at two hundred feet MSL over the dunescape. At the controls of the lead chopper in the flight of four was CIA pilot Jake Neely. He scanned the GPS inertial navigation array.

"ETA to the programmed destination around nineteen minutes. I'll have Spy Sat Net acquisition in 5 - 4 - 3 - 2."

A wide view of the desert base via the satellite started rolling across the LED screen. Neely made some adjustments and as the video transmission focused in on the area around the main facility, a concerned look broke out on his face and he turned to Clayton Reed who was riding in the co-pilot seat and holding the NLU in his hand.

"Sir, there's some intense military activity going on down there. It looks like a firefight."

"Can you zoom in a bit tighter?"

"Yes sir. We can get close enough to read their IDs."

Agent Reese popped her safety harness and leaned over from her seat in the rear of the cabin. "Ahneevah and the others are in trouble," she said as she processed the action visible on and around the wreckage that had been the base detention wing. "They're under attack from some kind of paramilitary force."

"And the motorized units have them surrounded and are beginning to tighten the noose," Neely added. "We can't risk firing. All the combatants are in critical proximity."

"If we don't stop it, they'll be slaughtered," Reese declared. "They won't have a chance. It's three against more than a hundred."

Reed glanced alternately at the blinking NLU and the digital display on the instrument panel. "We need a closer look." With that said, the NLU displayed a holographic image of the close combat taking place. "Jesus, make that *two* against a hundred. The archeologist is on the ground."

"He looks unconscious or ... worse," Reese added.

"Jake, we'd better get down there in a hurry ... full speed and minimal altitude. How low will she fly?"

Neely smiled, "Sir, we can win a limbo contest," he replied, then fire-walled the throttles and dove for the deck. Zoe re-secured her harness and exhaled heavily in an effort to take the edge off her apprehension.

Inside the command center Barrgrave was railing, "Wade, we can't just run and pretend none of this happened."

"We won't have to," Bixler snorted. "There's an advanced combat group of the upgraded F/A-22C Raptors stationed at Nellis. They can be here in less than an hour."

A hyper-intense Dax Wolf was charging down the base main corridor, clutching the remote access interface to his computer. He was heading in the direction of the command center and moving more quickly than anyone had ever remembered seeing him move. He burst into the com room and shouted, "The alien is tapped into an echelon of quantum mechanical science that's beyond anything that we can even begin to imagine." Bixler's blood pressure immediately soared.

Barrgrave recoiled as Bixler opened his briefcase and reached for the phone inside it. "This is Bixler XIB-VP-111. This is an order for a Harpoon II, special unit level *A* drill. I will enter the target coordinates for the air strike into the mission profile computer when it is ready to go."

"Wade, are you insane? You can't order nukes. This is American soil!"

Bixler dismissed Barrgrave with a wave of his hand. "We are way beyond that now," he sneered.

The discussion merely amused Wolf and he began to laugh. "Idiots … you know, you political hacks are so behind the curve. All you can think of is to go nuclear," Wolf spit out through his guffaws. "You and your damned WMD are no match for that green-eyed creature. He set his gaze on the mogul. "I'm telling you we are up against something so immense that it's way beyond your Morlock," Wolf's stare shifted to the politician, "and semi-Neanderthal brains to assimilate."

"You can't speak to the Vice President like that. It's treasonous," Bixler growled and pointed to several MPs standing at attention on either side of the door. "I can have you arrested for that kind of talk."

"Oh, who gives a damn? You can have me arrested for saying almost anything against you or any of the other high-placed, integrity-challenged morons in your cabal."

"There's no time for this now," Barrgrave sputtered. "We must get as far from here as we can."

"Sit down," Dax ordered defiantly as he punched a few buttons on his computer interface wand. "It takes a good hour to prepare a Level *A* F/A-22C drill out of Nellis. And I'm warning you that it would be a grave mistake on your part if you don't take the time to see and hear what I've learned before you go radioactive."

Barrgrave and Bixler were stunned by the otherwise taciturn Wolf's outburst. Reluctantly they plopped down into their seats.

"After returning from the alien ship crash-site I tested the samples I collected. Not a visible shred of the craft was evident."

"Yes, we know that," Bixler responded sharply and jumped to his feet. "That's nothing new."

"Don't interrupt," Wolf said firmly as he pointed the vice-president back to his chair. "Now pay close attention. When I put the various substances through the particle analyzer, I found traces of some striking and currently uncategorized subatomic particles along with positrons, anti-neutrons and negatively charged protons. Initially these infinitely tiny building blocks seemed to be in a static mode. But then ..." Wolf made some inputs on the remote device and the view screen in the command center came alive with incredible images. "As you can see, quite inexplicably, the various components began to coalesce around other selected nano-photonic fragments, which as far as I know have also not as yet been identified. Within minutes this interaction began to form a DNA helix."

"So? We've been able to produce a primitive life form in our labs," Barrgrave countered.

"Not within minutes, not a prayer," Wolf insisted. "And I'm not talking about a *primitive* life form. This genetic ladder is terabytes far more sophisticated than any I have ever seen or heard of ... including that of us humans."

"Sophisticated? How can inorganic matter form a sophisticated DNA helix in practically no time? I mean, it has to start with a low grade single-cell structure. It takes thousands, no, millions of years for advanced DNA development. Anything else is beyond the realm of known physical laws," Barrgrave insisted.

"You can throw out the book on your so-called known physical laws." Wolf pointed to the view screen. "Look at that helix. It isn't just an ordinary life-as-we-know-it-on-Earth double helix. It's a *triple* helix, comprising three separate entwined ladders!" Barrgrave was about to say something but Wolf put up his hand. "Yes, I checked the results six times." Wolf made a few additional entries on the computer link-up and more visual information flooded onto the LED. "These are some of the microscopic remnants of the craft. As you can plainly see, they are largely biologic and are no doubt building blocks. My guess is that the ship was born of ..."

"Born? Actually born? Like in childbirth? Impossible!" the Vice President exclaimed.

"Yes. Born! Like in living matter," Dax countered.

"Well, I'm glad we killed the damn thing," Bixler muttered.

"You would be," Wolf said with disdain. "That's because your sight doesn't go beyond your own nose. Look, I've got to get back to the lab. I still need to check the coding process, but we are extremely close."

"Close?"

"We are one computer run away from a genetically engineered *vaccine* of sorts." An uncharacteristic smirk leached onto Dax Wolf's face. "Perhaps an eventual countermeasure to our ... unusual competition. And Mr. Veep I suggest very strongly that you keep those Raptors with the nukes on the ground for now." With that, Dax Wolf rushed out of the command center. Bixler reached for the phone.

The pilots believed that the emergency scramble of their flight of Raptors at Nellis Air Force Base was purely an exercise using dummy ordinance. Their new F/A-22C variants included larger weapons bays to accommodate the modified Harpoon II short-range cruise missiles. Each super-jet carried one air-to-ground asset, and at wheels-up the afterburners were lit and bone-jarring sonic *booms* shook the installation as the four aircraft went hypersonic in bursts of fiery exhaust and shattering roars.

Leslee was able to parry the closed fist that was about to pummel her nose. Though the blow didn't land full force, it was enough to stun her for a second. Despite the contact, only a driblet of blood ran down from one of her nostrils, but it might as well have been steam.

"I already broke this nose once and my plastic surgeon, Dr. Birnbaum, called the repair work ... her rhinoplastic master-piece, you son-of-a-bitch," Leslee snarled and delivered a series of strikes that completely darkened her attacker's world and came perilously close to killing him. He went limp and crumpled to the ground.

Increasing numbers of hostile forces were scaling the debris wall on both sides. Leslee and Ahneevah had their hands full, and each time Leslee tried to shake herself free to go over and see what condition Zack was in, if any, another foe would clear the crest and come at her.

Amid the intense fighting, Zack showed no movement as he lay face down, bleeding in the ruins. Leslee grabbed an over-the-shoulder quick glimpse at him but a *quick glimpse* was all she could get before the next fist came flying. She reacted instinctively and knocked it down with such power that Ahneevah could plainly hear the *crunch* of bone shattering in the attacker's forearm. He turned white and collapsed in shock and grueling pain. Ahneevah frowned. "Sorry. It was automatic," Leslee said, sheepishly.

Then Leslee spotted a quartet of whirlybirds coming toward them, kicking up billowing trails of sand as they flew only a hairsbreadth above the desert floor.

"Damn! More trouble at five clicks," she shouted. Ahneevah was wrestling a machine pistol away from one of her opponents. She quickly short-circuited him and several others in quick succession. Then she focused her long-range green-eyed stare on the approaching helos.

"No, Leslee. They're friendlies. It's Agents Reed and Reese."

With the realization that some unexpected but highly welcome reinforcements were speeding in the direction of the battle, Leslee's adrenaline output was elevated even further. "The odds are starting to improve," she shouted as she violently smashed several sets of teeth with powerful spinning heel kicks before Ahneevah could rein her in.

"There's no need to allow your chemistry to get ahead of you. You almost killed the one who struck your nose. Remember, be better."

Leslee was surprised that with all that was going on Ahneevah was aware of her almost taking a life. However, after less than a second she wasn't surprised at all. "I can't help it. Zack got shot because he was trying to protect me," Leslee said ruefully. "If he hadn't jumped in the path of that bullet, I would be lying there, not him, and I can't even go to help him. He could be dying or even … already… de …"

"Just breathe. Keep your concentration on what is in front of you. Like they say, keep your eye on the ball," Ahneevah advised in an almost serene tone, and then continued to nonviolently cancel various consciousnesses. Leslee was puzzled by Ahneevah's seeming lack of empathy but then had to deal with several aggressors by using blurring combinations.

Back in the lab, Dax Wolf was again suddenly enveloped in the familiar incapacitating chill. He knew that he was being invaded by some inexplicable external force but had no way to isolate, withstand or terminate its power. However, he was able to resist it long enough to switch on the mega-laser and engage the prototype scaled-down particle acceleration unit. But the consequences were far different from those he had expected.

The resulting explosion threw Wolf into the air and he caromed off the ceiling. Then, like some three-dimensional billiard shot, he slammed into the far wall and slid down unconscious against it.

From a strictly tactical point of view, Reed's thirty-five-member task force seemed no match for the substantial firepower under the control of General Mitchell. Reed was well aware of this.

"Maintain your heading, Jake. We're gonna drive 'em to distraction. And tell the ground attack squads we're going in with faceplates, infra-red sensors and night goggles."

Neely smiled in recognition of the tactic, responding with a "Roger that."

When the four choppers arrived at the battle site, they slowed their forward motion and, with the engines revving at maximum RPM, executed a hover profile scant meters above the terrain. At the extreme high-rev setting, the whirring rotors began kicking up clouds of desert floor and debris. Added to that was a potent aural assault. A deafening rhythmic roar was generated by the pounding mini-sonic booms as the air molecules exploded away from the leading edges of the racing rotor blades.

In the cyclonic, ear-splitting, limited-vision environment, Ahneevah turned to Leslee and spoke mind to mind.

"Leslee, you love Zack, don't you?" she asked thoughtfully as Leslee threw a hefty sergeant over her shoulder and sent him tumbling back down into the crater.

"This is not the time," Leslee replied.

"It's always the time," Ahneevah answered with resolve, and then easily pulled the rug out from another opponent's ability to stand.

Then Leslee looked around and realized that the flood of Security Force personnel that had been coming over the debris pile was now down to a trickle, bringing a momentary lull in the action. She also noticed that the group of attackers from outside the perimeter still had a fair amount of distance to cover before they could pose any threat. In an instinctive reaction to the swirling dust and sand, Leslee shielded her eyes and started to move toward Zack.

"Don't worry about your eyes," Ahneevah advised. *"The debris particles will not harm them."*

Leslee blinked and was amazed that she indeed was not being affected by the whirling plumes of rubble, sand and dust. She wondered how this could be and then heard Ahneevah's telepathic voice, *"Your tear ducts will automatically compensate."* Then Leslee straightened up and took in Ahneevah's countenance. To fully absorb Ahneevah's tone of voice, she listened as the words digitally replayed in her mind. *"Leslee, you do love Zack, don't you?"*

"Okay ... Yes," Leslee confessed. *"I guess I've loved him from the minute he sent me out of his room when I tried to seduce him in Tel Aviv. It seems like a million years ago."*

Ahneevah smiled. *"A million years, hmmm ... Seems I've been there, and done that."* With even more urgency Leslee once again attempted to head over to Zack but was halted when additional mercenaries approached and she and Ahneevah had to go back to work. Several temporarily sight-challenged enemies were handily dropped by the one-two female punches. Though they might have been worlds apart, at this moment, Leslee Rose Myles of Beverly Hills, the 29th Configuration and the Earth and Ahneevah of the 28th Configuration and Lano Pahntri were as one ... and ... *in the zone.*

The Blackhawk choppers began touching down. Even before their wheels met the sand the strike units charged out of them into the battle area to begin securing Mitchell's choking, dazed and blinded combat forces. Ahneevah and Leslee saw the opening and sprinted down the incline toward the motionless Zack.

EPISODE THIRTY-THREE

"BEYOND THIS HORIZON"

As Ahneevah and Leslee raced closer to Zack …

… Leslee noticed a slight twitch of her fallen soul-mate's left hand and then a flexing of his fingers. First, she was breathless at the realization, then, an expansive grin unfurled across her face.

"Ahneevah, he's alive."

"Yes, I know."

"You know? Well … you could have said something."

"I sensed it but I wasn't really positive. Remember, I'm not all there yet. I only picked up his heartbeat this moment. I wasn't within range to detect his specific cardio-rhythm before."

When the two women arrived at the spot where Zack was lying he greeted them with a tortured groan and cautiously raised his hand up toward the searing pain over his left eye. It felt as if the hot, pointed end of a soldering iron was being jabbed in and out of his forehead. Zack tentatively touched the site of the open wound with his fingers and could feel the warm sticky liquid oozing from it.

The fact that he could feel anything at all was nothing short of a miracle. The bullet fired by Major Trent was headed straight between Zack's eyes. On impact, the shot's muzzle velocity and angle should have resulted in brain tissue spilling out of his shattered skull, along with considerably more blood than was now trickling down the side of his face. If the projectile had found its initial mark, Zack would now be aware of nothing. He would be dead. Inexplicably, the three-inch laceration on his forehead was only a flesh-wound, the consequence of the 9mm *bullet* dodging *him*. Somehow the original trajectory of the round was altered, and when Major Trent attempted to *click off* a second shot, his Beretta, a particularly reliable weapon, jammed and exploded. Then Leslee's double-hammer blow to Trent's temples made him a rolling blackout.

Subsequently, between the choking clouds of dust raised by the blustery down-drafts from the Blackhawk's whirling rotors, and the combined actions of Ahneevah, Leslee and the joint strike force, Mitchell's troops' desire to continue the fight had diminished to the point where Reed's battle group was able to quickly gain full control. Weapons were dropped to the ground and hands were raised in surrender.

Leslee kneeled down beside Zack and, having nothing else to use, she lightly dabbed with her sleeve at the rivulets of blood running down his cheek. When Zack attempted to stand he found that his legs were shaky and he staggered, but Ahneevah quickly steadied and helped him to his feet. Leslee instinctively brought her hand up to brush Zack's hair away from his injury. To her astonishment, as her fingers came within an inch or so of the bleeding gash, a web of blue tendrils leaped from them. This bio-electronic *brushing* instantly cauterized the wound.

Leslee threw a puzzled glance at Ahneevah, who wiggled the fingers on her both hands in open view signaling she did nothing. "It must be a residual charge from when you helped me disable the junction box in the hangar," Ahneevah said and casually gestured for Leslee to continue with what she was doing. Leslee took Zack in her arms and held him tightly, unaware of the mysterious processes that were taking place. "I thought they killed you," Leslee snuffled.

Zack wrapped his arms around her. "Yeah, I know … so did I. And I swear that when I got hit by the slug, my whole life flashed in front of me. Come to think of it, near-death experiences are becoming a regular thing for me these days … not good."

Leslee adoringly took Zack's face in her hands, looked into his eyes and spoke with great tenderness. "You jumped in front of the bullet to protect me … maybe to die for me."

Zack fixed his gaze on Leslee's hazel eyes and noticed that small pools were glistening in their corners. He placed his hand on top of hers. "Jeez, how could I let any harm come to the light at the end of my drunk? And … well …"

His hesitation to go where Leslee thought he was heading disappointed her and she dropped her hands away from his face. "Well? Come on … say it! You love me. Why is that so difficult?"

Zack shook his head and held her closer. "It's not difficult … it's just that telling you 'I love you' isn't nearly enough." Frustrated, he glanced skyward for an instant as if looking for some help, "Damn, I wish I read more Shakespeare." Zack said, as his eyes also began to well up. Then he took a deep breath and turned back to Leslee. "Look … Rosy, if I merely told you that I loved you it would be a major understatement. I'm way beyond *I love you*. When that bullet hit me and I saw my whole life, it wasn't the archeology, it wasn't the PhDs … it wasn't even the Kodiak find … it was you." Zack's words took Leslee's breath away and tears began to roll liberally down her cheeks. "Rosy, *I love you* doesn't even come close to saying what really I feel."

Leslee smiled, exhaled and brushed at the tears with the backs of both her hands. Then she took a deep breath, and put her arms around Zack's neck. "Well you just said it four times. That'll be perfectly fine for now," she sniffled. "We'll research it some more … together. I'm sure we'll come up with something."

"Well I'm glad that's finally settled," Ahneevah said. "I was beginning to wonder if you two would ever get on the same page."

"So was I," Leslee acknowledged.

Zack held Leslee tight in his arms and gently nibbled on her lower lip. "I haven't had a cigarette in … some time." he whispered. As they were about to seal the deal with a full mouth-on-mouth, the moment was interrupted by the familiar *buzz* that once again set Zack clawing at the air.

"Now the damned thing is following me."

"Maybe it likes you," Ahneevah said through a muted smile.

"It must. I think I'm making it grow. It seems to be getting bigger."

"Bigger," Ahneevah mused. "That's fascinating." The sudden roar of jet engines spooling up sidetracked the conversation. Ahneevah's long-range optics zeroed in on the active runway and spotted the Gulfstream and the B-2 Spirit starting their take-off roll.

"They're escaping," Agent Reed shouted as he raced toward the trio.

"No way, not gonna happen, not on my watch," Ahneevah launched back. Leslee and Zack glanced at her with amused looks in reaction to her choice of words.

"What? I'm just getting to review contemporary American English colloquial speech. Wasn't that correct?" Ahneevah asked, then removed the PET from the flight-suit hidden compartment and in her native language, reeled off a set of instructions to the PET. She held the device in the air and studied it for a moment, then gave it to Leslee and a look of uncertainty crossed Ahneevah's face. Then she shook her head and ran the fingers of both hands through her amber hair. "It may be slightly premature, but there's no other viable option."

The shaking, chattering, blackened, bruised and bleeding Dax

Wolf tried to get up but then weakly collapsed onto the laboratory floor. He remained prone for a few minutes, feeling his extremities for serious damage. Although much of his body was covered with blood he found that no arteries had been severed and nothing seemed broken. He finally struggled to his feet and then looked around to check on the damage to the lab.

Wolf determined that the explosion fortunately did not originate in the mega-laser or the mini-particle acceleration unit. Had that been the case, he himself, the entire laboratory area and most of the temporary research wing would have been demolished. After he reset the circuit breakers, a system diagnostic revealed that the malfunction had occurred in one of the auxiliary power units. With a high edge of urgency he ordered a replacement rated at twice the capacity. Relieved, Wolf began to tend to his injuries, which now oddly seemed far less severe than he first assumed.

EPISODE THIRTY-FOUR

"INDEPENDENCE DAY"

"I'm telling you, it's perfect," Bixler said as the G VII and B-2 Spirit ...

... climbed through thirty-six thousand feet. "It'll go down as an operation to thwart a terrorist plot aimed at a big city. The report will say that they were attempting to acquire classified weapons systems from a secret test facility to use them in a follow up to the incident near Albuquerque. We'll be heroes for Christ's sake. They'll give us a goddamned ticker-tape parade."

"How could you approve an operation like that? I thought that order could only come from the President, not the Vice President," Barrgrave said.

"You'd be surprised what *this* Vice President can do. And the beautiful part is that the American public is so worried about where and when the next terrorist attack will happen and how they're going to cover their credit card debt, their mortgages, health-care and energy costs; they'll accept any bullshit explanation we give them. Look at what we've been able to get away with already."

"What about Wolf?" Barrgrave asked, as the two aircraft leveled off at a cruise altitude of thirty-nine-thousand feet.

"We can lay the whole incident in his lap," Bixler hissed back. "He was simply another renegade scientist who couldn't handle the pressure of being part of the super-secret black project intelligence community. The main talking point will be that to reveal more would be to compromise national security. By claiming that all the information is classified, we can easily quash any congressional investigation. Without legislative oversight there will be no questions. So what the hell are you all bent out of shape about, Albert?"

A smile was about to creep onto Barrgrave's lips, but then his face suddenly turned ashen as if he just saw a ghost. He slowly raised his right hand and pointed out of the window. "That …Wade, we have company."

Bixler turned around and his face went two shades paler than Barrgrave's. "Impossible."

The word *impossible* self-destructed the instant Bixler uttered it. In a temporal reality where the 28th Configuration and Ahneevah intersected with the 29th Configuration, it was certainly nowhere near impossible.

Clearly visible at eleven o'clock off the Gulfstream's left wing was what must have at first seemed an apparition but undeniably—there it was—flying backwards and easily matching speed and altitude with the B-2 and the G-7—the StarStream. Bixler and Barrgrave rushed forward to get a better view. They entered the flight deck just in time to see the overgrown, airborne teardrop's frozen-plasma front windscreen converting into its transparent mode, giving them a clear view of Ahneevah, Zack and Leslee.

"But it blew up," Barrgrave bellowed. "We all saw it, and we couldn't find a single remaining visible shred of it. Jesus, it was dead … obliterated!"

Meanwhile, in the lab, Wolf was on his knees carefully overseeing the installation of the new high-capacity auxiliary power unit. Suddenly his video-com warbled. He rolled his eyes and pulled himself up into his chair. Strangely, he now had silver-gray streaks in his hair and looked like a man in his fifties.

Bixler and Barrgrave were on the lab LED display. Bixler spoke first. "Wolf, that spaceship is back. How could it be? We all saw it get blasted into nothing."

"That's right, it did get blown to atomic particles," Dax Wolf squeezed out in a scratchy tone. "But I made it clear that we are dealing with forces that are far beyond contemporary knowledge. If you recall, I told you that the craft was biological. Apparently it was capable of self-initiating a reanimation sequence within its remaining micro-anatomical systems. Even the sections of it that are not organic in nature must have been implanted or overlaid with artificial memory grains that could be rejuvenated as well."

"It cloned itself?" Barrgrave said with incredulity. Wolf nodded once in response.

Bixler radioed the next command to the B-2 Spirit. "Can we fire the Electro Magnetic Pulse wave now?"

Wolf, visible on Bixler's portable view screen, shook his head.

"Fire all you want. You're still not going to kill it. Don't you imbeciles understand? It can't die, at least not the kind of death that you're aware of."

Nevertheless, the order to fire was relayed to the Spirit crew and immediately executed. The pulse wave hit the StarStream amidships.

Zack closed his eyes tightly in preparation for a rerun of the last time that the StarStream was hit by the plasma beam. "Shit, not again," Zack squawked.

Ahneevah quickly reassured him. "No, Zack, not again," she said confidently.

After the mini-lightning did its leaping light-show on the outer hull, nothing further occurred. No loss of control. Not even a minor wobble. Zack slowly opened one eye, then the other. "The surviving StarStream genetic material was able to read and de-code the atomic particle composition of the destructive forces in the EMP plasma emissions," Ahneevah explained. "It was an easy step from there for the helix to develop chromosomal mod-ifications to enable the organic furnaces to absorb the pulse wave, redirect it to the power train, and remain intact."

"Easy? Wow, you mean it learned what could harm it and ad-justed by genetically mutating a countermeasure in practically no time?" Leslee asked.

"It's like natural selection, but at light speed," Zack suggested. "Jeez, Darwin was not only right, he was universally right." Zack patted the armrest on his seat as if it was a loyal pet dog.

"She survived for a billion years. A little EMP wave was child's play to her."

"Him," Ahneevah corrected.

"Him?" Zack and Leslee chorused.

Ahneevah thought for a split second, "If you remember the Disney *Love Bug* series of motion pictures in the sixties starring Sandra Duncan and then another one more recently with Lindsay Lohan, Herbie the VW was a *him*. *His* headlights would have probably drooped if he were called *her*."

Leslee smiled at Ahneevah's reference. "True, but it was Sandy Duncan, not Sandra," Leslee pointed out, but then she noticed a mischievous *scrunch* wriggle across Ahneevah's lips. "Wait a minute," Leslee said. "Sandra? Was that a joke? Zack, she made a joke."

"My civilization had a sense of humor. Laughter was very im-portant to us, just as it is to you. Simply turning the corners of your mouth up results in the secretion of beneficial enzymes and hormones throughout your body and most important ... it feels good."

"I love it," Zack chortled. "But why didn't you tell us that good old Herbie here wasn't lost forever?"

Ahneevah's reply had to wait as another blast from the B-2's Electro Magnetic Pulse cannon rocked the StarStream and lit up its living outer shell. This time the amazing craft compensated in a fraction of a second and steadied.

"Although … Herbie was conceived and constructed with a self-cloning program as a part of his inherent makeup, I couldn't be one hundred percent sure if he would regenerate or how extensive it would be. We were both exposed to the same time-continuum shifts and random element exposure. Those dynamics certainly affected my systems, but with the limited information I had available there was really no way to logically interpolate specific probabilities. The fact that Herbie was essentially vaporized and I was not … made any accurate outcomes impossible to calculate."

Zack's mental wheels were in overdrive. "Exactly how sure were you that Herbie would be back?"

"About ninety-eight percent that rejuvenation would be viable and could occur in one form or another."

"Ninety-eight percent? Tell me, Ahneevah," Leslee followed-up in a slow deliberate voice. "When you took an exam and got one question wrong out of a thousand, were you one of those students that would be disappointed?"

Ahneevah smiled because she knew Leslee had her pegged. "Yes, Leslee, I believe I was."

"I knew it. Well, as you might have figured, we are not perfectionists here. So you could have told us that you were ninety-eight percent sure that Herbie would be back."

"Perhaps that is so. But again, there was real doubt as to whether he would indeed successfully reanimate. It was uncertain even at the point when he was buzzing around Zack."

"Buzzing around me?" Zack digested this for a moment. "The mosquito!"

"Yes, and it is a good thing that he was buzzing. It was Herbie who made our escape possible by burning that hole in the wall of the detention area and then *helping* the building disintegrate. But most critical … Zack … was that the nine-millimeter lead slug with your name on it made contact with something else before it hit you."

Zack raised his eyebrows in total surprise and placed both hands on his head. "Herbie?"

"Right, although in a micro-mini state, the StarStream was still able to reach speeds beyond the sound barrier which generated bow and stern shock waves. In turn, the resultant nano sonic boom created pressure ripples with sufficient force to overcome the mass and velocity of the projectile and deflect it. If it had continued on its initial path, the bullet would have entered your cranium and penetrated through your cerebral frontal lobes. There would have been nothing we could have done to save you. Brain death would have occurred almost instantaneously. And of equal importance, Herbie also melted the front end of the gun barrel at the instant the trigger was pulled a second time. When the firing pin struck the primer, and the powder detonation propelled the high-velocity round forward, the combined force contained in the explosive charge and shot, blew the hand-weapon apart because there was no open barrel for that con-siderable surge of energy to escape through."

Leslee's eyes widened. "Wait a sec; did Herbie have anything to do with the UAVs crash and burn?" Ahneevah nodded once. "Certainly. He jammed their radio signals and took control over the flights from the remote pilots on the ground. The rest was easy ... *splat ... crunch.*"

Zack touched his forehead with his hands and then held them out with his palms up. "Hold on, splat ... crunch...what? What UAVs crashed and burned?"

Leslee shrugged at Zack. "It was while you were ... sleeping."

Ahneevah couldn't bypass such a perfect setup. "*While You Were Sleeping ... n*ow that was a movie with *Sandra* Bullock. Am I right?"

Leslee smiled and nodded in the affirmative but Zack still had a question. "Wait a minute, if Herbie was functioning, how come he didn't just do to the mercenary squads chasing us, what he did to the terrorists in New Mexico?"

"Not possible," Ahneevah said. "It was too soon after regeneration. Herbie was basically like a newborn and his electronics' range was limited to targets in close proximity. In effect his *teeth* hadn't come in yet and he could barely muster enough signal strength to block the four UAVs on a single frequency, let alone carry out a wide-scale, simultaneous jamming of multiple heartbeats."

The bleating of the aural warning system halted the conversation and the familiar NLU voice became activated. "We have an incoming flight of four fighter jets at 1,000 MPH plus. Their ETA is forty-nine minutes and they are carrying fissionable materials."

"Nukes?" Zack said incredulously. "Are they crazy?"

Leslee knew different. "No, they just want to get rid of the evidence. And make it almost impossible to investigate."

"That's just great ... Rosy ... *we* ... are the evidence."

Leslee gave a quick nod, "Precisely."

"The approaching aircraft are identified as F/A-22C Raptors," the logic unit voice advised.

"Raptors?" Zack blared. "They hardly ever used those fucking planes in combat against a foreign enemy, now they're flying them against us?" Zack turned to Ahneevah. "Can't you do what you did with the F-15s and shut 'em down?"

Ahneevah shook her head. "It's too soon. The most crucial segments of the StarStream's biotronic circuitry are still offline. The more sophisticated the system, the longer it takes to regenerate and become fully functional."

"You mean to grow up?" Leslee observed.

"Good analogy," replied Ahneevah. "A severe power drain would be the result if the remote electronics encoder and the inertia canceling network were activated prematurely, and without the avionics and inertial stabilization, the necessary high speeds for pursuit would be unattainable and reliable tracking data would be inaccessible."

"I remember," Leslee said. "Herbie won't let us go too fast because our bodies would be crushed by the extreme gravity forces at the excessive speeds and accelerations."

Zack caught her drift. "Yeah, we'd become oatmeal. What are we gonna do?"

While still flying the StarStream and considering other options, Ahneevah pulled the logic unit from the armrest slot and mentally linked up with the device.

"We deal with each crisis as it comes in front of us ... one thing at a time."

"Who are you kidding?" Leslee said through a chuckle. "You don't do anything *one thing at a time.*"

Ahneevah smiled to herself and the NLU began to hum and emit the familiar rainbow beam, which formed into a holographic message that hung like a road sign in the sky in front of the G VII and the B-2 Spirit.

RETURN TO BASE OR BE DESTROYED, it read.

Leslee and Zack were stunned to see Ahneevah make such a devastating threat. "But I thought unnecessary killing was against your principles," Leslee pointed out.

"It is. But *they* don't know that ... and given that the StarStream's weapons systems are still offline, what exactly do we have to lose?"

"You're bluffing?" said Leslee, surprised.

Ahneevah shrugged her shoulders and turned her palms up. "Hey, you hang around, you learn. Anyway, I could fib a little. I'm not exactly a Vulcan, you know."

Zack took the setup. "No, you're way better than that ... and besides ... you're real."

Ahneevah maneuvered the StarStream into an *attack* position above the two other aircraft and reconfigured the transparent area of the clamshell canopy to its solid mode.

Onboard the Gulfstream, the faces of Barrgrave, Bixler and the crew paled as they saw the vision now hovering above them like a cloud of doom.

"Do it now!" Bixler ordered. Within seconds both aircraft reduced power and began a one-hundred and eighty-degree descending turn back toward the base.

Zack and Leslee exchanged high-fives. "Smack-down," Leslee whooped.

"It moves like a blur, it has power that could save our planet, and it comes back from the dead. Is there anything the StarStream and its technology can't do?" Zack asked.

For the first time in a million millennia the corners of Ahneevah's emerald eyes began to well up in puddles of honey-hued tears. "It can't restore my original time-stream and allow me to hold my children's children or provide me with another embrace from all those that were dear to me."

In the laboratory, after the second the tech crew completed installing the new auxiliary power unit, Wolf sent them away and hurriedly brought all the equipment on line. This time the particle accelerator formed enough anti-particles to synthetically create an incredible army of micro-black holes. Like billions of invisible Pac-mans, the swirling laboratory-created phenomena ate up the basic photonic structure of the laser beam, causing it to disintegrate. Wolf was ecstatic but his celebration was short-lived as the biting cold struck again and Wolf lost control of his physical movements. *What the hell is it?* He wondered as he dropped to his hands and knees and with great effort, crawled toward the console.

EPIJODE THIRTY-FIVE

THE BEGINNING OF THE END
"GLORY ROAD"

The StarStream was hovering a few inches above the tarmac directly in front of the Gulfstream VII ...

... as it taxied to a stop on the desert base airstrip. The B-2 touched down at the far end of the runway and rolled up behind the G-7. Ahneevah, Zack and Leslee were standing in front of their flying teardrop. Ahneevah had removed her helmet and was holding it in her hand in its retracted, sliver-mode. Clay Reed, Zoe Reese and the other members of the Joint Strike Force, who were already waiting outside their Blackhawk choppers on a nearby taxiway, rushed over to the triumphant trio. In the meantime, Bixler, Barrgrave and the crews from the Gulfstream and Spirit had trickled out of their respective aircraft and onto the runway.

Ahneevah peered in the direction of Wade Bixler and Albert Barrgrave and purposefully headed in their direction. Leslee and Zack followed in her wake. As Ahneevah whipped past Inspector Reed, he handed the NLU section to her, and they exchanged subtle nods of mutual recognition and appreciation. Ahneevah did not take her eyes off the defeated Vice President and when she came within several strides of him she was not surprised to find that his demeanor projected no contrition whatever.

"Are you here as advanced recon for an alien invasion?" he growled.

Ahneevah stopped in her tracks. She had issues of true galactic proportions on her mind, but she considered that Bixler's *straight-line* called for a like response. Her eyes narrowed. "Yes, Earthling, this minor planet will soon be ours: now take me to your leader." Ahneevah stepped with intent toward Bixler who flinched. Then the intrepid 28th Configuration aviator looked back at the approaching Leslee and Zack, tilted her head, got up in Bixler's face and took his hand. "But first tell me about the Raptors."

Bixler felt a tingle. "They're carrying Harpoon AGM 84Ds," he blurted out but didn't know quite why. Zack and Leslee had arrived by this time and took positions on either side of the politician and the mogul.

"Harpoon AGM 84Ds," the NLU voice stated. "Twelve hundred pounds gross weight … Mach 0.85 with a range of 120 nautical miles. The missile normally carries a four hundred eighty-eight pound non-nuclear payload but these have been secretly retro-fitted to carry tactical nuclear warheads."

Zack moved in closer to the industrialist. "Don't tell me … Barrgrave Industries did the work, and it was listed as a black project so no one else knew about it. One thing, Albert, did you order that the engineers who did the modification work be executed to keep their silence?" Barrgrave opened his mouth to respond. "Never mind," Zack barked, and then turned to Bixler. "We need the recall code so we can signal the fighters to abort the strike … now."

"That won't do it. They're not on the guard channel. This exercise is to test the aircraft's performance under the extreme payload. The pilots think it's a routine milk-run with dummy warheads. They have no idea that they are carrying armed nuclear weapons."

"Armed?" Zack bristled. "I thought the pilot made the final decision to arm and fire," Bixler cleared his throat. "No more. A company in the private-sector found through research that most officers would have second thoughts about ..."

"... being responsible for starting a nuclear Armageddon?" Leslee interjected. "Another Barrgrave no-bid government contract, no doubt." She added with disdain.

At that instant, a Humvee skidded up and General Mitchell bounded out of the vehicle before the driver could even bring it to a full stop. The Vice President went on. "In the new rules of engagement we made both the arming and launch functions part of the flight computer system in case the human element decided against ..."

"... initiating the destruction of all life on Earth?" Zack mocked.

Barrgrave's shoulders slumped and he continued. "The idea was to be sure that upon reaching the initial aiming point the missiles would automatically launch and the mission would be accomplished."

Zack had fire in his eyes. "Mission accomplished? My God ... I've always believed that the ability to make a shit load of money doesn't necessarily guarantee brain power. Now I'm looking at the proof of that concept. Don't you assholes ever learn? American pilots flying American aircraft and carrying armed nukes while maintaining radio silence in United States airspace? What kind of moron has the authority to issue orders like that?"

Mitchell swallowed hard, and then spoke up. "The Vice President, through an obscure provision he slipped into Patriot Act VI."

"*He* slipped in?" Then Leslee tried logic. "What about the President sending the emergency recall code?"

"Negative," said Bixler. "Do you think we would actually trust him with that degree of responsibility? Besides, recall is locked out except when there are nukes involved, but this exercise profile says nothing about nukes."

"Shit ... of course," Leslee grumbled. "What was I thinking? You rigged the game. Pardon my French, Mister Veep, but with leadership being in the hands of greedy, psychotic imbeciles like you and your corporate flunky here, it's no wonder that this country and the rest of the planet is TFU." Bixler and Barrgrave looked quizzically at Leslee who turned up the volume and elucidated. "That's totally fucked up."

Then the NLU voice reported in once gain. "Thirty minutes to launch point on my mark ... mark. After deployment it will be another twelve minutes to target."

Ahneevah's eyes widened at Bixler and for the first time the bottle green orbs became tinged with a fiery red at their edges.

Wade Bixler got the message. "I can add two and two. Look, I'm standing at ground zero where four megatons of nukes will rain down in thirty-two minutes, for God's sake. We should get out of here."

Leslee, Zack and Ahneevah then turned their backs on Barrgrave and the Vice President. General Mitchell however, stepped nose to nose with Bixler. "I'm a soldier ... ready and willing to die for my country ... but I'll be damned if I'll allow my forces to get blown to kingdom come to cover up the treasonous acts of a pair of greedy, psychotic bastards. No sir, I didn't sign on for that!"

"General Mitchell, take charge of the evacuation," Ahneevah ordered with a nod of recognition to the CO. "Round up your troops and load them in the choppers, the Herk and the Gulfstream ASAP. Firewall the throttles and head east, away from the base."

"Yes, ma'am, and ... thanks." He saluted Ahneevah and with military snap she returned the salute and continued.

"Agents Reed and Reese, same story, head east. Zack, you're

going to fly in the StarStream. I'd send Herbie on auto but he's still … growing. I'll give you final instructions in the air."

Leslee was somewhat bewildered. "What about me?"

Ahneevah's eyes paled slightly. "I want you to go to a safe place in the Gulfstream. It's the fastest way out of the target area. This is not going to be a high-percentage operation."

Leslee put her hands on her hips. She was in firm argument mode. Then she thought better of it, softened her stance and stepped closer to Ahneevah. "You loved your mate, didn't you?"

"Like Zack said to you … it was *way more than love*."

"That's his voice and personality on the NLU, isn't it?"

Ahneevah started to answer but stopped herself, "How did you know?"

"I'm a woman … and no matter where … or when we're from, or what color we are, or how we're built, we are sisters. I've noticed how you react to his voice … how it eases you."

"Except for images, it's all that I really have left of him."

"What was his name?"

Ahneevah breathed deeply. It was a difficult moment for her. She turned to see that the evacuation was fully under way, and then she slowly exhaled. "His name was Ehzeelaan."

"Eh-zee-laan. Go on," Leslee gently coaxed.

Ahneevah took another look around. "We don't have time for this now," she insisted.

The lawyer in Leslee would not be denied. "There's always time for this."

Ahneevah sighed. "Very well … Ehzeelaan was an instructor in my preliminary aerial combat training phase and was my flight-leader on my early combat missions and also in the first of the three wars before the final one. But it was against military regulations and our oaths for us to have a relationship, and we obeyed that even though…"

"…even though you could hardly keep your hands off each

other?" Leslee offered intuitively.

"Yes," Ahneevah admitted. "As with your race, sensuality was an integral and joyous part of our lives."

This bit of news spurred Zack to pop in. "Jesus, now I gotta go up and face doomsday just when things are getting really interesting," Zack put his hands up, "scientifically that is."

Ahneevah's lips bowed up slightly at Zack's remark. "Zack, I noticed that you often refer to Leslee as Rosy. Isn't a rose a lovely but thorny flower?"

"That's her," Zack answered. "Rosy is her middle name ... Leslee *Rose* Myles. Do you have another name in addition to Ahneevah?"

"For record-keeping purposes we were given a family name-code that gave certain basic information about our birth. For example, my code is EBR-09Z in your language; E for the geographic location where I was born; B for the facility where the birth took place; R for the solar span part and 09Z for the daystar segment I first joined my circle. But I was always known as Ahneevah E."

"Did Ehzeelaan always call you Ahneevah?" Zack asked.

"Not always. Sometimes in softer, quieter moments he called me Neev and I called him Ez. "

Leslee put her hand on Ahneevah's shoulder. "Would you have gone with him on his last mission if you had the choice?"

"I did everything I could to get reassigned but we were ... married and it was forbidden."

"Well, it's not forbidden here," Leslee said and took Zack's arm with her free hand. "This could very well be our last mission and there's no way I'm running out on it. I'm going to be with Zack. Anything else is simply not acceptable."

Ahneevah smiled at Leslee's formidable reasoning powers and placed her hand on her *sister's* shoulder. "I just don't want to see you harmed ... I never had a sister. Now that I have one I'd like to keep her."

"I second that," Leslee said calmly, "I'd like to keep mine too … so … to that end I suggest you come up with a really good plan."

Ahneevah briefly considered Leslee's words and then stepped back. "Very well then, if the two of you are going to be the command crew of the StarStream, let's make it official."

With a photonic signal from the NLU com-link, Ahneevah created an opening in the opaque frozen-plasma canopy of the hovering StarStream. A luminous, fluctuating, spectrum of light beamed out from the cockpit area and danced on Leslee and Zack. As the pattern of the rainbow scan realigned, the combat fatigues the two were wearing morphed into flying gear similar to Ahneevah's, including the insignia from her Air Arm branch in the 28th Configuration. Zack wiggled his body and then smiled. "I see what you mean about not needing underclothes."

"This flight suit is like overalls and under alls," Leslee chimed in. "Am I right?"

Ahneevah nodded affirmatively, "Okay, let's get ready to launch," she ordered. Zack and Leslee saluted. Ahneevah returned the salute and watched her friends with great concern as they boarded the StarStream and sat side-by-side in the realigned cockpit which was now minus the third seat. Ahneevah then turned her attention to the rest of the air crews. "Who is the B-2 weapons officer?"

The two Stealth Bomber pilots stepped forward. "The Spirit has no specific weapons officer. I'm Lieutenant Colonel Noah Jax … call sign *Cracker*. And this is Captain Ed *Cool Hand* Stone. We are both rated to fly the B-2 and to operate all of its systems as well."

"Fine," Ahneevah said, "but it will be necessary for me to pilot the craft. I will need only one of you."

"I'm the aircraft commander, and with all due respects ma'am,

B-2, One-Niner is my airplane. I signed "Spirit of Kitty Hawk" out, and she's my responsibility," Lieutenant Colonel Jax said. He seemed sincere and a bit disheartened. "And ... uhhh ... sorry I shot you down."

"Me too," Ahneevah responded. "It was a ... new experience for me to use the Ejection Pod."

"I had no idea that we were on the wrong side of the situation," Jax offered. "Maybe now I can help set things straight."

The two Air Force officers saluted Ahneevah. She smiled in appreciation of the gesture, returned the salute, reactivated her helmet and started to put it on.

"Very well, Colonel, Captain," she said. "It's time to see about putting *possibility* back on the menu. As they say, let's kick the tires, light the fires and get your ... *Spirit of Kitty Hawk* into the fight."

EPISODE THIRTY-SIX

DAX WOLF AND THE CUSTODIANS
IN
"THE OUTER LIMITS"

***D**ax Wolf felt the sting of something immense, awesome and ...*

... all at once the entire magnitude of theoretical input on Earth became an infinitesimal fragment in comparison to the startling expanse of universal knowledge which his new alien-sensing radar had absorbed. Wolf detected that in preparation for the imminent application of the Null Quotient on Earth, the Custodians had already amassed the required elements together from the ambient matter in the universe and in their coalescing they created a dwarf star compacted down to a size small enough to fit in an average catcher's mitt. This unfathomable energy source was exactly what Dax needed to complete his terrifying work. He chortled demonically upon the realization that the galacticlally spawned *Supreme Beings* were playing right into his hands. How could they have known that they were making it all so simple for him? How could they even have the slightest notion that they were about to step off into a chasm that would send them straight back to their own *before*?

EPISODE THIRTY-SEVEN

"WAR GAMES"

"Passing through niner-thousand-five hundred," Colonel Jax advised as ...

... Ahneevah smoothly lowered the aircraft's nose to level off. The Lieutenant Colonel watched in awe as she effortlessly manipulated the controls on an aircraft she had never flown.

"Ma'am, the F/A-22s are ten minutes from Harpoon launch coordinates, and we're level at ten thousand feet."

"Roger, Colonel, this ship sure handles a whole lot better than the X2."

"If you don't mind me saying so, ma'am, you sure have a way with flying machines. But how did you learn our language? Were you somehow able to observe us from your home world?"

"You'd be surprised, Colonel."

"Did you have a rank in your military?"

"I was an Air Arm Commander ... much the same as your general officer."

"Then I'll call you general."

"You don't have to. I hear the respect in your voice. Ma'am is fine."

Lieutenant Colonel Jax smiled and nodded in the affirmative, "Noah is okay with me," he said and then made a few adjustments. "Now our signature won't be visible on the F/A-22's radar."

"Auto pilot on," Ahneevah said as she pulled the logic unit from its *invisible* pocket in her sleeve. Zack's face popped up as a 3-D holographic image. Jax looked on, fascinated.

"Zack, what's your current status?"

In the StarStream, Zack, in the right seat, slid the NLU into the armrest slot and Ahneevah's visage appeared before him. "We still have no indications of the weapons system coming on line, and we show nine minutes to launch point. Even if we get weapons back in time, how can we use them against the Harpoons? Won't the wave track the missiles back to the Raptors that fired them?"

"I'm not concerned with the weapons system right now," Ahneevah said. "It's the remote encoding interface unit in the auxiliary celestial nav-pack that we are going to need."

The flight of F/A-22s reached their launch coordinates and automatically fired their Harpoon AGM 84Ds. Then, as the mission profile dictated, the Raptors executed full afterburner, climbing one eighties and shrieked away. The missiles immediately showed up on the Stealth's scope. Colonel Jax was tracking them.

"We're fifty nautical from the targets," he said. "Three point four minutes for maximum EMP effect."

At ten miles distance, the light-speed particle bursts from the EMP cannon installed in the Spirit's bomb bay struck the first two incoming Harpoons, the rockets' electronics streams were instantly corrupted and both began to tumble out of control. The self-destruct program automatically initiated and the missiles exploded, sending a smoldering mini-hailstorm splashing down on the sea of sand. Things were looking better. Jax had the third Harpoon bracketed, but when he actuated the pulse cannon firing circuit, the EMP weapon malfunctioned. The Colonel made several adjustments and then tried again. This time there was an explosion, causing a hiccup throughout all the aircraft's systems and then B-2 One-Niner proceeded to rumble and shake its structural objections to the blast. The enunciator panel lit up with a chorus of chirping and pulsing over-temp warning indicators. Colonel Jax instantly went to work and began taking the necessary corrective measures.

Despite some of its main systems teetering on the brink of failure, the Spirit remained airborne. However, the EMP cannon continued burning and the flames started to ignite some of the adjacent sections of the weapons storage area. Additional fire warning alarms and lights on the instrument array began blaring and blinking. Jax activated the fire-suppression units and Ahneevah hit the button to jettison the EMP cannon but it remained hung up. "Fire-suppression engaged." He watched and waited for the system to begin operating.

"Re-sequencing the abort mode circuitry," the Colonel advised, "Try again." Ahneevah punched the switch and the pulse weapon separated from the belly of the aircraft and spun away.

"StarStream to Kitty Hawk … Ahneevah, we still don't have any indication that the remote encoding interface unit is up," Leslee reported over the logic unit.

"Roger that. It's time to enter the tactical cycle into the NLU. I have to transmit it in my language to be absolutely sure it is interpreted correctly."

Ahneevah proceeded to give the StarStream instructions via the logic unit. After she was finished, she again spoke to Leslee and Zack.

"Stay with the … with Herbie and have confidence in him. He knows what to do … his big sister gave him a good plan. As soon as the encoding mode activates, it will require a manual reboot. Just follow the light sequence."

Zack scanned the StarStream's panel. "Light sequence?"

"What light sequence?" Leslee inquired.

"It will come on in time," Ahneevah responded. "And remember, do only what's in front of you." She paused, as if going through a mental checklist. "One more thing … and this is critical. If Herbie gets too close to the Harpoon, you must abort. The free neutrons that are thrown off by Herbie's propulsion power grid will penetrate through to the radioactive material in the warhead and initiate a spontaneous nuclear chain reaction. You will have to stop your … uh … bogey using stand-off tactics."

In a different patch of sky, General Mitchell, in the C-130J and the other aircraft crews observing the chase from a safe distance, were witnessing a strange sight indeed. What appeared to be a teardrop and a boomerang were chasing two nuclear missiles in the pristine *blue room* high above the barren expanse of the Southwestern desert.

As Ahneevah turned the black, flying wing toward her objective, Zack and Leslee could see the flames shooting out of the B-2 *Spirit's* belly. Zack got right on it. "Ahneevah, we can see fire in the forward weapons bay."

"Roger," Ahneevah responded. "Fire-suppression isn't fully functional and we had to eject the EMP Cannon from the bomb rack assembly. It will be necessary for us to attack our target via direct contact. We must hit it and bail."

As the B-2 continued on an intercept course with the other Harpoon, Ahneevah had to fight to keep the aircraft stable.

"We're only gonna get one try at this," the Lieutenant Colonel said. "If we don't stop it, we can't catch it before impact. How's she feeling?"

"*He* is feeling sloppy."

"He?" the Colonel said, slightly bemused.

"I'll explain later. I think the primary fly-by-wire avionics are going off line. Is there any backup?"

"Only ejecting or landing."

"Not an option."

"Which?"

"Neither."

"The redundant central processing unit activates automatically," Jax advised. "If you don't have it, you're not going to get it. The fly-by-wire CPUs provide roll, pitch and yaw axial corrections from one millisecond to the next so that the aircraft can be flown using normal control inputs. No pilot alive can fly this ship without computer assistance. It's impossible."

Ahneevah searched through her mental network the shook her head.

"That's it. There's no cyberonic interface in the fly-by-wire array," she said quietly. "Okay then, Noah, whether I'm alive or not is sort of a gray area anyway … so … I'll have to take a shot at the impossible."

Colonel Jax could not begin to fathom the extraordinary dexterity and mind power that was at work. It had multi-terabyte capacity superseding the most powerful mainframe computers and robotics of the day. He marveled at the incredible way in which this paradox from another world—or time—or both—was able to control the aircraft; her right hand making the blurring stream of constant minute corrections with the stick, and her feet *boogying* on the rudder pedals.

Then, one of the plasma screens started flashing a dreaded warning of incipient *Ejection System Failure*. The fire was not yet out and had begun to burn into additional sections of the electric circuitry. Ahneevah and the Lieutenant Colonel both picked it up. "This mission is going south," he warned.

Ahneevah was racing through every level of her consciousness to find a solution. When she finally thought that she had arrived at one, everything was suddenly swept into an unfamiliar sea of inestimable nothingness.

EPISODE THIRTY-EIGHT

"WHEN WORLDS COLLIDE"

A lthough they were the Universe's main arbiters of time, the Custodians did not have a nanosecond to react …

… or even register or share their astonishment. At light speed, without warning, the photonic energy that was their essence transformed from white to red and crossed the entire spectrum from infrared to ultraviolet. Then … most inexplicably, the Custodians vanished into nonbeing.

Dax Wolf had successfully perfected a nano-bot particle accelerator, and the Custodians' creation of the magnetar neutronic dwarf star with its galacticlally powerful magnetic field was recognized by him as the necessary first phase in carrying out the Null Quotient. Wolf had taken advantage of the tremendous inner gravitational force generated by the extreme magnetic mass and utilized it to engineer organic micro-black holes and saturate the dwarf star with them, an accomplishment that challenged every theory that 29th Configuration science had postulated, from general relativity to quantum mechanics to string theory. These matter-and energy-consuming voids had a proportional gravity so powerful that they were able to combine in the core and form a Singularity which attracted the Spectronic particles that embodied the fragmental building blocks of the Custodians. This subatomic essence was pulled beyond the Event Horizon and toward the endless abyss of the cosmic plug-hole.

Paradoxically, the Nine were being *nulled* by virtue of their own creation.

EPISODE THIRTY-NINE

"THE DAY THE EARTH STOOD STILL"

The Micro Magnetar Dwarf including the Cosmic Singularity contained within … hung suspended between the infinite forest of time-neutral, matter and energy stanchions …

… that stood within the phantom temporal gulf. The spherical object appeared to be no larger than a baseball, though it had the mass and gravity of a medium star. The apparent magnitude was so great that if the celestial orb were situated in the same chronologic envelope and cosmic standard plane as the Earth and existed under normal physical laws, its gravity field would have torn the blue-and-green oasis apart and absorbed it in a trillionth of a second.

Without a single thread of a logical explanation, Ahneevah found herself out of the B-2 aircraft and in a frozen nightmare, being slashed by scores of razor-sharp mini-blades of ice which opened gaping wounds all over her body. Her flight suit was being shredded and was showing no signs of regeneration. The glacial cold was becoming unbearable.

Initially, Ahneevah conjectured that it was solely due to her multilayered thought processes that she was able to have any awareness whatsoever of the unexpected incursion of startling surroundings and miasmal discharges swirling about her. She was at once an outside observer but simultaneously immersed in an ocean of existence on a subatomic scale, and was using her enormous mental capacity to consider the varied possibilities of exactly what action was being taken against her, and—by whom. At first she reasoned that it must have been precipitated by the Custodians. However, if that were the circumstance, where were they? Further, it deeply troubled her that she was unable to acquire any traceable biological or thought patterns emanating from Zack or Leslee. As these issues were volleying between her numerous levels of analysis, she was staggered that she could identify only a single other active consciousness in her midst. Ahneevah could not fathom that within a stellar body compressed into the most compact *zip* file ever created, containing nearly seven-billion sentient life forms, all she could read was the unmistakable telepathic fingerprint of Dax Wolf.

Wolf was relaying selected visual images directly into Ahneevah's psyche. She could see the Nine Custodians assembled in the center of the Brazilian rain forest. Then, in a tera-span, stark astonishment shattered Ahneevah's concentration completely. Her multiple consciousnesses briefly flashed in and out several times as she *saw* the Custodians dematerialize.

"Your Nine Spectronic friends' fragmental neuonic-stream has already crossed the Event Horizon. It is now trapped in the dark-matter gravity field within the micro-magnetar and will be drawn into the Singularity at its core," was the message received by Ahneevah in a digital mind-to-mind transmission from Dax Wolf. For the first time in a billion years, since she received the report that Ehzeelaan was missing, every channel of Ahneevah's immense thought network was overflowing with a paralyzing dread. *"Why was Wolf able to function? What did he know of the Custodians and how could he have actually defeated them?"* She deliberated.

Dax Wolf *read* her questions and was faintly amused. What he had achieved was remarkable even by time continuum and intergalactic standards. By his actions, Wolf had instantly rendered moot the matter of whether or not the Custodians would spare and save or enable the demise of the 29th configuration.

Digital emissions radiating from the darkest corners of Dax Wolf's subliminal consciousness were launched eerily through the ganglia within Ahneevah's second inner skull and deep into the subatomic fragments of her cerebral mass. It transformed the battlefield into a phantasmic reality of a bizarre landscape of muddy, chemical craters and potent, high-pressure, airless vortices. Though Ahneevah now existed solely as pure energy, her physical shell remained present in a particle form making her susceptible to the severe corporeal battering.

The first manifestations of Dax's barrage was the searing pain, stinging stench and toxic anguish of the spewing acids and gasses, followed by the crushing weight of rampant, mega-force vacuum columns. Despite the fact that this was an extra-temporal battle, it carried with it the excruciating implications of severe bodily trauma. Rationally, Ahneevah knew that her wounds were not part of the reality plane of existence, but the afflictions were nonetheless unbearable and worse, they were mortally distracting. Dax was able to bring Ahneevah's consciousness back and forth between the full physical world and the elemental particle world. In a freezing liquid nitrogen environment, her limbs felt as if they were constantly shattering and her heart began pounding at over a hundred beats per minute to compensate for the severe sub-arctic temperatures. As a result of the relentless cyber-attack, Ahneevah was inflicted with palpable wounds to multiple areas of her body, and even the full weight of her wide-ranging intellect could not ward off Dax Wolf's debilitating strokes.

Ahneevah writhed in severe torture as she was ripped from one dimensional horror to another; interminable heat; stifling and repugnant environs with stinking, brimstone pools. At each agonizing, stop, Dax's ghostly digital voice continued to bombard every one of her mental levels.

"I used the biomechanical DNA that I collected from the crash site of your ship in combination with the genetic material from your hair samples to create a hybrid cell from the nucleonic mass in the StarStream's organic fusion furnaces. But the major key was provided by the Custodians themselves when they created the pulsar-magnetar neutronic body where the subatomic mechanics of everything on this world, including all living matter, is now in suspension." Wolf went on to describe how he was able to trap the Spectronic fragments that were the building blocks of the Custodians and their consciousness and being, and ensnare them between the temporal planes near the Event Horizon of the nano dark star. "With the Custodians neutralized, I also control all there is, or rather was, on the Earth and I have concluded that this civilization is not deserving of another chance to populate the stars. It would be more like contamination."

"If all life perishes, you will perish with it," Ahneevah moaned.

"My energy pillars will continue and I deem it well worth sacrificing my physicality, knowing that this failed, hopeless and useless planetary accident now called Earth and its wretched human parade of inferior civilizations will finally be excised."

Ahneevah's nervous system of silicon-flecks was overheating to the point of burnout. All of her levels of consciousness were fighting to stave off and compartmentalize the intense torment that was gripping her. As the ordeal became more relentless, Ahneevah found that she was becoming incapable of resisting it. She was shocked as never before when she heard herself screaming uncontrollably. The virtually invincible warrior felt as if she were being torn limb from limb and sensed that her life fluids were sadistically being drained out of her body—drop by drop. She couldn't know that though the physical agony was crushing, it was merely a distraction. Dax Wolf's assault on her was foreshadowing far graver consequences. She could feel her multiple levels of awareness being penetrated and fractured by the strong synaptic discharges carried in Dax Wolf's brain waves.

Wolf knew that the StarStream's biologic component was engineered directly from Ahneevah's DNA, enabling him to attack the unique creature far beyond the cellular level. Now he would move in for the kill. The renegade genius began raining a maelstrom of DNA anti-matter *particle arrows*—targeting the electrons which whirled about Ahneevah's nucleic under-pinnings. A contained chain-reaction was initiated. As a consequence, the subatomic pions that were holding together the nucleons of the atoms that made up the cellular components of Ahneevah's corporeal essence were being annihilated. The dazzling and crackling barrage of solid photonic fragments began eroding her chromosomal balance, thereby inducing it to constantly fluctuate between a one and two-particle state. This organic instability would result in the total destabilization and eventual obliteration of Ahneevah's physical and mental funct-ions. Wolf was successfully breaking down her subatomic being particle by particle and dismembering asunder her incredible mental and physical network. As she neared the Event Horizon, she knew that if her basic particle essence slipped past it and was absorbed into the Singularity, her being would be wiped out and lost forever. She would become the part of the stardust from which all living matter arose. Non-existence was overtaking Ahneevah at the speed of light and she was unable to stop it.

So be it, she reasoned as the fragmental sparks of her life continued fading. *I've been dead before.* Suddenly, as her sub-atomic core crossed the Event Horizon, she had a fleeting glimpse of Zack and Leslee in one of her last remaining mental conduits.

Where were they?

The stream of electronic outputs coming from Ahneevah's almost entirely exhausted intellect was reduced to a meager trickle. She contemplated the irony of her suffering defeat through a brain-wave pattern that Dax Wolf might have randomly picked up from one of the past Configurations. At least she had some concept of *how*. Along with the *how* was the remarkable realization that she had become ghostlike. It was quite puzzling to her that if she were indeed now merely a soul and part of the spirit world, why was there a force still trying to eliminate her? Horrific questions traversed her consciousness, which was now reduced to a single pathway; questions with no apparent answers. Had Dax Wolf intended to keep her imprisoned at the very edge of non-being? After surviving a billion years, instead of simply becoming stardust, would she otherwise be consigned to an ultimate fate of perpetual agony in a swirling multiverse? Stranded in forever: being relentlessly and repeatedly ripped to pieces with only enough mental perception left to suffer the evil, mind-bending offensive? Eternally being beaten to death without dying? She'd never heard of Hell until she absorbed the stored knowledge of the 29th Configuration, but the definition of Hell perfectly described her current harrowing predicament.

Ahneevah's last involuntary thought-stream before the encroaching blackness arrived was perfectly in accordance with her nature. Even at the end, Ahneevah was Ahneevah. Her one remaining mind track was flooded with fleeting images of her circle, her young ones, and, strangely Zack and Leslee—then— nothing as her last brain wave faded out a nano-second before contact with the Singularity.

EPIJODE FORTY

"STAR WARS"

There was a jolt ...

... and the sudden resistance rocked Dax Wolf. He reeled at the implication. Ahneevah's atomic structure had been nullified down to the most elemental particles, and should have already been absorbed by the Singularity. What could possibly explain the fact that she still managed to exhibit enough conscious will to resist his bludgeoning subatomic onslaught?

The backup was totally unexpected by Wolf and came as a complete shock to Ahneevah. At first she thought that she had been out of action again and might have missed another billion years. Then she recognized that Dax Wolf's unyielding mind-storm was still blasting at her, still pushing her toward her finish. She also was able to perceive that even though Wolf was attempting to increase the intensity of his assault, he was somehow unable to do so. Most telling of all was Ahneevah's realization that the depletion of her thought processes had somehow been reversed and most surprisingly, she picked up a growing incomprehension within Dax's own multifaceted brain network. She was able to zero in on highly fluctuating mental patterns that indicated—stress.

Maybe Wolf had overreached and was he running out of gas, she considered. *No, that wasn't it!* Remarkably, Ahneevah became cognizant of a series of nascent biotronic mental infusions gradually flowing into her from a source which in her current state she could not immediately identify. This new input was somehow counteracting Dax Wolf's powerful psycho-blitz and was lifting her energy elements away from the doom awaiting her at the plug-hole of the Singularity.

Ahneevah theorized that if the intellectual counterattack were coming from the Custodians, then it would be manifest as a torrent of cerebral download rather than a relative dribble. She concluded it was more likely that Dax still had the Custodian's fragmentized core imprisoned in the bowels of the myriad micro black holes. Whatever the situation, Ahneevah was thankful to be theorizing and *concluding* about anything. In truth she was glad to be functioning on any level at all. Threads of her enormous intellect were reemerging albeit very slowly. She was barely at one full processing level, which limited her to a defensive posture only.

I need to somehow repel Wolf's mental grip, she reasoned. *To survive and fight back it is necessary for me to reverse Dax Wolf's electrostatic battering. To do this I will require more resolve.*

Nevertheless, she was satisfied to still be *alive*—sort of—and realized she couldn't waste energy trying to figure out exactly why she was now in some state of conscious existence. Another of her mental tiers kicked in, then several more. Suddenly the answer came pouring into her brain in a burst of unmistakable rantings.

"Fuck, it's working," barked Zack. "I can feel it, Rosy. The creepy little positron son-of-a-bitch is losing his grip on her. Damned if you weren't right on the money."

"Just keep your concentration. Stay focused. We still have a while before TFLS."

"TFLS?"

"The fat lady sings."

As the majority of Ahneevah's mental levels sprang back into action, she realized what was happening. Although she never could have imagined the circumstances, she arrived at one unerring conclusion. The simple truth was that in all of nature, DNA knows. While Dax Wolf discovered through experimentation that Ahneevah's life strands possessed a dominating quality, he couldn't have realized or even considered the probability that both Zack and Leslee had acquired and absorbed certain key components of Ahneevah's genetic mechanism. When Ahneevah used her electrics to neutralize her adversaries, it was a limited burst and there was no permanent transfer. However, when she joined with Leslee to short-circuit the lights during the firefight in the hangar, she had to use a more benign force with an increased duration to accomplish her purpose. The combination of the reduced power and the augmented time exposure to her bio-electrics set up stabilized genetic mutations.

Zack's change came through Leslee. She passed it on when she inadvertently used the blue webs of mini-lightning to cauterize and close his head wound. Due to the nature of Ahneevah's remarkable genetic triple helix, her nucleotides were absorbed, aligned and fused perfectly with Leslee and Zack's DNA ladder. Among other properties, it enabled them to boost their mental acuity to a multi-level state—not as unlimited as Ahneevah's but more than enough to do the job of working together to liberate their friend from Dax Wolf's debilitating iron grip.

Due to Leslee and Zack's retaliation, Wolf's powerful psychic force was being minimized like a window on a computer screen. However, as Ahneevah was searching his psyche, she determined that he had indeed entrapped the Custodians. The war had now come down to a cybernetic Wrestlemania on a battlefield of pure energy within a chronologically-suspended, cross-dimensional magnetar. When Ahneevah's mental reservoir was at a sufficient enough level, she was able to join Zack and Leslee in the galactic mental tug-of-war.

The formidable trio's concentrated multiple-level brain wave bombardment slowly and steadily overpowered Dax Wolf. As a result, he was forced to gather the bulk of his cerebral reserves in an attempt to ward off the assault. This further degraded his mental control over the nano-bot particle accelerators, which destabilized rapidly. Suddenly there was a bloodcurdling digital scream that shook the temporal pillars and seemed to reverberate through the entire Universe.

"Rosy, tell me that wasn't the fat lady."

EPISODE FORTY-ONE

"TIME TUNNEL"

It was Ehzeelaan's familiar NLU voice that served to sling-shot Ahneevah's consciousness to ...

... the realization that she was back on the standard temporal plane. She returned to the exact millisecond she was taken and Colonel Jax had no awareness that she'd been gone. Ahneevah's flight suit repaired itself because Molecular Adhesion is an active function which is unaffected by temporal transversal. However, the mental and physical mutilations she suffered through Dax Wolf's crippling psychic blitz were still apparent. When crossing the temporal stanchions, any organic damage inflicted within the standard plane can be counteracted through a shift to the null-fragments, but the reverse does not occur. If the injury is imposed in the fragmental plane, that condition sustains in the transfer back to the standard. Had Colonel Jax been able to see the open wounds on Ahneevah's face there would have been a series of unanswerable questions. Fortunately, Ahneevah's flight helmet prevented the Colonel from becoming aware of her injuries.

Ehzeelaan's calm voice washed over the B-2 flight deck and brought some slight comfort to Ahneevah. "During this configuration's World War II, the Royal Air Force had to defend London from the Nazi bombing raids. In 1944 and 1945 the British were attacked by the German Luftwaffe's forerunners to the cruise missiles of today. These weapons were called V-1s—*V* for

Vengeance—but by reason of the sound emitted by their pulse-jet engines they were more commonly referred to as buzz bombs."

"Right," Jax declared. My great-grandfather flew a Supermarine Spitfire. Either the *Spits* or Hawker Hurricanes would track the V-1s and shoot them down with machine guns or cannons. Sometimes the pilots would run out of ammunition and so they came up with a tactic called *tipping*." The Colonel demonstrated by using his hands to simulate the two aircraft. "Great-granddad, Group Captain Nolan Jax, would fly the Spitfire right up next to the buzz bomb; slip his wing six inches or so under the enemy bird's wing and create an airflow disturbance, sort of like an aileron." Jax then used his thumbs to suggest wings. "The V-1's wing would *tip* up, the gyros would topple, and there would be one less attack asset to worry about."

Ahneevah instantly grasped the implications. "Yes, if we make the Harpoon tumble, the onboard computer will interpret it as a flight dynamics malfunction and will automatically initiate the self-destruct program."

Then Ehzeelaan's voice spoke up again. "There is a caution. The V-1 had over eight feet of wing for the British fighter planes to work with. The Harpoon only has eighteen inches, and it's more a directional vane than a lifting airfoil. The B-2's vortices won't be enough to overcome the rocket power. You will have to tap the fin with your wing tip, which is a one in a hundred move under the best of circumstances. Even if disruption of the Harpoon's course and stability is achieved, there is a second caution ... unpredictable collateral affects from the exploding out-of-control missile may cause catastrophic structural failure of your flight vehicle."

Maybe a crew of experienced *Spirit* pilots could accomplish the task Ahneevah had before her—if they were flying a perfectly functioning B-2—maybe. The maneuver that the wounded refugee from another existence had to execute was made exponentially more difficult because of her own injuries and the fact that she had to work with a significantly damaged bird. The stealth craft's fly-by-wire system was inoperative—and there was a fire onboard. Ahneevah considered that a 100-to-1 was unacceptable odds—but the alternative was unthinkable.

At this point the StarStream had flown to the horizon and was positioned in front of the other Harpoon so as to allow the teardrop craft's telemetry to probe the nuclear missile's brain and, hopefully, scramble it.

Ahneevah was in visual range and closing on the target missile. She was on the stick, and rudder pedals, making corrections faster than the eye could see. The cabin was starting to fill with smoke. The Colonel, on oxygen, was amazed that Ahneevah didn't seem to be bothered by the caustic fumes. He had no idea that she had practically stopped breathing and that the bulk of her respiration system was dealing with the task of filtering out all noxious substances.

Meanwhile in the StarStream, one of the remote encoding interface sequence lights came on. Zack passed his hand over it and another began winking. Leslee put her hand above that one and a third and fourth lit up. Leslee and Zack looked at each other and each *waved out* a succession of lights until Ehzeelaan's voice sounded from the NLU. "Remote encoding interface sequence will commence in ninety seconds."

In the B-2, Colonel Noah Jax was now concentrating on the approach-to-target vectors while Ahneevah, still in excruciating pain and continuing to weaken, dug down to the depths of her amazing skills to triangulate and orient the aircraft into the precise angle and attitude required. It was necessary for her to utilize every one of her functioning mind-paths to keep focused on the extremely complicated maneuver.

"Did I tell you that the B-2 is the most survivable aircraft ever built?"

"That's good news, Noah. But that's *built* on this Earth. What

I'd give for a StarGazer TSE right now—although I'm not exactly current in one. It's been over a billion years since I last flew it." Colonel Jax shot a puzzled look at Ahneevah, but then dismissed the remark as if she was speaking figuratively.

As she approached the Harpoon, Ahneevah gritted her teeth. "I've already lost one battle with Armageddon; and one is enough."

"Ten meters, one up," the colonel reported. "Now eight … okay … three more, level. Perfect, you're under the Harpoon center fin by less than a half of a meter. You've got to teach me how to fly like that."

"You're going to need more powerful computers on board," Ahneevah responded.

"On the ship?"

"Negative." Ahneevah pointed to her head. "Up here … perhaps someday."

The Harpoon's track remained steady and time was running out. This was the last option before ramming. Ahneevah's control input was so precise that when she tapped the right rudder pedal to keep the B-2 straight and flicked the stick to the left to pitch-up the right wing in order to make contact with the Harpoon fin, her hand didn't even seem to move at all.

The Spirit's right wingtip actually came up less than six inches at the end of a one hundred seventy-two-foot seesaw that without Ahneevah's guiding hand would have been a totally unstable aerial platform. As the Harpoon rolled and toppled, Colonel Jax immediately applied full power on the four engines, and the 69,200 pounds of thrust vaulted the craft into a maximum acceleration climb-out in an effort to distance the craft from the wildly gyrating missile, which quickly self-destructed. However, due to its proximity to the blast, the *Spirit's* right wingtip was partially ripped away severely compromising the composite skin surface. But even more critical, the wing tank and various fuel lines were ruptured, and almost fifty percent of the starboard control surface servos were inoperative. It was difficult enough keeping the B-2 under control when there were two full wings and totally operational control surfaces to work with; as opposed to the craft missing one meter of its right wing and having extremely limited banking and turning capability.

Because of her gnawing injuries, Ahneevah's magnificent wide-ranging consciousness had finally reached its limit and she blacked out. At that instant, the low-fuel indicator and a number of other audio and visual alarms came to life; beeping and flashing on the enunciator panel. The B-2 rolled to the left and entered a deadly flat-spin. The state-of-the-art bat-winged jet bomber was swiftly becoming uncontrollable.

Colonel Jax tried to neutralize the corkscrewing flight path by using the thrust of the two starboard GE 100 turbofan engines asymmetrically against the rotation, but the loss of the control surfaces due to the explosion aerodynamically cancelled the thrust vector. The graveyard spiral toward the ground continued unabated.

In the StarStream, Zack and Leslee watched helplessly as the B-2 spiraled earthward. Even if they could help the stricken craft they both knew that intercepting the Harpoon nuclear missile was their primary objective. Leslee was brimming with fear for her *sister* and Zack tried to comfort her. "She'll be okay Rosy. She always is, isn't she?" Leslee wasn't so sure.

Brusquely, Ahneevah was literally *shocked* awake. Ehzeelaan's voice spoke apologetically. "Excuse the crude method but a strong burst of current was the only way to bring you back. I have supplied you with enough electronic reserve to finish our mission." The one-time infusion of particle energy from the NLU was enough to temporarily diminish the negative effect of the wounds Ahneevah acquired from her mind-link encounter with Dax Wolf. She quickly assessed the situation and experienced a déjà vu.

"The rudder and elevon panels are frozen in a left-wing-high attitude. We have to change the airflow component some other way. Noah, I'm throttling back on all engines."

In mid-sentence Ahneevah was already taking action. In a micro-tic she cut the power, and began, in specific intervals, to alternately open and close the pod bay doors, raise and lower the landing gear and flaps. The extended surfaces were not designed to be deployed at high speeds and began shuddering as if they were about to peel away from the Spirit like a banana skin.

"Don't worry," the Colonel shouted. "She'll, uh, he'll hold together."

Ahneevah's eyes flashed. She had come full circle. She had applied the same pilot techniques that she used a billion years ago to save the StarStream. By deploying the B-2's various extendable components, Ahneevah successfully re-directed the air flow and created enough drag to slow the spiral and lower the airspeed.

"Now give me full power on one and two," Ahneevah commanded.

"Roger," replied Colonel Jax and fire-walled the number one and two throttles. This action resulted in stopping the aircraft's rapid, spinning descent. However, even though the B-2 was no longer falling out of the sky and was on a straight course, the jammed elevons made it impossible for Ahneevah to keep the wings level. Though holding a steady ground track the craft was in a steep right bank. As if to add a final nail to the bat-winged coffin, the fuel sensor began to chime.

"We're bingo on go-juice," Jax warned. "Also, the flaps aren't fully operative and can't be deployed to their normal landing configuration." Seconds later, engines one and two flamed out. Without the opposing thrust to keep the plane on course, the B-2 once again began veering to the right.

Ahneevah realized that accomplishing a dead-stick, belly

landing on the desert floor with the crippled *Spirit of Kitty Hawk* would be a disaster. With the airplane turning to the right and holding a thirty-plus degree bank angle, the dipped starboard wing would make contact first and hook the sand which would trigger a devastating ground loop and induce the craft to roll over and over until it disintegrated.

Zack's voice broke through over the logic unit.

"Can the StarStream provide any assistance?"

"Negative," Ahneevah responded. "Complete your mission. Destroy your target."

Without power and little means of control the B-2 was descending at over two thousand feet a minute. As it came down through two-thousand feet above the surface, all of Ahneevah's thought processes were scrambling to find a solution. None presented itself. There was nothing she could do.

"What is it with me and flight craft?" she wondered out loud. "Even after a billion years they keep trying to slip out from under me." Noah Jax gave Ahneevah a baffled look but was too busy to question her words. "If we get out of this, Colonel, I will explain everything."

The Colonel instinctively saluted, "Yes Ma'am."

Inside the StarStream, Ehzeelaan's NLU voice ramped up once more.

"Probing target control package, distance ten nautical miles … the target destruct sequence has been remotely activated. In ten … nine … eight …"

The B-2 was in a steep right bank, five hundred feet above the desert floor and traveling at an indicated airspeed of nearly four hundred miles an hour, much too great a velocity to touch down safely or even crash-land without ending up as a pile of shattered composite material. Both Ahneevah and Colonel Jax could see the explosion of the Harpoon that Leslee and Zack were chasing in the StarStream. They smiled.

"Well done, my friends. Take good care of Herbie."

Oddly, Leslee's upbeat voice came back over the air waves. "I'm afraid I can't do that. He's your puppy and your responsibility. Besides, I think that the three of us have a rather important meeting soon. You know … the Nine Halloween-refugee ghosty-ghosts."

Ahneevah was perplexed at Leslee's positive attitude and choice of topic given the dire circumstances but suddenly, at two hundred feet, she felt a slight tap and some vibrations quiver through her control yoke, and to her complete surprise, the stricken flying wing was beginning to level off. Then the communications channel crackled, "B-2, One-Niner … General Mitchell and Captain Stone here."

Out of the corner of her eye Ahneevah saw that the C-130J's left wing was tucked under the Stealth's crippled right wing, coaxing it back to a straight and level flight.

"Ma'am, Colonel … saw you were drooping a bit and thought you could use a little wing-to-wing kiss … to lift your *Spirit*. We've got some big tires on this bird and we can take you right down to the sand. And ma'am, when we get a few feet above the surface you might want to neutralize the lower elevon slats as much as possible to reduce contact with the ground."

"Roger that, Captain Eddie. At about three meters," Lieutenant Colonel Jax replied.

With the B-2 now flying somewhat under relative control, Ahneevah was able to raise the nose, thereby continuing to lower the airspeed. The bat-winged aircraft, leaning on the turbine and prop driven C-130 Herk, leveled off near the ground.

An instant before Spirit of Kitty Hawk's belly made contact with the desert floor, Ahneevah neutralized the rudder and elevon panels as much as she was able and Captain Eddie deftly reduced the Herk's power so that its left wing could smoothly slide behind and away from the B-2's right wing. "Thanks for being my wingman," Ahneevah said.

"No problem, ma'am," Captain Eddie replied. "And just for the record, if you were the pilot, I'd fly with you on a brick. You are an aviator's aviator no matter what planet you come from."

"Roger that, and also for the record, Captain, I was born on this planet, somewhere not too far north of here, but I ... I'm ... *older* than I look," Ahneevah responded and continued guiding her bird with a broken wing to a soft touch-down. It skidded along the desert terrain to a gentle stop. With no fuel on board there was no smoke or fire, only clouds of sand and dust. Ahneevah motioned for Lieutenant Colonel Jax to get out of the aircraft. When he was clear, she removed her headgear and could see the fresh blood stains from the deep lacerations on her face. The stalwart combat aviator was aware that by this time the transitory energy boost she received from the NLU had run its course ... then ... she was gone.

The choppers, the Herk and the StarStream landed nearby and the crews met Colonel Jax with exuberant cheers, congratulatory hugs and high-fives. However, Leslee and Zack knew that these symbolic gestures of victory were premature, for real victory was grimly in question.

The prevailing issue regarding the continuance or demise of the 29th Configuration was far more somber and teetered precariously on a singular fulcrum; a scale upon which twelve consciousnesses were positioned; three sentient beings on one side and Nine far more weighty extra-corporeal photonic life-forms on the other.

The Custodians again took action. Once more the revelation of the outcome all happened in an instant, but this time a part of the confrontation could be perceived by the survivors while it was occurring. The ensuing chasm in the continuum made the surreal the norm, and the norm ... nonexistent.

EPISODE FORTY-TWO

"THE TWILIGHT ZONE"

An almost infinite bridge of bleakness, devoid of any of the colors of life, connected the hemispherical horizons ...

... while the only recognizable features on the austere globe called Earth were the familiar shapes of the poles, oceans and continents. The Custodians were standing in an ashen desert that had been the Brazilian rain forest—the heart and lungs of the amazing blue-and-green miracle of the cosmos. As a direct result of the Null Quotient, this once lush garden, teeming with infinite varieties of animal and plant life, now matched the rest of the world's land masses as a grimly barren expanse of pallid gray. The stars were just beginning to be dusted from the heavens by the first rays of dawn. Golden shafts of light seemed to be reaching down from above, almost as if they were tugging the fiery solar disk upward—urging it, coaxing it to embark on its daily ramble across the sky. Peculiarly, though the figures of the Nine Custodians were spectral in nature, they somehow managed to cast elongated, crisply dark and eerie sunrise shadows on the monochromatic landscape.

An icy, whistling wind and swirling murky dust served as reminders that all of this was once a living, breathing body sailing through the cosmos with billions of living, breathing souls aboard. But the current life cycle on the miraculous orb of spinning-rock called Earth might well have reached its end. The

29th Configuration of sentient life had apparently breathed its last, and the third planet, circling a moderate-sized star, was once more reverted to its beginnings as a cradle of life for the succeeding inhabitants; a birthplace containing the definitive material which is the basic fabric of all that is or ever was, the ultimate molding clay of existence; the stuff from which everything in the Universe has been and will ever be made; stardust.

The Custodians observed their work and nodded with satisfaction as the full-scale StarStream flashed out of the baseball-sized micro-magnetar and hovered amidst the stark emptiness. The outer and inner canopies opened, and Zack and Leslee helped the grievously injured, barely conscious Ahneevah exit the craft. The green-eyed immigrant from a different world and another temporal existence was steeped in the pain of her multiple wounds and racked with mental exhaustion. She could not stand without having her arms around Leslee and Zack's shoulders for support. The three stared breathlessly at a panorama which could only be accurately described by the famous Apollo 11 Astronaut Buzz Aldrin's expression … *magnificent desolation.*

"It is done. The temporal columns have been realigned," the leader of the Nine advised as he floated in the trio's direction. "Our journey together is at an end."

"At an end? What end … and what about Ahneevah?" Leslee sobbed. "She's dying."

"No life can expire within the null-fragment stanchions, only in the standard plane." Then the Lead Entity glowed slightly brighter. "The three of you have shown great determination and power."

"Then what of us?" Zack asked. "We cannot exist here. Will Ahneevah die if you send us back to the normal temporal flow?"

We were able to acquire much unexpected insight from you," was the reply. "You defeated an overwhelming enemy and even rescued us from an uncertain destiny."

Leslee looked around at the bleakness. "Comforting, but more poetry," she said. "Is our *'thank you'* that we get to be stardust ... or slime ... or amoebas ... or some other one-celled life form?"

"Perhaps someday, but not *this* day," the Custodian answered. "We have decided to heed Dr. Carver's suggestion. Though far too many of those in your world exhibit greed, apathy, malice, dishonesty, gullibility, incompetence and ignorance, there are also those who display the nobler qualities such as mercy, compassion, integrity and justice. The compressed atomic structure of everything that was living or created on this planet is now contained in the spherical singularity whirling beside us in an extra-dimensional stasis."

Zack looked at the revolving body. "Wow! It's like the ultimate flash drive."

"Your entire world is temporarily suspended between the matter, energy and chronomic forces as were the three of you," the Custodian revealed. "It was the only way we were able to reset the Earth's ecological dynamics without canceling out all living and non-organic matter that was already present. We will null it all out if you so choose."

Leslee responded first. "That choice wouldn't be very merciful or just, now would it?"

Zack offered his two cents. "Come on, fellas. We've been through a whole lot already. No trick questions ... please."

The Custodian nodded. "A reasonable request, but we must warn you now that if the doom-point is reached again, we will return and will most definitely *take out the garbage*. At present there remains one more task. Ahneevah and the StarStream are a billion years out of phase and we have decided that they must unfortunately ..."

Leslee cried out, "No! Not a chance. Don't say it. Don't even think it."

Ahneevah, the sole surviving member of her kind and still the soldier, removed her arms from Zack's and Leslee's shoulders and took several wobbly steps forward. "I understand," she said obediently to the Lead Custodian. "I have no future here. I am worn down and all I had is gone. Perhaps it would be better if I were ..."

She turned around and painfully gathered a tearful Zack and Leslee in her arms and held them close to her, much as she embraced her children untold billions of yesterdays ago.

"Please, don't make it any more difficult than it is," Ahneevah solemnly urged.

"No problem. I'm all over this. It's what I do," Leslee whispered softly but confidently.

Counselor Myles was not about to accept the Custodian's judgment without an argument, no matter how high up on the *Supreme Being* scale they registered. She backed a step away from Ahneevah and held her unique *sister's* hands in hers.

"First, you're wrong, Ahneevah. All you have is not gone. We may not be much in the grand scheme of the universe but you have us." Leslee let go of Ahneevah's hands, kneeled down and scooped up a handful of the lifeless gray powder. Then she stood and let the *stardust* pour out between her fingers. "Do you think we saved you from being turned into one kind of nothing by Dax Wolf so you could be turned back into this? Nothing part two? N—O—T ... That's not a change I can live with ... at all!" Brushing a few errant tears from her cheeks, she spun around to face the Custodians. "It seems to me she's already had her nap ... totally ... for a billion years! By that measure, forever is more or less ... overkill."

"We will consider that," the Lead Entity said. After a heartbeat the Custodian nodded to the others and spoke again. "We will null the craft, but as for Ahneevah ... we have decided to take her with us on our future journeys. She shall be one of us."

Then Leslee began to laugh. "You think that's a promotion?

Going from being dust to wind up as matter-slash-anti-matter? You guys really don't get it, do you? I mean for entities that have been around ... well, nearly forever anyway, you sure seem to have the grasp of ... of a Homer Simpson."

The reference was lost on the Custodians, giving Leslee an opening to continue pressing her case. "Okay, how's this? Did it ever occur to you that being a bunch of fireworks and living ... or whatever you call your sentient stream ... uhhh ... existing in between tics and tocks for zillions of years might have caused you to lose touch with reality—any reality! Let me ask you something. Can you see into the future? And please answer 'yes' or 'no.' It would be refreshing."

Another Custodian floated toward Leslee. "The future is random and has yet to exist. If we were able to see time forward then we would know which configuration would succeed."

"Close enough. I'll take it as a 'no.'" Then, without hesitation, Leslee launched into a rapid-fire mode of questioning without a pause to allow the Custodians to answer.

"If Ahneevah wasn't here, would we even be having this conversation? How do you know that she wasn't supposed to be here and help lead our sorry-assed world out of the darkness? What the hell good can she do us as the tenth Sparkly? Never mind. Don't answer. You've been *Spectroning* around for billions and billions of years, and the best thing you did was when you screwed up and gave us Ahneevah. How can you not see that she unquestionably has a future here? She's *our* future! Why don't you consider that everything we've all experienced happened precisely because she belongs here? How do you know that it wasn't destiny that brought her across the Configurations because she was supposed to survive? This world must be told Ahneevah's story ... first person ... and hopefully learn and grow from it. And maybe ... just maybe, the grim reality and horror of seeing the extermination of an entire world will even shock those

322   THE TWILIGHT ZONE

on the executive boards of the military-industrial *complex* out of their *burning* need to create wealth by destroying life. You have the advantage of coming and going by starlight and perpetually being on the *road*. Tell me straight, have you ever actually witnessed the unending day-to-day struggle of intelligent life to survive?"

"No, we have not," was the answer.

"You ought to stick around a while and try it! It's no picnic … and has a much higher degree of difficulty than floating around on starlight." Leslee emphasized, and then continued. "With all due respect … uhhh gentlemen and … ladies, if left on our own, we probably will wind up as murky talcum anyway, but with Ahneevah we might have a chance. Don't take that chance away from us."

The Custodians consulted telepathically for a moment, and then the Lead Entity spoke, "Well argued, but as you say in your profession it is merely conjecture."

Leslee started moving in for the kill. "Conjecture? Just look what she did at the medical center in New Mexico. After she went into action, thousands of innocents were saved and no one was hurt, not even the terrorists."

"An isolated incident," was the lead Custodian's reply.

"No, I do not accept that," Leslee said, fuse lit. "You can't minimize the power of any isolated incident by simply dismissing it. With all of your stunning intellect, how could you have possibly missed that boat? If you really were paying close attention it would have been obvious. Events that seem minor can turn out to be monumental. Billions of years ago, the third planet in orbit around a moderate-sized star was struck by another world. In the unimaginable vastness of space, itinerant objects collide with each other all the time. This particular smashup happened in this particular solar system. Hey, maybe you even saw it … now in terms of the infinite universes it was a relatively minor occurrence but as we have theorized and you pointed out, that roving protoplanet, Theia, led to the formation of our Moon. Without the Moon this third rock from the sun would be mainly under water, and though you might have some very big and bad sharks, the Nine of you would have no job security 'cause you'd still be looking for a world that could think. I mean sharks are great at an *all you can eat buffet* but no shark on this world can write a book, paint a picture or play Scrabble. And even though whales can croon a tune and porpoises are super-smart, Willy can't engineer his own recording or file a copyright, and Flipper can't write down his history. Yes, our Moon coming into existence was a random event but a big deal for us and maybe at some point a big deal for the Universe as well. Then, somewhere in prehistoric times an early ancestor of our race probably saw a bolt of lightning strike a tree and set it aflame. Fire! The primeval hominid probably touched it, got burned and then carried it back to his ... or her people. There were no newspapers or twenty-four-hour cable television to broadcast the story, and the fire-finder certainly had no idea of the future world-altering ramifications of the discovery. But without fire our configuration and most other configurations would have been stillborn. Also, let's consider the rat's ass decision of five delusional Supreme Court justices to stop a state from counting legitimate votes. A politically motivated decision from *that* group of nine eventually brought us to the point where the Nine of you had to make another house call. Finally, it is my belief that along with the preponderance of radioactive fallout resulting from the nuclear destruction of 28th Configuration, it's nulling, precipitated by your own hands, if you have any, was most assuredly responsible for the survival of Ahneevah and the StarStream by keeping both in the state of temporal suspension that we found them. I submit it was a consequence of your own *isolated incident* that permitted Ahneevah to be here in the first place, and you cannot take her away from us. Consider the possibility that her distant past is the key to our entire future."

Leslee and Zack then stepped in front of Ahneevah, who was visibly touched by the gesture. However, Leslee was by no means through. She placed her hands on the Custodian's shoulders and was surprised to find that they felt solid even though they appeared to have no substance.

Another Custodian read her reaction and explained. "As matter and energy transform from one state to the other they vibrate at the speed of light. We came into existence at the precise instant of that transmutation of one to the other and continue to exist between them."

Leslee quickly found a handle. "I get it. You're like Certs ... a candy mint *and* a breath mint."

Zack smiled at Leslee's analogy. "Not bad. They're like the children of matter and energy, and retain the dynamic properties of both forces."

Leslee faced the Nine. As she set herself, the jaw muscles on the side of her face flexed several times. "Well, then somewhere within those dynamic properties you must realize that this mess is as much yours as it is ours. Logically, by prematurely turning Ahneevah into yet another Sparkly you will subvert an existence that has survived beyond anything you yourselves or theoretical science could imagine and quite frankly doesn't seem to be within the scope of your job description. I'm proud to be part of a culture which believes its most important contribution to posterity is contained in the words *Tikun Olam.* '*Repair the world.*' I get the impression the 'repair the world' concept is diametrically opposed to the one in your operations manual which seems to say, '*It's all screwed up anyway, so let's turn everything into gray Johnson and Johnson baby powder.*' Haven't you people ... or whatever ... learned anything? Maybe zipping around up there for untold billions of years made you a little goofy. You *were* useless, you know, but at this point you have the chance to make a difference. It was you in your own words … or digital impulses, who explained to us how unique our planet is and … how utterly alone we *all* are in this Universe. Knowing that, why would you even think of taking Ahneevah from us now?"

Silence … The Custodians had blinked. Leslee sensed their hesitation. They never expected anything like her, and more important, they had to consider the possibility that maybe there were many more Leslees and Isaacs. If true, that could represent a sea change in the continuum. "Excuse me," Leslee said, and then purposefully moved within the Custodians' ranks as if she were one of them.

"You are *the* jury of Nine. Certainly the most consequential arbitrators this world has ever known. Let's put aside the fact that in the future, if she survives, Ahneevah could possibly become the mother of a new race. Instead, I ask you to consider those leaps forward that you spoke of. The ones you said are built into the system, allowing one configuration to build on some of the discoveries from those that came before. Well here you are … almost twenty-nine big bumps down the road and there still hasn't been a Configuration that stood the test and went out to spread its seed. Have you ever asked yourselves why? Maybe direct information is needed rather than some isolated thought bursts."

Zack, moved by Leslee's appeal, felt tears well up in the corners of his eyes and most atypically, he found nothing appropriate to say, so he resolutely walked into the ring of Custodians to join Leslee. He took her hand and she squeezed his in response. Then she continued her plea.

"Just the technology Ahneevah possesses could be our first real step into the future that you yourselves envision for us. The energy source Ahneevah has brought us in the StarStream can do no less than end our dependency on fossil fuels … right now!"

Zack's mind winged back to the moment he first met Leslee in the Negev when she was a lost, needy, wreck of a college girl. Or maybe he was really there as he *replayed* their whole history and marveled at the extraordinary woman now standing next to him; a woman who was pleading the case for the existence of all humanity to Nine omnipotent beings almost as old as the Universe itself … and … winning.

"That's my Rosy," Zack whispered through a soft sob that barely crept out of his throat. Then he wiped the moisture from his eyes and wrapped his free arm tightly around Leslee, who motioned for Ahneevah to join her and Zack inside the Custodians' circle.

"With Ahneevah's help," Leslee went on as Ahneevah was barely able to shamble over to her, "we could have the power to fight the greed and intolerance that always lead to destruction. She will be an ally who can aid us in defeating those who have unlawfully seized control and will continue to poison our world with their avarice, hate and injustice. Hey, if you are really intent on having another galaxy-hopping companion out there, I've got a better Sparkly-in-training for you. Why not take Dax Wolf with you?—wherever he is." The lead Custodian flashed red for a brief second, then indicated the swirling magnetar.

"Definitely," Zack echoed. "He's a little bent but I'm sure you can straighten him out. After all, he proved that he's got the tools and the talent, and besides, there's really nowhere else for him to go."

"Yeah," Leslee added. "He sure as hell makes a lousy Earthling, and he has real issues with the *works and plays well with others* concept."

And so it was that Sanford Myles' once dysfunctional daughter outflanked a group of beings that existed almost since time itself. After an unusually long pause, the Custodians gazed up at the sky where the stars had now melted into a crystal blue dawn. The

Lead Custodian slowly raised his arm and turned to Ahneevah.

"You shall not create any more," he cautioned.

"Only the one," added another.

Ahneevah nodded once in acquiescence. "I understand," she softly replied.

The Custodian raised his arms which, to Leslee's surprise, now revealed hand-like appendages at the ends of them, and then the ancient celestial being lowered one hand and placed it on Ahneevah's shoulder. As it rested there, the toll taken by her battles with time, space, and Dax Wolf was instantly wiped away, her enchanting emerald eyes once again blazed, and her mental and physical scars were healed. Finally, without another word, each of the star-born life forms dispersed into Spectrons and flashed upwards. Ahneevah, Zack and Leslee gawped at their ascension. Zack cupped his hands around his mouth like a megaphone and shouted up to the clouds. "Don't be strangers!"

Ahneevah put her arm around Leslee's shoulder. "Leslee, that was quite remarkable. You are brilliant at your profession. I believe you would have been enormously successful even in my Configuration."

Leslee appreciated the generous compliment and put her arm around Ahneevah's shoulder.

"I was trying to keep from losing a sister and a friend. That always ups the ante, you know. It makes it more personal. I think they did catch me on what I said about you possibly being the mother of a new race." Ahneevah's brow wrinkled, and in response Leslee added, "Well, they said you could not create anymore, just the one ... only you. I certainly would have surmised that given their background as uh ... super beings ... they would know that you can't create anymore.

"I can't?" Ahneevah said. "It seems to me that based on everything that's happened ... you must be aware that our DNA is compatible."

Leslee, a bit perplexed by Ahneevah's words, looked at Zack for help. Zack merely shook his head. "No. It's not that," Leslee offered. "We figured out the DNA thing when we succeeded in stopping Wolf from turning you into star soup."

"It was your autopsy," Leslee continued. "The MRI lasted long enough to show that you don't have a reproductive system and couldn't bear children."

Ahneevah's confusion deepened another notch, and then she smiled and her eyes opened wide with clarity. "Dear Leslee, you've misunderstood. The Custodians were speaking of the StarStream. They were aware that it is to a great degree biological and could be cloned. I concurred that one of those was enough."

"Abso-F-ing-lutely," Zack said. "If there were a bunch of StarStreams running around, this rock would go right back to its standard global pissing contest. Who's got the biggest pee pee?"

"So then, can you still have children ... uhhh ... young ones?"

Ahneevah removed her arm from around Leslee's shoulder and turned to face her. Then she placed her hands on Leslee's lower stomach and spoke in a silken voice. "Under normal circumstances my reproductive system will continue to be active for many years. The processes that resulted in propagation were not random events to my race. They were thought-initiated measures and occurred only when a conscious choice was made by both partners to do so. You see, the system within me for conception and prenatal development is not always present like yours is. It comes online in one lunar cycle and only when our shell detects a mutual psychological intent to introduce new life. It lasts only during the gestation time span."

Zack was right there. "Mental contraception ... talk about *real choice*. I wonder if the religious lunatic fringe would object to that or would those nut-cakes bring out the thought police?"

"Okay ... let me get this straight," Leslee continued. "You're saying that you were part of a civilization populated by women who never had to worry about birth control or having their periods. And had no possibility of PMS … no menopause, and you blew yourselves up anyway?"

Ahneevah thought for a moment and then smiled in recognition. "Females were not the problem," she replied.

Then a light bulb went on inside Leslee's head. "God, I got to get me one of those *on demand* gestation thingies."

"Possibly, "Ahneevah offered, "but since it is a dominant trait, your female children will most certainly have it." Leslee gave Ahneevah double thumbs up. "Brilliant."

Suddenly, two columns of Spectrons poured down from the clouds, shimmered in between Leslee and Ahneevah, and re-materialized into the star-born Lead Custodian.

The ethereal Lead Entity seemed to take a breath, then turned and faced the two women.

"I neglected something," he said, and for the first time his mouth actually formed the words.

Zack bored right in. "Yes, I guess you do that once a Configuration."

The Lead Custodian placed a *hand* on the side of Leslee's face and stared hypnotically into her soft hazel eyes. In that gaze, Leslee felt an exhilarating magic course through her. In an instant that would last in her mind forever, she swore that she had glimpsed the entire Universe, its beginnings and beyond.

"I now stand with you on your chronological plane. Perhaps you are correct, Leslee Myles. We shall see. Stardust is stardust," the Custodian said.

Then the Custodian motioned for Zack to come and stand next to Leslee. He put his free hand on Zack's shoulder and moved the other from Leslee's cheek to her shoulder. All at once, the archeologist stood tall and looked more like a man in his middle thirties.

"You shall have much joy and will experience bold adventures together," the Custodian announced.

The Lead Entity's words surprised Leslee. "Is that a wish or a prediction?"

"It is both."

"But you said *shall have* much joy. I thought that you couldn't forecast the future."

"It is not a guarantee, just a … a feeling."

Leslee jumped right in. "A feeling? A feeling! Good. Work on those feelings. If you can manage some more of them … it might be a positive step for humanity and the known and … unknown universes. And BTW, as a personal request," she smiled serenely and added, "in case you come back to check up on us … keep the hands. They make you *feel* more … human … and frankly … right now … we're all you've got."

For the first time in as close to forever as an ethereal consciousness can get, a slight smile bloomed on the Custodian's otherwise stoic face. "Perhaps some day, if you wish, you *all* may join us," he said.

"Hold that thought. But please don't rush it, okay?" Leslee responded.

All of a sudden, Dax Wolf spilled out of the whirling micro-magnetar behind them.

Leslee looked at Wolf with distaste. "Hey, I tried. I wanted them to take you. What in the hell could we charge you with? If I told a grand jury that you were guilty of aiding and abetting the destruction of the Earth and plotted the end of time, they'd never indict anyway."

The Custodian placed his hand on the wayward genius and was about to invoke a thought but before he could they both dissolved into nano-fragments of light and streaked upward.

Zack, reveling in what had just transpired, took Leslee's hand, pulled her close and they kissed. Ahneevah beamed and both Leslee and Zack wrapped their arms around her. Leslee eyed

Ahneevah and flashed a mischievous grin. "So," she whispered, "between us girls, exactly how old are you …in 29ᵗʰ Configuration years?"

Ahneevah thought for a brief moment. "If you don't count the billion or so years I was caught between the null fragment stanchions and the … well, between the tics and tocks … twenty-nine."

A somewhat surprised Zack said. "Twenty-nine? You don't look twenty-nine."

An unusual touch of vanity washed across Ahneevah's face. She ran her hand through her honey-colored hair. "Well I looked a wreck before, but now after the Custodians … wait, do I appear to be … more advanced than twenty-nine?"

Leslee laughed heartily and drew Ahneevah closer, "Welcome to the 29ᵗʰ … no maybe the 30ᵗʰ Configuration and our planet Earth."

Out of the blue, Ahneevah picked up a barely audible high-frequency warble. A look of profound curiosity perched on her face and she lifted her head skyward. Zack and Leslee were oblivious but even if they had perceived the rapidly quavering sound, they would not have been able to understand it right away. When Ahneevah figured out exactly what she had heard, she shook her head in disbelief.

Zack and Leslee caught Ahneevah's peculiar look. Zack spoke first. "What?"

Ahneevah answered, with visible reluctance. "As they were flashing through the sky, I heard a baffling vocal exchange between the lead Custodian and Dax Wolf."

"What?" Leslee prodded.

"I heard Wolf say, 'we are now ten.'"

"So? Maybe it was Wolf's way of acceptance that sailing around the stars with the rest of the Sparklies would be more preferable to him than staying here and being Dr. Evil. There's nothing mind-bending about that. Lighten up."

Ahneevah shook her head. "No, that's not it. It's the Lead Custodian's response that really intrigued me." Leslee had now gone from simple prodding to urging and then to one small step below exasperation. "Spill!"

"When Wolf said, 'we are now ten,' the Custodian's reply was, 'Once more, as we should be.'

As astonishing as the possibilities of this revelation might have been, they were immediately overshadowed by the miracle that was beginning to unfold around them. The contained micro-magnetar suspended nearby began to spin rapidly. As it whirled faster and faster it took on the appearance of a spiral galaxy and when it flattened, a growing funnel of Spectrons began to emerge. Some of the vibrant kernels of light settled in Ahneevah's honey strands of hair and glittered like gilded, phosphorescent snowflakes. Then the tornado of whirling radiant nuggets began to expand and bathed the nulled area and far beyond in a sea of tiny golden globules. As each brilliant seed of sparkling energy danced on the gray terrain, abundant life sprang from it. The garden began to sprout again with the touch of each splash of the wondrous cosmic dew, which coaxed a profusion of plant and animal life to start reappearing, blossoming and growing, flying, swimming, walking and crawling all around. The gray Earth once again was becoming cities and forests and jungles and mountains and deserts. Not a creature on the planet missed a beat or had any awareness of what had taken place.

EPILOGUE

THE END OF THE BEGINNING
"BACK TO THE FUTURE"

An armada of news and law enforcement helicopters was whirling, twirling, and rickety-racketing in ...

... the airspace above the rural Tennessee community of Whitwell. Even one chopper would have been out of place in this pastoral town of less than two thousand. Zack, Leslee and Ahneevah thought it fitting to have their first press conference at the Whitwell Middle School, where in 2001 the school Principal, several teachers and student volunteers created the Children's Holocaust Memorial to shine as a beacon against intolerance and evil. The undertaking was centered on the collection of six-million paper clips from all over the Earth to represent the Jewish victims who were exterminated under in the shadow of the *final solution*. Due to the project's world-wide renown through extensive press and television coverage, twenty-nine-million paper clips were ultimately received. As a result of the overwhelming response, the organizers rigorously sought and acquired a German railway cattle car to serve as a memorial. The wooden car was constructed in 1913 and actually used in the conveyance of holocaust victims to the death camps. It would eventually house eleven-million of the paper clips that were contributed in memory of the six-million Jews and five-million Catholics, gypsies, homosexuals and others who were transported in similar railroad vehicles and perished amid the horror, brutality and insanity of the despicable Nazi regime. A sign placed on the memorial read:

"AS YOU ENTER HERE
WE ASK YOU TO PAUSE AND REFLECT
ON THE EVIL OF HATRED AND INTOLERANCE."

Leslee, Zack and Ahneevah were deeply moved by this unique expression of grace that blossomed in this southern hamlet, which at the time the project was envisioned and enacted, had not a single Jewish person living in it.

Every major news outlet and every important journalist was jammed into the relatively limited space that encompassed the school grounds. But who wouldn't show up for a gathering rumored to reveal an *alien* creature to the whole world? There were two rows of chairs in front of the railcar. Sanford, Pinky, Jason and Elliot Myles and Inspector Clayton Reed, Special Agent Zoe Reese, CIA pilot Jake Neely, Snow Smith and Joshua Dov Benjamin and Nurse Lynne Daniels were seated in the first row. Seated in the second row were General Ethan Mitchell, Colonel Noah Jax, Captain Eddie Stone, Doctors Oliver and Amelia Carl, along with Doctors Ilias J. Solomon, Abbie Diamond, Ruthie Becker and Maxine Pearl.

As well as the event that was about to take place, the crowd was also murmuring about the resignation and subsequent arrest of the President, the Vice President, most of the cabinet officials, and the apprehension of Albert Barrgrave II. Reed and Reese saw to it that classified files, which the perpetrators thought were protected by Executive Privilege, mysteriously turned up. They would implicate the band of conspirators in committing highly treasonous acts: purposely withholding knowledge of terrorist movements from the proper investigative authorities and using an elite U.S. armed forces unit to declare war against two American citizens so as to maintain and advance the stranglehold of the ruthless corporations over the people of the United States. Not to mention invoking martial law under completely false pretenses and canceling two elections. The Speaker of the House, the next in the line of succession, was sworn in as President and appointed a new attorney general who would see to it that all those of dubious character who committed criminal acts against the U. S. Constitution were prosecuted.

There were no opening speeches. Zack simply walked up the six stairs to the platform in front of the railcar. Ahneevah and Leslee followed. The three were wearing their flight-suits but the military insignia were no longer visible. Camera strobes were flashing so furiously that even in the daylight it appeared that the trio was under a single constant artificial light source. The buzz from the crowd dissipated into a stunned silence as the army of press began to fully absorb the other-worldly beauty and elegance of Earth's newest and yet oldest known living resident. Zack stepped up to the microphone.

"I am Dr. Isaac Carver." After being so prevalent in the news, Zack and his narrative were well known by the crowd and they shouted back. "Hi, Isaac."

Zack smiled and continued. "This is acting Attorney General, Leslee Rose Myles." Zack reached out and took Leslee's hand. "And this … is Ahneevah, who is most definitely not an alien. Ahneevah has been here on our Earth since a very, very long time ago … before it was even called Earth." Ahneevah, with grace and dignity, glided over to the podium and through her wide, jade eyes, slowly scanned the throng. Those in attendance and those watching throughout the world would later swear that her soft but somehow inexplicably penetrating gaze burrowed deeply inside every one of them and touched the very essence of their humanity.

"It is most appropriate that we are at this place because my world ended as a result of hatred and intolerance—those same evils that this magnificent and yet quietly elegant memorial shines so firmly against. This creation and others like it will forever serve as a constant reminder for us to keep the promise that the souls here represented will never be silenced."

A sparkling smile lit up on Ahneevah's face and seemed to flow from her into the hearts of those gathered. Her green saucer eyes shined as she placed her arms around Zack and Leslee, her new brother and sister. Then she continued, "Through the three of us you will all have a voice and will always hear the truth."

Leslee looked out at the wonder of a new hope and added, "We pledge that we will stay here in this venerated place and answer all of your questions even if it takes ...well... a billion years."

The usually unflappable men and women of the fifth estate at once stood and erupted into applause. They knew that this event might well mark the beginning of an age that the world could never have imagined.

Leslee leaned over to Ahneevah, pointed in the direction of her family and softly whispered, "That's my brother Jason—cute, isn't he? He's single, what do you think? He's a pilot too."

"Well," Ahneevah answered through a warm and infectious smile that lit up her emerald eyes, "like the sparkly one said, we are all stardust."

A palette of colors like a mini-aurora borealis swirled about Ahneevah's head and then seemed to blossom out like fireworks—or was it merely the reflections of the barrage of camera strobes?

The questions came in droves, and Ahneevah answered every one of them in the language that it was asked. She explained the operation of her Neuronal Logic Unit and the StarStream and to show some of its awesome capabilities, she put the craft through some of its paces high overhead. As a powerful expression of the blistering terror of Armageddon, she telepathically guided the

StarStream to hover silently above the multitude and project holographic images showing the *holocaust lilies* and the fiery death and destruction which ended the 28th Configuration.

"In the far distant past I watched my old world die. This is what the end of everything looks like. It has been said that war is the very gates of hell opening up and destroying the future; the result of leadership's failure in all of its guises. I saw them ... deception, stupidity, greed and arrogance. Those impostors were my world's unavoidable destiny, and it could be yours ... ours. To those who believe we must always look forward and not backward, I can only repeat the words of Dr. Carl Sagan, 'You have to know the past to understand the future.' Failure is the greatest teacher so I beg you to be vigilant and to not allow the same mistakes to be repeated. Those in the past who acted with ignorance, incompetence and criminality must be held accountable. Now, this is what the colors of reemerging life look like," Ahneevah declared as the hologram changed from carnage and ruin to stirring reflections of the blank alien-gray stardust canvas of Earth being repainted with the recognizable dazzling shades of rebirth. "Dr. Carver, Counselor Miles and I witnessed a second chance ... a world being reborn ... this world ... your world ... our world." The incredible images of resurgence continued to play on the serene and chastened faces of those present and billions of others throughout the Earth.

After a slew of other technical and political questions, Wolf Blitzer of CNN had a more basic inquiry. "Ahneevah, what does your name mean in your language?"

"I might ask you the same question." A playful look glinted in Ahneevah's eyes.

"Uh ... Wolf, is it?" The gathering laughed and the CNN reporter smiled.

"First, let me give you the correct pronunciation of my name."

Zack gave Leslee a little nudge. "This should be interesting," he gushed. Agents Reese and Reed also exchanged knowing grins.

Ahneevah accurately recited her name for the first time in front of the ginormous global audience, and the average blood pressure of the human race dropped nearly thirty points.

"With regard to my name … my forebears have told me that the day I was born I tried to stand up almost immediately. Ordinarily it took at least one lunar cycle, a month, before our legs could support our weight. They thought I was purposely attempting to signal my own arrival … to announce myself. So they gave me a name that captured the quintessence of that attitude. It was an unusual name among my people because it really was not a name at all. It was merely a pronoun and a verb connected together to form a name. I believe the direct translation into your words is … *I exist* or more straightforwardly … *Ahne* means *I* and *evah* refers to a state of being, *is,* or more correctly, *am.*"

Zack and Leslee came to the same realization at the same instant and turned to each other.

"I am?" they softly whispered. "I am," Ahneevah said humbly making it simply an answer and not at all a statement.

Leslee's eyes opened wide, "oh … my …God!"

Far beyond the Earth, outside the Heliosphere, and more than one-billion miles above the orbital plane of the Sol-3 System, a digital-telepathic exchange took place. Dax Wolf initiated the mind-stream conversation. "Have our new allies been enlightened as to the existence of the Time/Dimension Wormwells?"

"They have not," was the Lead Custodian's response.

"Perhaps they should be. After all they've been through, they do have a right to know that which we know."

"I am confident that they will be able to deal with anything that might happen. That is precisely why they were tested," crackled the Custodian.

"The inherent forces of the universes were unleashed against them and they were the first Sentients to survive, Wolf countered. "They must be forewarned that recurrent temporal fluctuations between the Wormwells can provide standard and non-standard conduits for Configurational transitioning."

"That is a valid observation," the Lead Custodian replied. "I will consider communicating with the green-eyed one ..."

"Ahneevah ... *her name* is Ahneevah," Wolf interrupted with an uncharacteristic show of reverence. "Of course," the Custodian consented. "I ... we ... shall convey the information regarding the existence of the Time/Dimension Wormwells and any inter-Configurational transit events to Ahneevah."

*ETCETERA

WAR OF THE WORLDS

Meanwhile ... at another temporal continuum crossroad ...

... Jroz N'y-Greedjia, a malicious despot and the last planetary leader in the 27th Configuration, knew that his world's water resources were nearly exhausted. Hundreds of millions were suffering the misery and death brought on by tongue-swelling thirst and acute dehydration. But instead of calling for science to immediately develop and put in place solutions such as desalinization and reverse electrolysis to restore the life-sustaining liquid, N'y-Greedjia chose to devise a plan that would reserve the precious remaining supply for those that he deemed the *deserving* one-percent of the population. He dictated that his scientists synthesize and release a deadly viral-toxin and further decreed that the *chosen* receive inoculations with an antivirus serum. The virulent strain spread quickly throughout the global population. Within days, the unchecked epidemic of death left billions of decomposing, disease-ravaged corpses strewn throughout the land masses and floating on the seas. However, Jroz N'y-Greedjia had not anticipated that this particular microorganism would mutate into a super-bug which proved impervious to the antivirus vaccine. There was nothing that could provide protection against the rampant killer-strain. This forced the dictator and scores of his minions to retreat far, far underground in an effort to flee from the pestilence that they had unleashed on the surface. They eventually discovered a Time/ Dimension Wormwell which provided an escape route from their doomed world. N'y-Greedjia and his evil legions were prepared to skip from one Configuration to another raiding, conquering, committing wanton genocide and leaving massive destruction in their wake. Their first stop was the 28th Configuration.

EPISODE TITLES

ARE ACKNOWLEDGEMENTS OF THE GIANTS WHO INSPIRED THE AUTHOR:

"THE LOST WORLD" Novel by Sir Arthur Conan Doyle

"TIME AFTER TIME" Novel by Karl Alexander, Film Written by Steve Hays & Nicholas Meyers

"THE DAY THE WORLD ENDED" Film Written by Lou Rusoff

"THE WHEELS OF CHANCE" Novel by H. G. Wells

"DESTINATION MOON" Film Written by Robert A. Heinlein

"WELCOME TO THE MONKEY HOUSE" Novel by Kurt Vonnegut

"SOMETHING WICKED THIS WAY COMES" Novel by Ray Bradbury

"THE CREATURE FROM THE BLACK LAGOON," Film Written by Harry Essex & Arthur A. Ross

"CLOSE ENCOUNTERS OF THE THIRD KIND" Film Written and Directed by Steven Spielberg

"THE THING" Film Written by John W. Campbell Jr. & Charles Lederer

"PLANET OF THE APES" Film Written by Michael W. Wilson

"STAR TREK" Television Show Created by Gene Roddenberry

"ALIEN" Film Written by Dan O'Bannon Story & Screenplay, Ronald Shusett, Story

"CONTACT" Novel by Carl Sagan

"A BRIEF HISTORY OF TIME" Book by Stephen Hawking

"MENACE FROM EARTH" Novel by Robert A. Heinlein

"BLOWUPS CAN HAPPEN" Short Story by Robert A. Heinlein

"THE END OF ETERNITY" Novel by Isaac Asimov

"STRANGER IN A STRANGE LAND" Novel by Robert A. Heinlein

"AGAINST THE FALL OF NIGHT" Novel by Arthur C. Clarke

"PROJECT NIGHTMARE" Novel by Robert A. Heinlein

"HITCH HIKER'S GUIDE TO THE GALAXY" Television Show Created by Douglas Adams

"THE FUTURE IN QUESTION" Novel by Isaac Asimov

"TUNNEL IN THE SKY" Novel by Robert A. Heinlein

"A GRAVEYARD FOR LUNITICS" Novel by Ray Bradbury

"TIME BANDITS" Film Written by Terry Gilliam & Michael Palin

"REPORT ON PLANET THREE" Novel by Arthur C. Clarke

"FANTASTIC VOYAGE" Film Written by Harry Kleinman Jr.

"ORPHANS OF THE SKY" Novel by Robert A. Heinlein

"THE CAVES OF STEEL" Novel by Isaac Asimov

"THE FLY" Film Written by George Langelaan & James Clavell Sr.

"THE WINDS OF CHANGE" Novel by Isaac Asimov

"BEYOND THIS HORIZON" Novel by Robert A. Heinlein

"INDEPENDENCE DAY" Film Written by Dean Devlin & Roland Emmerich

"GLORY ROAD" Novel by Robert A. Heinlein

"THE OUTER LIMITS" Television Show Created by Leslie Stevens

"WAR GAMES" Film Written by Lawrence Lasker & Walter F. Parkes

"WHEN WORLDS COLLIDE" Film Written by Sydney Boehm

"THE DAY THE EARTH STOOD STILL" Film Written by Edmund H. North

"STAR WARS" Film Created and Written by George Lucas

"TIME TUNNEL" Television Show Created by Irwin Allen

"BACK TO THE FUTURE" Film written by Robert Zemekis and Bob Gale

"WAR OF THE WORLDS" Novel by H.G. Wells

LaVergne, TN USA
11 March 2011
219679LV00002B/5/P